FOUR MEALS

MEIR SHALEV, one of Israel's most celebrated novelists, is the author of three other works of fiction – *Roman Russi*, *Esau* and *The Big Woman* – all of which have been notable literary and commercial successes in Europe and beyond. His novels have been published in over ten countries – most recently *Four Meals* was awarded the Juliet Club prize in Italy. Shalev is also a columnist for *Yediot Achronot*, a leading Israeli newspaper and is the author of five children's books, also published widely on the international front. He lives in Jerusalem.

BARBARA HARSHAV has translated books of poetry, fiction and non-fiction for twenty years. Her translations include works from German, Yiddish and Hebrew, including Shalev's second novel, *Esau*.

FOUR MEALS

Translated from the Hebrew by
Barbara Harshav

Meir Shalev

CANONGATE

First published in Great Britain in 2000
by Canongate Books Ltd,
14 High Street, Edinburgh EH1 1TE

10 9 8 7 6 5 4 3 2 1

The publishers gratefully acknowledge general subsidy
from the Scottish Arts Council towards the Canongate
International series.

British Library Cataloguing-in-Publication Data
A catalogue record for this book is available on
request from the British Library

ISBN 0 86241 862 3

Typeset by Palimpsest Book Production Limited,
Polmont, Stirlingshire
Printed and bound by WSOY, Finland

First Meal

1

On warm days, a soft smell of milk rises from the walls of my house. The walls are plastered and whitewashed, tiles cover the ground, but from the pores of the walls and the cracks of the floor, the smell rises to me, persists, steals in like the sweat of an ancient love.

Once my house was a cowshed. The house of a horse and a she-ass and a few milk cows. It had a wide wooden door, with an iron bolt across it, concrete troughs, yokes for cattle, jugs, cans, and milking stations.

And a woman lived in the cowshed, she worked and slept in it, dreamed and wept. And on a bed of sacks she gave birth to her son.

Doves walked back and forth on the ridge of the roof, in the remote corners the swallows were fussing over their nests of mud, and the fluttering of their wings was so pleasant I feel it even now, softening the expression on my face, smoothing the wrinkles of age and anger as it rises in my memory.

In the morning, the sun illuminated squares of windows on the walls and gilded the dust particles dancing in the air. Dew gathered on the lids of the jugs and field mice scurried over the bundles of straw like small grey lightning bolts.

The she-ass, as my mother told me the memories she wanted to preserve in me, was wild and very wise, and even in her sleep she would kick, and when you wanted to ride on her back, Zayde, she would gallop to the door, bow down, and pass under the bar of the bolt, and if you didn't jump off her back in time, Zayde *meyn kind*, the iron bar hit your chest and brought you down. The she-ass also knew how to steal barley from the horse and how to laugh out loud and how to rap on the door of the house with her hoof to get some sweets.

And a mighty eucalyptus tree rose up in the yard, its boughs wide, fragrant, and always rustling. No one knew who had planted it or what wind had borne its seed. Bigger and older than all its brothers in the nearby eucalyptus forest, it stood in its place and waited long before the village was founded. I often climbed it because crows nested in its crest and even then I was observing their ways.

By now my mother is dead and the tree has been cut down and the cowshed has become a house and the crows have taken off and new ones have come, returning to their dust and hatching out of their eggs. And nevertheless, those crows and those stories and that cowshed and that eucalyptus – they're the anchors, the eternal pictures of my life.

The tree was about sixty feet high, the crows' nest was close to its crest, and in the thicket of its lower branches you could see the remnants of the 'Tarzan hut' of children who climbed up and nested in it before I was born.

In the old aerial photos of the British air force and in the stories of the villagers it is clearly visible, but today all that's left of it is an immense stump, with the date it was cut down seared in it like the date of death on a tombstone: December 10, 1950. Moshe Rabinovitch, the man whose yard I grew up in and whose cowshed I live in, the man who gave me his name and bequeathed me his farm, came back from burying my mother, sharpened his big axe, and put the tree to death.

2

For three days Rabinovitch chopped down the tree.

Over and over again the axe swung up, and over and over again it came down. Around and around the man chopped, moaned and swung, groaned and struck.

A short man, Rabinovitch, taciturn and broad, with thick, short hands. Even today, in old age, the villagers call him 'Rabinovitch the Ox' because of his strength and his passivity, and the third generation of children play the 'awful bear' with him: in one hand, he holds three thin arms of three children, and shrieking and laughing, they can't get out of his grip.

Chips and sighs flew, tears and sweat dripped, snowflakes swirled around, and even though differences of opinion erupt here about every memory – they don't argue in our village about that act of vengeance, and every baby knows the details:

A dozen towels Rabinovitch used to wipe his face and the back of his neck.

Eight axe handles he broke and replaced.

Twenty-four quarts of water and six pots of tea he drank.

Once every half hour, he honed the blade of the axe with the whetstone and a steel file.

Nine loaves of bread with sausage he ate, and one crate of oranges.

Seventeen times he sank onto the snow and sixteen times he got up and went on hitting.

And the whole time, his thirty-two teeth were clamped and his ten fingers were clenched and his weeping breath steamed in the cold, until the great screech of the break was heard and the loud sigh of the onlookers, like the murmur that arose in the community centre when the lights were turned out, but louder and more scared.

And then the shouts of alarm and the patter of feet fleeing and afterwards the clamour of death, and there's no simile for it except to say the thing itself: the clamour of the fall and death of a big tree, and everyone who heard it will never forget it – the explosion of the splitting and the roar of the fall and the whiplash of the crash to the ground.

Those aren't like the sounds of a human being's death, but then the sounds of the life of a tree and of a human being are also different, and they leave behind different silences after they go.

The silence of the hewn tree is a curtain of darkness soon rent by the shouts of people, by the rippling gusts of wind, and by the cries of birds and beasts. And the quiet that filled the world at my mother's death is thin and clear, and so, lucid and crystal, it stands and doesn't melt away.

Here it is, with me, next to all the noises of the world. It doesn't swallow them and they don't blend with it.

3

Flikt di mame federn,
federn un pukh,
zaydelen – a kishele
fun helln-roytn tukh.

I knew that song even before I understood what it meant. It tells of a mother plucking feathers to make her son a down quilt with a pink cloth cover.

Many mothers, I imagine, sang that song to their children, and every one put in the name of her own child. 'Zaydele' was me. That wasn't a nickname that stuck to me, but my real name. 'Zayde,' which means grandfather, is the name my mother gave me when I was born.

For years I've wanted to change it. But I don't. At first I didn't have the courage, then I didn't find the strength, and finally we gave up, my name and I, and we've made peace with one another.

I was only a few months old when Mother sewed the cover and sang me the song, but even so, I seem to remember those nights well. Winters were cold in Moshe Rabinovitch's cowshed, and in summer Mother negotiated with our neighbour Eliezer Papish, who raised geese, and in exchange for his goose down, she sewed down quilts for him and his whole family.

By the way, we called Eliezer Papish the 'Village Papish' to distinguish him from his rich brother, who sold tools and building supplies in Haifa and was called the 'City Papish,' and maybe I'll tell about him, too, later on.

So, my name is Zayde, Zayde Rabinovitch. My mother's name is Judith, and in the village they called her Rabinovitch's Judith. A good smell of lemon leaves wafted from her hands and a blue kerchief was always wound around her head. She was hard of hearing in her left ear and she got mad when anyone talked to her on that side.

My father's name nobody knows. I am illegitimate, and three men claimed me as their son.

From Moshe Rabinovitch, I inherited a farm and a cowshed and yellow hair.

From Jacob Sheinfeld I inherited a fine house, fine furnishings, empty canary cages, and drooping shoulders.

And from Globerman the cattle dealer, I inherited a *knipele* of money and my gigantic feet.

And despite that complication, my name was crueller for me than the circumstances of my birth. I wasn't the only child in the village or the Valley sired by a father who was unknown or a father that wasn't his; but in the entire country, maybe even in the world, there wasn't another child whose name was Zayde. In school they called me Methuselah and 'Gramps', and every time I came home and complained about that name she gave me and wanted to know why, Mother explained simply: 'If the Angel of Death comes and sees a little boy named Zayde, Grandfather, he understands right away that there's a mistake here and he goes someplace else.'

Since I had no choice, I was convinced that my name protected me against death and I became a child who knew no fear. Even the primeval dreads that reside in the heart of every human being before he's born were eradicated in me.

Fearlessly, I would hold out my hands to the snakes nesting in the crevices of the chicken coop, and they would watch me, winding their necks inquisitively, and didn't hurt me.

Often I climbed up on the roof of the cowshed and ran along the steep slope of shingles with my eyes shut.

I engaged my heart to approach the village dogs who were always tied up and had become thirsty for blood and revenge, and they wagged their tails amiably at me and licked my hand.

And once, when I was an eight-year-old grandfather, a pair of crows attacked me as I climbed up to their nest. A hard black blow landed on my forehead and I spun around and lost my grip on the branch. Swooning with delight, I dropped down and down. Soft embraces of branches slowed my fall, and my landing was padded by the expected bed of leaves, the soft ground, and my mother's superstition.

I got up and ran home and Mother applied iodine to my scratches.

'The Angel of Death is an orderly angel. He's got a pencil, he's got a notebook, and he writes down everything,' she laughed, the way she laughed whenever I was saved; 'but you can't count on the *Malakh-fun-shlof*. That Angel of Sleep never writes down anything and never remembers. Sometimes he comes and sometimes he falls asleep himself and forgets.'

The Angel of Death would always pass by me, and I felt only the hem of his cloak grazing the skin of my face. But once, in the autumn of 1949, a few months before my mother's death, I also saw him face-to-face.

I was about ten years old. The Village Papish's enormous mare was in heat, our stallion heard her neigh and her rutting and started running wild inside our fence. He was a good-natured chestnut-coloured horse. Moshe Rabinovitch, who did everything 'just right', and therefore didn't fraternize with his livestock more than was acceptable and proper, indulged him with caresses and carobs, and once I even saw him plaiting the horse's tail into a thick yellow braid, with blue ribbons woven in as decoration.

He even refused to geld the stallion despite all demands and advice. 'That's cruelty to animals,' he said.

Sometimes the stallion would get an erection and bang his member against his belly. Hour after hour he would do that, with great and desperate persistence. 'Poor soul,' Globerman the cattle dealer then said; 'his balls they left to him. A female they don't give to him. And hands he hasn't got. So what can he do?'

That night, the stallion leaped over the fence and mated with the mare, and in the morning, Moshe gave me his halter and sent me to bring him back.

'You'll look him straight in the eyes,' he said, 'and tell him c'mon-c'mon-c'mon-c'mon. But if he'll make eyes at you, don't have nothing to do with him – you hear me, Zayde? Leave him alone at once and call me.'

It was early in the morning. The bleating of hungry, impatient calves was borne on the air. The scolding of farmers at their dreamy milking was heard. The Village Papish was already running around the pen, shouting and cursing, but the couple didn't pay any attention to anything. Their eyes were misty with love, their loins were dripping, their horse smell was enriched with new tones.

'You came to take the stallion?' exclaimed the Village Papish. 'Rabinovitch has maybe lost his marbles? To send a little boy?'

'He's milking,' I said.

'Milking? I could be milking now, too!' The Village Papish's voice was loud enough to reach our yard so Moshe would hear it.

I went into the pen.

'Get out of there fast!' cried the Village Papish. 'It's very dangerous when they're together.'

But I had already lifted the halter and was intoning the magic words.

'C'mon-c'mon-c'mon-c'mon . . .' And the stallion approached and even let me put the straps on his muzzle.

'He's gonna go nuts right away, Zayde,' called Papish. 'Leave him right now!'

Just as we were leaving the yard, the mare whinnied. The stallion stopped and pushed me to the ground. His eyes bulged and turned red. A loud snort erupted from the depths of his chest.

'Drop the rope, Zayde!' shouted the Village Papish. 'Drop it and roll out of the way fast!'

But I didn't let go.

The stallion rose up on his hind legs, the rope grew taut, and I was lifted up and dropped supine on the ground. His front hooves kicked the air and tamped the dirt next to me. A heap of dust rose and beyond it I saw the Angel of Death, his notebook in his hand, his eyes fixed on me.

'What's your name?' he asked me.

'Zayde,' I answered, not letting go of the rope.

The Angel of Death recoiled as if stunned by an invisible slap. He moistened his fingertip and leafed through the notebook.

'Zayde?' he fumed. 'How can you call a little boy Zayde?'

My body was shaken and beaten; the awful hooves whistled by me like the axes circus performers toss at their blindfolded girls. My hand grasping the rope was almost pulled out of my shoulders and my skin was flayed off on clods of dirt, but my heart was serene and confident.

'Zayde,' I said once again to the Angel of Death. 'My name is Zayde.'

In the shining white light, I saw him lick his pencil, examine his notebook once more, and understand that there was some mistake here.

His jaws gnashed in rage, and with a gasp of wrath and menace, he went somewhere else.

The loud whinnying and the yells of the Village Papish rushed Moshe Rabinovitch to me. He ran heavily across the ten metres between the two yards, and what I saw then I shall never forget.

With his left hand, Rabinovitch grabbed the stallion's halter and pulled him down until their heads were level, and with his right fist he struck the white star in the centre of the horse's forehead with one blow, and no more.

The stallion jerked back, stunned and surprised, and the majesty of his virility fell as if it were lopped off. He dropped his head, his eyes sank back, and with a moderate, ashamed pace he returned to our yard and went inside his fence.

The whole thing lasted no more than thirty seconds. But when I stood up, safe and sound, my other two fathers were already there: Jacob Sheinfeld had run up from his house and the dealer Globerman came in his green truck, collided, as he always did, with the big eucalyptus tree, and jumped out, yelling and waving the nail-studded *bastinado*.

And mother came tranquilly, stripped off my shirt, shook the dust off it, washed and disinfected the scratches on my back, and laughed. 'A little boy named Zayde, nothing will happen to him.'

So it's no wonder that as time went on, I became convinced that my mother was right and I came to believe in the power of the name she gave me, and so I take the precautionary measures it entails. Once I lived with a woman, but she ran away from me, amazed and despairing, after a few months of abstinence.

'A son will bring a grandson, and the grandson will bring the Angel of Death,' I told her.

At first she laughed, then she got angry, and in the end she left. I heard she married somebody else and that she's barren, but by that time I knew all the jokes and mockery of fate, and my heart was inured to it.

That's how my name saved me both from death and from love. But this has nothing to do with the story of my mother's life and her death, and stories, unlike reality, have to be preserved from all excess and addition.

A slight melancholy may be woven into my way of talking, but it isn't evident in my life. Like every person, I create moments of grief for myself, but the pleasures of life aren't alien to me, my time is my own, and as I said before, three fathers showered their benefits on me.

I've got a *knipele* of money and a green truck bequeathed to me by Globerman the cattle dealer.

I've got a big beautiful house on Oak Street in Tivon, the house bequeathed to me by the canary breeder, Jacob Sheinfeld.

And I've got a farm in the village, Moshe Rabinovitch's farm. Moshe Rabinovitch still lives there, but he's already registered it in my name. He lives in his old dwelling, facing the street, and I live in the pretty little house in the yard, the house that was once a cowshed, where bougainvillea twine around its cheeks like colourful sideburns, where swallows flutter yearnings at its windows, and a soft smell of milk still rises from the cracks in its walls.

In bygone days, doves hummed in it and cows gave milk. Dew collected on the covers of the jugs, dust in dances of gold. Once a woman lived in it, laughed and dreamed, worked and wept, and in it she brought me into her world.

That, in fact, is the whole story. Or, as practical people say in their deep, loathsome voices, that's the bottom line. And everything that will sneak in above it from now on are details with no purpose but to satisfy the pair of those small, hungry beasts – curiosity and nosiness – who nest in all our souls.

4

In 1952, about a year and a half after her death, Jacob Sheinfeld invited me to the first meal.

He came to the cowshed, his shoulders drooping, the scar on his forehead gleaming, and the moss of solitude darkening the wrinkles of his face.

'Happy birthday to you, Zayde.' He put his hand on my shoulder. 'You'll please come to me tomorrow for dinner,' he said, and turned and left.

I was then exactly twelve years old, and Moshe Rabinovitch gave me a birthday party.

'If you were a girl, Zayde, we'd make you a bat-mitzva today.' He smiled, and I was surprised because Rabinovitch didn't tend to talk in 'ifs' and 'what ifs.'

Oded, Rabinovitch's older son, who was already the village truck driver, brought me a silver-plated Bulldog model of a Mack diesel. Naomi, Rabinovitch's daughter, came specially from Jerusalem and brought me a book titled *The Old Silver Spot*, with pictures of crows and the notes of their calls. She kept kissing and crying and hugging and stroking until I was filled with embarrassment, desire, and dread all together.

Then the green truck appeared, collided, as always, with the mighty stump of the eucalyptus where big scars, mementos of all the previous collisions, could be seen in its flesh, and another father burst out: Globerman the cattle dealer.

'A good father doesn't never forget a birthday,' declared the dealer, who never failed to fulfil any parental obligation.

He brought some premium cuts of beef ribs and bestowed a sum of cash on me.

Globerman brought me money for every event. For birthdays,

holidays, the end of every school year, in honour of the first rain
of the season, on the shortest day of the year in winter and on
the longest day of the year in summer. Even on the anniversary
of Mother's death, he would thrust a few shillings into my hand,
which horrified and disgusted everybody, but it didn't surprise
anybody because Globerman was known throughout the Valley
as a greedy, coarse man. And in the village people said that five
minutes after the English expelled the German Templars from
nearby Waldheim, Globerman showed up there with his truck,
broke into their abandoned houses, and looted the crystal and
porcelain dishes they had left behind.

'And by the time we got there with the wagons' – the narrators
were enraged – 'there wasn't anything left.'

Once I heard the Village Papish scolding Globerman for the
same thing. The word 'robber' I understood, 'Hashbez' I guessed,
and 'Akhen' I didn't get.

'You stole! You plundered!' he rebuked him.

'Me steal? I didn't steal.' Globerman chuckled. 'I obtained.'

'You "obtained"? What does that mean, you "obtained"?'

'Some of it I obtained by pulling and some of it I obtained by
dragging. But steal? Not me. I didn't steal nothing,' roared the
dealer, with a laugh I can still recall clearly to this day, many
years after his death.

'I'll tell you what's the difference between just a gift and a gift
of cash,' he said now in a loud voice so everyone would hear. 'To
think up what gift to buy somebody *iz a lokh in kop*, a hole in
the head. But to give somebody cash *iz a lokh in hartz*, a hole
in the heart. Period.'

And he closed my fingers around the money and declared:
'That's how my father taught me and that's how I'm teaching
you. It'll be just like you yourself was born on the *klots*, the
butcher block.'

Then he pulled out the flat bottle he always carried in his
coat pocket and I recognized the smell of the grappa Mother
loved to drink. He poured a lot of liquor down his throat and
a little bit of liquor on the fire, roasted the ribs he brought, and
sang aloud:

Zaydele went walking down the street
Went with a penny to buy himself a treat
Oh, Zaydele, it's only a deceit
The penny went off and there's no treat
Daddy, Daddy, he is bold
Mommy, Mommy, she will scold
They'll beat poor Zaydele till he's out cold.

And Moshe Rabinovitch, the strongest and oldest of my three
fathers, caught me and tossed me up in the air over and over
again, threw and caught my body with his thick, short hands.
And when Naomi yelled, 'And one to grow on,' and I soared for
the thirteenth time, I saw a swarming cloud of wings threatening
to cover the village.

'Look,' I shouted. 'Starlings in summer!'

And at first glance, the raging nimbus did indeed look like a
flock of starlings that had lost its sense of time. But it soon turned
out that, thanks to the swings of Moshe Rabinovitch's strong
hands, I saw the locusts rising on the Valley that year, 1952.

Moshe's face became melancholy. Naomi panicked. And
Globerman said for the *n*th time: '*A mentsh trakht un got
lakht* – man makes plans and God laughs.'

Within five minutes the dull drumming of the Arab peasants
was heard beyond the hills, coming out of their houses to the
fields, armed with screaming women, long sticks, and noisy,
empty gasoline cans to rout the enemy.

Globerman sipped more and more grappa from his bottle and
served Moshe more and more meat, and in the evening, when
all the children went to the fields with torches and bags, spades
and brooms to kill the locusts, my third father, Jacob Sheinfeld,
came, laid his hand on my shoulder, and invited me to dinner.

'All the gifts are nothing. Money gets used up. Clothes you
rip up. Toys get broken up. But a good meal, that stays in your
memory. From there it doesn't get lost like other gifts. The body
it leaves fast, but the memory slow.'

That's what Jacob said, and his voice, too, like the voice of
the dealer, was loud enough to reach everyone's ears.

5

'A strange bird,' that's what they called Jacob Sheinfeld in the village.

He lived all by himself, he had a little house, a garden which was once well-tended, and a few empty canary cages, relics of an enormous flock that was now dispersed.

His field, which had once boasted a citrus grove and a vineyard, vegetables and fodder, was now leased to the village for common cultivation. His incubator he had already closed. His wife, who had left, he had already forgotten.

Jacob's wife was named Rebecca. I knew she had left him because of my mother. Never did I see her, but everybody said she was the most beautiful of all the women in the village.

'What do you mean, all the women in the village?' the Village Papish amended. 'All the women in the Valley! All the women in the country! One of the most beautiful women in all the world and in all times!'

The Village Papish was one of those admirers who is devoted to female beauty, and in his house he had splendid art albums he used to leaf through with washed, caressing hands, and sigh: '*Sheyner fun di ziebn shtern* – more beautiful than the seven stars.'

Like a distant, glowing nebula, Rebecca was sealed in his memory and in the common memory of the village. To this day – even after she had gone off and re-married and come back in old age, and managed to bring Jacob back to her before her death – they still talk about her here. And whenever a handsome woman comes to visit or a new baby is born who is very beautiful to behold, memory immediately compares her with that reflection of the beautiful woman who once lived here, whose husband was unfaithful, and who went off, and left us all behind, 'wallowing in ugliness and desolation and the black soil'.

*　　*　　*

Twelve years old I was then, and in the way whose beginning is hazy and whose end is painfully sharp, I understood that I was responsible for Jacob's catastrophe and for his solitude. I knew that, if not for me and the deed I did, my mother would have granted his suit, given in to his pleas, and would have married him.

As in a box, I hid from my three fathers the secrets concerning them and her. I didn't reveal to them why she behaved as she did or why she chose the one she did. I didn't tell them that, sitting in my observation-box, camouflaged with branches and grass, I saw human beings, too, and not only crows.

Nor did I tell them about the mockery and scorn, my lot in school.

'What's your name?' laughed the little children.

'What's your father's name?' teased the big children, guessing aloud which of the three was my real father.

They were scared of Rabinovitch and Globerman, so they clung to Jacob Sheinfeld, whose isolation and mourning made him an easy target. He also had a strange custom which stirred pity and disgust in everyone's heart: he would sit at the village bus stop on the highway, saying either to himself or to the dusty casuarinas or to the cars passing by, or maybe to guests visible only to him: 'Come in, come in, friends. How nice of you to come, friends, come in.'

Sometimes he seemed to greet them, stood up formally, and as if he were reciting an ancient slogan, he said: 'Come in, friends, come in, we're having a wedding today.'

Often, when I went on a trip in the village milk-truck with Oded Rabinovitch, we'd see him sitting there.

'Look at him how he looks,' said Oded. 'If he was a horse, they would have shot him long ago.'

But not to Oded, and not even to his sister Naomi, did I reveal what evil I had done to Jacob in my childhood.

The next evening, after I finished my homework and helped Moshe with the milking, I washed, put on a white shirt, and went to Sheinfeld's house.

I opened the small gate and was immediately wrapped in the

strange and wonderful smells of a meal. They slipped out of the house, but didn't go over the hedge, and stayed in the yard.

Jacob opened the door of his house, and when he said, 'Come in, come in,' the smells grew stronger, winding around my neck and ankles, bearing me from the yard inside the house and filling my mouth with the saliva of excitement.

'What were you cooking there, Jacob?' I asked.

'Good food,' he said. 'A gift for you on a plate.'

Jacob's gifts weren't frequent or public like the dealer's gifts, but they were more interesting. When I was born, he gave me a pretty yellow wooden canary that was hung over my crib. When I was three, he folded yellow paper boats for me and we'd sail them together in the wadi. For my eighth birthday, he prepared a surprise that made me very happy: my big observation-box, painted with camouflage spots, equipped with holes for observation and ventilation, two handles, and a pair of wheels.

'From that box, you can watch your crows and they won't know you're there,' he told me. 'But don't use it for watching human beings. That's not nice.'

Inside the box, Jacob had put up clips for paper and pencils, and arranged a place for a bottle of water.

'And you've also got places to stick branches and leaves here, Zayde, so the crows wouldn't feel nothing and wouldn't run away,' he said. 'By me, the canaries sit in the cage and I'm outside. And by you, you sit in a cage and the crows are outside.'

'They don't run away from me,' I said. 'They know me by now and I know them.'

'Crows are just like human beings.' Jacob smiled. 'They don't run away, but they put on a show for you. If you'll hide in the box, they'll act like normal birds.'

The next day, I asked Globerman to take me and the box in his truck to the eucalyptus forest.

The forest stretched over the eastern edge, next to the common fields of the village, and beyond it was the slaughterhouse. The forest was dense and dark, and only one lane bisected it, the lane where the dealer would lead his livestock to their fate.

In its high crests, crows nested, and in that season you could still make out offspring who were almost as big as their parents and were beginning their flying lessons. The old crows showed them various exercises; and the young ones, who could still be easily identified in their first year by their dishevelled feathers, sat bunched together on the branches. Now and then one of them would slip off his perch, flutter in a panic in the air, screw up his courage, and return to his place, pushing his neighbour on the branch until that one would also fall and fly a little.

I sat in the box, I saw everything and the crows didn't sense me. In the evening, when Globerman came to take me back home, all my limbs would be shrivelled but my heart would be broad and happy.

Jacob sat me down at the kitchen table, a big, smooth table, where white plates gleamed like full moons, and silver dishes glittered next to them.

'In honour of your birthday,' he said.

His eyes tracked the expression on my face as I ate, and I neither could nor would hide my pleasure.

By the age of twelve, I knew what I loved to eat and what I hated, but I couldn't imagine that food could give such profound and poignant pleasure. Not only my tongue and my palate, but also my throat and my guts and my fingertips sprouted tiny taste buds. The smell filled my nose, saliva flooded my mouth, and even though I was still a child, I knew I would never forget the meal I was eating.

Strangely, my pleasure was accompanied by a thin grief that gnawed at the bliss and the taste and the smell that filled my body.

I thought of the simple meal I ate with my other father, with Moshe Rabinovitch, who generally stuck to potatoes, eggs, and the chicken soup he boiled so violently, as if he wanted to make sure that the chicken whose neck he had wrung and whose feathers he had plucked wouldn't come back to life.

A man of habits and ruts is Rabinovitch. As always, even now he doesn't talk during a meal. He chews his food very thoroughly, rolls it from side to side, and when his hand

loads the fork again, I know that in another six chews he will
swallow.

Only he and I were left at home. Mother was dead now;
Naomi was married and lived in Jerusalem; Oded didn't leave
the village, but he lived in another house. As always, even now
we sit alone, Moshe and I, eat and are silent. After he eats, he
drinks a few cups of boiling tea, one after another, and I wash
the dishes and straighten up the kitchen just as Mother would.

And when I finish, I get up and say, 'Good night, Moshe,'
because I didn't call any of my three fathers 'father', and I go
out to the little house in the yard, and there I lie down alone.
In my bed, which is her bed. In her cowshed, which became
my house.

6

Jacob didn't sit at the table with me. He fussed around me,
served, watched me as I ate, talked incessantly, and now and
then, if there was a space between two words in his mouth, he
stuck in a piece of the omelette he had made for himself.

I was afraid he would tell me about my mother, because most
of the people in the village felt a need to tell me about her or to
ask me about her, but Jacob sat and told me a story; parts of it
I already knew, about his childhood in the Ukraine, about his
love for birds, about the river where the girls would wash their
clothes and the fellows would sail little paper boats to them,
with words of love written between their folds.

'Koreblik lubvoi,' he said; 'love boats.'

'I was a little boy then, littler even than you, Zayde. And for
me, that Kodyma River was big like the sea. Children have eyes
like magnifying glasses. That's something I once heard from
Bialik. He was here in the village giving a lecture, and here's
what he said: the Alps in Switzerland are really high mountains.
But they aren't as high as the garbage heap in my grandfather's
yard in the village when I was five years old. The whole thing

Bialik said in much nicer language. But Bialik's words I don't have, and to talk like him I can't talk.'

Big maple trees grew on the banks of the Kodyma. In the shadow of their branches the ducks paddled, their heads shiny green. In the thickets of reeds, the wind rustled, and the peasants said it was repeating the moans of the drowned.

At the bend of the river, a heavy black slate rock canted, and a weeping willow bent over it. Here the girls knelt to wash clothes, their knees pressed to the dark stone, their fingers turning red in the icy water, and their noses running from the cold. Jacob hid behind the blossoming branches on the river bank and peeped at them. From the corner where the little boy was hiding, the movement of the water made the girls washing clothes look as if they were sailing on a boundless yellow-green sea.

One couple after another, the storks were plucked out of the sky and landed on their old chimneys and nests. They leaned their necks back, capered in their dances of wooing and fidelity, to show that another year had passed and their love still endured. They pecked their red beaks together, exchanged gifts of spring, and their legs blushed with lust.

'Because love is love, for ugly storks just like for my beautiful canaries.'

The spring wind played with the dresses of the girls washing clothes, stuck the cloth to their thighs and then let go, and the sunbeams limned the bluish shadows of the veins in their wrists as they wrung out the clothes. The light, clear and fragile as porcelain, sketched the picture Jacob would call with surprisingly florid language: 'The eternal picture of love.'

'A child who looks at beautiful women he doesn't want what a grown-up man wants,' he explained to me. 'See, you're still a child yourself, Zayde, and soon you'll be a man, so you got to know all these things. It's not the *tsitskes* and the *tukhis* a child wants, it's much more than that. It's not the beauty of this one or that one he wants, it's the beauty of the whole world he wants. To pick the stars out from the sky he wants, to hug the whole earth and the whole life and the whole big sea he wants. And a woman, she can't always give all those things. Once I had a worker here in the yard and I tell him what I'm telling you now. And he says to me: "There may be six women in the whole world who can give those things, Sheinfeld. But children don't know them yet and grown-ups don't meet them anymore." You remember that fat worker I had here?'

The love pecks of the storks were heard aloud, like periods and commas inserted by an invisible grammarian into the laughter of the laundresses. The bachelors gathered upriver to send love letters. Each one wrote something and then folded the paper.

'Here, Zayde. Like this they would fold.' Jacob took a sheet of yellow paper from one of the drawers. 'Like this and like this ... and now like this ... You turn it around and you open it, here and here, and again like this. And with your fingernail you make it smooth. And you got a – *koreblik*,' and he gave me a handsome, smooth paper boat, the boat a father folds for his little son.

Sometimes a whole letter was in a *koreblik*, sometimes only the sketch of a broken heart, a nightingale dripping blood, or clumsy pictures of yearning: a house, a tree, a cow, a baby.

The fellows put the paper boats on the water and let them be swept up in its flow. About two hundred feet separated them from the laundresses, and many boats absorbed water and fell apart, others capsized and sank, or were pushed to the bank and hit the thickets of nests. The few that did arrive were snatched up by the girls, who were so eager for them they would poke each other's eyes out to get a *korbelik lubvi*.

'A love boat,' Jacob explained again.

You didn't sign the love letters because everyone knew it was fate that saved the paper boat from the wrath of the water and led it to the girl it was meant for. It was fate that strengthened her hand in her war with her girlfriends. And it was the same fate that would make sure to inform her who the writer was, the boy meant for her.

The story smoothed the parched grooves of disappointment of his face and made his chin quiver.

It wasn't until years later that I realized he was testing me, explaining to me, tempting me, and maybe apologizing for the sin he hadn't committed and the blame that wasn't in him, and he didn't know it was in me.

'Maybe you'll drink a little something, Zayde, eh?'

He also said 'a little something' the way Mother and Globerman and Moshe Rabinovitch did.

'Moshe will get mad,' I said. 'I'm only twelve.'

'First of all, I'm also your father, Zayde, not just Rabinovitch. And second of all, we just won't tell him.'

He took two shot glasses out of the kitchen cabinet. They were so thin and transparent that only after the cognac was poured into them did I discern their roundish shape. Even today, when they're mine and stand in my cabinet, I'm afraid to hold them.

I drank a little and sneezed. My shoulders shivered and a warmth spread in my bones.

'Good?'

'It burns horribly,' I groaned.

'Your mother liked to drink very much,' said Jacob. 'She drank strong pomegranate liquor, and also cognac. And even more than cognac she loved grappa. That's a kind of liquor of the Italians. Globerman would bring her a bottle sometimes, and once a week they would sit and drink together. And he would put little chocolates in her mouth and tell her a little story. More than half a bottle they could finish like that together and then get up and go to work like nothing happened. Believe you me. Half a bottle in the middle of the day isn't a lot, but it isn't a little either. In the beginning she hated him like poison, the dealer. If she would meet him on the street or in the field, she would want to poke out his eyes. But from that drinking, one day a week, they was once-a-week friends. Listen, Zayde, you don't need big things to be friends. And to hate, too, very little reasons is enough, and even to love.'

Jacob's voice cracked a moment: 'See, here in the village everybody used to ask why I fell in love with her. Behind my back they were asking it, and to my face, too. How come you fell in love with Rabinovitch's Judith, Sheinfeld? How could you let your Rebecca go, Sheinfeld?'

He said those words as if he were repeating a question, even though I hadn't asked it, not aloud and not in my heart.

'See, that's what I just told you a minute ago, Zayde, you don't need big reasons to love a woman. And the size of the love has nothing to do with the size of the reason. Sometimes one word she says is enough. Sometimes only the line of the hip, like a poppy stem. And sometimes it's how her lips look when she says "seven" or "thirteen". Look and see, with "seven" the lips are starting out like with a kiss. Then you see the teeth are touching the lips a moment to make the "v". And then the mouth is opening a little . . . like this . . . se-ven. See? And with "thirteen", the tip of the tongue is peeping out for the "th". Then the mouth is opening and the tongue is touching the top of the mouth at the end.'

He stared at me as if he wanted to see if I caught the meaning of his words.

'To understand that thing, hours I stood looking in a mirror. I stood there and I said all those numbers very slow, and I watched very careful how every number looks on the mouth. And once I even said to her, Tell me, Judith, how much is three and four? just to see the seven on her mouth. But she probably thought I'm nuts. And sometimes, listen, Zayde, just the eyebrows, just the eyebrows of a woman, can grab a man for a whole life.'

He poured himself another glass of cognac, closed the bottle, and put it back in the cabinet. 'You don't get any more today, Zayde. That was only for you to taste and for a time to remember. I'll leave that bottle for you, let it lie here and wait with me until our next meal. It's good for cognac to wait. And the glasses and the dishes and everything that's here, you'll get it all from me after I die. Meantime, you go on growing up and playing and running after the crows. And the three of us, me and Rabinovitch and Globerman, we'll make sure you get a good childhood. Because what does a child have except childhood? Strength he hasn't got and sense he hasn't got and a woman he hasn't got. All he's got is love that breaks his body and his life.'

7

Jacob washed the two shot glasses, dried them carefully, and held them up to the light to examine their transparency.

'I always had a weakness for birds, too,' he said. 'And my mother died when I was a little boy, too. But me, Zayde, I didn't get a childhood. My father married another woman and she threw me out of the house right away. Sent me off to her brother, my foster uncle. He had a workshop in the big city, far far away from home and the village. Better he should learn a trade, she says, and not walk around the river near the laundresses. And with her brother in the workshop I worked like a slave, from morning to night. His children went to school and wore fine clothes with the gymnasium buttons, and I barely learned how to read and write and to this day I speak a broken Hebrew. So broken that all the years I'm ashamed to open my mouth at the village assemblies. Sometimes on purpose I put in a nice word to make it sound pretty. Then everybody would laugh. Once I said "yours truly" instead of "I", and the Village Papish said to me, right in front of everybody: "Your yours truly, Sheinfeld, along with all the rest of your language, is like a pearl on a heap of garbage." He stinks himself from the *kvatsh* of his geese and me he calls garbage. When he would pass by here on his wagon with the garbage barrels he'd bring from the prison camp for his geese to eat, the birds would fall dead out of the sky from the stink. And me he calls garbage. So when I was a little boy, the birds was all I had to cheer me up. Why were birds created at all except to make men happy? Does the God of the Jews care if animals are flying around in the sky? There's not enough room on the ground? In Uncle's yard, there were poor sparrows. In the morning I'd see them freezing just like me. Little grey sparrows with their feathers all puffed up with cold. They also had little black *yarmulkes* on top of their heads. They also didn't have a drop of sense inside their heads. That's why people call a fool a birdbrain. But if you can fly, what do you need a brain for? Those sparrows, they look so grey. But when the sparrow husband feeds the sparrow babies, the sparrow wife is fooling around with another guy right in front of his eyes. You knew that, Zayde? So, the piece of bread they'd give me, I'd hold it in my mouth like this and lie on the ground in the yard on my back, like this, Zayde. And the sparrows would come and stand right here on my chin and on my forehead, and they would peck the bread right out of my mouth. Give me your hand now, Zayde, help your father up from the floor.

'And once the neighbour's little boy caught a finch in a trap, and he says he's going to poke out the bird's eyes with a needle so he'll keep on singing. You knew that, Zayde? A songbird, if you'll put out his eyes, he sings and sings, and he doesn't stop until he dies without a drop of strength. So I steal a penny from Uncle to ransom the bird. And Uncle catches me and gives me such a beating – "*Shmendrik!*" he says. "You want to starve us to death?" – And I run away to the river and I don't come back for two days. For food I'm eating grass, and for water I'm drinking from the river. And I'm sitting and making paper boats and writing on them: *Tateh, Tateh, kum aher un nem mikh a haym.* You know what that is, Zayde? Because of your name, I forget you don't know Yiddish. *Father, Father, come and take me home*, that's what I'm writing. And boat after boat I'm putting in the water, until Uncle finds me and drags me back to the workshop. And once more he's killing me with his smacks: "Such things you'll write about me?" he says. And he sends his own sons to chase after my paper boats, because he knows how far *korbliki* like those could go. What can I tell you, Zayde? You can hit and you can punish a child, but you won't break his spirit, and you won't murder his dream. To tell everything I went through with this evil uncle, a person really has to be Dostoyevsky. But one thing, Zayde, I'm telling you that you should know: I didn't part from the birds. I grew up with them. And I always had a bird to sing to me. That's just something you make up your mind about. I just made up my mind that every bird that's flying, for me he's fluttering his wings. And every bird that's singing in the tree, for me he's singing. The uncle's children were students in the gymnasium, and I was only a tinsmith's assistant, a little boy with hot tin burns on my hands, and my skin white and grey like a corpse. And coughing from coal dust. And out of the window that boy sees them walking in the street in nice clothes, the uniform of the gymnasium with buttons. But the birds, Zayde, for him they're singing. Out of the window I see them and so I says: How did you make such a thing, Lord? A bird that sings and flies? And why didn't you make me like that, too? Here I am, Lord, here I am, answer me!

'Here I am, here I am, answer me,' Jacob repeated, as if he were savouring the taste of the words along with the omelette, and them, too, he said in the Yiddish way, tearful and captivating, just like Mother would say them.

8

'And so I was envious and I was covetous. Oh, how jealous I was. Jealous of the children for their suits, of the birds for their wings. The water of the Kodyma River I envied because the girls dipped their hands in it. And even the black rock I envied where their knees touched. Even today, I take nothing from nobody and I steal nothing from nobody. But I do covet, Zayde, I do covet and I do envy. 'Cause passion and desire, these are birds nobody will catch and nobody will cut off their wings. The girls were on the black rock doing their laundry, and the wind peeped under their dresses, and the fellows went down and stood in the water and sent them the paper boats with the words of love. When you grow up and become a man, Zayde, you'll see: you can run after a girl, you can send her all kinds of little gifts, you can sing her songs at night, like the Italians do with a guitar. You can put a paper boat for her in the water, and best of all maybe do all of them. Because you never know what she really loves. For instance, the son of the miller back home once saw a carriage on the road going along the river. Just

then he's standing next to the big mill wheel and two green eyes
are looking at him from the carriage with such a look that even
you, at your age, Zayde, would understand. So a whole day he
sits and thinks what the eyes says, until finally he goes nuts and
starts chasing every cart and every wagon that goes by in the
street. And once he's running like that, chasing the coach of
the mistress of a cossack officer. She was a Jew who followed
her officer to every war and every place the cossack went. She
had a coach and horses and all the luxuries you need for love
she had there – a bed with a velvet curtain, and the silk sheets
that keep a man strong all night long. Maybe you're not old
enough yet to hear stories like this, eh, Zayde? And every single
kind of sausage and food and bottles she had there, 'cause love
gives you a big appetite. And everything was nice and neat and
on its shelf. 'Cause if a woman is loved very much she'll also
be very tidy. Exactly the opposite of a man. For a man, with
love comes a mess right away. And terrific eyebrows she had,
eyebrows that men who know about such things would kill for.
All you need is just one terrific thing in a woman to hold onto
a man. We men need to stand like cattle in the meat market to
show everything we got, outside and inside. But a woman, it's
something else. You can love the whole woman for a whole life
just because of one terrific little thing she's got. Just remember
that women don't know that, and you mustn't tell them. Did I
tell you that already, eh, Zayde? Did I already say that? Never
mind. It's not so terrible. Some things you can say twice. The
first time you say it as soon as it comes into your head, and the
second time you say it as soon as you understand it. And you, if
you think the God of the Jews cares about our love, just imagine
this: a cossack battalion is passing by, the horses are galloping,
noise, dust, and then the wagon with the Jew and her officer in
the silk bed. And that fool of a miller's boy, who's chasing after
every cart and carriage because of the green eyes, he runs after
that wagon, too. Well, the cossack officer didn't bat an eyelash,
and you'll forgive me, Zayde, he doesn't take his *shvantz* out of
his Jew, and he leans on one hand like this. And the other hand
with the sword he sticks out the window of the carriage. And
right in the middle of everything, he splits the boy's head open

with one stroke, like a water-melon, and all his brains spill out on the ground. And all his love and his questions and everything inside there pours out, too. 'Cause love, like I told you, Zayde, it's in the mind, it's not in the heart like people your age still think and that's where they look for it. Come on, eat now, *meyn kind*, eat, my orphan. Too bad your mother isn't here to see us father and son happy and eating together. Forgive me if maybe I ruined your appetite with such a tale. *Ess, meyn kind*, eat.'

And I ate.

9

Moshe Rabinovitch, the father who gave me his name and left me his farm, was born in a small town not far from Odessa. He was born late in his parents' life, the youngest of their seven sons.

His mother, whose hope for a girl was disappointed, dressed him in little girl's clothes, grew his hair long, plaited it into a golden braid, and wound blue ribbons in it, and Moshe didn't protest.

He grew up in the kitchen, enveloped in women and smells, and the years of sewing and knitting, listening to the intimate conversations of the maids and the cooks, and playing with lace dolls, made him into a muscular, quiet little girl, who was marvellous at embroidering loops and who knew she was bound to disappoint her mother.

And indeed when Moshe was eleven years old, she rolled up the muslin sleeves of her dress, knocked down her big brother, and beat him to a pulp because he had pulled the braid her mother had plaited and called her *Maydele*. And when she was twelve, when other girls are already sprouting breasts, her chest grew only reeds of hair. A fair masculine down budded on her cheeks, her Adam's apple and voice grew thick, and her manhood was obvious to everyone.

At first the mother resented her daughter for her betrayal, but one morning, when she saw her observing the behind of the servant girl who was leaning over the well, she understood that her anger was illogical and her expectation in vain. The night before her bat-mitzvah, the mother sneaked into her sleeping daughter's room and cut off the glory of her braid. Next to the bed she put a boy's suit and ordered one of the carters to teach Moshe to urinate standing up.

That night Moshe dreamed a dream little girls don't dream, and the next day he woke up earlier than usual because of the chill at the back of his neck. He put his hand there and the feel of the stump of braid filled him with awful panic. From there, he brought his hand down and felt his groin, and the smell that stuck to his fingertips was so strange and frightening that he jumped out of bed naked. Since he didn't find the dress he had put out in the evening, but the new trousers of a strange boy, he hid his manhood with his other hand and with bare buttocks, he ran to his mother.

But a stocky female servant was planted in the kitchen door, a black frying pan upside down in her hand, and the naked boy was driven away, attacked again and was hit, fell and got up, until he accepted the verdict and withdrew. And like all short men with broad shoulders, his weeping turned into growling and his regrets into strength. His purloined braid wasn't returned to him, a new braid he didn't grow, and to the kitchen of his childhood he didn't return except in his dreams.

That week, a teacher was brought to the house to teach Moshe to pray and to read a book and all the things he hadn't had to know as a girl. He didn't become a great scholar, but a few years later, by the time his father died, he was an experienced fellow, taking care of the family business.

Only two things remained from his childhood: he didn't bless God for not making him a woman, and he didn't forget his golden tresses. Sometimes, with a gesture even he himself didn't sense, his hand went up to his scalp and came down to the back of his neck, and explored, hoping and wanting, just as he gropes around there to this day.

And sometimes he was beset by a fever of searching and would rummage in the cellar and the attic, the pantry and the linen closet, just as he searches to this day.

But the severed beautiful golden braid he didn't find.

One day, Moshe went on family business to the wheat market in Odessa. And here, in a Greek restaurant on the street of the port, he saw a Jewish girl who was so much like him in her looks and her gestures that she seemed to have emerged from his mother's old hopes.

Moshe understood that he was standing before his female reflection, the famous twin imprisoned in every man's body, the twin sister every man dreams of and talks with, but only a few get to see her and even fewer to touch her.

For a whole day he walked behind her, stroked in his imagination the plaited gold of her hair, and breathed the air her body passed through, until she noticed him and laughed at him and sat with him on a park bench.

Her name was Tonya. Moshe peeled roasted pumpkin seeds and gave them to her, he pulled out his penknife and sliced Astrakhan apples for her which he had bought for the two of them, and cut her strips of the hard cheese his mother had given him for the road.

'Sister,' he told her with an excitement that didn't suit his heavy build; 'my sister that I never had.'

It was summer. The fragrances of the market were borne on the air. In the port, seagulls and ships blasted. Tonya's face beamed with love, with sun, and with joy.

Moshe told her he wanted to bring her to his mother as a gift, and Tonya laughed and said she'd come.

A week later, Moshe returned to Odessa with two of his older brothers and took her, accompanied by her two older brothers, to his mother's house.

When the mother saw the girl, she was flabbergasted. She called her 'my daughter' at once, and six clouds immediately darkened the faces of her six daughters-in-law, for she had never called any of them 'daughter'.

The widow laughed, then she wept, and finally she said that now at last she could be gathered to her husband.

And indeed, seven days after the wedding, she took leave of

her sons and her daughters-in-law, and, as was customary in the Rabinovitch family, died in a bed that was set up under the linden tree in the yard. She divided her fortune and property fairly and honestly among her sons, her jewellery among her daughters-in-law, and to Tonya she bequeathed a locked wooden box, inlaid with mother-of-pearl.

Moshe, who knew what was in the box, trembled but didn't dare say a word.

On the thirtieth day after her mother-in-law's death, Tonya went off to a corner and there, all alone, she opened the box. The splendid childhood tresses of her husband dazzled her eyes and filled them with tears. So smooth and gleaming were the locks that they seemed to be crawling and moving by themselves.

Tonya was frightened and closed the box, and when she caught her breath, she cautiously opened it again.

'Hide his braid from him,' instructed a vague note floating on the shining waves of hair, 'and give it to him only if necessary.'

When the year of mourning ended, so did World War I, and Menahem Rabinovitch, Moshe's oldest brother, came to visit with his wife Bathsheba. Menahem had immigrated to the Land of Israel before the war. He had worked in the agricultural settlements of the Galilee and Judea and ultimately settled in the Jezreel Valley. His stories and songs were so exciting, and the gigantic Cyprian carobs he brought in his bag were so plump they dripped honey on the floor and enticed Tonya and Moshe to follow him.

They immigrated to the Land of Israel and bought a house and a plot of land in Kfar David, near Menahem's village. A gigantic eucalyptus tree stood next to their hut and Moshe wanted to cut it down immediately. But Tonya, in the first and only quarrel that broke out between them, clung to the trunk, shouted, and hit, until she repelled her husband's axe.

In Kfar David, too, people were amazed at the resemblance between the two of them. Everybody said they looked like they were born to the same mother. Both of them were short, strong, and ravenous as bears, broad of face and neck. They were distinguished only by Moshe's premature baldness and Tonya's breasts.

The Rabinovitches, the neighbours added, never got tired, not even of things that everybody else was weary of – work and expectations and communal life. Moshe was equal in strength and diligence to three men and immediately acquired the nickname of 'Rabinovitch the Ox'. And Tonya raised chickens; in the citrus grove, she grafted a row of fragrant pomelo trees, a fruit that wasn't yet widespread in the country in those days; and in the yard, she planted two pomegranate trees: the sour 'Wonderful', and the sweet 'Mule's Head'. Moshe built a baking oven in the yard and she heated it with corn husks and the bark that peeled off the big eucalyptus.

In the good times, the villagers called them 'my Tonychka' and 'my Moshe', for that was what the two of them called each other. They had a son and a daughter, Oded was the first-born and then came Naomi, and on that rainy day, in the winter of 1930, that day when Moshe and Tonya went down to the citrus grove beyond the wadi, Oded was six and Naomi was four, and they didn't know that by sundown they would lose their mother and their world would turn dark.

10

Some say that the purpose of every story is to give order to reality. Not just chronological order, but also degrees of importance. Others say that every story comes into the world only to answer questions.

In school, the teacher once told us that the story of Adam and Eve in the Garden of Eden explains why we hate snakes. At the time I thought: why make up a big story with such weighty matters as the creation of the world, the Tree of Knowledge, man, and God, simply to explain such a trite and trivial issue as hating snakes?

One way or another, my story isn't a story of the Garden of

Eden, but a small, true story. My Tree of Knowledge, big and rustling as it was, has already been cut down and is no more. The animals of my garden are cows and canaries, and the only snake I can find in it is the viper that stung Simha Yakobi in the great fire, and I'll tell about that in a minute. His strike, too, was evil, but he didn't have the malice or cunning of his ancient forefather.

'For me, that fire at Yakobi's is the beginning of love,' said Jacob Sheinfeld, counting off events on his fingers; 'after all, for everything you need a starting point, Zayde, even for love.'

'For instance, Zayde,' he went on, 'when you grow up and get married, and you want to give the woman you love a wedding gown, you can go to the dress shop and buy her a gown there, or you can plant a mulberry tree and grow silkworms on it, and spin the threads by yourself and weave the cloth by yourself and dye it by yourself and cut it out by yourself and sew it by yourself. You see, you decide where it all starts. You understand that, Zayde?'

I didn't, but Jacob saw the smile of curiosity spread over my face, bent down to me, and asked again: 'You like the meal?'

I looked at him. His eyes were smiling, but the terrified corners of his lips were trembling, waiting for my answer.

A child I was, a child with three living fathers and one dead mother. An illegitimate child whose belly was full of delicacies and whose heart was empty of answers.

I looked at him, I smiled, but I guarded my guilt in my heart of hearts.

11

Simha and Yona Yakobi came to the village and left it many years ago.

Simha Yakobi immigrated to Israel from St Louis in America. There he was a locksmith and a bachelor, and here he got married and became a poultry breeder. His wife was a girl from the Galilee named Yona. Incidentally, that phrase – 'a girl from the Galilee' – made quite an impression on me in my childhood, and to this day I feel a special excitement whenever a girl from the Galilee crosses my path, either in story or in fact.

It was soon evident that the first names 'Simha' and 'Yona' confused the villagers because both names are used for men and women, and people often called Yakobi by his wife's name and his wife by her husband's name, and I may be mixed up, too, maybe Simha was the girl from the Galilee and Yona the locksmith from St Louis.

Since they kept making mistakes, they decided to call the two of them by their last name; more precisely, they called Simha 'Yakobi', and Yona 'Yakoba', or maybe vice versa. One way or another, in that great fire, the viper stung Yakobi. But the real thing, the thing that concerns Jacob Sheinfeld, was done by the fire and the snake, many years after the one was put out and the other fled.

The Yakobis' big poultry coop was the pride of the village, and one of the attractions shown to guests. In a time when spotted Arab hens ran around in farmyards laying one tiny egg every three days and poking around in the garbage, the white American brooders of Yakobi and Yakoba sat in splendid wooden cages, lay on chutes that robbed them of their eggs with a cunning slope, and enjoyed tin basins, hanging feeding troughs, and immaculate breeding boxes.

Tragedy, as always, wasn't impressed by all that, and swooped down on its prey by surprise. One night, terrified clucking came from the coop. Yakobi lit the kerosene lantern and rushed outside. As he entered the coop, he trod on the viper who was scaring the hens and who immediately bruised his heel.

It was spring, the season when vipers are overflowing with the venom and evil they amass throughout the winter months. Yakobi fell flat on the ground, the lantern slipped out of his hand, smashed, and set fire to the coop. Feathers and walls caught fire, clucking and smoke rose to heaven, and the snake, in the sneaky way of his kind, immediately fled.

'He did and he went away,' explained Jacob. 'What other business did he have there?'

The neighbours were summoned to help, but in the raging turmoil, no one knew what had happened. Instead of looking for Yakobi, they all tried to put out the flames and rescue the brood hens. Only after it was all over did Yakoba find her husband lying among the smouldering firebrands and the singed carcasses of the birds. By some miracle, only his hand and leg were seared, but smoke had gotten into his lungs and the snake's venom almost killed him.

His size, his strength, and his good fortune saved Yakobi from death. But he never really recovered. He lost his power and his energy, refused to work, and all day long he hummed a children's song whose monotonous tones irritated the entire village.

Yakoba, determined and diligent, tried to run the farm on her own, but weeds and thorns grew in the garden, the yard became a garbage pen, the four cows stopped giving milk and were sold to Globerman one after another, and the afflicted man didn't leave his wife alone.

The viper's venom kept on bubbling in his veins. All day long, he dragged around behind her, sang his nonsense to her, and doted on her with the pesky persistence and desire of four-year-old children wooing a beloved kindergarten teacher.

After two years of torments, Yakoba locked up the house and went to the fields without turning to look back. Yakobi toddled along behind her, humming his song, and trying to lift her dress. Thus the two of them reached the highway, crossed it, vanished among the oaks on the northern hills, and were never seen again in the village.

For months the Yakobis' hut stood empty and waiting, and no one knew what for.

The rosebushes went wild and turned into prickly vines, their flowers grew smaller and stank, and shrikes impaled the carcasses of mice and lizards on their thorns.

Passionflower shoots crawled on the floor of the porch, choked the gutters with the clasp of tendrils, and finally prised the windows open and crept into the rooms.

Weeds and screwbeans flourished in the yard, as in every abandoned place, until they covered the remnants of the burned coop. The hedge turned into a tangled wall, where black snakes hissed and cats dragged their prey.

Gangs of tiny murderers – geckos and spiders, praying mantises and chameleons – lurked in the wild bushes. There was always rustling and quivering among the leaves, and more than once, when a child's ball fell there and someone put a hand in to get it out, he got a bite or a sting or both.

Some people suggested burning down the yard along with its inhabitants, and then, one summer day, at dusk, the distant and strange sound of a songbird was heard approaching the village.

Man and beast stopped, raised weary heads, cocked amazed ears.

The sound, so foreign, so attractive, wonderful, and sweet, kept growing louder.

Then it was joined by the squeak of tortured springs, the rattle of pistons, and the gasps of an aging motor that had lost the compression of its youth. From distant mists of dust, a rickety green truck burst forth, big and swaying as a ship, and slowly rose from the fields.

In the driver's seat was a fat man, about forty years old, his hair white as snow, his skin pink and delicate as the skin of baby mice turned up onto the earth by a plough. He was swathed in an old black suit and protected by sunglasses just as black. Old suede patches shone on his sleeves, and in the back of the truck, spacious cages full of canaries singing with tremendous excitement, like children on their annual outing, were bumping up and down.

Jacob put his hand on my shoulder and said: 'Fate, Zayde, doesn't make surprises. It makes preparations, it makes signs, and it also sends out spies, but only a few people have eyes to see these things and ears to hear and a brain to understand.'

The strange stranger went straight to the forsaken hut of the Yakobis like someone who knew where he was headed. When he arrived, he put a broad-brimmed straw hat on his head and got out of the truck. The noise and agitation that always came from the tangles of the hedge and the high grass stopped all at once.

For a brief moment, the guest took off his sunglasses, revealed two pink eyes of an albino, and fringes of darting, ragweed lashes, and immediately hid them again behind the black lenses. He was short, with a double chin; his smile was pleasant and his looks were terrifying.

He took one cage and then another, and vanished with his birds into the hut. Even before the sound of the closing door had died out, startled caravans of centipedes, wolf spiders, and small angry vipers began leaving the yard and disappearing into the fields as if on command.

'Because,' said Jacob, 'animals sense more than human beings. Someday I'll tell you about your mother's cow, and how much she could sense.'

Only after sundown did the albino come back out to the yard and survey the task that awaited him. He immediately took a sickle out of the back of the truck and a file from the toolbox, and honed the curved blade with unexpected expertise. With long, smooth movements you wouldn't have guessed from his looks, he mowed the grass and stacked it at the edge of the yard. Then he took a tin pack of Players from his shirt pocket, lit a cigarette, inhaled the smoke with great pleasure; and he didn't blow out the match, but tossed it onto the pile. The straw, the grass, and the thorns burned, as they do, noisy and enthusiastic, and tinted the faces of the onlookers with their red glow.

Then everybody went away and the albino went on working all that night and the nights that followed. He trimmed the hedge, pulled up the passionflowers, cut down Yakoba's rosebushes, and grafted new strains onto the stumps. He turned over the soil of the yard with a pitchfork, and when dawn broke, he scurried into the shelter of the house. The crows, to whom every excavation and hoeing prophesies a plethora of plunder, hurried to land in his yard, hopping around and searching for the earthworms and mole crickets brought up to the surface of the earth by the pitchfork's teeth.

'And that,' said Jacob, 'that's how it all started. Nobody knew, even my wife Rebecca didn't know. And Rabinovitch the Ox didn't know. And Globerman the dealer didn't know. And I myself, I certainly didn't know. Only later on I understood that was how it started.'

He got up from the table, went to the window, and spoke with his back to me.

'The coop burned down, and the albino came. And Tonya Rabinovitch drowned and your mother Judith came. And Rebecca went, and the canaries flew off, and Zayde was born, and the worker came, and Judith died, and Jacob stayed. There's something simpler than that? That's how it always happens at the end of every love. The beginning is always different and the middle is always complicated. But the end is always so simple and so much the same. In the end, there's always somebody who comes and there's somebody who goes and there's somebody who dies and there's somebody who stays.'

12

Black clouds gathered, a wind blew, the wadi overflowed, and Tonya and Moshe didn't sense anything and didn't worry.

The rain played its cold songs on the roofs and hummed in the tin gutters. In the shelter of the sheds the livestock huddled together. Sparrows with puffed-up feathers and narrowed eyes entrenched themselves in lattices. A pair of crows, creatures who have no fear in their heart but only curiosity, practised hovering and climbing in the gusts of wind against the piercing downpour.

At three o'clock, Tonychka got up and Moshe emerged from his brief afternoon nap; they ate, as usual, a few oranges and a few thick slices of bread with margarine and jam, drank, as usual, a few cups of boiling-hot tea, and when the rain stopped they hitched the mule to the cart and went to bring grapefruit and pomelos from the citrus grove.

A sharp, cold wind, painful as a wet canvas sheet, came down from Mount Carmel and slapped their faces. The mule's hooves sank in the deep mud and were extracted from it with a sticky noise, leaving slushy pits in it. In the fields were the outline of new little channels which the water, in its endless downward affinity, cuts in the earth every year.

Tonya and Moshe passed the vegetable patch and the vineyard, crossed the wadi, and came to the citrus grove. Together,
they loaded the heavy crates, and when they turned to go back,
Tonya grabbed the reins and Moshe pushed the wagon from
behind and helped the mule get it out of the black mire. Tonya
turned her head around to look at him. Steam rose from the
skin of his face, which was flushed with the effort.

She loved her husband's strength and was proud of it. 'Please
just wait a minute, right away I'll call my Moshe,' she would
declare whenever one of the neighbours had to struggle with
a heavy sack or a recalcitrant animal. Near their house, next
to the wicket in the fence, lay a rock that weighed about two
hundred and fifty pounds, and Tonya made a florid sign on
it that said: 'Here Lives Moshe Rabinovitch Who Lifted Me
Up from the Ground'. Wags said that such a sign should have
been put on Tonya herself, but the rock was famous in the area
and now and then some fellow would show up from one of the
towns or the English army camp or the Druse villages on Mount
Carmel and try to lift it up. But Moshe was the only one who
was strong enough and Moshe was the only one who knew how
to kneel down and embrace the rock with his eyes shut and
Moshe was the only one who knew how to groan as he lifted it
and how to carry it like a baby against his chest. Everyone went
back to his place downcast and limping – downcast because of
the failure, and limping because everyone, without exception,
kicked the obstinate rock furiously and broke the big toe of his
right foot.

The rain began coming down again. When they returned to
the wadi, Rabinovitch saw that the water had risen a lot. He
climbed onto the wagon, took the reins from Tonya, retreated,
and guided the mule so that it would cross the river-bed at a
right angle. But the moment its hooves trod on the steep, slippery
bank, the mule groaned in a voice that sounded surprisingly like
a woman's, and stumbled.

From now on, things moved in the horribly familiar course
of catastrophes:

The mule sank down between the shafts. The wagon tipped

onto its side and turned over with a slow but very determined movement. Rabinovitch fell under it and his left thigh was trapped and crushed.

He yelled in pain. The broken kneecap tore the flesh and the skin and was exposed to the cold touch of the water. He almost blacked out, but dread – one of those dreads that is clear even before its reason is understood – turned his eyes to Tonya.

Most of her was lying beneath the overturned wagon. Only her head and neck were sticking out. Her skull and the back of her neck were sunk in the mud, her hair was clogged with water, the skin of her face, which always looked ruddy and healthy, turned grey all at once.

In the water, so close to her head, grapefruits and pomelos bobbed around as innocently as toys in a bathtub.

'Get me out of here,' she whispered.

She was hoarse with fear. A tongue of blood poured from the corner of her mouth, bright and thin. Only her eyes moved and looked at him.

Moshe, his crushed leg pinning him to the mud, thrust his hands under the side of the wagon and estimated the load.

'Get me out, my Moshe . . .'

Her voice was choked, it wanted to be a scream but didn't succeed.

'Listen to me, Tonychka,' said Moshe. 'I'll raise the platform a little, and you'll crawl out.'

Now the head also moved, nodded slowly, and the eyes opened wide in understanding and agreement.

'Now!' groaned Moshe.

His face grew dark with the effort. Veins and sinews stood out in the thick joints of his hands. The wagon creaked and was raised a little, and Tonya twisted, struggled, and gave up.

'I can't,' she moaned. 'I can't.'

The pain cut Moshe's trapped leg and the wagon came back down.

Some say that, in moments like that, time stands still. Others say that it passes doubly fast. And even others say that it is broken into a thousand tiny splinters that won't ever be put together again. But on that rainy day, on the fall of the

overturned wagon in the wadi, time didn't pay attention to
those hackneyed conjectures – it didn't slow down and it didn't
speed up, it just passed by in its path, huge and nonchalant,
wings beating and hovering as usual over the world.

A thin mist dripped dotting the surface of the water with
pockmarks, the wintry sky grew dark, and meanwhile the wailing of the mule and the scent of fear wafting from its body
attracted a few jackals, and they recoiled from Moshe's shouts
and the clods of mud he pitched at them.

One jackal leaped and sank its teeth in the mule's hind legs,
and Moshe, who had managed to pull out one of the posts of
the side of the wagon, hit him and broke his back. The others
were frightened and retreated, but later on they understood
that the man couldn't get up, and since they're clever and
hunger sharpens their intelligence and makes them brave, they
approached the mule from the head, where the pole was too
short to reach, and they leaped and tore pieces from its muzzle
and lips.

'The pomelos are floating,' Tonya said suddenly.

'What?' Moshe trembled.

'The grapefruits are sinking,' Tonya explained. 'And the
pomelos are floating.'

'The villagers will come soon and save us. Keep your head
out of the water, Tonychka, and don't talk.'

It rained harder, the wadi rose, the grapefruits turned yellow
like tiny faded moons under the water. Tonya, who lay on the
other side of the wagon, now had a hard time keeping her head
above water. Moshe tried to support the back of her neck with
the pole, but couldn't.

The sweat of fear bathed his bald scalp. He saw how the water
was rising, how the nets of muscles on the side of his wife's neck
were trembling, and he understood what was going to happen.

Suddenly the head sank and immediately floated up again, as
if kicked by the dread of death.

'Moshe . . .' a little girl's voice was heard. 'My Moshe . . . *der
tsop* . . . the braid in the box . . .'

'Where?' shouted Moshe. 'Where's the braid?'

The water climbed and the head was covered, and rose up

once again, and this time the voice returned and was Tonya's voice.

'My end has come, Moshe,' she murmured.

Rabinovitch turned his eyes and squeezed his jaw and his eyelids shut until the air bubbles stopped slipping out of her mouth. Then the sun also declined, yellowish grey beyond the clouds, and only after she disappeared, and the twilight and the rain wiped out the memory of the horrible sounds of her death, did Moshe once again look at the dark place where his wife's head had vanished. He was attacked by a horrible coughing. Tears of grief and failure flowed from his eyes. Lizards of regret, quicker and more slippery than any feelings, were already mining burrows in his body.

Out of horrible anger he once again clutched the edge of the wagon and hurled and roared – 'Get out now, get out, Tonya!' – to the astonished jackals and the dying mule.

The wagon slipped out of his hands onto his broken leg and Moshe fainted, came to, and fainted again, and a few hours later, when his own shouts woke him up, he saw as if in a dream the hurricane lamps approaching and heard the shouts and barking of the search party. But by then he had already been so struck by night and sadness and cold and pains that he didn't have the strength to call to them. It was only the mule's groans of distress that showed them the way.

13

Two years passed from that day to the day my mother came to work in Moshe Rabinovitch's house, take care of his orphans, and milk his cows.

I know only a few details about those years in her life, where she was and what she did.

'A *nafka mina*, who cares.' She'd dismiss me whenever I'd ask her about it, and would immediately get annoyed. 'Now hurry and sit on the right side, Zayde, you heard!' Because once again I had forgotten and was sitting on her deaf side.

When I grew up a little, I also asked my three fathers, and they gave me three different answers.

Moshe Rabinovitch told me that she had worked for a time in the winery of Rishon Le-Zion, 'and there she also learned to drink her liquor,' he smiled.

The cattle dealer Globerman, who had eyes and access all over the country, told me that my mother's parents 'stayed in exile after they heard what she did in the Land of Israel, because they didn't want to see her anymore.'

And when I kept asking and wanted to know more, the dealer said that men mustn't investigate their mother's past.

'What went on between Lady Judith's legs before you came out of there, Zayde, isn't any of your business, you don't have to know, period,' he stated in his usual coarse way, which I still had trouble adjusting to, but which didn't offend me anymore.

And the canary breeder, Jacob Sheinfeld, my mother's suitor and victim, served me his fragrant dishes one after another and told me simply: 'Rabinovitch's Judith from heaven she came to me, heaven, and she went back there from me.'

That's what he said, and his hands drew circles on the table, and the white scar on his forehead suddenly turned red, which always happens when he turns pale.

'You're still little, *meyn kind*. But you'll grow up and you'll learn and you'll know that in love there are rules. And it's better you learn those rules from a father, so you don't need later on to suffer because of love itself. How come a child has a father? So he'll learn from his father's troubles and not from his own troubles. How come all us sons of Israel is the sons of our father Jacob? So we'll all learn from his love. People are going to tell you lots of things about love. First of all, they'll tell you it's something for two. No, Zayde. For good hate you need two. But for love, you only need one person. And one little thing is enough for love, like I already told you. And someday, when you fall in love with a woman because of some one little thing, her eyes, let's say, somebody's going to come along and say: you fall in love with her eyes, but in the end you have to live with the whole woman. No, Zayde. If you fall in love with her eyes you'll also live with her eyes. And all the rest of that woman is like the closet for the dress.'

He dropped his eyes under my amazed look. His hand stopped stroking the table, but his mouth went on talking: 'Those things even God doesn't understand. The God of the Jews, loneliness He understands very good. But love He don't understand at all. One Lord all alone up in heaven, no kids, no friends, and no enemies, and the worst thing – no woman. In the end He gets crazy from so much loneliness. So He makes us crazy, too, and calls us whore and virgin and bride and all kinds of names a dumb man calls a woman. A woman is none of those things. In the end she's flesh and blood. It's too bad, only now I understand all that. Maybe if I understood it back then, if I understood that love is from the brain, not from the heart, is laws and rules, not dreams and craziness, maybe I would have had a better life. But understanding is one thing and succeeding is something else. If one man is going to get the one woman he really wants, somebody's got to run the whole world for that, and all parts of the world got to move and fall into place. 'Cause nothing goes by itself. And sometimes a person drowns in water here in the Land of Israel so that in America somebody else will win at cards. And sometimes a rain cloud comes here all the way from Europe so on a stormy night a man and a woman will be together. And if somebody commits suicide, it's a sign that somebody else wanted him to die very very much. And when a crow screams, somebody hears that scream. And when I saw Judith coming, when I saw the wagon going real slow, and the sun shining straight down – I looked on her and I knew: this is the woman my eyes could raise from the earth. Could raise her up and take her to me. In the land of India, there are people like that. They can move a cup on the table just by looking on it. You knew that, Zayde? In the children's newspaper at the Village Papish's house, I read about it. In his house they kept the old issues. Over there in India they got whatchacallit, fakirs, who don't feel any pain. They stop their breath and their heart. And they can move a cup on the table to the left or the right just with a look. Believe you me, Zayde, with a look. Right and left.

Left and right. Move the cup like that. And a cup, you should know, Zayde, it's a lot harder to move a cup than to move a woman.'

14

It was Moshe's older brother, Menahem Rabinovitch, whose stories and sweet carobs led Moshe and Tonya to immigrate to the Land of Israel, who knew Judith and advised Moshe to bring her to work in his house and farm.

Only after I grew up did Uncle Menahem tell me the name that was forbidden to mention, either in speaking or in writing, the name of my mother's first husband. He said the name and told me the story.

'They were living then in Mlabes or Rishon, I'm not absolutely sure.'

My mother's first husband was a soldier in the Hebrew Brigades, and when World War I ended, he came back to the Land of Israel and didn't find work.

Every day he went out to the main street of the town to look for work. A proud man he was, and didn't plead with the landlords, but rather fixed them with that soldier's look he had acquired in the war and which had now become a stumbling block for him because he didn't know that that look wasn't good in peace-time.

'People use what they've got, even if it's not exactly fitting,' Uncle Menahem explained. 'They smile when they should cry, pull out a gun when they should give a smack, and envy their lady loves instead of making them laugh.'

Long hours that man lay in bed and kept silent. They lived in a rented room which had previously been a pen for Turkish ducks. Feathers that were already crumbled to dust turned his eyes red. The old stench of poultry droppings slapped his face like unforgotten insults.

Judith suggested he grow vegetables and sell them in the

market, and the man got up and sowed a few garden beds behind the shack. But even among the sprouts he found no rest. A big tree rose in the yard and crows entered it in the afternoon for their noisy encounters, shouted and hovered over the crest of the tree like evil tidings. Their wings and their shouts blackened his hopes so much he hurried back to the room. Sometimes, he'd make a supreme effort and go sit on the banks of the Yarkon River, hug his knees, and close his eyes as if he were seeking consolation within his own body.

If not for Judith, who went on taking care of the vegetables, and raised a few brood hens in the yard, and made jam from the citrons that dropped in the landlord's citrus grove, and was marvellous at patching and resurrecting any tattered garment, they and their little daughter would have died of pride and starvation.

At last the man said he wanted to go to America, work there for a year at the Wilmington Foundry in the state of Delaware, a metal plant that belonged to the father of an American friend he had met in the Hebrew Brigades.

'I'll make money and I'll come back home,' he said. 'One year, Judith, two at the most.'

At the time, she was sitting at the table shelling lentils for soup, and she immediately turned her deaf ear to him. But he grabbed her shoulders and shouted, and she was forced to listen.

'Even in America there's no work.' She was angry and alarmed. 'And people will jump off roofs there.'

Two mounds piled up in front of her, a big brown one of lentils and a small grey one of splinters of dust and stone, husks and dried worms. Between her knees stood their two-year-old daughter, her eyes on her mother's nimble fingers.

'Don't go,' Judith implored. 'Don't go. We'll manage. Everything will be fine.'

Her hand found the knot of the blue kerchief on her head and tightened it. Dread and prophecy were in her voice. But that man, whose name I mustn't remember, didn't heed her terror. The journey was already seeping into his body and sealing his skin.

Short, with blurred features, he is drawn on the inside of my eyelids: he packs a few clothes in a small wooden suitcase, takes the provisions of poor travellers – hard white cheese, oranges, bread, and olives – takes leave of his wife and daughter, and goes to Jaffa. Here's Mother, leaning on the doorpost. Here's the little girl, leaning on her leg, my half-sister, but faceless like her father.

In Jaffa, he bought himself a cheap, deck-passenger ticket and went down to the little ship that took Shamouti oranges and sweet lemons to England.

It was a grey day, but the smell of sun latent in the oranges rose from the belly of the ship and accompanied the passengers, intensifying their regrets and remorse.

From Liverpool the man sailed for New York. Scared and in a hurry, he walked from the docks of the Hudson to Grand Central Station, and because in a foreign land his pride was diminished, he walked around in its enormous labyrinths calling out, 'Wilmington, Wilmington,' in the loud chirp of the helpless, until good people showed him the way to the ticket window and the platform.

The train slipped along in the belly of the earth for a while. Then it burst into the light, rumbled over a big river, and crossed a strip of reeds and swamps, the sort of thing the man hadn't expected to see in America. He sat by the window, counted the electrical poles as if he were scattering crumbs to show him the way back, and murmured to himself the names of the cities that passed by: Newark . . . New Brunswick . . . Trenton . . . Philadelphia . . . And three hours later, when the conductor shouted 'Wilmington' he hurried off.

He trudged from chimney to chimney and didn't find his friend's foundry. But he scouted and asked and found Columbus Street, where his friend had told him he lived, and he reached the house, whose number he remembered.

A fine house surrounded with a fragrant wall of trimmed finta bushes, and even though a Dutch clothing merchant lived there, the man thought it looked exactly how a Jewish foundry owner's house should look. He hoisted his hand and knocked on the door.

Fate decreed that on that very day the Dutch merchant had made a lot of money. He was in such a good mood that, when he saw the strange guest, he was struck with generosity, invited him in, and fed him a marvellous dinner of steamed fish and potatoes, seasoned with butter and nutmeg.

I often thought how strange it was that Uncle Menahem and Oded Rabinovitch and Jacob Sheinfeld knew all those small details they didn't witness. Did Oded hate my mother so much in his childhood that he embroidered her world with such precision? Did Jacob roll her chronicles around in his imagination so much that he created them anew? Did so much contrition fill the body of Uncle Menahem after her death? And if those potatoes had been seasoned with sour cream, coarse salt, and chopped dill, and not with that butter and nutmeg, would my mother's life have been changed because of it? And me, would I have been born?

One way or another, the Dutch merchant and my mother's husband drank aquavit with laurel berries, and after dinner they smoked thin cigars and played checkers. The host explained to his guest that his great-grandfather had built that house, and his grandfather, his father, and himself had been born in it, here, my good friend, in this very bed, and that in every city in America you could find a street named Columbus, and that Jews, you must know, my dear sir from Palestine, are not likely to have anything to do with steel foundries. In short, he hinted affably and politely that his friend from the Hebrew Brigades was nothing but a liar.

And indeed, that comrade-in-arms was simply a small fabricator seeking honour, the son of haberdashery peddlers from Chicago, who had never seen Wilmington except in the atlas. Like most liars, he hadn't investigated the falsehood, and some time later, as Uncle Menahem mocked him, he immigrated to the Land of Israel, introduced himself as 'the adjutant of Ze'ev Jabotinsky in the bloody battles of the Jordan Valley', rented a room in Tel Aviv, and made a living from dispatching articles titled 'Letters of a Pioneer from the Galilee' to Revisionist newspapers in America.

At any rate, the Dutch merchant, good-hearted with drink, gave his guest some old clothes and a loaf of seven-grain bread heavy and fragrant as a baby, and put a few addresses and letters of recommendation into his hand, and after trudging around some more and pleading some more, my mother's first husband became a guard in a department store that sold cheap goods.

There he rose to the high priesthood, from guard became a messenger and from a messenger became a salesman, and in a short time he became head of a department. Then he bought himself some brown and white shoes, became friendly with small liquor dealers, and started smoking cigarettes. Thus it happened that the one year in America, which promised not to be more than two years in a steel foundry, stretched into three years of smoking and selling.

Nevertheless, the man didn't forget his wife Judith. Once a month he sent her a letter and a little money, and he didn't stop this practice of his even when she stopped answering his letters. About the two women who loved him in Wilmington he didn't write to her because he knew his wife well and knew that she was graced with common sense and the power to guess. But from the two women, the man didn't conceal a thing. Over and over, he told them he had a wife and daughter in the Land of Israel and would be going back to them.

15

Shlaf meyn meydele, meyn kleyne
Shlaf meyn kind, un her tsikh tsu
Ot dos feygele dos kleyne
Iz keyn andere vie du.

My mother would sing that song to Naomi.

Oded would get mad. Naomi would enjoy it. Moshe was silent. I wasn't born yet.

Earlier, I imagine, she would sing the song to her daughter, afterwards to herself, and the words waited inside her until they found a new little girl.

'That means, Zayde, that you've got a half-sister in America,' Oded told me a few years after her death.

We were riding in the village milk truck then, on one of those night trips I went along on.

'I wish I had, too,' added Oded.

Oded dreams a lot about America and American trucks and American roads and American women, and a whole wall of his house is covered with all the road maps of the United States, which he cut out of the Rand-McNally Atlas and covered with plastic sheets. For hours he stands facing them, memorizing routes, sticking pins and flags, and preparing trips for an imaginary fleet, heavy and many-wheeled.

'You see this highway, Zayde? That's highway number ten. In America, they call such a highway an interstate. See this stretch, Los Angeles, San Bernardino, all the way to Phoenix, Arizona? Right here is the biggest truck stop in the world. With everything you need: diesel, food, beer, and oil. As we say: fill up the car and the man. Five hundred heavy trucks come there every day.'

'So why don't you just go to America?' I asked him.

'That's all I need,' replied Oded, 'to make my dreams come true.'

'She's pulling to the right,' he added, stopped, and got out to check the wheels. We walked around the tanker, Oded hit the tyres with a big wooden hammer and listened to the tones. He lingered at one of them, spat on his finger, poured the saliva on the mouth of the valve, and carefully examined the bubbles.

'A little bit of air is escaping,' he said. 'Who needs that trouble, to make dreams come true? . . . What do you think, I don't know that America's not a hundred per cent good as I imagine? At some time, every little boy wants to be a truck driver when he grows up, and a lot of grown-ups still dream of that, too. But only an idiot like me makes it come true. Remind me in an hour to stop and check that valve again.'

Two years old that daughter was when her father went, and by the time he came back she was five. A pretty little girl she was, stiff of neck and hard of eye; in her hands she grasped a rag doll and didn't recognize the small, splendid man who came into the old Turkish duck coop, smiled, waved a bundle of money, and called out: 'I came to take you to America!'

If the little girl hadn't grown, you might think he had been gone only half an hour, since, when he came in, her mother had been sitting in the same chair at the same table and picking over lentils, which, as lentils are, were much like the lentils she had been picking over the day he left. That same deep line was still ploughed between her eyebrows, and that same offensive stench of coops was in the air, and the small heaps, the grey one and the brown one, were piling up in front of her like an hourglass that had stopped.

He wanted to go to her, but Judith stood up, and with a heaviness that amazed her husband, she stood the little girl in front of her, as if to defend herself, and perhaps to be hidden behind the little body. Her fingers stroked the child's back with scared, long strokes, and the man noticed her new, big belly which rounded before his eyes.

'You're pregnant,' he exclaimed joyously, and suddenly his own words struck him, and the mocking awareness that he hadn't been home in three years, and he understood the cry for help of her first letters and the coolness of the middle ones, and the lack of the last ones, and the eyes of the landlord, which were lowered to the ground when he came in, and the ugly course of the crow who landed from the tree like a black rag and croaked derisively at him.

His knees buckled, but he recovered immediately. He quickly put his money in his pocket, grabbed his daughter's hand, and said to her: 'Come, Daddy will take you to America.'

'I want to take my doll,' said the child with a quiet and a coolness that surprised both her parents.

'No need,' said the man. 'You'll have a new doll, you don't need to take anything from here. Come, now.'

He turned to leave and the child left her doll and followed him.

Judith didn't lift her eyes. Her stroking hand remained hanging in the air. Dread riveted her to the spot. She bent her neck a bit and the expectation of a blow trembled at the base of her spine.

Before he closed the door, my mother's first husband turned
his face, smiled with the affability of American salesmen, spat
on the floor, and said to her: '*Shmutzige pirde!*' – a curse
so abominable it can't be translated even by someone whose
mother tongue is Yiddish. Even Globerman, whose daily bread
is coarseness, cleared his throat a bit before he explained it to
me in its full sharpness.

The man closed the gate of the yard, crossed the neighbour's
vegetable field as the neighbour was crawling on his knees in
the red loam mud and pretending to be deep in his onions and
carrots, and disappeared with his daughter beyond the wall of
cypresses. On the road, he stopped a little truck coming from
Ras-El-Ayn, stuck a dollar bill in the hand of the amazed driver,
and ordered him to take them straight to the port of Jaffa.

In the evening, Judith's lover came and saw her white and alone,
her head like a stone among the lentils scattered around.

'He came back?' he whispered.

Judith didn't answer because the man was talking on her
deaf side.

'And took her?' he shouted.

'Came back and took her,' she wailed.

'I'll go after him, I'll catch him, I'll bring her back to you!'
The man got excited.

Judith looked at him. The warmth of his body, the fury of
his heart, which had won her and helped her in the time of her
loneliness, now seemed miserable to her like a field of stubble.

'Don't go after him, don't catch him, don't bring back the
child,' she said. 'It's not your games, you men.'

In front of her closed eyes stretched the empty prophecy of her
life. 'The child didn't recognize him,' she finally groaned. 'But
she went with him without a word to me. Not even good-bye.'

The man sat down next to her, put his arm around her, cradled
her head in the hollow of his neck, and put his hand on her belly
button.

'Now it's us, Judith,' he whispered. 'You and me, and soon
we'll have a new little girl.'

'Yes,' said Judith. 'I'll have a new little girl.'

A great cool force suddenly filled her whole body. A month and a half later she gave birth without a shout and without surprise to a big, beautiful boy who was already dead.

'We'll go there and find her,' said her lover over the grave of the stillborn baby, and once again he started shouting. 'We'll go to court. You can't simply take a child away from a mother like that. In America there's a law.'

'We won't go there, the verdict has already been passed and carried out,' said Judith. Her lover looked at her and was terrified because he saw the hardness rising from her flesh, climbing the capillaries of her body, and sinking like chalk in the cracks of her skin. He saw and knew that he had to leave her alone.

16

So that's how the lying Revisionist from the Hebrew Brigades changed things, and if you're interested in questions of 'if' and 'what if', as I am and as they are in me, you'll find diversions of Chance and Fate here to respond to. For if he really did have a foundry in Wilmington, my mother's first husband would have gone back home on time and I wouldn't have come into the world, and if I had come, I would have had one father, and they would have given me another name and the Angel of Death would have caught up with me long ago.

Uncle Menahem, who saw my childish occupation as the irony of fate, told me a wonderful story about the three brothers, If, What If, and What If Not, who walk every night in the traces of the Angel of Sleep. 'The *Malakh-fun-shlof* puts people to sleep, and the brothers If, What If, and What If Not wake them up, dance around them in a ring of questions, and don't let them sleep anymore.'

But the dealer Globerman, whose nocturnal tranquillity is not injured by any issue, exertion, remorse, or regret, repeated his motto to me: '*A mensh trakht un Gott lakht* – man makes plans and God laughs.' That is: questions will be asked, answers will be given, the three brothers will dance over my unsleeping eyes – the same as for Judith, for she never saw her daughter again until the day she died.

So I've got a half-sister somewhere in big America, and not even her name ever appeared on our mother's lips. And if I asked and persisted about her, Mother's standard line stopped me: '*A nafka mina.*'

The ship sailing from Jaffa took the father and his daughter to Genoa. There they stayed a few days in a cheap hotel that stank of fish, anise, and garlic, and big cats sat in geranium boxes on the balcony like nesting birds.

From there they sailed to Lisbon and from there to Rotterdam and from there to America and because of the other passengers in their cabin who lay in their bunks all day, laughed in strange languages, played cards, and reeked of vomit and sweat and filth and tobacco – they walked along the deck rail a lot.

Meanwhile, as will often happen to such men, the little girl had already changed from a plundered prize to a hindrance to him, and his anger and desire for revenge weren't satisfied, and their murmurs even overcame the roar of the waves, and the man would smack his daughter's face hard. Such smacks were so fast and short that no one noticed them and no one heard the ugly words that were sprayed out with them: '*Punkt vi deyne mame di kurve* – just like your mama, the whore.' And if I may once again be permitted to say something about the heroes of my life and the creations of my imagination, I will say that if it were up to me, we wouldn't meet that despicable man again. If he had stayed with them, he might have become the hero of this story and another son would have told it, but since he did what he did, he exiled himself from my chronicles and spared me the need to unfurl the rest of his history.

And as for my mother's forgotten lover, I know neither his name nor where he came from, and since three fathers is enough for me, I don't even look for him. But once, about fifteen years after Mother died, on one of my visits to Naomi in Jerusalem, she pointed out an old man who was very stooped, looked like an upside-down L, and was leaning on two wooden canes, stumbling down the street of Beit-HaKerem in Jerusalem, not far from the teachers' seminary.

'See that man? He was your mother's lover,' she said.

And if the shock of such a sentence isn't enough, that was the first and only time I understood that Naomi also knew something about Mother's history.

How did she know that was the man? I don't know.

Why did she decide to tell me he was the man? I don't know that, either.

Should I have been offended? Naomi, who sensed my embarrassment, said: 'Let's go back to the house, Zayde, and make a big salad like we used to eat at home.'

I always bring her vegetables and eggs from the village, and a jar of sour cream and slices of cheese, and I always come to her at night, in the big milk truck, driven by Oded.

I've grown up, Oded has gotten old, yet I still love those night-time trips with him and his stories and his complaints and his dreams, which he shouts to overcome the roar of the motor.

The roads have become wider, the trucks pass by one after another, but the nights remain cool as they were, and Oded still villifies the man who married his sister and took her away from the village, and he still asks me: 'You want to honk, Zayde?' And once again I put out my hand to the horn cord, and once again I'm jolted and softened when its bleating rises, enormous and gloomy, into the night air.

Two little children were skipping around that stooped man and a horrible hidden burden lay on his shoulders. But who would assure me that that burden was my mother? And who doesn't bear such burdens? For against the few men who loved her is a whole world of people who didn't know her, and every one of them tottered down his street, and every one is bent over like an upside-down L, bowing under the load of his soul.

17

'That was a great tragedy with Tonya,' said Jacob. 'A very great tragedy. We had a few other catastrophes, but a thing like that? To drown like that in the wadi? Is a wadi to drown in? In the Kodyma River you drown, in the Black Sea you drown, but in our wadi? In how much, twelve inches deep? A catastrophe like that doesn't just happen. Eat, Zayde, please eat, you can eat and listen at the same time. Once I thought maybe because they looked so much alike and there was rain and fog there, so the Angel of Death made a mistake and Tonya died instead of Moshe. But she died and he remained with all that failure and regretting, and that's really something, Zayde, 'cause you got to know how to miss a dead woman. That's not like missing a live woman. Those two regrets I know real good and I know exactly what I'm talking about 'cause I missed your mother both when she was living and when she was dead. How old are you today, Zayde? Exactly twelve and you're also an orphan yourself, so maybe you can understand these things even without me confusing you. What can I tell you, Zayde, like a black shadow fell over the village. A young widower, two little orphans . . . and nothing matters to the God of the Jews. At the end of the winter she died and a month later spring came with joy and dancing. Buds flower, larks sing, cranes call. Kroo-kroo . . . kroo-kroo . . . you know the sound of the cranes in the fields, don't you, Zayde? Their voice isn't loud, but you hear it far, far away. Once, during World War II, I saw an Italian prisoner-of-war from the prison camp dancing there in the field with three cranes. Birds immediately feel that Italians aren't like other men. From far away, I thought it was four people, they was so tall and have a kind of royal crown on their head. And when I started coming close, the prisoner-of-war picked up his feet and took off for the camp and the cranes opened their wings of nine feet across and started flying. *A yener* – oh that – prisoner-of-war camp . . .

you remember it? You were a little boy then. They had a hole in
the fence and they would come out like my poor birds from the
cage I'd leave open, and they'd run around here in the fields, and
nobody guarded them because they didn't really want to escape.
Have another helping, Zayde. Come on, open your mouth, *meyn
kind*. I remember how my foster uncle's youngest son would
eat. From the day he was born his mouth was always open
and his first word was "more". Not "mother", not "father",
but "more". At the age of six months, he pointed to the pot of
food and said, "*Nokh!*" Anybody who can say "more" doesn't
need many other words to get along good in life. There are
people who get along fine all their lives with just two words,
the word "that" and the word "more". That boy would eat to
gobble up a bull like they say, like a bottomless barrel, and his
mother really loved to see him eat and say more and more, and
he grew and grew so much that she was scared of the evil eye,
and would call him to the table only after everybody else had
already finished eating, and then she would stand in front of
him with a big sheet spread like this in her hands, to hide him
while he was eating, so nobody would see him and, God forbid,
give him the evil eye. So eat now, Zayde, open your mouth big
and eat and I'll sing you a little song for your appetite:

> At the window, at the window,
> Stood a bird today,
> A boy ran up to the window—
> Pretty bird has flown away.
> Weep, child, such dismay,
> Pretty bird has flown away . . .'

18

At first Moshe Rabinovitch's catastrophe was the property of
the whole village. During the week-long mourning period, his
friends mobilized, milked his cows and picked the fruit left in

the citrus grove. And in the next few weeks, until his broken leg healed, they came to give him a hand and a shoulder, and lent him a mule or a horse for the day until he found a new work animal. The orphans were invited to eat by all the neighbour women, and Aliza Papish, the wife of the Village Papish, showed up to glorify the floor of the hut, to do the laundry, and to clean.

But time passed, the helpers dropped off until they stopped altogether, and the neighbour woman's husband told Moshe he couldn't afford to feed the children.

Rabinovitch, who was still encased in plaster from his chest down to his ankle, got very angry. After all, from the start he had offered to pay the neighbour for the meals, and when he now asked him again how much money he'd want, the man blurted out a sum that could support an army brigade. Moshe threw him out and made an arrangement with the wife of the manager of the village warehouse, and from that day until Judith came to his house, Oded and Naomi ate dinner there for a reasonable price. Sometimes a few English officers also ate there; and the albino book-keeper, who dared come out of Yakoba and Yakobi's old hut after sundown, also dined there.

The narcissus bulbs Moshe pulled up from the bank of the wadi and buried in the earth of Tonychka's grave bloomed quickly. New baby crows were noisy in the nest at the top of the eucalyptus tree. The world went on as usual, moved and revolved in its orbit, bore its dead and its living like a ship in search of a port.

The sun climbed up, the air grew warm, and every afternoon, Moshe wallowed like a calf in the emptied field, chewed grass and bared his wounded flesh to the spring.

Lapwings drummed near him on long legs, presenting their splendid, ever-clean suits. Chirps of bliss of the field mice, those who were saved from the wrath of the winter, were heard rushing under the grass. A smell of blooming assaulted from the fields, quickening the blood in the veins, and downed the deformed finches in their flight.

From that custom of lying naked in the field and absorbing the beams of spring, he isn't yet weaned. Years later I would see him come to the field, take off his clothes, and stretch out in the high grass. And once, when I stationed my observation-box behind the field and watched the larks dancing, Moshe came, stripped, and lay down right next to the box.

His thick short body breathed slowly, his hand smoothed the hair on his chest and belly, and when the heat rose, the hand moved his testicles from side to side.

Two big flies walked around on his face and he didn't brush them off.

So close and exposed and innocent he was, and he didn't sense that I was there at all, for the branches and the grass hid the box even from the birds, and although I was almost baked by the heat of the sun, I didn't dare move, for Moshe suddenly began saying to himself, 'My Moshe, my Moshe,' leaned on his side a bit, and a smell like the smell of Uncle Menahem rose in the air, but I was too young to understand it, and I thought they smelled alike because they were brothers.

Rabinovitch's broken thigh mended fast, but when he asked the doctor to take off the cast, the doctor claimed it wasn't time yet. Moshe didn't argue with him. He returned home, went into the cows' big trough, and lay there until his bonds melted and the water in the trough turned as white as milk. A few days later he hitched up the wagon and went to the next village with his children for the Seder with Uncle Menahem and his wife Bathsheba.

Uncle Menahem and Moshe were different from one another. Menahem was tall and thin, and even though he was older than his brother, he looked younger. He had long fingers, whose delicacy wasn't damaged by working the land, and thick brown hair, and a warm, pleasant voice, and a trimmed moustache the family called an 'American moustache', even though no one knew precisely what that was.

And he also had the biggest farm of Cypriot carobs – the juiciest and lushest carobs. I remember how he would proudly break such a carob and let it drip dark honey.

'If Bar Yokhai had a tree like this in the clearing, he would have been satisfied with one single carob from one Sabbath eve to the next,' he said.

Uncle Menahem talked about his carobs the way a dairy farmer talks about his livestock. He had a lush 'herd', a few 'bull' trees, and a few score 'cows', and he said that if he could, he would take his trees out to pasture, walk behind them, and pipe on a flute.

'One day, Zayde, we'll invent trees without roots. When we go for a walk or to work in the field, we'll whistle at them and they'll run behind us, and we'll always have shade,' he told me.

He also had a tale he loved to tell and I loved to hear, about a gentile farmer who wandered around the Ukraine with a gigantic, blossoming apple tree, which he planted in a big wagon, full of soil, drawn by four oxen, and bees flew behind it.

At any rate, Uncle Menahem didn't rely on the wind to carry the bull carob pollen to the cow carob flowers, but fertilized them himself. In late summer, he climbed the male trees, shook the fragrant pollen into paper bags, and quickly scattered it among the female branches. Because of that, the heavy, dusty, ineffable smell of sperm stuck to him, embarrassed the neighbour women, amused the neighbour men, and drove his wife, Aunt Bathsheba, out of her mind.

Aunt Bathsheba loved her husband to distraction and was sure that all the women in the world felt the same way about him. Now she feared that the smell of sperm, which didn't leave his body even after she shoved him into the shower and scrubbed him with a brush until he turned red and shouted in pain, would attract strange women to him. So every woman who got within sight of Uncle Menahem was called a 'hoor' by his wife, and since the village was small and the jealousy was great, the hoors multiplied and Aunt Bathsheba's anger rose.

'A husband like Menahem has to be quiet in the spring,' she explained. 'It would be better if he were quiet all year, but it's especially good for him to be quiet in the spring and not start doing everything he knows – telling tales, lying lies, and confessing confessions . . . All those things are very dangerous to do near the hoors in the spring.'

And thus it happened that in the third year of his marriage, Uncle Menahem was afflicted with a strange allergy, which would attack him every spring and was not expressed in the usual way, with sneezing and itching and tearing, but with a complete silence of his vocal cords.

Tonya once said that Bathsheba put a curse on Menahem, but the aunt denied it: 'A wife shouldn't do such things. That's why there's a God in heaven.' She smiled with the righteousness of someone whose task is done by others.

One way or another, every year, one morning between Purim and Passover, Uncle Menahem would wake up with his voice gone. The first words he said on the first morning of his muteness misled him into thinking he had gone deaf, but later he understood that his lips moved, but his voice didn't emerge.

At first, his forced muteness turned him into an irritable, short-tempered man, and turned Bathsheba into a quiet and satisfied woman. But in later years, Uncle Menahem calmed down and got used to it and learned to use notes to talk with those around him, while Aunt Bathsheba was once again filled with her jealousy and dread. Now she feared that the spring that muzzled her husband's throat would impel him to run after the hoors in new ways.

'After all, he's a decent bird,' she kept saying.

And once, when I was six or seven years old, I told Uncle Menahem that I knew what was the difference between him and Jacob Sheinfeld.

'What's the difference, Zayde?' asked Uncle Menahem in a note.

'Both of you are birds,' I told him, 'but you're a decent bird and Sheinfeld is a strange bird.'

Mother smiled, Naomi laughed, Menahem's body quivered with pleasure, and his hand wrote me a note: 'Ha ha ha.'

'A man who doesn't have words will jump around and put on an act like monkeys in the woods,' said Bathsheba, who was frightened herself by the mighty result her jealousy could produce.

Uncle Menahem didn't jump around and didn't put on an act, but was silent and withdrew into himself, with that kind of withdrawal thin men experience at the end of summer, when the days begin to grow short.

A kind of protective humour of mutes was also created in him. 'I don't need to recite your boring Haggadah,' he announced in a big formal sign he waved in front of everybody at that Passover Seder.

Oded and Naomi and the three sons of Bathsheba and Menahem laughed. And so did Moshe, who hugged his brother when he came in that year; he wept and said: 'This is the first Seder without a wife and without a mother, Menahem,' and he smiled.

'Menahem thinks you should get married again right away,' said Bathsheba and Menahem nodded.

But Moshe wasn't even willing to talk about that, and certainly not, as he said, in front of the children.

Moshe and Bathsheba sang with the children all the songs they remembered from the old country, Menahem drummed them on the table, and Oded found the the *Afikommen matzo* Menahem had hidden, and asked for 'Mother to come back'.

Moshe was shocked and turned pale, but Menahem tapped the boy on the back of his neck and wrote: 'That's a fine wish, Odedi, but in the meantime, you'll get a pocket-knife.'

19

Sometimes, Moshe wanted to grieve, to be weak, for he felt that a flourishing body didn't suit a mourning soul.

He wanted to collapse, but he couldn't. On the contrary, after Tonya's death his body seemed to grow even stronger. As if the muscles that despaired in her neck grew strong in his, as if shoots of green life sprang suddenly from the ashes of mourning and – shameful as it was – glimmers of relief, and explicit and embarrassing twigs of a flourishing of widowers; no one admits that, but everyone discerns it and knows what it means.

Moshe's speech, which was generally heavy, became fluent and faster, his slow peasant's gait started dancing sometimes, and thin new hair sprouted on his smooth head – not a thick new mane of youth, but an infant down that darkened his bald pate.

His body had healed by now and grew so strong that he went back to work as if nothing had happened. He harvested and picked and hoed and ploughed, and in the evening, after milking, he once again hung the four milk jugs on a pole he had made from a two-inch pipe, loaded it on his thick shoulders, and took it to the dairy.

From there, he went to fetch his children from their supper. The empty milk jugs dangled at the ends of the pole, clanged with a hollow gloom, and Moshe's thoughts echoed them in his heart.

He entered the warehouse manager's home. The albino book-keeper said hello and Moshe growled some reply. He despised everything outside the normal order of the world, and the book-keeper, with his owlish life, the hues of his hair and eyes and skin, made Moshe uneasy.

But the albino didn't want to endear himself to him or to anyone else. He tended to his birds and did his work and didn't bother anybody. Once a week, the treasurer brought a wheelbarrow full of receipts and papers to Yakobi and Yakoba's old shack, and knocked on the door. The book-keeper, with his pink eyes and his black suit, opened the window a crack and whispered: 'Please come in quietly so you don't frighten the poor birds.'

After the treasurer left, the albino would swoop down on the papers, calculate accounts, sharpen pencils, and weigh the balance sheet of the outside world, which was flooded with light.

The song of his birds and his closed shutters protected him from the wrath of the sun, and only at dusk, when his enemy declined, looking weary and yolk-like, to rest for a moment on the horizon before departing from the world, did he come out of his shelter to stretch his bones and inhale some fresh air.

First the door would open. An arm in a long sleeve, terrified and quivering like a mole's muzzle, sniffed the light and the air, slowly turned over, assessed the ire of the dying sun and the dissolving heat of the earth. And when the hand was assured, the rest of the albino came out behind it, his sunglasses looking up and his step hesitant. He retreated inside immediately, and came right back out again, carrying canary cages, as if he were taking his dogs for a walk.

After he hung the cages on the tow chain of the truck, which stretched from the corner of the house to the trunk of the nearby cedar, he sat down in a chaise longue and set out a tray of peeled cucumbers cut lengthwise, white pepsin cheese, herring, a bottle of beer, and a worn-out book that wrung bloody tears from his eyes and soft groans of pleasure from his throat.

Meanwhile, the children began showing signs of their orphanhood. Oded wet his bed every night and Naomi lost weight.

'Nominka doesn't eat,' the warehouse manager's wife said to Moshe.

'Her food isn't any good,' Naomi said later as they walked home.

'Tell me what you like to eat,' said Moshe after a long silence. 'And I'll tell her.'

'It's Mother's food we want,' said Oded.

'We all want Mother's food,' said Moshe.

The summer was hot and fragrant as always. The darkness of the village surrounded them with the silence of owls' wings. Tiny slivers of straw flew from the barn floor and scratched the skin of Moshe's neck like last summer, when his Tonychka was still alive and went with him to the threshing.

Three more times the moon would fill up and empty out and then, Moshe knew, his firm body would soften and fill with autumn. Storks would glide in the sky, a dewy wind would come from the mountain, the squills would feel it and rise up at the edges of the fields.

He loved the circles of memory the storks sketched in the sky, the devotion of the squill in its earth and the vibrating longings of its twigs. Never was he an eloquent speaker, and those two, the squill and the stork, defined for him – one with its wings and the other with its bulbs – the passing of time and the eternity of place that words can't describe.

*   *   *

The last hornets assembled on the young grapes of the vineyards, new clouds piled up, the robin, the tiny fighter, returned from the north. He came back and took charge of the pomegranate tree, and his furious battle chirps were heard from the thicket, delineating the borders of his estate and his tolerance.

Cold, damp winds moved the cypresses, small, supple acorns dropped from them and bounced on the roof of the shed. The wadi overflowed again, and every day, like a wounded animal seeking a cure, Moshe searched his house and his yard for the box with the braid, that braid the dead women of his life had hidden from him.

In the village sky, clouds of starlings rose up like smears of enormous brushes, in flocks that met, spread out, merged, and separated. In the morning they flew east over the valley and at night they came back. They landed for the night on the canary pines near the water tower so fast that the big trees seemed to suck them into their foliage. Only the quiet chatter was heard among the branches, the chatter of birds and children before they fall asleep, until that, too, fell silent.

In the house, there were still a few jars of jam that Tonya had made the summer before her death, and no one remembered they were there. But Moshe, in his grim search for his braid, found them in some corner and brought them to the kitchen. Oded swooped down on them and that very evening, his father discovered him in the cowshed, all smeared with jam and twitching like a poisoned jackal from so much sweetness.

'It's good,' said Oded, and offered him a spoonful. 'Open your mouth, Father, and close your eyes.'

Without thinking, like everyone who was once a child, Moshe shut his eyes and opened his mouth, and Oded stuck on his tongue a spoonful of jam that scalded his throat and pressed tears out of his closed eyes.

Naomi, who followed him into the cowshed unnoticed, looked at the two of them and shuddered.

'Want some, too?' asked Oded, and offered her the spoon. 'Mother's jam, eat some.'

But Naomi was suddenly filled with the vague, mute rage of

orphanhood, and before they could stop her, she snatched the jar and smashed it on the concrete floor of the cowshed, and then fled into the yard.

20

'*Ess, meyn kind.*'

His hand put another plate before me, and on its return, it dared to stroke my head.

Jacob never called me 'my son', but only '*meyn kind*', as if Yiddish intimidated him less. As for me, I didn't call any of my fathers 'father', not in any language.

Globerman often scolded me for not calling him 'father', but Jacob didn't care. He asked me only one thing, not to call him by his last name – Sheinfeld – like everybody else, but only by his first name.

'Now I'll tell you a story about another Jacob so you'll understand,' he said. 'Not about Our Father Jacob, the one all us Jacobs is named after, but about another Jacob Sheinfeld, who was the brother of the father of my grandfather. In our family, in every single generation there's a Jacob Sheinfeld, the Sheinfeld stays and the Jacobs change. If I told you how that Jacob Sheinfeld made a living, you'll laugh. He was a soap taster. Did you ever see how they make soap, Zayde? They got a big vat, big as this room, and they pour into it all kinds of filth and ashes and fat from dead animals, and it all stinks and boils on the fire, and bubbles come up from that porridge, bubbles big as watermelons, and if you ever saw that nauseating stuff, you'll never want to wash with soap again in your life. And that's what he'd taste. Again you laugh? When I was little, if a boy said naughty words, they'd wash his mouth out with soap to punish him, but in the factory they had to taste the soap porridge so they should know when to turn off the fire, or else all the soap wouldn't come out right. How do they know? That's a secret. It's not written in any book. A thing like that is written

only on the tongue and the memory of the specialist. He'll smell
and he'll taste and he'll make faces and he'll say what's missing,
and finally he'll say: "*Itzt!* Now!" And then right away they got
to turn off the fire. And you had to taste from the middle of the
vat, not from the sides, and so that Jacob Sheinfeld would hang
like this on the rope like a monkey over the boiling vat and put
in a spoon, and taste on the tip of his tongue and spit it out
and say whether to wait or to put out the fire. With them, the
profession would be passed down from father to son, but that
Jacob Sheinfeld was an old bachelor and he didn't have children,
and when he started to get old, the owner comes to him and says
the time has come for you to teach somebody how to taste the
soap. See, if, God forbid, something should happen to you, who
would give the sign and say the "*Itzt*"? Jacob Sheinfeld hears
that and he doesn't say a word. And the next day he comes to
work like every day, hangs on the rope over the boiling vat of
soap, tastes, spits, and says: What this needs is a little bit of fat
from an old carcass, and before anybody can figure that out, he
lets go of the rope and falls into the boiling vat of soap. Will you
eat something sweet now, Zayde? I'm sorry I told you that story
now. I maybe should have waited a few years. I maybe should
have told it to you at our next meal. Now I'm going to make
you something sweet that I once learned from an Italian man.'

He scurried up, as if he wanted to wipe out the impression of
his story.

'Very simple. Now all we got to have is an egg yolk, wine,
and sugar. Come to the sink with me and watch.'

Into the palm of his hand, he broke an egg, poured the white
between his spread fingers, and then bounced the yolk gently in
the concave surface of his palm.

'See, Zayde?' he said. 'It doesn't break and it doesn't spill.
That's how it is when the egg is fresh and the yolk is strong.'

He separated two more yolks like that and put them in a bowl,
added a little sugar and some fragrant wine.

'What's better than a mixture like that? The yolk is food from
mother and the memory of life, and the wine is the soul and the
future, and the sugar is the lust and the strength.'

The whisk was a blur and became a silver circle with so much speed, and Jacob put the bowl on the pot of boiling water and went on beating. 'That smells a lot better than soap and it tastes a lot better than soap and one day I'll teach you how to make it. You understand what I'm talking about, Zayde?' He took the bowl out, stuck a finger in it, and told me to do the same.

'That's what the Italians do.' He licked his finger with pleasure. 'You like it? Eh? Me, too. Rabinovitch gives you something sweet at home?'

'Not much,' I said.

In those days, people didn't eat a lot of sweets. At Rabinovitch's house, we sweetened our bread only with jam, and with our tea, we bit on a sugar cube. To this day, that's how I drink tea, because then bitter and sweet aren't blended with one another, but exist side by side.

Moshe, who regarded a yearning for cake or chocolate as a sign of corruption, used to tell that in his childhood his parents' home was so poor that when they drank tea they would hang one sugar cube on a string over the table.

'And you dipped it in the cup?' I asked.

Moshe smiled with the pride of the poor. 'No,' he said. 'We would drink the tea and look at the sugar.'

'Don't believe my father, Zayde,' Naomi told me. 'They had tons of money in Russia. They had forests and warehouses, and a mill and businesses, and my father, when he was a boy, ate more sweets than all his children put together, and that includes you, too, Zayde.'

21

Soft and persistent, the rain fell, fell without stopping. Moshe made burlap hoods for himself and his children, and he built a small wooden sled shaped like a shallow trough, with a tin-lined bottom. Every evening he put the milk cans in it and dragged it through the mud to the dairy, and every evening, after he chatted there with the other farmers about this and that and the other thing, he went to fetch his children from the warehouse manager's house.

The kids sat with the empty cans in the sled and were dragged home. The first few times, they laughed and shouted, 'Giddyap, Father, giddyap!' But they soon grew short-tempered and Moshe's patience gave out, too. The straps of the sled cut the muscles of his shoulders. His firm, short legs got stuck in the mud and were pulled out of it with a nauseating noise. Every day he worked in the yard and the field, and in the evening, he no longer responded to his children's pleas and didn't play the 'awful bear' with them, but lay on his belly and groaned until Naomi came and walked on his back with her little stockinged feet, kneading and soothing his flesh with her heels.

Then the children went to sleep and Moshe boiled some eggs and cooked potatoes in their skin, crumbled laundry soap into flakes, lit a bonfire in the yard, and boiled Oded's stinking wet sheets. He cleaned and tidied up and searched for his braid, and didn't go to bed until after midnight, his limbs languid and his spirit sullen.

That was a year of blessing, but not on the Rabinovitch farm. There were two miscarriages in the cowshed, a marten found a crack in the wall of the hatchery and murdered scores of chicks, the drainage in the orchard didn't work, and rainy days clogged the roots of some trees.

By day Moshe tramped around in the soil of his fields and at night his dreams dug through to his wife's grave, touched her bones, brought up the wooden and mother-of-pearl box, stroked the golden braid, and drew strength from it.

Then the dreams stopped and returned to their cages and Moshe woke up, for Oded came to his bed and pressed against his body. He waited until the child fell asleep, and then he got up and took him back to the bed he shared with Naomi. But Oded would wake up again, and his father would hear the squeak of the bed again, and the jam spoon striking like a clapper against the side of the jar, and the drumming of the little feet coming back to him and climbing into his bed.

And in the morning, Moshe woke up, his skin soaked with the cold childish urine of orphanhood and neglect, and his heart entreating and shouting: Where is Tonya, his wife – his twin? And where are his embroidered little dresses? His amputated plaits of hair? The tresses of his childhood and his strength?

22

And so in 1930, in Kfar David in the Jezreel Valley, there was a widowed farmer who had to plough and milk and cook and sew and play a game with his children and read them a story. And get up every night to make sure the blankets hadn't slipped off them, and send them to school every morning, washed and combed and sated, and bury his face every day in his dead wife's clothes, bats of fabric and memory hanging in the cave of their closet – and, great as his physical strength was, it didn't help him at all.

And in the colony of Petakh-Tikva, or maybe Rishon Le-Zion, there was a poor, deserted woman whose little girl was taken away from her, and her heart was shrivelled in her rib cage and the tears melted burrows in her flesh.

'So what's the big deal here?' asked Jacob Sheinfeld, and cleared the big plates from the table. 'See, now everything's clear, Fate wanted that encounter.'

And indeed, from now on, it's only a question of time until my mother gets to the village.

'And I ask you, Zayde: for that you take a little girl away from her mother? For that you drown another woman in the wadi?'

Encounters like that, he added bitterly, Fate doesn't tend to leave in the hand of Chance or even in the hand of Luck. It was the hand of Uncle Menahem that was entrusted with what was going to happen.

Uncle Menahem heard about Judith and was sensitive enough and smart enough to talk to Moshe about her, to tell him what he had to know and to leave out what needed to be left out, and afterwards he also took the trouble to go to her. He wanted to keep that secret, but Bathsheba raised an awful fuss in the middle of the village and shouted that her husband 'is going to jump on a new hoor'.

Menahem proposed to Judith to come to Kfar David and work for his brother, where she would find bread to eat and clothes to wear and a house to live in and children to raise and cows to milk and pots to scour and a man to drink tea with, and to look into his eyes to read his brow.

'It'll be good for both of you,' he told her.

But neither Moshe nor Judith was eager to accept his proposal. Each of them withdrew into the armour of grief and both of them said 'maybe', and 'what for', and 'we'll see', and other such wary words, as if their hearts prophesied it but advised: 'Wait!'

A year had passed since Tonya's death and it was almost Purim. Closets and trunks were opened, fabrics were pulled out, dye and trimmings were prepared. The big Purim costume contest was held, and three candidates made it to the final stage.

The first was a vague bluish figure calling itself 'King of the Indian Ocean'.

The second was the albino book-keeper, who surprised the whole village just by participating. He dressed up as 'a young girl doing laundry in the river', and mounted the stage with bare knees, whose mottled redness stood out in his white skin, clutching a laundry basket in one arm and a washboard in the other, and he never took his pink eyes off Jacob Sheinfeld.

The third, of course, was the Village Papish. Every year, the Village Papish surprised everybody with his original costume, and that year he dressed as 'Siamese Twins'. He made up his eyes and wrapped himself in colourful rags, and to the great joy of the audience, he announced that his twin suffered from stage-fright and had stayed home. But the ovation was immediately interrupted and the audience fell silent, for suddenly Tonya Rabinovitch also appeared and climbed up on the stage.

In simple, everyday clothes, the deceased woman thrust her way in and stood among the trio of competitors. She looked so much like herself that the master of ceremonies wanted to tell her to get off the stage because she wasn't in costume, but everyone immediately moaned in horror and anger because they remembered that she was already dead and they understood that it was Moshe Rabinovitch, who had dressed up in memory of his wife. They looked so much alike that all the widower had to do was put on the dead woman's dress, stick a pair of big wool balls in it, and put a kerchief on his head.

'Get down, Rabinovitch, get off the stage,' someone shouted.

'You should be ashamed of yourself!' the Village Papish scolded him between clenched Siamese teeth.

But Tonya stared at him with the fearless eyes of the dead, came close to him until he backed off; she wiped her hands on her apron with that familiar gesture neither death nor time could erase, and said in a thick voice: 'Right away, I'm going to call my Moshe and he'll make mincemeat out of you.'

'Get off! Beast!' shouted the audience. There were also whistles and a few angry men came to the front of the auditorium.

Tonya dropped a few curtsies with a bearish grace and got off the stage. Like a heavy blade, she ploughed through the audience and left the celebration, and the people immediately fell apart into small, grumbling groups, which also hurried off.

At home, Moshe didn't take off his dead wife's dress. He searched in closets, rummaged in corners, plucked the hair off the back of his neck, and shouted at the wooden walls. The children looked at him in fear and didn't say a thing.

At last he went out to his rock, clasped it in his arms, and picked it up, pressed it to the woollen breasts and the mighty muscles underneath them, and paced with it in a circle of roars and growls, until he dropped it back in its place.

'What can I tell you, Zayde? That really was a great tragedy, because besides the mourning and the regrets, there's also the pity they had for him here. And in human beings, the distance between pity and cruelty is very small, and so they started talking behind his back of how miserable he was, and from there to talking about how he was crazy is also very small, and here in the village everybody tries to act how the group thinks of him. So because of that I act today like a dummy and Rabinovitch acted then like a crazy man and we'll wait and see how you'll act, too, someday.'

And on one of the following nights, Rabinovitch went to the

Village Papish's yard, grabbed a goose by the neck, and carried it out of there. He wrung his victim's neck, poured its blood on the ground, stripped off its skin, lit a bonfire of bark and twigs, which were always piled up at the trunk of the eucalyptus, and put Tonya's big black pot on it. When the pot was heated, Moshe put the pieces of skin in it, turned them over and over, and now and then he poured the melted fat into a big bowl at the side. He did that until the strips of skin shrivelled and turned a nice brown and then he sprinkled them in the bowl of hardening fat.

At dawn he ran to the bakery and brought a loaf of bread, tore pieces from it, and dipped them in the *shmaltz*, which hadn't really hardened, and ate them like a maniac, with the scorched and brittle crusts of skin.

Not from hunger and not from revenge or repentance did he do what he did, but because of his grief, which refused to abate, and because of his flesh, which refused to be consoled.

The tears melted the lump in his throat, the fat mixed with the leaven of regrets in his guts, and he began wailing and vomiting. The sounds woke Naomi, who came and stood over him and she, too, began weeping with panic.

And when Oded also came, wet with urine and all stinking, and said, 'I wet my bed again, Father' – Moshe got up from the ground and shouted: 'Why? Why? How much do I need to wash up all your stink?' And suddenly he swung his hand and slapped the little boy's face.

The good smell of the *shmaltz* drew many of the villagers into Rabinovitch's yard. They gathered around the big black kettle and understood where their dreams of the old country had come from and woke them up. Unfortunately, they also saw the awful blow Moshe had struck his son.

Everyone was astonished. Rabinovitch never raised his hand against anyone. Only once did he bring down a butcher, one of the coarse friends of Globerman the cattle trader. That butcher was known for being able to cut the thigh bone of a bull with one blow of his axe, and he came to challenge Moshe's rock and pick it up from the ground. When he couldn't do it, he was filled with wrath, and instead of kicking the rock and breaking his big toe, as people usually did, he tried to drag

Moshe into a wrestling match and was immediately pinned to the ground.

Now that Oded was slumped against the trunk of the eucalyptus with his eyes rolled up and white and his body sagging, Moshe turned pale, hurried over to pick him up, and cradled him in his arms. But Naomi shrieked: 'Don't touch him! Don't touch him!' And Oded came to and wiggled out of his father's arms and clung to his sister and to the eucalyptus in turn.

Beyond the fence, the people were whispering to one another, and Rabinovitch, wanting to get away from them and from the terrified eyes of his children, ran to the haystack, pounded it with his fists and kicked the bales of hay, rummaged around among them and threw them all over until they came undone into flying packs before the amazed eyes of the cows and he himself lay supine on the ground.

'Come out now, come out!' The awful bleating was heard all over the village and brought all those who hadn't been drawn by the smell.

Everyone stood at that distance where people stand when a mad dog appears in a neighbourhood or when an uncastrated bull breaks out of its fence. They didn't come close, but they shouted soothing words to Moshe and asked him to get up and go back home.

At last, Oded, who had recovered, ran to the pile of straw, and when he grabbed his father's hands and pulled his thick heavy body to him, Moshe became light as a feather and was lifted off the ground.

Moshe let his little son lead him home and there he dropped onto his bed and fell asleep, and didn't wake up until the next day, to the irritated cries of the cows. He got up to milk, sent the children to school, saddled the horse, and rode to the next village.

'Tell that woman of yours to come,' he said to Menahem without even getting off his horse.

'Wait a minute, Moshe, let the horse eat something, drink, sit down and let's talk a little,' Menahem requested.

'Not today, Menahem.' Moshe drew his horse back. 'Write fast and tell her that she should come.'

'It's almost spring, Moshe,' laughed Menahem. 'If we don't talk today, we'll have to wait until after Passover.'

'I'll wait. Today, write to the woman. Let her come.'

He dug his heels into the horse's belly and galloped back home.

23

'More dessert?'

'Yes,' I said.

Once again the water was boiled, the yolks were separated, the wine gave its fragrance, the finger was dipped.

'Every time it comes out a little different.' Jacob chuckled. 'Maybe it still needs a little bit of fat from an old carcass, eh?'

He brought to the table a shining goblet transparent as a dragon-fly's wing, stuck a spoon in it, and pushed it over to me.

He didn't tell me to do it, but I shut my eyes and opened my mouth wide. I heard him panting as he put the spoon on my tongue.

Words can't describe that sweetness, which I haven't managed to achieve again to this day. Many years have passed since that first meal, but the memory of the dessert still caresses my palate and is so strong and clear that sometimes, when I pick my teeth with a toothpick, I still extract from between my molars a sweet grain left there from back then.

'You know what you're eating?' asked Jacob.

I shook my head no.

'It's an Italian dessert.'

I was afraid that if I opened my mouth, the good yellowy taste would fly out.

'Once I had a lot of canaries,' said Jacob.

I nodded and shut my eyes again and Jacob poured another spoonful of bliss and amazement into my mouth.

He observed me as if he wanted to know what else I knew. I

expected him to ask: 'Why did you do that to me, Zayde?' But Jacob didn't suspect and didn't know and didn't ask, not during that meal and not during the ones that came after, and he only said: 'You like it?'

I had come to the moment when I'd have to swallow what was in my mouth. 'Very much,' I said. 'The best thing I ever ate.'

'Maybe you also want to hear some music?' asked Jacob. He dipped two fingers in the bowl and licked them with pleasure. 'How strong the yolk is,' he said. 'And so much life in it.'

It was late by now. From the wall the most beautiful woman in the village looked at me with her scary eyes. The treat Jacob put in my mouth made me drowsy.

'It's good,' I said.

He put a record on his phonograph, guided the arm, and scratchy dance music spread through the room.

'That's a tango,' said Jacob. 'Here in the village, they don't dance that. That's a dance of love and weddings, of a man and a woman. Tango is touching. You know what that is, Zayde?'

He didn't stand up, but his two fingers whirled like little legs on the table, leaving yellowy tracks of sweetness on the wood.

'If you want, Zayde,' he said, 'I'll teach you that dance.'

'Not now,' I said.

'This tango,' said Jacob, 'it's a dance not like any other dance. It's the only dance for couples which a person can also dance alone, and even sitting down you can dance it, and even lying down, and even in your dreams. The Village Papish said that once, and I can't forget his beautiful words: the dance where no one leads, the dance of repressed lust and inflated yearnings. Sometimes he talks so beautiful, Papish, that your heart really aches to hear him.'

Twelve years old I was, and now I was a little scared and I wanted to go home.

'I don't want to learn how to dance now,' I announced, and stood up.

'Of course not now, Zayde.' Jacob laughed. 'See, you're only a child. Someday, if you get married, I'll teach you. A man's got to know how to dance the tango at his own wedding. I'll teach you all you got to know before you get married.'

'I won't get married. I mustn't!' I said firmly as my legs were already leading me to the door.

We went out into the little garden. The big poppies were already withered. The high yellowing grass tickled my legs with its slow wind dances. Jacob Sheinfeld put his hand on my shoulder and bent down to me until his cheek grazed mine. I felt his lips seeking an answer and rest, barely touching my temple, and when he felt my recoil, he also recoiled, straightened up immediately, and took his hand off my shoulder.

'You don't have to visit me, Zayde,' he said. 'You don't even have to say hello to me in the street. I'm used to it by now. Ever since Rebecca left, ever since Judith died, I'm alone. But in a few more years, when I invite you to another meal, you'll come.'

The thin white scar that could be seen on his brow despite the darkness suddenly vanished, and I knew that he was blushing.

'All right,' I said.

I went home. A warm early summer night enveloped my body, and the feeling was so pleasant I imagined I was swimming. A sweetness of wine and sugar and egg yolk reigned in my mouth and I knew it would never evaporate from there, not even after it was erased from my memory.

A smell of smoke and scorching rose in the air. In the distance, bonfires gleamed, and black and red silhouettes circled around them.

I ran there. It was my classmates dancing and burning the larvae of the locusts.

'You'll come?' Jacob shouted behind me.

'I'll come,' I shouted back.

I smoothed my tongue over my teeth, from right to left and from left to right, back and forth, over and over. I ran from there. I pressed my tongue to my palate, and swallowed the sweet saliva that came into my mouth.

Second Meal

1

The second meal Jacob cooked for me about ten years later, after I got out of the army.

I didn't have a distinguished career in the army. My name gave me trouble in every drill and my immunity from death didn't make me a brave fighter, but rather a lazy, quarrelsome fellow who didn't accept authority.

The night before I was inducted, Jacob lay in wait for me next to the tree where the crows gathered and suggested we go together to my mother's grave.

'Don't bother me, Sheinfeld,' I said.

I was no longer a child and I could recognize an expression of pain and offence, but I wasn't yet grown up enough to change my mind and apologize.

Jacob recoiled as if I had smacked his face, and then he said: 'Just watch out, Zayde, and don't tell the officers there what your name means, because then they'll send you across the border for all kinds of dangerous things.'

I laughed and told him he worried too much, but I did take his advice. I didn't tell anyone what my name meant, not even after the traffic accident I survived intact, as usual: I was sleeping in the backseat of a jeep that turned over. The driver, a grey-haired reserve officer with a pot-belly, who showed me a picture of his grand-daughters when we'd started out, was crushed and killed. I was thrown into the nearby ditch and walked away without a scratch.

As a recruit, I revealed a talent for target shooting I didn't know I was graced with. I was sent to a course for sharpshooters, and afterwards I stayed there as an instructor.

The training base was a small camp, with straight angles and white-washed stones. Eucalyptus trees surrounded it, and their strong smell evoked memories, depressed me. Ancient abandoned crows' nests were turning black in their crests, and when I asked why the birds had deserted the place, one of the instructors said to me: 'If you were a bird, would you live next to a sniper base?'

My days passed with blocked ears, stolid isolation, and constant shooting at thousands of cardboard enemies and not one single live human. I spent hours endlessly setting sights, endlessly shooting bullets into the same hole, and endlessly writing letters, some I sent to Naomi in Jerusalem and some I kept. I have the ability to write backwards and forwards, with regular writing and mirror writing, and because of this strange talent, Globerman once told me that maybe I wasn't the son of any of my three fathers, but of some fourth man. One way or another, I especially love the writing that Meir, Naomi's husband, once told me is called 'Bostropeidon', meaning 'the ox's gait': one line in regular writing and the next line in mirror writing, just as the ox ploughs the field, back and forth on his traces along the previous rut. And I was so devoted to that writing that Naomi complained she was fed up standing at the mirror to read my letters.

She would send me packages from Jerusalem, with funny drawings, terrific poppyseed cakes, and stories that didn't interest me about her husband Meir and their little son.

Jacob also sent me letters – short and rare, in a twisted handwriting and with spelling mistakes that suited the way he talked. Globerman, as usual, sent money, and on every bill, next to the signature of the bank director, he added his own signature and a word or two. And Moshe didn't send me anything, but always went with me to the dairy on Saturday night when I left to go back to the base. Now I was much taller than him. He hugged me when he parted, shook my hand in his rough bear paw, and I climbed into the heights of Oded's truck and went off.

In 1961 I finished my service, returned the snipers' Mauser to the arsenal along with my telescopic sight, came back to the village, and turned down Globerman's offer to study cattle dealing.

'It's good work, Zayde,' he told me. 'And it was always a

profession passed down from father to son. You'll learn from
me everything you need to know, you'll be a *finer soykher*, a
fine dealer, just like somebody born on the *klots*.'

With all my affection for Globerman, it was good enough for
me to be born on the floor of the cowshed. Being born on a
butcher block didn't seem to me to be an improvement in family
pedigree. But Globerman was a generous father, a fascinating
conversationalist, and an unfailing source of tales, diagnoses,
and opinions, and now and then I'd accompany him for a day
or two of work and stories.

'My mother would turn over in her grave,' I told him, 'if she
knew that I was with you in the slaughterhouse.'

At the time, we were riding in his ancient green truck on the
dirt roads of the Valley and the dealer was imparting moral
lessons and memories to me.

'*Gib a kook*, Zayde – take a look,' he said. 'The camp for the
Italian prisoners-of-war used to be here. Here, right where the
little hill is, they had their own kitchen, and those red bricks is
all that's left of the chimney of the oven. All day long they'd sing
here and cook and dance, and the best smell in the world would
come out of that chimney of theirs, and in the fence there was
a big hole everybody knew about, where the prisoners-of-war
could leave quietly and return quietly without bothering the
guards.'

'Ask Sheinfeld sometime,' he added. 'He knew those Italians
better than I did.'

There was some cunning mixed into his voice. I understood
what it meant, but I knew that Globerman was testing me and
I didn't respond.

The truck circled and shifted on its worn-out shock absorbers
and the poor cow standing in the back was hurtled between
the wooden sides. The cattle dealer was a terrifying driver,
who kept swerving out of the lane and bumping into stones,
trees, and animals which weren't quick enough to get out
of the way. Oded, who had taught him how to drive years
before, told me more than once: 'Be careful when you drive
with him. Globerman's sure the gearshift is a stick for stirring
the oil.'

The dealer asked me if I had had 'all kinds of *tsatskes*, chicks' in the army.

'I don't like *tsatskes* very much,' I said.

'In the end everybody gets the woman he deserves. How did they used to say back home? Reuben gets the *tsatske* and Simon gets the *klavte*, the bitch, and Levi gets the *balabuste*, the housewife. Maybe the time has come for me to look for some decent *tsatske* for you, a woman with power, Zayde. With flesh like the shoulder of a year-old calf. A woman who, when she closes her legs on you and laughs, your whole body sings like a bird. Someday, when you understand flesh, you'll also understand what I'm talking about now. Meanwhile, wait until luck introduces us to such a woman.'

'And if we don't have any luck?'

'The world is full of radish women and potato women and hard-boiled egg women,' said Globerman. 'And I already told you, Zayde, everybody gets what he deserves, period.'

His proximity to blood and money made the dealer very dogmatic about various kinds of life, especially from the aspect of gluttony and flirting.

'Everybody's wrong!' he declared. 'A beautiful woman, when she's dumb, she's the dumbest, and when she's smart, she's the smartest. Because in a woman beauty goes together with sense and in a man beauty comes together with stupidity.'

He looked at me and smiled, I smiled back, and the old truck, which was only waiting for such an opportunity, burst into the nearby orchard and broke an apple tree.

Globerman cursed long and leisurely, turned off the motor, and in the silence that prevailed, he said: 'And besides that, Zayde, with every woman there's some secrets that only the eye and hand of a *fleysh-handler*, a meat dealer, can know. The time has come for you to know that, Zayde, 'cause you're twenty-two years old now, and if you would work like you should, with the flesh of the cow and not with her milk, you'd already have known all these things a long time ago. A normal person looks at nonsense in a woman, at lips and eyes, and if he's a little bolder, he also watches how her *tukhis* – her backside – moves when she walks and how her udders dance when she works. But a person who was born on the *klots* knows, for instance, that at the end of her back, right where if she had a tail it would grow, there every woman's got like a little hill of fat. The first chance you get, let's say, when you're dancing with her, you give her a tap there, Zayde, here, *tappen* like this.'

He stretched out a nimble hand and tapped the place where I don't have a tail.

'Right here. Men ain't got nothing there. But in a woman, from her little hill here you can tell about her other little hill, the one she's got in her Paradise in front. There she should have a fat and beautiful and happy hill. *A ziesskayt*, a sweetness of flesh. If she hasn't got a hill there, the whole body is very sad, period.'

He got out to check the damage.

'This truck's got a bumper like a bull's forehead,' he declared proudly.

Globerman's world was clear and sure, the letters and signs were unequivocal, the hints broad and decisive, periods bellowed at the ends of sentences.

'And one more thing you can learn now from your father, that if she's also got a little hair on her upper lip, not a real moustache, God forbid, Zayde, only like a shadow of grass, that's also a good sign that that woman is a warm woman with a beautiful forest on her beautiful hill.'

He took a bill out of his pocket and nailed it to the trunk of the broken apple tree.

'That'll be enough,' he said. 'So they shouldn't say Globerman isn't honest and doesn't pay for damages in cash. You understood what I told you about the hill? So, even before she takes off her clothes, you already know important things about her that even her own mother doesn't know.'

The truck went back onto the dirt road, its belly raking the thorny spine between the banks, and we started across the eucalyptus forest. The lane, where the dealer and his victims used to leave traces of hooves and boots, had already been expanded from the width of a cow to the width of the truck, and only the rings of the tyres were visible in it now.

'Already the thief's standing there,' the dealer said to me when we emerged from the forest and saw the butcher waiting at the gate of the slaughterhouse. 'Don't you say a word, Zayde, you just look and learn. That dog is a big swindler, and who do you think he learned to be a swindler from? Like all of us, he learned from his father. And how do I know they're a family of swindlers? From my father, who taught me who I should watch out for. In their butcher shop, when some pious jerk would come in to buy kosher meat, his father would stick his hand behind his back deep into his pants and put it on his own *tukhis* like that. The customer would look at the meat and ask: '*Dos iz glatt*? It's smooth kosher?' And he'd stroke his *tukhis* in his pants and say: '*Yo, yo, dos iz glatt.*' And if you asked him later why he lied, right away he'd pull down his pants without no shame, turn around, and say: 'Is that *glatt* or isn't it? Touch it and feel how smooth it is.'

Satisfied with my hoot of laughter, Globerman parked the truck and led the cow out of it.

'Right away you'll hear the same thing,' he whispered to me through clenched jaws. 'He *fanfatehs*. Talks through his nose. That's also a sign you should know, Zayde: anybody who talks through his nose is a swindler, period. But we'll do everything honest and faithful, right? Just remember, don't mix in. And especially don't tell him how much we bought it for.'

The butcher who talked with a nasal twang observed the cow, made her walk, tapped the points of her spine, felt her rump and the nodes in her neck, the whole examination Globerman used to do at our village.

'How much do you want for this carcass?' he asked at last, and they grasped each other's wrist and the ceremony began.

'Seventy pounds?' shouted Globerman, and hit the butcher's hand hard.

'Thirty-five!' twanged the butcher, and hit Globerman's hand.

'Sixty-eight!' exclaimed Globerman, and struck the butcher's hand.

'Forty!' exclaimed the butcher, and his hand whipped the dealer's hand.

'Sixty-five!' replied the dealer with a loud smack.

Those sounds were very loud. Small grimaces of pain crossed the faces of the two hagglers.

'Forty-three and a half!'

'Sixty-four!'

'Forty-six!'

There was a brief silence. The two of them looked at one another; their hands were red by now and wanted to part.

'*Benemones Parnussa?*' asked Globerman.

'*Benemones Parnussa,*' the butcher agreed.

They dropped their hands and rubbed their tormented palms.

'Fine,' said the butcher. 'May you have seven pounds from it, you thief.'

'Fifty-nine pounds,' said Globerman.

The butcher paid, Globerman took his rope off the cow and put it back in its regular place on his shoulder, and said to me: 'The minute he said "and a half", I knew it would end with *Benemones Parnussa*,' and we left.

'You understood what happened here?' he went on. 'You know what *Benemones Parnussa* is?'

'No.'

The dealer nodded his head at me: 'Listen. *Benemones Parnussa* means a decent living. If the butcher and I can't agree on the price, he says how much I deserve to make on the cow. If I bought it for fifty-two pounds, and he says *Benemones Parnussa*, seven pounds, then he's got to give me fifty-nine pounds.'

'So why didn't you tell him you bought it for fifty-five?'

'No. Lying is forbidden.'

'Lying is forbidden? That's what your father taught you back then and you're teaching me now?'

'*Fleysh-hendler un fish-hendler un ferd-hendler*, meat-dealers and fish-dealers and horse-dealers, those are professions without much honour, but they are passed down from father to son,' said Globerman. 'And if you want to be a dealer, you should know that we also have principles in life. You can lie about everything. Cheat about the weight, cheat about the health, cheat about the age. We give it water and feed it salt and starve it and fatten it and loosen its bowels and stick a nail in its leg and make it *glatt* on our own *tukhis*.

But with *Benemones Parnussa* we are forbidden to lie, period.'

2

I enjoyed those lessons and stories and trips, but I didn't want to be a cattle dealer.

I read books, I worked on the farm with Moshe Rabinovitch, I went back to observing the crows, and I struck up an affectionate relation with a girl from the nearby agricultural school, who worked at fattening geese for the Village Papish and looked so fertile and dangerous that I didn't let her touch me below the belt.

In those days, I started to suffer from insomnia. I didn't understand where it came from, from inside my body or from outside it, but I did remember what Mother used to say – that the Angel of Death is orderly and very careful, and the *Malakh-fun-shlof* is forgetful and lying and you can't count on his promises.

I took advantage of the insomnia to prepare for the university. I spent many nights lying and reading and reciting – my yellow wooden bird hanging over me, hovering eternally, and a small lamp at the head of my bed.

And at dawn, when at last the book dropped onto my face and I fell asleep, Rabinovitch would come into my room, grope in the dark, explore and seek, and I would wake up.

He paid no heed to me, peeped in the closets, rummaged in the kitchen shelves, opened cans and jars.

'What are you looking for there, Moshe?' I finally asked him, even though I knew what the answer would be.

'*Der tsop*,' he replied. 'The braid.'

In his voice, the force repressed in the hard fibres of his flesh and the feeblemindedness that was to attack him in old age were embroidered together, and even then were twined in his voice like a thin prophecy.

'*Der tsop*,' he repeated in that voice which was many years older than its owner's body. 'Where is the braid Mother cut off me? My Tonychka didn't tell you where it is?'

I shuddered. I knew, of course, that the living miss their dead, converse with them, and weep for their loss, but I didn't know that the dead also act like that with their live loved ones.

Even today, when the braid has been found, he again comes to me at night and again I am terrified by his words. Nothing has changed: I am still lying there and reading, and the *Malakh-fun-shlof* still tarries, and Rabinovitch still comes in, mutters, '*Der tsop . . . der tsop . . .*' and seeks the braid 'Mother cut off me'.

It's strange to see such an old man saying 'mother'. But I don't tell him that and I don't remind him that I didn't know his mother and that I was born years after his Tonychka died. He's an old man, and why should I disturb his last days with inane details? So old that I don't bother to hide the braid from him. First his mother hid it, then his wife, and now, when it is out in the open, it's forgetting that conceals it from him.

Jacob is dead now, Globerman is dead now, Mother is dead now, and Moshe is still alive. His memory has grown weak, his legs are heavy, but his arms are still as strong as an iron vice.

Every day, like a hunter returning to the carcass of the lion, he goes off to the gigantic stump of the eucalyptus he cut down in the yard, walks around it and examines it carefully, and plucks out every green shoot that sprouted from it.

'That's your punishment, murderer,' he mutters to the tree trunk. 'Not to die completely, you won't, but not to sprout again, either, you won't!'

Then he sits down on the stump, puts a wooden board across his lap, and on the board he heaps up crooked, rusty nails he gathered in the yard and on the street. And even though I'm used to that sight by now, I still don't believe my eyes when old Rabinovitch straightens the nails by pressing them with his thick fingers and then puts them in another pile. Afterwards, he polishes them with sand and uses motor oil until they gleam again as on the day they were born.

*   *   *

I get out of bed, take the wood and mother-of-pearl box from
its usual, open place on the shelf, and open it.

'Here's the braid.'

The gold of the hair glows in the dark. Rabinovitch puts out
a coarse, shaking hand and says: '*A shayne maydele*, a beautiful
girl, eh, Zayde?' And strokes his own tresses.

Then he tells me: 'Close the box, Zayde, and don't hide it
from me no more.'

Zayde closes, and Rabinovitch goes, and silence reigns once
again.

3

The invitation to the second meal came to me from Jacob's
taxi driver, who used to take him wherever he wanted to go.
The driver came to the Rabinovitch farm, knocked on the door
of the cowshed, and handed me an envelope.

In those days, Jacob was living outside the village, on Oak
Street in nearby Tivon, in the big house that is now mine. We
often saw his taxi waiting in the shade of the casuarina on the
highway, and him sitting there at the village bus stop, saying
his 'come in, come in' to people and cars. He didn't go into the
village anymore.

I decided to walk to him. I left the village in the morning, after
milking and breakfast, so I could take my time, linger on the way
to my heart's content, and get to him before sundown.

It was an early autumn day. On the taut electrical wires along
the road, hundreds of swallows were strung, like notes in a
music book. The dust of the road had been tamped down by
a thousand summer wheels, and bundles of flying stubble were
borne in the air.

The first rain hadn't yet fallen and the water in the bed of the
wadi was so low that fish skeletons were already emerging in the
dry mud of the banks. The few that survived gathered together
in some hollows and were so easy to catch that the crows and

cowbirds pecked them as adroitly as kingfishers. Blackberries grew in abundance here, winked black, ripe end-of-summer eyes at me, and I, in my enthusiasm, ripped my shirt on the hooks of their thorns.

I walked along the wadi to the experimental farm near the village. At that time, the agronomists there were busy growing spices, and tantalizing smells of food frequently rose from there.

I crossed the small valley beyond the farm and climbed north on the path between the big oaks, remnants of the forest that once covered the hills. Under one of them I lay down to rest and drink the water I had brought along.

The place wasn't strange. Two forests accompanied my childhood. The forest close by was the forest of eucalyptus that came between us and the slaughterhouse. A few pairs of crows nested in it and before dawn, the warbler sang there. I learned to follow the rusty red signs of its tail, and so I discovered its nest on an old stump of eucalyptus. New branches, that grew under the cutting and that hadn't been pulled out, rose and formed a hidden, greenish cone which is the best thing for birds who seek isolation. Vultures and bustards were also seen in the skies of the forest, hunting carcasses of cattle that were dragged here, and I also saw Uncle Menahem there a few times, showing his spring notes to laughing women, some I knew and some I didn't. I imagined that those were the famous hoors, but Naomi's order prevailed with me and I didn't tell Aunt Bathsheba a thing.

The second forest, the one farther away, was a forest of oaks where I walked now to Jacob. I used to visit it in my childhood, too, but that forest was too far for me to drag my observation-box there. I loved to lie on a bed of dry leaves and look up.

Jays with principles lodged here, those who chose to give up the refuse from man's table. They were as bold and curious as their brothers who moved to the villages all around, but they seemed smaller, the blue of their wings looked less splendid, and their young creatures appeared veined and wild. They hid acorns, flew less, and preferred secret hopping among the branches. The males, as I often saw, still maintained the practice their brothers in the village had already abandoned, of building a few nests and letting the female choose one of them.

My old friends the crows didn't reside here, but blackbirds were seen and heard, the males all fitted out in their black raiment and orange beaks, and the females modest and camouflaged in grey and brown.

'The boy's in the forest again?' Rabinovitch would shout.

'There are wild animals there!' Jacob Sheinfeld scolded. The river of his childhood still flowed in him and the howling of the hungry wolves and the dread of northern forests hadn't yet vanished.

'Come on, take the truck fast and go look for him,' Globerman urged Oded.

And Mother laughed: 'If the Angel of Death comes and sees a little boy named Zayde,' she reminded my three worried fathers, 'he'll understand at once that there's some mistake here and he'll go someplace else.'

A quiet, busy murmur of leaves and birds, small animals and wind rose from the forest. But as soon as I reached its border, the ringing warning shouts of woodpeckers were heard, and everything immediately fell silent.

I sat down on the ground and stretched back. The sheet of silence fell from the tops of the oaks and covered my body.

Spiderwebs gleamed, beetles plodded along, a damp warmth rose from under the layer of leaves on the ground, testimony of the slow fermentation of mulch. Slowly my ears grew accustomed to the silence and now I could make out the cracks between its layers: the constant rustle of the dry oak leaves, the gnawing of a worm in the trunk, and the grating of the seeds in the throats of the turtle-doves, who stuff themselves in this season and strengthen themselves for their winter journey to Africa.

A few minutes of terror and observation passed until the creatures of the forest grew used to my presence and calmed down. The wood-pecker resumed his role of town crier, with a rapid drumming that ripped open the silence. Then the tit-mice raised the angry metal of their voice, and all the rest of the forest creatures immediately followed suit. The world split into a thousand thin noises, spilling out of a torn sack.

All the wheels of nature were clicking around me as in a clock shop. The small hands of the seasons showed late summer with the last shouts of the cicada, the warm arid smell of the dust of the ploughed fields, the beating of the wing of young partridges whose colours, boldness, and size numbered the days that had passed since they hatched. The big hands showed the hour with the sun that was beginning to decline, and the west wind that whispered it's-already-four-in-the-afternoon-and-I-will soon-grow-strong, and the shriek of the swallows seeking provisions and heralding the approach of evening.

I remember the first time Mother taught me to read those hands. I was six years old and I asked her to buy me a watch.

'I don't have money for a watch,' she said.

'I'll ask Globerman and he'll buy me one,' I said. 'He's my father and he's got as much money as he wants.'

Despite my young age, I already had a good understanding of the position of the three men who took care of me, brought me presents, and played games with me.

'You won't ask anybody for anything,' said Mother in a hard, quiet voice. 'You don't have a father, Zayde, you've only got a mother, and what I can, I will buy for you. You've got food to eat, you've got clothes to wear, and you don't go barefoot.'

Then she softened, took my hand, led me outside, and said: 'You don't need a watch, Zayde. See how many watches there are in the world.'

She showed me the shadow of the eucalyptus that said nine in the morning with its size, its direction, and its chill, the little red leaves of the pomegranate that said mid-March, the tooth that wiggled in my mouth and said six years, and the small wrinkles in the corners of her eyes that capered and said forty.

'You see, Zayde, this way you're inside time. If they bought you a watch, you'd only be next to it.'

A sudden rustling was heard, crawled into my ears, and seemed to open my eyes from inside. It was a cat. A house cat that slipped past me, one of the cats who withdraw for a time from human society and test their strength in forest and field. He was very big, truly gigantic, and his coat was black and white. Despite the murderousness that forest life already restored to the shape of his back, you could still discern the grace and laziness and stuffed softness of a thousand years of domesticity.

I, who even got around nesting crows, didn't budge, and the cat didn't notice me until I called him with a tempting 'psst . . . psst . . . psst'.

He froze on the spot, turned green eyes to me, and barely kept from coming to me and surrendering to my caresses.

'C'mon-c'mon-c'mon . . .' I chanted to him in a whisper, and at the sound of my voice, a human voice, the cat reconsidered, leaped up, and disappeared.

I got up and walked away, too.

4

'You got bigger.' Jacob opened the door for me.

We had exchanged a few letters when I was in the army, but it had been more than three years since we had met.

'You got bigger, too, Jacob,' I said.

'I got old,' he corrected me with a smile, and immediately uttered his line: 'Well, come in, come in.'

His new house was handsome, big and roomy, with a small lawn in front and a big garden in the back. But it was the kitchen I liked most. A big table sat in the centre, pots and skillets hung on shelves and weren't hidden away in closets. Here I sat down. I'm one of those people who like to sit in the kitchen, both in my own house and in other people's houses.

'I worried about you when you was in the army. You didn't answer the letters I sent.'

'You don't need to worry about me. I'm a little boy named Zayde, did you forget, Jacob?'

He looked at the rip in my shirt from the blackberry thorns.

'Fast,' he said. 'Take it off and I'll mend it for you. A person can't walk around the street like that.'

Despite my protest, he didn't relent until I took off my shirt. He threaded a needle, and in a few minutes he stitched the rip with tiny, nimble stitches that were even and regular, and that amazed me.

'Where did you learn to sew like that?' I asked.

'When you have to, you learn.'

The big white plates I remembered from our first meal were already set out, reflecting the light of the big lamp with a round green card-player's shade hanging above them.

'Food, Zayde, you serve only in a white plate, drinks – water and tea and juice and wine – you pour only into a colourless glass,' Jacob stated resolutely. 'There's rules for those things. If you see a restaurant with candles, you don't go in. Candles are not for romance, it's a sign that the cook's got something to hide. A person's got to see what he puts in his mouth. He sees, he smells, he gets saliva. There are six little faucets of saliva in the mouth and they start working right away. Saliva is a really wonderful thing, Zayde, even more than tears, more than any other liquid in the body. With food it's longing and with a kiss it's love and with spitting it's hate.'

While I ate his treats, Jacob stood at the sink and went on talking, fussing with the next course, or tasting his own food standing up – that vegetarian meal of an omelette and a green salad with a lot of lemon, black olives, and cottage cheese – which somehow made me jealous, despite the delicacies he put on my plate.

'You remember our first meal? It'll soon be ten years.'

'I remember, but I don't know what we ate.'

'Poor cook, eh?' said Jacob. 'You can't whistle the courses he cooked or recite the meat or dance the soup.'

'You can't whistle a book, either, and you can't eat a tune,' I tried to console him.

'Yes, you can,' said Jacob.

Then he added: 'And a tune is always a new thing that never was before in the world, and from the violin and the flute comes sounds even birds can't make, and the painter, like God, he can paint things that aren't in the world at all. But food? Even without the cook there's food. And a whole day he'll stand and cook, and in the end the first cucumber after Passover will always taste better than his roast, and a black Santa Rosa plum with a little crack in the skin is better than his sauce, and even just a thin slice of raw meat is better than all his dishes.'

On the wall hung a picture of Rebecca. Now and then, I looked back at her, but I didn't say anything to her.

Once, before I was born, Rebecca Sheinfeld was the most beautiful woman in the village. So beautiful that even people who weren't born then still talk about her. So beautiful that no one still remembers the lines of her face, the colour of her hair, or the shade of her eyes, but only the fact of her beauty.

When she was young, she refused to be photographed because of her beauty, and when she came back, many years later, she refused to be photographed because of her old age. Only one picture of her remains from those days, the picture that hangs to this day in the kitchen of the house in Tivon, and the teeth of time have damaged that, too, for Rebecca in her frame isn't as beautiful as Rebecca in stories and memories and dreams.

'The cook,' Jacob summed up, 'is, after all, a matchmaker.'

'Between meat and spices?' I asked.

'No. Between the meal and the one who eats it,' said Jacob, wiping his hands on his apron and sitting down across from me.

'You like it, Zayde?' he asked after a brief silence.

'Very much.'

'So the match worked. *Ess, meyn kind.*'

5

Judith's reply came to Uncle Menahem through a man from the kibbutz marketing cooperative who used to buy carobs from him.

Menahem opened the envelope, read the letter, rushed to his brother, and announced: 'She'll come next week.'

Moshe was perturbed. 'Do I have to prepare something special for her?'

'Never prepare something special for a woman you don't know,' said Menahem. 'You won't succeed, and the two of you will get angry. She asked only for a corner of her own and a day off sometimes. Call the children now, I want to talk to them.'

He sat Naomi and Oded on his lap and told them that a 'woman-worker' would soon come to the house, and added, 'I know this woman and she's a very good woman. She won't be your mother. She'll just live and work at your house. She'll cook for you and wash your clothes and help in the yard and the cowshed. It'll be easier for all of you. For Father and for you and for that woman, too, it'll be easier. She'll come soon and we'll all go together to bring her from the railway station.'

That night, Rabinovitch awoke to the sound of dragging and banging, and when he went out to the yard, he saw Oded building a floor of boards in the lowest branches of the eucalyptus.

'What are you doing?' he asked.

'I'm building a nest in Mother's tree,' said Oded.

'Why in the middle of the night?'

'Got to get done,' said the boy gravely. 'By the time the woman-worker comes, I'll have me a house.'

The days peeled off one after another, until Judith came, and on the last evening, when only a few hours separated him from her, Moshe took clean clothes out of the closet, lit the wood in the oven, and boiled bathwater.

'We'll wash real good,' he said, and scrubbed his children with his big, good hands.

'The woman-worker shouldn't think poor dirty people live here,' said Naomi.

Oded was sullen and dejected and his body was hard and recalcitrant under the water, but Naomi enjoyed the washing and the touch of her father's hands. The warm vapours, the smell of soap, the nap of the towel on the skin of her stiff back gave her a pleasant shudder of anticipation.

The next morning, Moshe didn't send his children to school, and after the milking he washed, too, the very same way he washes today: he stands on a wooden crate under the awning of the cowshed and showers with a rubber hose. He stood on the crate, like a bear on a rock in the river, the water pouring over his body, a big loofah in his hand and a foaming cube of laundry soap at his feet. Then he sat down on the milking stool in the fragrant shade of the eucalyptus and Naomi used scissors to clip the thin yellowish tendrils growing wild on the back of his neck, and combed the crown of hair around his bald pate.

'Now we're all pretty.' Moshe got up from the stool. '*Dayosh!* Come on, let's go!'

He threw a bundle of straw on the wagon, Naomi put in a few folded sacks and sat down next to him, and Oded agreed to come down from the tree and join them in exchange for a promise to be allowed to hold the mule's reins all the way.

'All the way except for the wadi.' His father granted his request.

Oded was crazy about wheels and trips and driving. When he was three, he was already running in the village streets holding an iron hoop as a steering wheel, and when he was five he learned the principles of steering on a wooden board with wheels at the corners, which he galloped madly on the slope from the supply warehouse to the entrance to the village.

'Today, too, that whole semi-trailer is just a horse and wagon!' he laughs. 'It's a little bigger, but I learned to go in reverse back then, with a real horse and a wagon with shafts.'

For years now I have been riding with him at night and I'm still impressed at how he can manoeuvre the tank in reverse. 'It's easier than you think and it's more complicated than it looks,' he says. 'But people don't really understand what it is to drive a rig this size. Look at him, look at that shitty little Prince, cutting me off before the intersection, like a cockroach on my mirror. Does he know what distance I need to brake? In America they'd shoot him for a thing like that. There they respect trucks.'

When they got to the wadi, the regular silence prevailed. The water flowed slowly, shallow and transparent and pleasant, and as water does, it carried memories, wiped out smells and traces.

Moshe took the reins from his son's hands. Well, he said to himself, the water that drowned Tonya isn't here anymore. It flowed to the sea, will evaporate, thicken, and become clouds again, will pour and overflow, will drown another woman and orphan her children.

Naomi's and Oded's faces turned glum, as if they were painted with their father's musings. The cart wheels clattered across the channel and silt rose from the bottom and muddied the water.

From here the road turned and continued along the other bank of the wadi until it connected with a bigger one a mile or so later. Tadpoles capered in the mud, strange gnats with long, straddling legs rushed around on the skin of the water, and beyond the bend of the river-bed the heralding whistle of the locomotive was heard, startling frightened herons, and pillars of smoke ran wild.

In a grey cotton dress, with a blue kerchief on her head, her eyes squinting with dread and light, Judith got off the train.

She stood erect, but she looked so tense and scared that Moshe's heart froze with pity and terror, for he worried that instead of helping him, she would be another burden on his hands.

'You saw right away that she didn't have a penny to her name. She wore old shoes and stockings that had once been white, and I decided right off the bat that I loved her,' Naomi said.

She had a big, tattered leather bag, and Uncle Menahem, who also came to the railway station to greet her, hurried to take it from her.

'Welcome, Judith,' he said. 'This is my brother, Moshe Rabinovitch, and these are the children, Oded and Naomi. You say hello, too, Oded, say, "Hello, Judith, welcome."'

Judith climbed onto the bundle of straw that had been put in the wagon especially for her, and when she placed her foot on the connections of the shafts her left knee came up, and the delight in the movement of her leg was depicted on the fabric of her dress. The children looked at her and Moshe concentrated on the mule's shining rump as if he were reading the future in it.

When they crossed back through the wadi on their way home, Judith suddenly felt Naomi's hand stealing into hers.

Moshe steered the mule so that they would come straight to the yard from the fields, and wouldn't go through the highway and the village street, but everybody knew and they were waiting and watching, and the wagon cruising slowly among quiet waves of gold and green, wild chrysanthemum and mustard, and the woman with the tired face sitting on the straw throne, was clearly seen by eyes waiting in fields, at windows of cowsheds, and through winks of curtains.

When they reached the yard, Oded announced that he was going up 'to my new house in Mother's tree', and Moshe, Judith, and Naomi went into the hut. Two rooms and a kitchen were what it had in those days and Moshe told Judith that at night she could sleep in the children's room or put up a bed in the kitchen, which was quite big.

'If we decide you'll stay here, maybe we'll build another room,' he said, and Judith didn't answer, nor was it clear if she considered it a promise or a threat, but she did tell him that she didn't hear well on her left side.

He was embarrassed and wanted to get to her right side, but Judith turned and went out to the yard. While his words were still hovering around her and seeking an opening, she went into the cowshed, looked at the empty north-east corner, with only a few sacks and some tools, put her big leather bag down, and said: 'I'll live here.'

'With the cows?' Moshe was amazed.

'I'll be fine here,' said Judith.

'What will they say in the village?'

'I'll clear it out and clean it up, and you'll bring the bed and the crate for my clothes.'

And with sudden boldness, she added: 'And if you would please put two nails in the wall for me, here and here, I'll put up a curtain from here to here. A woman also needs a corner to herself, without eyes looking at her and fingers pointing at her.'

6

Once every two weeks, the albino started the old green truck and disappeared for a mysterious night.

He was careful to come back before sunrise and in the village they said he was visiting a 'restaurant where they serve more than food'. So, when he returned, the book-keeper trailed vapours of alcohol and women, which made the canaries hoarse, made the farmers cry, and attracted stray dogs from the fields. In the village office, they knew by now that it was better to leave him in his dark room the next day, and let his wine and his weariness and his odours wear off before they gave him more work to do.

That night, the *Malakh-fun-shlof* passed over Jacob's bed, and in the pre-dawn silence, he suddenly heard the slow throbbing of the truck returning its owner to his house, and he immediately leaped to the window. The pair of headlights capered dull orange, drew tipsy circles in the fields, and Jacob was filled with excitement.

'What are you looking at there at this hour?' Rebecca murmured from their bed.

'In spring, nineteen hundred and thirty-one it was,' he said. 'That night I couldn't fall asleep and the next day Judith came. I remember that day very well. Rebecca and I had a little kerosene incubator back then, for three hundred chicks at the same time, which in those days was really something, and a few brood hens for the house, and three cows, and we had a grove of oranges with a row of grapefruits and a row of King walnuts, because in those days they didn't have this rage for pecans yet, and two rows, one of apples and one of pears, and a little vineyard of grapes. I remember everything. Just then we were working in the citrus grove, we were weeding and sawing branches that died in the winter, and all of a sudden Rabinovitch's wagon came from the fields, and right then I lifted my head and I saw her. So you'll

ask me now how come I fell in love with her, come on, ask,
Zayde, ask and don't be scared. How come I fell in love with
your mother, you ask? So I'll tell you exactly what happened,
Zayde, and you'll understand whatever you'll understand. It just
so happened by chance that I was wiping my brow, you know
with my hand like this, you see? And at the end of the gesture,
it just so happened by chance that I picked up my head, and
then I saw her like my hand opened me a window. The cart
passed by like a boat, not stopping, and right then, it really just
so happened by chance, a space opened up between the clouds
and the sun peeped out for one moment. I keep saying, it just
so happened by chance, but if so many things just so happen by
chance together, it's a sign there's some plan here, some trap like
they set for birds. A trap like that is a very simple thing, Zayde,
but if it just so happens by chance that there's also a crate there
and it just so happens by chance that there's also a string and it
just so happens by chance that there's also a stick and it just so
happens by chance that there's also a lid and if it just so happens
by chance that somebody put a few grains inside there, then, all
in all, it can't be it just so happened by chance anymore, and the
bird is caught there completely on purpose.'

The fruit trees blossomed and Jacob, half hidden behind the
bright petals and the transparent walls of their scent, watched
the cart approaching, and because of the place and the angle,
Judith seemed to him to be sailing slowly on a broad, yellow
river that had no banks.

He didn't know his own mind. The light, bright and fragile
as porcelain, sketched the shade of the blossoming walnut
branches, fell on the field, illuminated the thin ivory nape,
described the bluish shadows of the veins standing out on the
backs of the hands, and hinted at strength of soul and torments,
and the stockings that drooped a bit over the strong, delicate
ankles.

Judith leaned forward a little and the spring wind, as I imagine
it, played with the fabric of her dress, pressed it to her thighs and
let go of it, and as always happens at the moment when you fall
in love, an old picture surfaced from Jacob's depths and sought
and found its mate.

He was right. Those traps are very simple. It's enough for a cloud to float over the sun, for an echo of a fleeting scent, for a fragile angle of light. Enough for her reflection to be realized in the frames of memory – and the string is pulled, the wire is tripped, the door falls, and the trap is sprung. This is how fate hunts his prey and bears it off, a happy fluttering victim, to his lair.

'What happened, Sheinfeld?' asked Rebecca.

Like many women in those days, she called her husband by his last name. If she had called him by his first name, she would have understood the dispositions of his soul better and their lives would have turned out differently. But, as the Village Papish used to say: 'Who thought of those things in those days?'

Jacob was jolted out of his thoughts.

'Nothing,' he told her. 'Nothing happened.'

His trembling hand once again wiped his brow and unwittingly spread a thin strip of black planters' ointment, as if drawing the scar to be cut there in the future.

'I wasn't lying, I just didn't understand. None of what happened I didn't understand. I didn't understand that Rebecca would leave the house, I didn't guess the whole hard life I would have because of Judith.'

And then Rebecca also noticed Rabinovitch's wagon.

'You're a fool, Sheinfeld.' Her face turned glum.

She bent over again, picked up the hoe, and didn't say another word.

7

'Sometimes – you'll forgive me, Zayde, for saying such a thing – I even thought that maybe Tonya died so I would meet Judith. It's awful to talk like that, eh? It's awful even to think it. But love makes very strange thoughts and against thoughts there's nothing you can do. That's something even the cruellest king knows. The thought is inside the cage of the head and there's

no way you can get it out of there, but inside its cage it's the
freest bird and it sings there whatever it wants and whenever it
wants. And that's how I used to think that thought, and right
away I would rip it out like you tear up weeds, and you can't
leave even one single piece. 'Cause at Rabinovitch's, it really
was a great tragedy, the children was crying and sometimes
you'd also hear blows coming from there. Naomi he never
touched, not once, but when he'd give Oded a *flosk*, the boy
would shut his mouth tight and not a sound would come out,
and the little girl would cry instead of him. 'Cause, you know
yourself, Zayde, that Rabinovitch isn't a man to raise a hand
to a child, but in a situation like that you can go nuts, you can
lose all your patience. How much can a human being drag on
his back? The house and the yard, and the kitchen, and the
cowshed, and the field, and the citrus grove, and the cows, and
the children? Once he runs into me in the street, takes a hold
of my shoulder, and it's like he wants to tell me something, but
there's only tears in his eyes and the marks of his fingers stayed
on me for a month afterward. I think that was the only time
I saw the ox really in tears. 'Cause, even at Tonya's funeral
he didn't cry. In general, Rabinovitch and I, both of us loved
one woman and we got a lot of disagreements and differences
between us, but all in all there was some sympathy between
us even before your mother came to the village and something
remained even afterward. I have affection for people that are
built like him. In the village on the Kodyma River, there was
a farmer who was just like him, a *goy*, short and thick like a
box – as tall as he was wide and just as thick, everything the
same. When that *goy* would castrate a bull, first of all he would
give the bull a *zetz* on the forehead with his own forehead, bam!
And another one, bam! And another one, and once the bull falls
and gets up and another time the man falls and gets up, until
finally the bull's eyes would turn up and his knees would
shake, and by the time he figured out with his beast mind what
happened and where all that dizziness was coming from, the *goy*
already came up to him from behind with the knife and the bull
was already passing out from so much pain and his balls were
already in the frying pan with potatoes and garlic and onions,

and he was already hitched up to the plough and working in the field like a castrated bull should, walking and ploughing forward and turning around and going back, and turning around again and ploughing forward and backward and forward like that and not looking to the side. When others are eating your balls, Zayde, you don't look to the side no more, you just go and go and come back in the rut with the plough. So you should know, Zayde, I think because of the blow Rabinovitch gave Oded back then, he got scared of himself and brought Judith to work 'cause he was scared maybe one day he'd do something awful. 'Cause, people like Rabinovitch don't know their own strength. A blow from the *lappe*, the paw of the beast, that can be the end not only of a child, but even of a grown-up person. And believe you me, Zayde – after Tonya died he became even stronger than he was before. That's a thing that happens sometimes, a man becomes a widower and he gets so strong it's like he flourishes with grief. There was a tree like that there, I don't know what the *goyim* call it, but we called it *der blumendiker olman*. You know a little Yiddish, Zayde? She didn't teach you a word of Yiddish? That's funny, a person called Zayde and he knows no Yiddish at all. Never mind. *Der blumendiker olman* is the flowering widower, and that tree, every year it would break and freeze in the snow, really die, and every spring it would put out a whole lot of little green leaves with buds straight from its poor trunk and bloom again. It happens like that sometimes with widowers, too, and that's how it was with Rabinovitch. All of a sudden he's flourishing, his teeth are white again, and when he walks he walks with big strides, and when he breathes he can smell things very far away, far in time or far in distance, and also, believe you me, Zayde, from all that grief and cold, his bald head even grew a little hair. What can I tell you, Zayde? Sometimes grief is the best manure. Some people say something wasn't right here – there are always people who will turn up their nose at everything – a person in mourning shouldn't look so good. But if you ask me, Zayde, maybe that's how a person heals himself. Sometimes the soul is the doctor of the body and sometimes the body is the doctor of the soul. If they don't help each other, who will? And once at night, maybe twelve-thirty, when I was standing in the dark and waiting maybe Judith's shadow would pass by the window of the cowshed for a moment, all of a sudden I saw Rabinovitch come out of his house and into the yard, I thought he was going to her, but he just went in under the wagon and waving both hands, he yelled, and believe you me, he picked it up from one side maybe three feet high. Unbelievable how much strength and how much anger can be in one person's body, how strong his body can get, all the pain and all the memories and all the regrets, everything a woman can hold in her womb when she's pregnant, a man can hold in his bones and muscles, but give birth he never will and puff up he never will, he just gets hard and heavy inside, like he's full of stones, another stone in the belly and another stone and another stone, men get like a quarry from all those children we're never gonna give birth to. I once heard about a *shiksa* like that, who was pregnant forty-five years and never gave birth. Sometimes I don't believe these stories myself, but they're my father's memories, and a father's memories you've got to believe. If you don't believe the memory of your father, your own flesh and blood, what will you believe? When she was seventeen some man working in the lumber mill raped her. He grabbed her by the hand, laid her down on a bag of sawdust, and got on top of her by force, and when she finished wiping her eyes from the tears, and her legs, forgive me, from all the filth and the blood, the poor thing told her father what the man did to her, and right away she got so many slaps on the face from him that she lost an eye, and the man, her brothers grabbed him and killed him with a pitchfork from the barn with all four teeth through his ribs. Well, after a few weeks she was already puffed up with the pregnancy like a barrel and the father said, this is really very good, she won't get a husband anymore now, the *kurve*, so at least let me get a grandson out of her who will work hard like his poor father and help me in the field. Days go by and weeks go by and months go by and that one never had a baby. The nine months go by, and ten months, and a year go by, and two years go by and three and four, and she's still got a belly like a pile of wheat in the barn, with her breasts like watermelons,

throwing up every morning like a drunk in a bucket, walking
all the time with her hands like this on her hips from such a
backache. At first people thought maybe she was like a cow that
sometimes puffs up from clover, and they wanted to stick her
with a *trokar* like with a cow because of the gasses, but with
her it wasn't air. If you put a hand, you felt it kicking. What
didn't they do with her? They went with her to the church, to
their witches, they brought one woman who rummaged around
in her there and with special grass made her smoke down there,
they even came to our rabbi, and he told them – listen well to
what he told them, Zayde – this is what he says to them: you lay
her down on the table and you put a bottle of schnapps, forgive
me, between her legs, 'cause a *goy*, even if he's little and even if
he hasn't even been born yet, when he smells the schnapps he'll
come out from anywhere he is. Well, ten years like that, twenty,
and the years go by, and she's still pregnant. Her father dies, her
mother dies, and she's already sixty years old and she's still got
that belly, and the baby's inside, what can I tell you, already a
grown-up foetus, more than forty, and he'll never come out. So
now you understand, Zayde, how come I fell in love with your
mother?'

'No,' I said, and irritation at the unknown began bubbling
up in me.

'How come I fell in love with her?' Jacob whispered with
pleasure.

The slice of bread in his hand moved in the plate, besieging
and flanking and heaping, his eyes stared at me above his salad
and omelette, seeking signs and proofs in me.

'You know, Zayde, from this side you look like me, from that
side like the *soykher*, and from here sometimes you look like
Rabinovitch. And how do you like the meal?'

'The meal's good,' I said, with my lips dry.

'So you want to know how come I fell in love with her?' he
asked for the third time and his voice was so much like mine he
seemed to be repeating my own question, even though I hadn't
asked it, at any rate, not aloud.

''Cause that's what Fate decreed for me.' He stood up solemnly.

He put his plate in the sink, standing with his back and his shoulders to me, like my shoulders, bowed.

''Cause you've got a Fate that comes from above,' he went on. 'And you've got a Fate that comes from the side and there's a Fate that attacks you from behind and there's a Fate of somebody else that goes off and comes to you. And with me, the worst Fate, the Fate a person brings on himself from inside. It's like somebody who reads the Ten Commandments in the Torah, and then right away he gets ideas about how to do sins, and somebody who buys a first-aid kit and then right away accidents start with him, and somebody who takes canaries home gets caught up in love. It's just like a person's name. Your mother thought a child named Zayde will never die, and I'm telling you, Zayde, somebody whose name is Jacob will never have it easy with love, that's how it was from the first Jacob to the last Jacob, from Jacob Our Father to Jacob Sheinfeld who used to taste the soap and to this Jacob Sheinfeld, your father, who once in ten years has to cook you a meal for you to come visit him and agree to talk with him. That's how us Jacobs make ourselves a hard life with love. Our Father Jacob even changed his name to Israel, and did that do him any good? Outside the name changed and inside the troubles remained. Eat everything on your plate, Zayde, or else you won't get the egg yolk dessert you love so much, and you should know just one thing: it was impossible for me not to fall in love with her. The sun shined from here, and the wagon came from here, and the eyes looked from here, and you see all at once both what was in the eyes and what was in the memory: a woman comes sailing in a river like in green-gold water, and the wind just then is playing with the cloth of her dress, sticking it and letting it go from the body, and the shadow falls right here on her neck ... So, not to fall in love with her? Like a yellow leaf in the water I was swept up to her. So, can such a thing happen by chance? I ask you, Zayde, can such a thing happen by chance?'

8

That night, too, Judith's first night in the village, Rabinovitch had a hard time falling asleep.

And as usual with insomniacs, he knew what fate had in store for him, and had already despaired of reading a book, which had now become a mechanical leafing of pages, with no words but only pages, and of reviewing memories, and counting the imaginary geese that leaped over the fence of the Village Papish's yard.

As usual, he thought of his braid, and of his Tonychka who died without telling him where it was, and again he wondered whether she would have shown it to him if she had lived and whether she would have lived if she had shown it to him, and once again he felt the waters of fear flooding his lungs, and close to midnight, when the awful wailing rising from the cowshed and besieging the air was heard, the brothers If, What If, and What If Not stopped dancing their tormenting dances above him, and he saw Naomi jump out of bed and he got up, too.

So strange and surprising was the wailing that, at first, it was impossible to understand that it was the weeping of a woman and not the nightmare of wolves or the scream of a calf who saw the smiling Globerman in a dream.

Moshe wrapped the sheet around his body and rushed into the yard, but he didn't dare go into the cowshed. He paced around in the dark next to the wall and after a minute or two, he went back to bed, and it wasn't until Naomi asked him, 'Father, why are you trembling?' that he himself noticed it, and he didn't answer her.

'Who screamed?' asked Naomi.

'Nobody,' said Moshe. 'Nobody screamed. Sleep now.'

By dawn the wailing vanished, the air above the cowshed

congealed again, as the skies are stitched together after the blade of a falling star.

The grey crow uttered his first shout from the eucalyptus and the bulbul immediately joined him with his clappers and the falcon with his trills, and sounds of a kitchen waking up rose in the air. When Moshe returned from milking, he saw his two children sitting at a neat, clean table, smelling of lemon peel, and the plates on the table had pieces of cheese brought by Aliza Papish, the Village Papish's wife, both out of the goodness of her heart and because she wanted to get a good look at Rabinovitch's worker before the rest of the village women caught sight of her.

A sliced radish, too, with grains of salt sparkling on it, coloured the plates red and white. And a good smell of pressed olives and eggs frying already rose all around. At dawn, Judith cleaned Tonya's old *taboon*, the smoke of the burning eucalyptus bark came back to the yard in its full force and bitterness, and the loaf of bread baked in it hunched like a tiny mountain of joy in the middle of the table.

'Now you eat the olives Mother once made?' Oded grumbled at Naomi. 'Her jam you didn't want to eat.'

'And as soon as you smelled Judith's food, you rushed right down from the tree,' said Naomi.

They ate and went to school, and Moshe went back to the cowshed and stuck two nails in the walls where Judith had showed him. She asked where she could get curtain rings, and she immediately saw him pacing around the yard, his body bent over and his eyes searching for rusty nails. After he straightened and polished them, he went to the cowshed and asked her how many rings she needed.

Before her amazed eyes, Rabinovitch rolled the nails between his fingers one after another, and a dozen rings were quickly strung together and threaded on a wire he stretched, the curtain was hung and spread, and a sort of isolation chamber was created between the cement wall and the cloth wall, and the good smell of lemons already rose from there, made its way in the dense air and the heavy smell of manure.

She spread a cloth cover on the iron bed, and at noon Naomi

came home from school holding a pink-purple bunch of wild clover and storksbill. She put the flowers in a can and put the can on the case in the cowshed, and added a brief note: 'For Judith'.

'And what will they say in the village?' Moshe argued after dinner. 'That I sent you to live in the cowshed?'

'And what will they say in the village if I live with you in the hut?' said Judith.

Naomi was collecting breadcrumbs from the table, and Oded didn't budge. Rabinovitch was silent and wondered if Judith knew he had heard her scream at night.

'Explain to them whatever you want, Rabinovitch,' she added. 'I don't have to explain anything to anyone.'

She finished washing the dishes, shook the drops off her hands with two decisive waves, and wiped them on the cloth apron around her waist with a gesture all women had in those days and now they don't have anymore, a gesture that disappeared along with the apron.

'Come show me how to untie the cows.'

She went out. And when the embarrassed Moshe followed her, arguing once again, 'It looks bad,' she turned to him and said: 'You're a good man, Rabinovitch. I wouldn't have counted on any other man, but here is where I'll live.'

They untied the iron yokes and Moshe tapped the rumps of the milk cows and shouted, 'Get out! Get out!' to chase them out into their dark yard.

Judith did the same and then took the blue kerchief off her head, quickly moved the curtain aside, and the decisive rustle of the electric sparks of her hair and the metal rings on the iron wire said, Done.

Moshe shouted again, 'Get out, bagobones! Get out!' even though that wasn't necessary anymore.

One more minute, he waited on the other side of the curtain, and then he returned to the hut, lay down on his bed, and waited.

9

Rebecca Sheinfeld was the most beautiful of all the beautiful daughters of the Schwartz family of Zikhron Ya'akov.

She had suitors not only from her own hometown and from the villages of the Galilee, but also from distant villages in Judea, from Haifa, and from Tel Aviv, and men gathered in Zikhron Ya'akov because of her, 'like thirsty wanderers to an oasis'. There were horsemen and wine-growers, young teachers and farmers' sons. At night they ate roasted grains they took from the barn and drank wine they stole from the winery, and played their ocarinas and mandolins.

Women would also come there because that was how they met men returning at dawn, the softest, most vulnerable time, after longing and fatigue melted their legs and the shining sun illuminated their disappointment. And quite a few couples, they said in the colony, made matches there because of Rebecca.

Every night, her father locked her in her room, climbed up onto the flat roof, and sat down there, an earthenware jug of water at his side, the head of the palm tree rustling next to his own head, and a hunting rifle loaded with grains of salt in his hands.

Rebecca looked at her suitors from the window and was filled with pity for them and for herself. But one afternoon when she went to the butcher, near the line of Washingtonia palm trees of the village, she met Jacob Sheinfeld, a labourer who had immigrated to Eretz Israel a week before, and had come to Zikhron Ya'akov not knowing anything at all about its most beautiful girl.

'Listen to an experienced woman and live in the city,' said her mother when Rebecca announced her intention to marry him and go with him to a new place named Kfar-David. 'There's no worse fate than the lot of a beautiful woman who lives in a small place.'

I asked the Village Papish to interpret that statement and he explained to me that every settlement can include and digest only a certain amount of beauty, that it depends on its size and the number of its inhabitants.

'Jerusalem,' he said, 'can bear a dozen beautiful women, Moscow seventy-five, and the village barely one.' And he added that it was like the ability of an animal to absorb snake venom, which depends on its size and its weight. 'The horse will live and the dog will die,' he said.

A bitter and quarrelsome old man was the Village Papish, as often happens to people with lust and humour who live beyond their allotted time. Now he claimed that it would be better for beauty itself if it were divided up among many women, but happily it didn't tend to dissolve and spread out equally and fairly in all the daughters of Eve.

Rebecca married Jacob and went with him to Kfar-David, and within a few days, her mother's words proved to be right. She didn't find peace either in her marriage or her new place. As soon as she came to the village, the men stopped sleeping because their dreams of her were more exhausting than insomnia, and the fantasy was easier than the looks they gave her when they were awake.

> And on that day or that night,
> the brawls began,
> between the woman
> and her man.
>
> Knitting their socks, women whispered,
> silently, not to be heard,
> and old men peeped around,
> quietly stroking their beards.

And Rebecca, who also knew that she was more beautiful than all the women of the village, remembered her mother's words and didn't leave her house very much. She gave herself the hardest and ugliest work to do, she didn't comb her hair, and when she did have to go into the centre of the village, she wore her husband's work clothes. But that only increased her charm because, said the Village Papish, you can't blur beauty like they blur the truth here, and Rebecca's walk was the walk of a beautiful woman, and the fluttering of her eyelashes was the fluttering of a beautiful woman, and the way the consonants 'p' and 'm' were launched from between her lips and the capering clapper of the 'l' on the tip of her tongue was the way they yearned to be uttered in the mouth of a beautiful woman.

And when she strode, the coarse grey cloth flapped on her limbs like the wings of birds never seen in the village. And the wind pasted it to the shape of her hips and breasts and to the little hill of her groin, as it can delineate only the shape of flesh of a beautiful woman.

But Rebecca refused to know all those simple things, and when she saw her husband looking at the woman on Rabinovitch's cart, her weary body bent forward, the wind playing with her clothes, and the light nestling in the shadows of her veins – Rebecca said in her heart that maybe she had been so cautious that she lost her charm with her own hands.

Things, in their hinting way, began to take shape in her mind. Lines began to be drawn and to connect the dots. Tonya in the wadi, the albino and his birds, the fire, the poppies, the woman cruising on the sea of chrysanthemums. All those, Rebecca knew, were merely the onset of evasiveness, like the emerging heads of buds, just the modest onset of what was coming, but after them what would she be? her heart asked her. After them what would she be and who would behold her?

A wise woman she was and could imagine the future and sense what was coming before it was completely clear. In dread mixed with curiosity, she waited for what was going to happen.

10

Sometimes an elegant English officer appeared in the village, dressed in a white navy uniform, driving a rattling wood-plated Morris Minor. He went to the albino book-keeper and bought birds from him.

One day another guest came: a blind goldfinch hunter from the Arab village of Illut beyond the eastern hills. No one noticed his blindness because his confident steps led him straight to the hut of Yakobi and Yakoba.

The Arab knocked on the door, and the albino opened it immediately, something he usually didn't do.

'How did you find the way?' he asked.

'As a man goes up a river until he comes to the source, that's how I came to the birds,' said the blind man. And with a happy grin, he added: 'And I didn't fall down, not even once.'

He savoured the sound of the canaries' song and told the albino that the *fellahin* feed their finches and their *bandooks* on *umbuz*.

'That's hashish seeds,' he explained. 'The *bandook* takes the hashish in his mouth, forgets he's in a cage, and then he's happy and sings like a bridegroom, doesn't give a damn about the whole world.'

On his next visit, the goldfinch hunter brought a few *bandooks* – hybrids of wild goldfinches and canaries – along with the hashish seeds that were good for their singing.

Like mules, *bandooks* can't produce offspring either, and so their wild blood doesn't get thinned out in generations of domestication and prison. Their breeders can't boast of pedigrees and hereditary titles, but the colours of the *bandooks* and their song are always loud and fresh, and the enchanted albino decided to feed them nourishment even more inspiring than hashish.

He sowed poppies in his yard and began extracting the sap from their stems. The big flowers quickly turned red at the top of their stalk, rose up, and set fire to the yard with a sinful splendour, and as poppies will do, they moved slowly even in the gustiest winds.

Jacob looked at the poppies, listened to the *bandooks* and the canaries, and couldn't get his mind off the woman who came to work on Rabinovitch's farm.

Poppies have an amazing quality: they don't disappear from the eye of someone who looks at them, even after he turns his eyes away from them. Red and black, they look at him even if he closes his eyes. And Jacob stared at them, blinked long and short blinks, and didn't know how dangerous were the experiments he was making.

One night, a few months after Judith came to the village, the old green truck returned to its stable in a straight, sure line, and the albino, sober and fresh as a baby, got out and unloaded sacks of cement and plaster, bricks and boards, and iron scaffolding from the back.

Behind the fence, Jacob heard the sounds and looked into the darkness. The fair head gleamed like a buoy in the dark air, and the rhythmic noise of the work told Jacob that the book-keeper was an experienced builder and could see in the dark like a cat.

For a few days, he followed the construction, and it seemed to him that the albino was watching him and even paying attention to him. And indeed, one evening, when the book-keeper sat down to rest in his garden, leafed through his book, sighed, and sipped his drink, he suddenly took off his dark glasses and gave Jacob a long, reddish look, that ended in a smile.

Excitement assaulted Jacob's torso, and fear nailed his feet to the spot.

'What are you doing there all day at the fence?' asked the most beautiful woman in the village.

There was no anger in her voice, not even any wonder, just fear and worry.

'Nothing,' said Jacob.

At night she heard the pounding of his heart, the prattling of the snakes that whispered longings inside him, and by day the birdsong prophesied ill to her. She was alone, wrapped in the fabric of her beauty and in the mantle of her dread, and now she understood what her mother had told her years before: beautiful women don't have real women friends.

The Village Papish told me that in her first days in the village, the women sought Rebecca's friendship. Some stood at a safe distance and observed her, and some dared to approach and touch her arm and open their mouths a bit, unaware that they were trying to gulp the air she exhaled.

'And after they saw that beauty's not a contagious disease, they kept away from her,' he said.

But even he couldn't prophesy the full force of the love that gripped Jacob's heart or all the wild sprouts and branches that would grow up.

> Abigail and Sarah,
> Leah and Yael—
> everybody in the town
> was perfumed by her smell.

The Village Papish sang his song to Rebecca, his fingers drumming on my knee and his voice growing louder.

11

Nobody knew what Rabinovitch's worker carried in her heart or what she had up her sleeve.

Everybody watched her with their own eyes, observed things that usually hint and reveal a secret: smells of new dishes, a strange perfume, an unfamiliar and revealing garment waving on the clothesline.

But only the scream rose from the cowshed at night, and it certainly didn't solve anything.

Soft agreed signals of warning were exchanged among the women, like the choked whistles of spring that field mice exchange when the jackal cleaves the tall grass.

But there was nothing predatory about her. There was some mystery, unintentional, and there were brief, fragrant movements of her hands as she worked, and touches she exchanged with Naomi; and that stubborn shell of hers, sometimes opaque as plaster and sometimes transparent as a grape skin, carried with her and around her.

Obviously, the pitchfork and the reins, the needle and the ladle weren't strangers to her hands, and she quickly learned how to milk. At first she milked like a beginner, only between the finger and the thumb, and when the cows got used to her touch, and she got used to their closeness, Moshe taught her how to milk with four fingers pressing the teat one after another, from the index finger to the pinkie. Her arms ached from the effort and her fingers shook, but then her muscles grew strong and from the melody of the streams of milk in the bottom of the bucket, you could hear the milking of an experienced hand.

One after another, like the pages turning in a book, the secrets of the cowshed were revealed to her. She learned to anticipate the cow's intention to kick even before the animal itself knew, she remembered the caprices of the two old milk cows, managed to decipher all the hints written on the nose and rump of a sick calf and to recognize the hierarchies of authority and respect that prevailed among the cows.

A few months later, Rabinovitch instructed her to take a cow in heat to mate at Samson Bloch's, in the next village, not far from Uncle Menahem.

Samson Bloch was an expert cattle breeder. More than once he saved a calf from dysentery with a simple mixture of flax soup, olive oil, and scrambled egg. Everybody knew the ingredients, but he was the only one who knew the order, temperature, and quantities to blend together.

Bloch rivalled Globerman in assessing the weight of livestock by looking, he castrated calves and colts better than the veterinarian, and rumour had it that he sold the castrated testicles to that Haifa restaurant where the albino bought more than food.

He had a stud bull named Gordon, 'an old bull, but he works just like the young ones,' Bloch explained proudly to anyone.

'Did she give you any trouble on the way?' he now asked Judith.

'She was a little nervous,' she said.

'Now, after a rendezvous with Gordon, she'll go back home like a baby,' said Bloch. 'She'll be quiet and happy as a bride.'

In the afternoon, when Judith brought the cow back to the cowshed, she felt that all the other milk cows looked at her in a new way and she smiled to herself. She loved the cows and, as for them, they didn't look at her suspiciously, didn't talk to her on her deaf side, didn't ask her where she came from, nor did they make any remark when they saw her sipping from the bottle of liquor she hid among the bales of hay.

And at night, when the wailing ripped out of the innards of the woman who was to be my mother, tore her throat, and woke her up, the cows turned their big, slow heads, looked at her with patient eyes, and went back to their rest and their rumination.

12

On the other side of the village, the albino kept up his nocturnal construction.

Within a few weeks, next to Yakobi and Yakoba's old hut rose a new room with a smooth cement floor, double wooden walls, and a white-washed slate roof, with a small sprinkler to cool it on hot days. That was the room for breeding canaries. The screen on the windows was dense enough to keep a cat or a snake from getting inside, and on the lattices of its shutters, the book-keeper installed a special system for opening that allowed effective ventilation of the hut without blinding its owners.

And when he completed the construction, the albino came and knocked on Jacob's door.

Rebecca opened it and her face turned gloomy when she saw the guest, but the albino saw Jacob over her shoulder and asked him if he wanted to visit 'the birds' new house'.

Already in the new room there was a dusty hot smell, the smell of sawdust and feathers familiar to everyone who breeds birds and chicks. The new birdhouse had no cages. The canaries flew in the open space and the book-keeper told Jacob that he intended to put the nesting material there and let them couple by themselves, except for the special mating for sale, and for those he had set up separate family cells.

When Jacob entered, the canaries were startled, flew and fluttered in the air.

'They'll get used to you right away and will calm down,' said the albino.

In the following days, Jacob began knocking from time to time 'with the tip of my little fingernail' on the door of the hut, going in, looking, working, and studying. With the devotion and willingness of an apprentice, Jacob helped the albino record layings and hatchings, cleaned the breeding and birth cages, and washed troughs and lattices.

'Everything you should be doing in our incubator, you do for his birds,' Rebecca remarked to him one day, and Jacob looked at her and didn't answer.

The albino taught him to recognize the various seeds that composed the canaries' food – turnip and radish seeds, hashish and grains – to crumble the hard-boiled egg, the carrots, and the potatoes. To soak the poppies in milk and feed them to the singers 'because their digestion is very nervous'.

He taught him to recognize the mating song of the male, for experienced breeders know that it's not a love song, but a sign that it is time to supply him with jute and wool scraps to build a nest.

The albino lodged the growing fledglings with the males because the mothers tend to pluck off their feathers to pad the new nest.

'Look what good fathers they are,' he said

And indeed, as soon as the nestlings were in their fathers' care, the males turned into devoted and strict trainers, took pains to feed the little ones and to teach them to sing. Jacob remarked that not all birds acted like that, and the albino was surprised because, aside from the canaries he bred, he didn't know any winged creature. 'He could hardly tell the difference between a crow and a goose.'

Jacob told him about the monogamy of storks, geese, and cranes, and praised the crow's famous fidelity to his mate, and even told something that Menahem Rabinovitch had once revealed to him, that 'the ancient Egyptians used to paint a crow as a symbol of married life'.

The albino loved to hear about the customs of the finches, who flinch from coupling with their mates in the winter. When the females migrate south, the males remain in Europe, freezing with cold, loneliness, and longing. Some of them join their women later, and some meet up with them again only in the spring.

'For a male to stay alone in the summer is no big deal,' said Jacob. 'But in the winter, that's another thing altogether. That's when he learns what it is to be alone. And when she comes back, beautiful and tired, full of love and sun and stories, he learns how much gratitude there is in love.'

The ways of the finches painted a sweet expression on the book-keeper's plump face.

'They meet in the spring,' he repeated. 'It's lovely and wise for a couple to meet only in the spring.'

Jacob remarked that the canaries are also very faithful to their mates, and then a pink smile of derision spread over the face of the albino: 'That's how it is with a couple when you close them up together in the same cage,' he said.

White juice spilled from the stems, gathered and congealed and turned dark. Then the red silk petals withered, wrinkled, and dropped off, the ovaries of the poppies puffed up, turned dark, and toughened. And at night, the book-keeper went out with a little pruning hook clicking in his hand, chopped the rigid capsules, and cracked them with his fingers. He cooked the small black seeds in the congealed sap and fed the dough to his birds.

Every few weeks, the little Morris Minor came from Haifa with the navy officer in it who bought a few pairs.

'Poor birds,' the albino meditated aloud after the officer left. 'Now they'll go down into Egypt.'

With warm oil he cleaned the pale down on the backside of one of his rollers, and said: 'This one's got diarrhoea, Jacob. Don't give him any carrots or potatoes today, just hard-boiled egg white and a little poppy-seed to eat.'

He suggested that Jacob abandon agriculture and devote himself to breeding canaries.

'It can be a good livelihood,' he said.

'It's a livelihood that doesn't suit the ideas of the village,' said Jacob.

'Chickens or canaries, they're both birds,' said the albino.

'It's not the same thing,' said Jacob.

'Nonsense,' said the albino. 'I'll teach you everything I know, and after I leave, you'll stay.'

'Where will you go?' Jacob asked apprehensively.

But the albino smiled impatiently and asked Jacob to go to the centre of the village and bring him a half-inch faucet from the warehouse.

'Go, get out,' he urged him. 'They're going to close right away.'

Jacob went to the centre, and here came Rabinovitch's Judith toward him, striding straight opposite him with the flowers of her dress and her blue kerchief, and she looks and approaches just the way she looks and approaches in his imagination. Never did she chance upon him like that, walking opposite him, in a surprisingly empty street, towards him, straight towards him. He wanted to calculate the point of their meeting but couldn't because his feet counted his steps and his eyes counted her steps, the brain added them together and the heart divided the sum in two.

When one last metre separated them, he gathered his strength and asked her how she was, and even said: 'My name is Jacob.'

'I know,' answered Rabinovitch's worker as she walked.

Her face was so close he could faint, the burn of a look, a fleeting profile, a white neck, and heels. Her dress flapped on her limbs, her back, so erect, went off into the distance.

13

He stirred with a wooden ladle, put his face close to the pot, and sniffed.

'What's the secret of the taste, Zayde? That everything will be fresh. That everything will be delicate. Just to touch. Just to put one on top of the other. Just to show the food its seasoning: nice to meet you, I'm potato. Nice to meet you, I'm nutmeg. Please meet Mr Soup, nice to meet you, Mrs Parsley. Seasoning, Zayde, it's not a smack in the face, seasoning's got to be like a butterfly's wing touching your skin. Even in simple Ukrainian borscht, the garlic shouldn't change your expression, just give you the feeling of a smile. Once I told you a story so you'd eat my food, and now I make you food so you'll listen to the stories. That means you aren't a little boy anymore, Zayde, so pay attention to your name, start being careful.'

Time, indifferent, mighty, and benevolent, bore away the initial curiosity on its stream. Gossip and guessing started boring even those who invented it. The sense of danger also passed on.

By now everybody had learned that you didn't approach Rabinovitch's Judith on her left side and you didn't ask her anything about who she was or where she came from.

Oded and Naomi came to school clean and neat. The movements of Moshe's body were once again calm and confident. The blessing, that blessing inspired only by a woman's hand, returned to his farm.

Each of the three men who were to be my fathers was tending to his own business.

Jacob Sheinfeld, who bequeathed me his drooping shoulders and his house and his dishes and the wonderful picture of his wife, meditated on Judith and learned how to breed canaries.

Moshe Rabinovitch, who bequeathed me the colour of his

hair and his farm, listened to her screaming and searched for his braid.

And my third father, the cattle dealer Globerman, who bequeathed me his money and his enormous feet, started placing cunning little gifts in the cowshed: a small bottle of perfume or a new blue kerchief or a mother-of-pearl comb for her hair.

'For Lady Judith,' he would repeat.

The dealer was a tall, thin man, his hands were stronger than they were thick, and his face concealed intelligence. Winter and summer he wore a big, worn leather jacket, and on his head was always an old beret that looked like he also used it to blow his nose. In those days he didn't yet have the truck. He always walked and sometimes he sang strange songs to himself, and their language sounded foreign even if they were sung in Hebrew. Some of them I remember well:

> Two horses, on they came
> one is blind
> one is lame
> on one's back rides a cat
> his tail is plucked
> his whiskers flat
> and he's pursued by a little mouse
> wearing trousers and a blouse.

He covered enormous distances on foot, his pockets full of bills and coins that were heavy enough to keep him from flying away in the late summer wind, with a notebook full of cows' names that kept him from forgetting anything, and with boots full of gigantic feet big enough to keep him from sinking in the mud.

Sometimes he walked alone and sometimes along with a cow, who had a rope tied to her horns, dread in her heart, and whose bleating jolted the air. East of the village, the old forest of eucalyptus turned blue, and in it was the path where traces of cloven hooves and big boots were clearly marked. Beyond it waited the butcher, the knife, and the meat hook. Every hoofprint, Naomi showed me, turned in one direction, and the traces of the boots went back and forth. On that path, the cows walked their final road. Except for one cow, the cow Rachel, who walked the path one night and then came back on it. Because of that night and that cow, I came into the world and I shall tell more about her later.

The cattle dealer always had a filthy rope wound around his shoulder, and he had his 'baston', a thick walking stick with a steel tip. He used to lean on it as he tramped around the yards, and he also used it as a cattle prod and as an index finger and as a weapon against vipers and dogs. They would run after him in the fields, crazed by the smell of blood and terror of the cows that stuck to his clothes and even wafted from his skin.

The cows also sensed this smell, the smell of their own death, coming from the body of the dealer like vapours rising from the underworld, and when Globerman appeared in one of the yards in his hat and with his rope and his notebook and his stick, a quiet snort of warning and dread rose in the air, and the cows would huddle together, their spines tense with fear, their bodies clutching one another, and their horns lowered menacingly.

Like every cattle dealer, Globerman could estimate the weight of a cow with one furtive look, but he was too smart to offer to state the weight to the farmer.

'First of all, Zayde,' he taught me the mysteries of give and take, 'this way he'll think he's cheating you, and second of all, the farmer always gives less weight than there really is there. Because buying a cow is theatre and in this theatre the farmer wants to be the saint and the dealer doesn't care if he's the sinner. Because of that, even if the owner thinks a thousand pounds, he'll say nine hundred, maximum nine hundred fifty, period. So, if he loses money and enjoys that, too, who are we, Zayde, to disturb him?'

Until his dying day, he kept hoping to bring me into his business.

'A *soyd*, Zayde, a secret.' He bent down to me. 'You're the only one I'll tell it to because you're my son. Every dealer knows you got to check the cow, but only somebody like us Globermans who was made on the *klots* knows it's even more important to examine the dairy farmer, period. You got to know what he thinks about the cow, and it's even more important to know what the cow thinks about him.'

'Love and trade are alike but they're also the opposite. Because love isn't just heart, it's mainly sense, and trade isn't just sense, it's mainly heart,' he explained. 'When a farmer sells me a *bik*, a bull, it's only flesh without a soul, at his price only weight and health are important. But when a farmer sells me *a kuh*, a milk cow, well, Zayde, that's another story. To sell this cow is like selling your mother, period. Oy oy oy, how bad to part from her, Zayde, how their eyes talk. *Oy meyn kind, oy mamenu –* oh how can you let me go, oh how she looks at him.'

'How come you're selling such a beautiful cow?' he would ask the farmer venomously.

It wasn't an answer he wanted, but rather to hear the tone of voice and to see how the face turned yellow with disgrace.

'Walk her,' he would demand. 'Let's see, maybe she swallowed a nail.'

Theoretically, this examination was designed to discern a limp or a pain that would indicate an internal injury, which could make the cow declared unkosher after it was slaughtered, but in fact what the dealer wanted was to see how the farmer approached his cow and how she responded to his presence and his touch.

'If he loves her, Zayde, he's got some regret, and if he's got some regret, he won't haggle over the price. That's how it is. You won't tell that to nobody. If you ask a trader where he makes a profit, he's got only one answer: you buy a cow on the hoof, you sell the hoof and you're left with the cow. Period.'

'I brought Lady Judith a little something,' he declared.

'Lady Judith' was my mother and 'a little something' was the general name for all the gifts the dealer gave her. At first he just happened to leave them on the ledge of the trough in the cowshed, and when Judith told him, 'You forgot something here, Globerman,' he answered her: 'I didn't forget.'

'What's that?' she asked.

'A little something for Lady Judith,' the dealer repeated the definition, and then bowed and retreated three steps, turned aside, and left, because he knew that Lady Judith wouldn't touch the gift in his presence.

Sometimes he added something like: 'Lady Judith is alone among the cows and needs a little something to remind her that she's a woman.' And on days when he was in an especially romantic mood, he said: 'You need a man to make you the queen you really are, to carry you in his arms like they carry a baby, period.'

But Lady Judith, who loved her cows, loathed the cattle dealer's manners, his gifts, his smell, and his periods.

14

'You'll eat slow, not fast, no faster than I talk, 'cause otherwise both of us could choke. You'll eat and I'll tell you about Naomi, to make it taste even better. A lot of times I saw her standing at the book-keeper's fence just like me, and finally one day I asked her: "You want to come in with me?" He didn't let no child come close, he always says birds don't like the kind of children we got here in the village. But when I brought her, he says to her: "You're Rabinovitch's little girl? Come in, please, come in." And that's how she came with me, didn't say nothing, just looked. Her head would move back and forth because the canaries sing from all sides of the room, one to the other, this one talks and that one answers. Everybody's got his own voice and his own song, and that's how they learn, too. Everybody learns his father's songs. There are also birds who learned from music they heard or from other birds outside. They imitate, like the worker I once had here, and he could imitate everything: a bird, a cat, a person, voices and movements both. You remember him, Zayde? You were a little boy when he came. And once Naomi asked the book-keeper if she could take a canary as a gift for Judith and he told her – listen, Zayde, what he told her – "Judith's going to get her bird, but not from you." And she cried then and went away and came back again. It's very hard for a little girl whose mother died and it's even harder for a little girl whose mother died and all of a sudden she loves another woman. It's so many years since I saw Rabinovitch's little girl. Once she says to me: "You got such a beautiful wife, Jacob," like both of us was guilty, she's cheating on her mother and I'm cheating on my Rebecca. She was a little girl with a lot of sense. Too bad she married that city boy Meir. He's not for her and Jerusalem's not for her, but they've got a child, I heard. Oded still takes you to her in Jerusalem? He's a good boy, Oded. Not bright like his sister, but he deserved a better life and a better woman, too. To make a long story short, when Naomi was a little girl, it was interesting to see how she ran after Judith, just like me and the dealer. Believe you me, she would look at her from far away, too, and would bring her gifts, too. She couldn't bring her clothes and perfume and cognac like the dealer, and she couldn't make her a big wedding like I did, but she could touch her and we couldn't, and she understood something I myself never understood, something only my worker explained to me many years afterwards, and that's the most important thing, that love is not some free-for-all, that love has rules and love has laws. To make a long story short, Rabinovitch's little girl would hug Judith and would take her hand and stroke it, and would bring her flowers from the field. Maybe she was afraid that we, me and Globerman, would take her away and do what her father should have done. Things like that nobody knows. Sometimes your mother used to take her to Tonya's grave. Alone she wouldn't go. Little children don't go alone to Father or Mother's grave. And not only on the anniversary of her death did she take her there, 'cause then that was with Rabinovitch and Oded, and also Menahem and Bathsheba would come and a few other people from the village; there were also times when just the two of them would go, and I used to stand and peep at them from far away. I can tell you this 'cause you also used to peep. You sat in the box I made you for watching the birds, but you also peeped at human beings. At me you peeped too. It gave me a strange pleasure that you were looking at me, 'cause there, at the bus stop I was the strangest *faygele*, the strangest bird to look at. So what did your mother

have to look for at his Tonychka's grave? That's something I
never understood. But she used to take the little girl with her,
and I saw them standing, the two of them, there at the grave,
and all around all the cyclamens were in bloom. Like anemones
always grow on old ruins, that's how cyclamens love cemeteries.
Wherever you see a lot of anemones, people once lived there,
and wherever you see gravestones, that's like rocks for the
cyclamen, just like that cowshed is like a cave for the swallow
and the case of the shutters became a hiding place for the
sparrow. The crow's the only one that doesn't leave the trees
God made for him in the six days in the beginning and doesn't
build himself a nest anywhere else. On one side, he lives near
people and isn't scared of them at all, but on the other side he
won't really live together with them like the dove does, the one
bird I can't stand. It stands with an olive branch in its mouth,
the symbol of peace for the whole world, but at home they
just murder each other. You yourself saw how doves when
they fight on the roof, they kill each other to death. It's just
horrible. If one dove is half dead, broken in pieces and can't
stand up, the second dove won't let him get away. Wolves give
up, but not the dove. He'll go after him and hit him and won't
let go of him until he's totally killed him. Crows also do things
like that sometimes, but the crow, on the other hand, doesn't
brag that he's the symbol of peace. To make a long story short,
they used to stand there at the grave, didn't talk much, but you
saw how Judith's hand was on the little girl's back, stroking,
stroking, stroking, and the child didn't move, enjoyed it like a
cat does, and then the two of them used to come back from
the path in the fields to the casuarina of the road, and the
little girl used to run all around like a little calf at Passover,
jumping with her tail up and kicking the air, and your mother
with her erect back and her straight, shining forehead with the
one deep line between the eyes, the line of the secret and the
pains, which cut the air like a knife. Believe you me, Zayde,
on cold days I could see where Judith walked, from the traces
her forehead cut in the air. In summer it used to disappear right
away in the heat, but in the cold a strip of trembling air used
to remain wherever she passed with that line. Well, and now

she's there herself with the cyclamen and the narcissus, not far
from Tonya, and her eyes and the line have already been eaten
by the worms, and Rabinovitch has already got two graves to
visit there – his Judith and his Tonychka – but strength to go
there he hasn't got anymore, just to sit on the stump of the
eucalyptus he cut down and straighten nails with his hands, for
that he's got strength, to straighten nails and to feel regrets.
'Cause somebody who wants to regret has got so many kinds
of regrets. There's regrets for somebody who went away and
maybe he'll come back. Then there's regrets for somebody who
already came back, but he isn't the same, and worst of all is to
regret somebody who just died and won't come back anymore.
Those are exactly the regrets I've got for your mother, Zayde,
regrets like that aren't even exercises for resurrection. Those are
regrets that come out of themselves and go back into themselves
and are like a cancer growing in the soul. And only in one thing
are they like each other, all the sorts of regrets, that they don't
have food to satisfy them and they don't have drink to make
them forget and they don't have a cure to stop them and they
don't have reasons, either, 'cause they don't need them. What
I'm telling you, Zayde, maybe someday you'll understand this
thing and maybe you never will, but one thing you got to know
about these regrets even if you don't understand, and that's that
regrets don't need reasons. My poor mother used to say: "*Oyf
benken darf men nisht keyn terutz*, to regret you don't need no
excuse." That's very important to know. That's like the king
doesn't need any reasons, and the police chief doesn't need any
reasons, and all the generals in the army don't need any reasons,
either, and my uncle, too, whose factory I worked in like a slave,
he didn't need reasons, either. Just a stick and shouts, that's all
he needs. Somebody who's got as much strength as regrets, he
doesn't need any reasons.'

15

I was a young man then. Youth and immortality bore me beyond Jacob's torments, his table, and his memories. In my eyes, I was like a big falcon, wandering and dancing on the warm spring air.

Only today, lashed to the doorposts of my own longing, returning to the dust of my regrets, I understand those words of his, know the obstinate heart of memory and all the struggles of contrition.

It was himself he described and about me he prophesied, and about that man, my mother's lover, the man Naomi showed me in Jerusalem, the man bent in two – he was talking about him, too.

He also told of Moshe, under the collapse of the wagon in the wadi. And he talked about Oded, Oded the orphan, eternally forsaken, a Sinbad of anger and milk and another big land.

And of my mother he talked, of her and the memory of her stolen daughter, and of all the armour she wore on her body. She always turned a deaf ear to every bad word, and always, when a stranger came to the village, she closed herself in the cowshed and sent Naomi as an antenna before her: 'Go, Nomele, go see who's coming.'

Her calculated caution didn't provide her with a perfect defence. She carefully avoided any encounter with a rag doll in a girl's hand, and until her dying day, she refused to sift lentils and left them out of the soup. But her daughter seemed to be lying in wait for her and attacked her and smote her in the groin. She saw her when she blended the milk powder in the calves' watering pail and when she smelled the pea flowers, and she thought about her when she saw a cloud approaching or a flower blooming and when the crows conversed aloud and when the sun rose and the moon died, and at night her eyes were open, remembering in the dark, and her insides were ripped apart with her scream, because in the dark there's room, she once told me when I was still too young to understand and too naive to forget, in the dark there's room, Zaydele, for all open eyes and all regrets and all screams.

'You can hide everything in a box, Zayde, in a box and in a cage and in a closet and in a room. Even love you can close up like that,' Jacob told me. 'But memory has all the keys, and regrets, Zayde, they even pass through walls. They're like the magician Houdini, they know how to get out, and like ghosts they know how to get in, when and where they want.'

But Mother's regrets didn't stick to me. I have a half-sister in America and I've never seen her face, not in my fleshly eyes and not in my mind's eye. Not even a picture of her remained with my mother, nor do I even know her name. Never did I try to find her or to meet her. Of course sometimes I ask myself all the right questions: Where does she live? Does she look like me? Will you come back someday? Will we see each other? But my insomnia isn't for her, and my regrets, my half-sister, don't sail to you.

16

Almost three years passed since the day Judith came to the village, and she would sometimes laugh now or make some comment, and in the afternoon she would take a box out of the cowshed and sit on it in the shade of the tin awning. With a spoon she ate the cheese she made in dripping cloth sacks, and chewed on salty-spicy little cucumbers she pickled in jars in the window of the cowshed. A pleasant west wind blew and said four-thirty, and the hand of the taste of the cucumbers said four days.

Many times I have tried to make pickles like hers, and didn't succeed, but I can evoke the memory of their smell in my nose and then I slide my tongue over my teeth, from right to left and from left to right, back and forth, like walking in a rut, salty salty salty salty salty salty salty ytlas ytlas ytlas ytlas ytlas ytlas ytlas—

And then, when I press it to my palate, it swims in saliva with their precise taste.

Mother wiggled her bare toes and sighed with pleasure, and with her eyes closed she slowly drank her grappa. Then she would get up and go distribute food for the cows, milk, cook, straighten up, and clean, and just before midnight her screaming rose again from the cowshed as if it were her first night there.

Oded used to wake up and grumble: 'She's crying again, looking for pity.' And Naomi breathed only in the intervals between the sobs, and imagined she stopped them because they threatened to rip her own throat, and she felt that her body was turning to stone and growing cold.

'Only after she got pregnant with you did she stop screaming,' she told me many years later, in Jerusalem.

'That was the first sign that she had a baby in her belly. But then, when she came, on those first nights – how old was I then? six or something – and I remember, when Judith would scream, it would hurt me here, inside, under my belly button, and here in my chest, you feel it, Zayde? Touch it. That was my first sign that one day I would be a woman.'

We were riding on the train then, from Jerusalem to the small station of Bar-Giora, where, she told me, there was a wonderful stream and we'd stroll by it.

The locomotive sprayed sparks and steam, puffed on the slope of the track, we ate sandwiches of omelettes, cheese, and parsley that Naomi had wrapped in the rustling paper from a margarine package.

She didn't forget to take some coarse salt wrapped in newspaper and we dipped the tomato in it and laughed.

'My father loves salt, too,' she said.

'So does my mother,' I said.

'I know,' said Naomi. 'I love people who love salt.'

Younger than all of Judith's lovers, she loved her with a love that was better and deeper than all of them, the love by decision.

'The minute she got out of the train with her big funny-looking suitcase, I decided that I loved that woman, no matter what. That wasn't love for a mother or for a friend or for an aunt. So what was it? What kind of a question is that, Zayde? A kind of blend it was. A blend of a cat and a cow and a very big sister.'

The train-crossing guard said: 'Watch out, there are terrorists here.'

We walked on the shady path above the channel. Naomi laughed and my heart stood still. Sixteen and a half years old I was then, and she was about thirty-two. Time, the great ripener, made her beautiful and slowed her down and deepened her voice and my love, and made her husband Meir rich and old and withdrawn.

Only two years later, when I was a soldier and went to them on leave, did I dare ask her: 'What's going on with your husband lately?' And she said: 'I feel so good when you come to visit, Zayde, let's not talk about Meir.'

The lake of her beauty had already started a retreat from the banks of her forehead and the pillar of her chin, and was now centred in her lips, in the corners of her eyes, where it was especially sweet and thick, and in the two smooth eyebrows on the sides of the bridge of her nose.

Mother and Oded hated him, but I like Meir. His wife I love, him I like, and their son I try to ignore. Even today, when I go meet with my red-haired professor – the 'head rook', as Naomi calls him – to bring him my observation journals and to get compliments and new assignments from him, I try to talk a bit with Meir. He still has the thin figure and the straight well-formed shoulders and the thick hair, parted in the middle, and that light walk, the walk of a man who lives in peace with his own body.

Naomi suddenly tilted her head, and for one moment, she put her sweet salty lips on mine.

'Tasty.' She laughed and tapped the back of my neck.

'You've grown up nice,' she said. 'You've already got the shoulders and hands of a man.'

We were sitting in the shade of the mulberry tree. The warm air of her mouth gathered and trembled in the hollow of my neck. Her hand dropped gold between my shoulders. A partridge roared off with a beating of its wings.

'She used to sing to me, listen to this, *shlaf meyn feygele, meyn kleyne, lig nor shtil un her tsikh tsu.* You understand? Then she would translate, like this: "Sleep, sleep, my little bird. Hush, lie still and hear my word."'

The red branches of the mulberry tree looked black to her against the sky above them, she announced all of a sudden.

'Her first Purim in the village she told me, "Come on Nomele, I'll make you a special costume." I thought I was going to be dressed up as the queen of England, but all she did was sew me some plain little girl's dress, did my hair in a brand-new way, and put a rag doll in my hand. I asked her what kind of costume that was, and she said: "You're dressed up as another little girl." And that's what I said in class. Everybody was dressed up properly, as kings and heroes, and when they asked me what I was dressed up as, I said just what she told me, that I was dressed up as another little girl. And proudly, you know, not ashamed, and with all the love that I decided to love her. Because that's the most important rule of love, that it's a matter of decision. I already told you that once and I'll tell you again: you just have to decide – now, that's love. Just like that. Now, that's love. Everything I hear and smell and see and think – is love. Look Naomi and smell and touch and taste and listen carefully. What's happening now, that's love. And to say it aloud, when nobody hears: now, that's love. And to talk as in love and to look as in love and to act as in love. Like our neighbourhood milkman, a wonderful old religious man, once told Meir: if you, Mr Klebanov, if you just adore the Holy-One-Blessed-Be-He all the time, and how He created the world, you'll remain a heretic as you are, but if you curse the Lord every morning, God forbid, and at the same time put on a hat and keep kosher and honour the Sabbath for a month, that'll make you a good Jew. Just like that. Love of commandments and rules. Touch her all the time, hug her three times, think what Judith is doing now, imagine her hands when you eat her sandwich at recess at school, here, on these slices they were, this cucumber they peeled and cut. This salt they sprinkled. Put a blue kerchief like hers on your head, and steal a small sip from her bottle and cough. Maybe, if I had decided to love Meir as I then decided to love her, my life would have been easier afterwards. Sometimes I thought she loved me, too, and she really did hug and kiss, but she never stroked. The stroking she kept in her hand. You remember how the old folks in the village used to put it? Loving doesn't cost money. I hated that saying so much. If loving doesn't cost money, then why are they all so stingy with love?'

'I'm not,' I said.

'You're not stingy, Zayde, you're just stupid, and I don't know what's worse,' said Naomi. 'But your mother was stingy. Stingy with love. Did you notice how she'd sometimes walk around with her fist clenched? At first I thought she wanted to hit somebody and then I understood that she was keeping something there. Maybe that caress I wanted so much and she kept for another little girl. Do you ever think of that half-sister of yours, Zayde? I'm also your half-sister, maybe. Only at my mother's grave did your mother caress me. Every month she used to take me there. Father used to come with us only on the anniversary of her death, you know that yourself, Zayde, but then, in the first years, she used to take me every time, and only there, at the grave, was her hand on my back open and caressing and caressing. And I loved most of all to sit on the cement walk my father paved for her and eat pomegranates with her. You remember how nice it was to eat pomegranates with her on the walk?'

17

Once every two weeks, on Tuesday, they showed a movie at the town hall. Oded would bring the round flat box from Haifa, and sometimes he would go to Mother, lower his eyes, and say: 'It's a movie from America.'

She didn't go to the town hall very much, but when a movie came from America, the two of us went. Together we looked at the pictures of an American street and American houses and American roads and trees, and together we inserted her little girl into their frame.

As will often happen, the daughter went on growing in her memories. She saw her adding height and intelligence, saw her change the way she did her hair and the way she looked, was stabbed by the buds of her ripening breasts, screamed in fear with her at her first menstrual period, and along with her, forgot her mother tongue and her mother, and one night she even dreamed of her married to a man and giving birth to twins, who, to her horror, looked like that cursed man whose name I was forbidden to say then and am forbidden to remember even now.

On the way back from the town hall, she didn't say a word, and at home she took a small sip of her drink and sighed without knowing how loud and sharp her sigh was, and then she lay down and heard the dances of the three brothers, If, What If, and What If Not, and the laughter of the *Malakh-fun-shlaf* and Moshe's nocturnal rambling: from the kitchen cabinets to the clothes closet, door after door, and from there to the space between the beds to the floor and from there to the space between the hut and the ground. Then he went out to the yard and gently knocked on the walls of the storehouse, moved sacks, and lifted bales of straw in the haystack. He didn't go into the cowshed, where his entrance could be interpreted as improper, but he peeped again into the hatchery, and went back to the storehouse, because in those days, he attributed to the braid the ability to move and evade, and even thought it contained a measure of cunning.

And so he walked and searched and surveyed and came back. To the rack of his bed, to the little girls' frocks his mother had put on him, to the bubbles of death in the cold water, to his wide-open eyes wandering in the dark.

The cement walk from the house to the cowshed, Moshe Rabinovitch paved for Judith before I was born. The little hand of big time has brought forth spots of lichen in it now and sprouted screwbeans in its cracks. But I remember as if I were there because there isn't a day that I don't walk on it.

'That walk, my father made for your mother. From the house to the cowshed. That's a nice gift, isn't it? You should've seen her face when Father finished the work and said to her: "That's for you, Judith." If he were Globerman, he would certainly have bowed and told her: "Lady Judith doesn't have to get her wonderful feet dirty in the mud, period!" And if he was Sheinfeld, he would have lain down in the mud and told her to walk on him. But my father paved her a walk. Without any fooling around and the way it should be.'

One day, at the end of Judith's third summer here, Rabinovitch brought cement and sand and gravel and boards, built a form, inserted iron stakes, and poured squares that combined into a strip of cement from the hut to the cowshed. Then he smoothed and watered the cement and when the work was done and the walk dried, he invited Judith to come to it.

And suddenly, Mother was filled with a spirit of joy. With one hand, she lifted the hem of her skirt a bit, gave the other hand to Naomi, and the two of them inaugurated the new walk with a few light, bouncy steps.

'And that winter we didn't drown in the mud between the house and the cowshed. You can't imagine how happy we were about that walk.'

'For Mother you didn't make a walk,' Oded said to his father.

He boycotted the new walk and for two years he strode alongside it. Then he gave in and stopped, but in the ground his feet had already trodden a thin short path of orphanhood and rebuke, still visible there to this day.

Before Passover, Tonya Rabinovitch's pomegranates blossomed in a plethora of tiny leaves, then they glittered and bloomed red, and in the June *hamsins*, the scarlet ovaries puffed up and decked themselves out in their crowns.

Judith made newspaper cones, took Naomi, and together they covered the tiny fruits, and in the autumn when that summer came to a close, the two of them sat on the new walk and ate pomegranates.

The first pomegranates, with big pink seeds, were ready to eat by *Rosh Hashanah*, and the dark sourish ones Judith picked after *Sukkoth*, squeezed them and strained their juice with the white laundered cloth they used for straining milk, and taught Naomi how to make wine from it.

Years have passed since then, but I can easily picture them
sitting on the grey cement, the woman who's dead now and
the little girl who has grown up now, blue cloth kerchiefs on
both their heads and their four knees bare. Their strong, bare
feet are still pricked by the tiny spinning tops of the eucalyptus,
which was still standing there, and by the hard little hedgehogs
that kept dropping from the casuarinas.

Judith picked up a pomegranate, tapped it gently all around
with the wooden handle of the knife, and decapitated it. She
peeled a bit around the stump, cut around the rind, and cracked
the fruit with her fingers.

'Never cut it with a knife, Nomele,' she said. 'Metal gives
pomegranate a bad taste.'

With the pad of her thumb, she loosened and spilled the seeds
into the palm of her other hand, and from there she poured them
into her mouth.

'Those are my mother's trees,' grumbled Oded.

'So you eat them, too,' said Naomi.

'Don't let a single seed fall,' Judith warned her, as she warned
me, too, a few years later when I was also in the world and the
two of us sat on that same walk and ate pomegranates. 'Don't
let a single seed fall. Anyone who drops a seed has lost.'

Even today she warns me like that in my mind, but today I
don't eat the fruit of those pomegranates. All winter they are
occupied by robins and all spring they bloom red and they still
ripen into a plethora of fruit. Out of a vague sense of obligation
I cup them in paper cones every year, but I don't pick them when
they're ripe.

Summer passes, the birds and the wind tear the paper cups,
and the tiny fruit flies, who go nuts from the sweetness and lust,
hover over the oozing cracks in the rind of the fruit and tell me
it's autumn.

Then the pomegranates dry out and harden in their torn
wrappers like mummies whose shrouds are undone. Their black
rind tells me it's winter and their seeds crumble like corpses' teeth
in its winds.

18

Shlaf meyn Nomele, meyn kleyne,
Shlaf meyn kind, un her tsikh tsu,
Ot dos feygele dos kleyne,
Iz keyn andere vie du.
Ay li lu li lu li li.
Shlaf meyn Nomele, meyn kleyne,
Lig nor shtil un her tsikh tsu,
Sleep, sleep, my little bird,
Hush, lie still, and hear my word.

'Maybe you'll stop singing to my sister all the time,' grumbled Oded.

He was a little boy, but rage and fear aged his features with premature wrinkles, strengthened his body, and gave him the gait of a grown man.

At night, Judith put him and Naomi to bed and told them stories, but the love and attention in Naomi's face wasn't to Oded's liking, and he complained.

His voice was bitter and dull: 'Our mother told us nicer stories.'

'I'm not your mother.' Judith folded the blanket down off his face.

She gave him a look he hasn't forgotten to this day, and when he describes it to me now, an angry, frightened little orphan still dwells between the words.

'If you want to fight with me, Oded,' she told him, 'don't hide under the blanket. You're not a baby anymore. Come out and fight seriously.'

And when she saw the embarrassment spreading over his face and smoothing the anger out of it, she stroke his amazed cheek, said, 'Good night, children,' and went to the cowshed: to her cows, her bedroom, her bed, her screaming.

*　　*　　*

'Go to her, Father.' Naomi got up one night and stood at her father's bed.

Moshe shook his head no.

'I'll go with you,' said Naomi. 'We'll go in and ask her why she's shouting like that.'

'We shouldn't go to her,' said Moshe.

'Then I'll go to her if you won't.'

Rabinovitch sat up with a start. 'You won't go to her. Nobody will go to her. Grown-up people don't cry to make you come to them. She'll cry a little and it'll pass.'

One night, Naomi couldn't help it anymore. She sneaked into the yard of the cowshed, held onto the waterpipe, and tried to stand on the trough and peep at the bright figure, with gaping mouth and eyes, huddled in her corner.

Moshe's heavy hand blocked his daughter's mouth. He picked her up and held her tight.

'She shouldn't know that we know,' he growled into her ear as he carried her to the house.

And when he took his hand away, a flock of words burst from her mouth like a bevy of finches from the thicket.

'The whole village knows, Father!' she shrieked. 'And she knows that everybody knows. Even the children in school are talking.'

'Never mind what they're talking.' He put his hand on her again. 'But she mustn't see you going there.'

'They think you're doing things to her!' The words bubbled up from her mouth and scalded the skin of his hand.

'Shut your mouth or I'll tie a towel on your face! When you grow up you'll understand.'

And the screaming melted away. The gashes she ripped in the air were stitched back together. Scars were visible but only a moment and vanished at once.

'It's like the flesh of a woman down below that doesn't get any marks,' Jacob told me.

He poured the cognac. 'Only births leave traces there,' he said. 'But not love and not infidelity. Not us men. Only on our mother's flesh do we leave marks, not on the flesh of our wives. Look there someday, Zayde. You're a grown man now. Look and see for yourself. On the skin of the face and on the skin of the hands, all the stamps of life remain. Even on our *shmuckele* nothing is erased. Anybody who can read, reads the marks on his *shmuckele* like a diary. Globerman told me that once. Like the rings on a tree trunk they stay there. Here's the good years and here's the bad years, here's the names and here's the times. There's a rock like that in Lake Kinneret that shows you marks of how much water there was every year. That's how it is with us. But with a woman down below, nothing. No mark. There it's just like the Kinneret. You see the old storms in the lake? You see in the air of the day the screams that passed through it in the night? See? You don't see there, either.'

19

Like a cuckoo's fledgling, Judith pressed and pushed all other thoughts out of his mind. He thought only of her, her and her screaming and her body and her cart cruising in the greenish yellow sea of chrysanthemums, and he didn't understand, he told me, how she could be in two places at the same time: 'With Rabinovitch in the yard and with me in my head.'

Sometimes he saw her on the street or in the centre of the village, and he would nod hello to her and torment his heart with naive plans and childish hopes to meet her in another way and another time and another place.

And one day Moshe Rabinovitch came to Jacob to hatch two hundred chicks for him, and asked if Sheinfeld could wait a few weeks to be paid.

Jacob was so happy he said: 'The money is nothing, Rabinovitch, never mind the money.'

He hurried to the incubator, dismantled it, washed and disinfected its parts and dried them in the sun, and when the chicks hatched and the incubator was filled with chirping, Jacob came to tell Rabinovitch to prepare the coop for them.

'I'll bring them tomorrow,' he said, his eyes roving and searching.

But Judith didn't appear and Jacob went off.

The next day, he hitched up the wagon and brought the chicks in two closed cases. The smell and the chirping drove the cats out of their minds. Some of them assembled in Rabinovitch's yard and besieged the coop, looking for a crack. But Moshe poured cement all around, right on the edge of the screen, and fastened every single joint with wire because he knew that hunger makes cat limbs supple and their murderous impulse gives them the ability to squeeze inside like snakes.

The concrete floor was already covered with sawdust and Jacob bent over and gently emptied the case of chicks onto it. The yellow block, dense and chirping, scattered into dozens of frantic little balls and immediately banded together again in a murmur of fear and excitement.

And then the door suddenly squeaked. The chicks fell silent all at once and that shudder again penetrated the back of Jacob's neck. He knew it was Judith who came into the coop and was standing behind him.

His heart fluttered. That's what will happen to the human heart when fear shrinks its chambers and, at the very same moment, when happiness expands its top floors.

'And the heart – you knew that, Zayde? – the heart melts. And right away, a mess in all the hands and all the feet. Here some muscle shakes, bones are like milk powder in water, blood is like soup, agitated and boiling.'

'Very simply, I couldn't breathe,' he recalled. 'I was very simply choking. That's how a man tells himself he's in love.'

'How did Rabinovitch live with her there in the yard and not go nuts?' he wondered. 'You understand that, Zayde? When he saw her working, when he saw how she moved, when she lifts up a jug of milk or drags the buckets to the calves and her body is straining under her dress . . . How can a person lie like that in the hut and know she's in the cowshed, right behind a wall of wood and a wall of air and a wall of cement? You can just go nuts.'

*   *   *

That evening, when Judith was milking and Moshe was unloading the clover off the wagon, he suddenly asked her if she had noticed Jacob's looks.

'He likes you,' he stated.

'*A nafka mina*,' said Judith.

'Well,' said Moshe. 'What joy. The whole village is dreaming of Sheinfeld's wife, and Sheinfeld is making eyes at you.'

Judith finished washing and hardening the teats of the milk cow. In straight white jets, the milk sprayed into the bucket, and the high-pitched ping of its initial impact grew deeper and more muffled from one spray to the next.

The cow turned her head and looked at Judith. Her big tongue thrust out and was inserted into her nostrils with the sound of a wet cork. The warm, sweetish smell rose in the air and was absorbed in the walls and Judith's eyes blazed.

She leaned her sweating forehead on the cow's belly, and when the cow gently lifted her hoof, hinting at some discomfort, she said: 'Shaa ... shaa ...' and stroked the big thigh, pressing gently on the point that paralyses the intention and the ability to kick.

Years later, when I was seven years old, she told me that the horse gets love in exchange for his love and the dog gets authority for his loyalty and the cat food for his charm, but the cow doesn't get anything, except rebukes and kicks. She gives her milk and her strength and her children while she's alive, and afterwards they take her flesh and skin and horns and bones.

'They don't throw away any of the cow,' she summed up.

And Jacob said: 'That's how it is with a great love. With a great love only one person always gives everything. Always there's nothing that gets lost.'

He lay in his house, his head asleep, his heart awake, and his eyes two holes gleaming in the dark.

Crows, swallows, canaries, and sparrows slept their slumber. The barn-owl, white queen of the gloom, spread silent wings and emerged from her hiding place.

Rebecca was also awake, for insomnia is contagious.

'Sleep, Sheinfeld, I don't have any strength anymore,' she said. 'When you don't sleep, I'm tired in the morning.'

But Jacob was silent. His bones squeaked and his flesh hurt.

'And I said thank God my eyes, wide open in the dark, don't shine thoughts on the wall. Just imagine that, Zayde, that she would see my thoughts and I would see her thoughts like in the cinema or with a magic lantern.'

With a strange clarity, he felt his ribs pressing together in his chest and, like long teeth, chewing the flesh of his heart.

'What's with you lately, Sheinfeld?' asked the most beautiful woman in the village.

And Jacob didn't answer. For what good are words for love?

20

One evening, the door didn't open. The groping hand wasn't stretched out. The albino didn't emerge.

The canaries were singing as they usually did, but Jacob was worried. He waited a little and moved out of Yakobi and Yakoba's yard and put his face up to the lattices of the big hut. Then he knocked on the door. The singing stopped and a dreadful silence reigned. Jacob was afraid to go in, convinced himself that the book-keeper was still asleep, and left.

The albino wasn't seen the next evening, either, and Jacob was scared because the wheelbarrow of papers from the treasurer's office was standing at the door, and the truck was parked in its usual place and its hood was cold. He called the Village Papish who didn't hesitate to break down the door of the hut and, in a tempest of the turbulent shrieks and struggles and feathers of the canaries, the book-keeper was lying naked on the floor, cold and fat and stiff.

'He's dead.' The Village Papish straightened up from the body.

He ran to summon the medic, and Jacob was left alone with the pinkish grey albino. The hair on his snowy white corpse was snagged with flying grains of sawdust, birdseed shells, and droppings.

The smell of death began to be felt in the air. Jacob immediately poured water into the tiny porcelain basins and scattered all the varieties of seeds and crumbs there in the feeding troughs, seeking consolation and serenity in the routine movements of work.

Then came those who took care of such matters, and they very matter-of-factly took the corpse away.

The birds, who were terrified by the turmoil in their hut, had calmed down now. The thin shrieks of alarm vanished. The last particles of down stopped dancing around in space and settled on the floor. A slightly encouraging sound of singing began rising from the cages, a fragmentary conversation at first, a tiny bit here and a tiny bit there, and they went on in a loud and defiant song. And Jacob, who had been sitting alone on the floor of the canary house for a long time, was infected with the ancient faith of all bird breeders – that their singing is a sign of thanks and love. A faith like that will also be found among kings and kindergarten teachers, drill sergeants and village choirmasters.

He got up and went back home. Rebecca served him dinner, but Jacob didn't pay any attention to his food and took no pleasure in it, either. Finally, he left most of his dinner on his plate, got up from the table, and said he had 'to go take a look and see what was going on with the poor birds', and didn't notice that that was the second time that day he had imitated the dead albino's style of speaking.

He didn't observe his wife's weeping, got out of her embrace, dragged a folding cot to the canary house, and lay there all night in the gloom, waiting fearfully for some heir or relative to pop up, brandishing a signed will and white eyelashes, proof of relationship, and demand the poor birds.

But the albino was childless and no one showed up. The council published an obituary notice in the newspaper and addressed the Mandatory court in Haifa, and even those relatives who usually come to light only after death, those cousins even the dead person himself doesn't know – even they didn't come.

The council sent two representatives 'to check the inventory'.

In the albino's kitchen cabinets were a few Czech government yearbooks, five pairs of sunglasses, dozens of tubes of stinking skin lotion, and two pairs of shoes.

After rummaging through the dead man's clothes closet, they discovered that the threadbare black suit he always wore was in fact five identical black suits, all cut the same, and all equally threadbare, and on their ten sleeves were the same shiny old suede patches.

In the pantry were pots and skillets, heavy as rocks and very dirty, and a yellow wooden canary, marvellously precise and carved, which Jacob immediately took for himself without telling anyone.

He remembered the worn-out book the albino used to read and weep over as he sat in the yard of an afternoon, and after a feverish search, he found it, too, hidden in a closet in the canaries' hut. To his surprise, it wasn't a personal diary or a love story or a book of poetry, but old schedules, carefully bound, of trains that had once travelled between Prague and Berlin, Vienna and Budapest.

The next day, Jacob went to the nearby village to ask Menahem Rabinovitch why a person was interested in schedules of trains that never travelled here. The carob grower leafed through the book and smiled and explained to him that everybody has his own ways of taming regrets and sharpening memory, and everybody, in his own way, tries and fails.

21

Every afternoon, the crows assemble for a meeting.

They come to find out what's new, and I come for the same purpose. To human eyes all crows look alike, but I know every one of them by name and by his history. Some I recognize as I recognize people, by their face, and others by the borderline between the grey and the black on their chest. So I know who died and who disappeared, who was born and who got married.

They come from all around for meetings and conversations that go on almost until dark, and then each goes off to his own tree and his abode.

Until the day my mother died, they used to congregate on our big eucalyptus tree. After Moshe cut it down they still hovered over its ruin for two more days, black and screaming as if their world were destroyed, and on the third day, they transferred their meeting to the old railway station beyond the wadi, and to the plot of anemones.

There, the young crows, who are as big as their parents, but whose wings are still tentative, show off their progress in flying. The old ones utter well-turned caws. The scouts and the guards supervise what goes on in the area.

Now and then, some of them swoop down on a cat who came out of the village or pester an owl who appeared in the light. Some take off to pursue a buzzard and even pick a fight with an eagle circling in the sky. What a fine spectacle that is. Six or seven crows fly to the eagle, but only one of them does battle. Eager for excitement and fearless, light, and nimble, he swoops down on the eagle, attacks him from the side, rises underneath him, and the eagle, when his patience runs out, tries to clash with him, to hit him and bring him down, in vain. The crow evades him and turns over, lands like a rock, and immediately rises again and attacks and he's supple and bold, craving entertainment and honour.

But back then, when the albino died, the eucalyptus was still standing in the yard, and seven days after his funeral, the crows cut off their regular meeting, and suddenly they all landed in the cow yard. Excitement and suppressed violence were obvious in their behaviour. They ran around on the rails and screamed bizarre, coarse screams that startled the doves out of their regular lodging on the roof.

Now I'm tempted to say that they wanted to herald my birth. And secretly I'm proud that it was a noisy black flock of crows and not white doves that prophesied my coming into the world. But back then no one paid attention to such stretches of time, and no one connected it to the death of the canary breeder, especially since everyone knew that such a gathering of crows in the cow yard could mean only one thing: the impending birth of a calf.

The crows are mad about cow placentas. Their senses are so sharp and their passion is so great that they're often the first to discern labour pains, sometimes even before the pregnant female herself. Now they danced on the fence, hopped, and shrieked on the roof of the cowshed and terrified the cows in heat.

Moshe heard them, went out to the yard and noticed the breathing of the cow and the swelling of her loins. A thick rope of mucus was already stretching under her tail.

'Well, children,' he said. 'Ask nice that we'll have a heifer.'

'What difference does it make?' asked Naomi.

'A farmer is glad when females are born in the cowshed and males in the house,' said Moshe.

He noticed the reservation spreading over Judith's face and wanted to appease her, but he didn't yet know the keys to her anger or the preludes to her wrath.

'Well, Judith, that's only a saying of farmers.' He was embarrassed, put on his rubber boots, and went back to the cow.

The birth was long and hard. Rabinovitch tied a rope around the foetus's legs and pulled hard for a long time.

'You're hurting her, Father!' cried Naomi. 'You're pulling too hard.'

But Moshe didn't answer and Oded said: 'Shut up, Naomi, you don't understand anything about it. Giving birth isn't any business for women.'

The cow groaned. Her eyelids seemed to pull down. The other cows looked at her with heavy faces.

'Here, it's coming out,' said Moshe. He put his hand in up to the elbow, turned the body of the foetus to a more comfortable position, and pulled out a fat calf that was already dead.

'Dammit.' He tossed the carcass aside. 'Hitch up the horse, Oded, and drag it to the eucalyptus forest.'

He went into the cowshed, but Judith was looking at the cow, whose eyes were shut with weakness and whose legs were trembling, and she said: 'She's got another one inside.'

'How do you know?' asked Oded. 'How come you understand more than my father?'

'I know,' said Judith, and she touched the cow's nose and added: 'She's cold as ice. Fast, go call your father to come back. She's haemorrhaging inside.'

Suddenly the cow's knees buckled and she knelt down, and when she turned over helplessly on her side, a heifer burst out of her guts, followed by a spring of blood. She spread her hooves and her neck, shook and groaned.

'Father, Father!' shouted Oded. 'There's also a heifer—'

Moshe rushed to the yard. One look at the dying cow and the flowing blood was enough for him. He ran to the cowshed and came back with the corn scythe.

'Take the children away from here so they won't see,' he said to Judith. 'And run and get the dealer. I think he's wandering around in the village today.'

His broad body hid the act, but a new puddle of blood immediately collected at his feet.

Off to the side, the heifer started trying to stand up. She was strong and nimble, and when she made it, the typical physical features of a barren heifer appeared. She was tall, her shoulders broad and sloping, her legs long, and her face the face of a male.

'Sonofabitch,' Moshe cursed. 'The calf died, the mother passed away, and now this *tumtum*, this androgyne.'

Fifteen minutes later, Mother and Globerman came.

'Did you manage to slaughter it in time?' asked the dealer.

'I did.'

Then Globerman noticed the dead calf and his peculiar twin.

'Troubles come in threes, eh, Rabinovitch?' he said.

Moshe didn't answer.

'Look at that *maydele* how she looks,' said the dealer. 'It's always like that when there's twins – a little heifer and a little calf. It's her brother's blood that made her half a boy. She won't give milk and she won't give birth. I'll take her, too.'

'Her you won't take,' Judith said suddenly.

'I'm talking to the boss now, Lady Judith.' Globerman took his filthy beret off his head. 'That heifer is half a calf. If you give her to me, Rabinovitch, we'll make a deal for the old lady, too. I've got an Arab who'll give a good price for the carcass.'

But the heifer already started walking, shaking and wet, stumbling and searching for a teat. Her feet led her to Judith, and Judith took a sack and started wiping the mucus and blood off her.

'Rabinovitch,' she suddenly said, 'I've never asked you for anything up to now. Don't give him this heifer.'

'That's the most beautiful sound in the world,' said Globerman. 'The voice of a woman pleading.'

'Leave that heifer here,' said Judith. 'I'll take care of her.'

'It's not a heifer, it's a calf, and I'll take him now,' said the dealer. 'He can already walk by himself.'

'No!' shouted Judith, and her voice was loud and shrill and strange.

Moshe looked at her, at the dealer, at the heifer, and at his feet.

'Listen, Globerman,' he said at last. 'You say she's a calf? So I'll sell her to you like we sell a calf. We'll raise her, we'll feed her a little so she puts on weight, and we'll sell her to you in half a year.'

The dealer took out his notebook, pulled his pencil from behind his ear, and asked: 'What will you name her?'

'Roast Beef,' said Oded.

'Shut up, Oded!' said Naomi.

'We won't name her,' said Moshe. 'Only milk cows have names.'

In the yard, the crows hopped, bloody fragments of placenta dripping from their beaks.

'I need a name,' said Globerman. 'Without a name, I can't write in my notebook.'

'We'll call her Rachel,' said Judith.

'Rachel?' Moshe was amazed.

'Rachel,' said Judith.

When I grew up and my Mother told me the rest of the story about her and her cow Rachel, I realized that Rachel may have been the name of my sister who was taken to America, and when I said that to my mother, her face became glum and she said: 'What are you talking about, Zayde? What strange ideas you have.'

'So what is her name?' I asked. 'Maybe you'll finally tell me her name.'

'*A nafka mina*,' replied Mother.

I was sure that was a Yiddish word, and only when I grew up did I learn it was Aramaic for 'who cares'.

22

'In the end, Lady Judith, you'll be mine.'

'No, not even if you were the last man on earth.'

'Lady Judith, you need a man with heart. With money. With a generous hand and a generous heart. Who's like that here except me?'

Very slowly, the cunning livestock dealer focused his attempts, his remarks became sharper, all his expertise in human and cattle souls he invested in Moshe and Judith. He started giving her the little something he brought in Rabinovitch's presence to see how the two of them would react.

Once he came and when he saw that Judith wasn't in the yard, he said to Moshe: 'Reb Yid, I brought a little something for Lady Judith, you'll please give it to her when she comes back, and don't forget to tell her who brought it.'

Another time, he dared to bend down to Moshe, who was a head shorter than him, and ask in a mocking tone: 'Reb Yid, how is it that you live with that woman in the yard and don't go nuts?'

Judith and Naomi were crossing the yard, carrying tin buckets to water the young calves. The dealer looked at my mother and said with a coarseness unexpected even in him: 'From that udder the doctor wouldn't reject even the smallest piece.'

Judith left Rachel to the end. The strong, wild orphan bleated impatiently, and when Judith approached her she stuck her head in the bucket so eagerly she almost spilled its contents. Judith stroked her neck and whispered affectionately to her.

'Don't give her so much,' Naomi whispered so her father and Globerman wouldn't hear. ''Cause then she'll gain weight and Father will sell her to the dealer.'

'He won't sell her, Nomele,' said Judith. 'This heifer is mine.'

A few days after the albino's funeral, the Council held a sale of the dead man's belongings.

One man – 'a weird character', as the Village Papish defined him – came from Haifa and haggled for hours over the five suits.

The blind Arab, father of the *bandooks* from the village of Illut, bought the sunglasses and some empty cages.

Jacob took the filthy pots and frying pans that nobody wanted, and said he'd go on taking care of the birds, because nobody knew what to do with them.

And the green truck was sold at auction.

A special auctioneer was brought from the city and the whole village gathered to see the spectacle, but only two buyers showed up: the treasurer of the nearby kibbutz and the dealer Globerman.

The treasurer saw who his rival was at the sale and started laughing. 'Globerman,' he said, 'since when do you know anything about cars? You don't even know how to drive.'

But the dealer walked around the truck, gave a few '*tappen*' on the fenders and the hood, and felt the tyres to see if they had any bones in them. Then he asked one of the men to drive the truck in a circle. Everybody chuckled and somebody shouted: 'The truck swallowed a nail, Globerman!' But the livestock dealer stood in the centre of the circle, importantly waving his thick *baston*, listening to the motor, and watching the spinning wheels.

'It'll hold two cows in the back and one woman in the cabin?' he asked. And when they told him it would, he was satisfied, pulled the legendary *knippl* out of his pocket, and everybody stopped chuckling because the thick bundle of notes immediately put an end to the planned auction.

The truck became the property of the cattle dealer, the embarrassed treasurer went back to his kibbutz, and Globerman gave
the auctioneer half a pound and a case of beer for his *Benemones
Parnussa*, and sent him home.

23

Now that his chicks were growing up at Rabinovitch's farm,
Jacob decided he had an excuse to visit there, and after a week
of cogitation, he appeared and proclaimed: 'I came to see if the
chicks are growing good.'

He asked Judith what she was giving them to eat, made all
sorts of recommendations and gave all sorts of advice, and after
all that, he gathered up his courage and asked if she wanted to
learn how to make paper boats so she could play with Moshe's
children and win their hearts.

Before she could answer, Jacob took out a few pieces of paper,
sat down, and started folding them with a surprising agility,
folding them and turning them over and smoothing their folds
with his thumb-nail, and four beautiful paper boats immediately
stood gloriously on the table.

'If you'll go out to the yard with me, we'll put them in the
cow trough,' he suggested.

The boats bobbed on the water of the trough, looking solid
and sure.

'Boats like these can also sail on the river without sinking,'
he promised, and then, with a boldness that surprised both of
them, he put his hand on her middle finger and said: 'I'm not
a great sage, Judith, not handsome, and not rich. And when
God was passing out brains and beauty, I wasn't the first one
in line. Not altogether the last one, but not the first one, either.
But when God was passing out patience, I waited in line until
everybody else didn't have patience to wait any longer. That's
how it is with us Jacobs. I'm not Globerman, not Rabinovitch,
not nobody, but seven years for me is but a few days to wait.'

And suddenly the cognac in his glass was agitated, tears came into his eyes, his face bent down, he was almost hidden in his plate.

'And see, more than seven years I waited, until she died I waited. And afterwards I didn't wait anymore. What's there for me to wait for a dead woman? A dead woman you should miss, but to wait? She's dead and ever since I only think about all the questions. What happened? How did I lose her? And what if I did this, and what if I did that, and maybe that? Everything I did so good, everything I planned by the rules. Maybe she said something to you once, Zayde?'

'Nothing,' I answered, dreading the next question.

Jacob squinted at me.

'I've got to go now,' I said.

'Sometimes a mother tells her son something,' said Jacob.

'Not that mother,' I said. 'You know much more about her than I do.'

'You were with her more than me.'

'I've got to go, Sheinfeld.'

Jacob smiled with a grimace of pain.

'Sheinfeld,' he said. 'Sheinfeld . . .' And a few minutes later, he asked: 'How will you go now? After midnight, there aren't any buses. Here, Zayde, I'll make up a couch for you in the other room.'

'I'll walk,' I said impatiently. 'I know the paths and the short-cuts. I'll get there right in time for the morning milking. To help Moshe.'

'From here to the village by foot? Through the forest at night? That's dangerous.'

'Dangerous?' I laughed. 'The Angel of Death is a very orderly angel. He sees a little boy named Zayde and immediately goes off to look for somebody else. Watch out, Jacob, when you stand next to me. Maybe that's how he'll get to you.'

'You aren't a little boy anymore.'

'I'm not a grandfather yet, either.'

'The Angel of Death is like a farmer who's got an orchard,' said Jacob. 'Every morning he goes and walks around among the trees and looks for the ripe fruit. There was a *goy* like that back

home. He would tie coloured ribbons on the trees as a sign that
he had to pick here. And he had another very funny habit, he
always took food for the road. Even if he was only going to the
store, he would make himself a little bag with bread and cheese
and something to drink so he wouldn't have to ask anybody for
a favour, and once—'

'Jacob.' I stood up. 'You'll tell me some other time. I've really
got to go now.'

'You don't want me to make you the dessert, the Italian one,
with egg yolk and wine, that you love so much?'

'No, Jacob, I've got to go.'

'Then go, Zayde, go. Just don't say your father forced you
to stay.'

'You liked it, the meal?' His shout pursued me.

'A lot,' I called back into the darkness as I ran. 'It was
very good.'

'I'll invite you again, and you'll come, right?' the darkness
called to me.

'I'll come, I'll come.'

I slid down the eastern slope of the hill, stumbled, and tripped
on bushes and rocks. I sank into the smell of elecampane in the
ditch, I leaped over its pebbles, I climbed the other bank and
the ridges beyond it, and when I reached the road, the roar of
the truck motor was heard in the distance, and the halo of light
was creeping up the hill, and the orange lamps and the glowing
triangle were twinkling on the roof of the big horse of the village
milk truck.

The ascent ended, Oded shifted gears and shifted gears again
and shifted gears again, and speeded up, and I climbed among
the trees to the road, jumped into the beam of the headlights, and waved both hands, because I knew what his braking
range was.

The horn honked in loud recognition, the heavy milk truck
just slowed down, and I jumped up, and grabbed the ladder,
and clambered inside, excited and annoyed.

'What are you doing here, Zayde?' shouted Oded. 'Where did
you come from all of a sudden? You got some chick in Tivon?'

'I haven't got a chick anyplace.'

'You were with your idiot again?'

'If you talk like that about my father, I'll talk like that about our father.'

'Did you eat delicacies?' shouted Oded. 'Did you at least bring me some leftovers?'

Life with a big diesel engine had made him used to speaking at a shout both in and out of the truck's cab.

'There are hitchhikers who get scared of my shouting and ask to get off in the middle of the road.' He laughs. 'And that goes on at home, too. I remember how my Dinah used to get mad at me. "Why does the whole village have to hear what you say to me?" she used to say. "I'm right here, right next to you, I hear everything." But what can I do? One day, coming up from Wadi Milek, I discovered that even when I talk to myself I don't hear one single word, so ever since then I shout.'

This is how I heard my history. From Globerman with money, from Jacob with treats, from Rabinovitch with straightened nails, from Menahem with the notes of mute uncles, from Naomi with caresses, and from Oded with shouts.

'One of these days you'll write about all those things,' he used to shout at me. 'Otherwise, how come I'm telling you everything? About my father and about your mother and about Naomi and about Uncle Menahem and about Globerman and about all that? You'll write down all those things so everybody'll know, you hear, Zayde? You'll write!'

Third Meal

1

The third meal I ate at Jacob's house twelve years later. Two of those years I spent at the university in Jerusalem and ten in Rabinovitch's cowshed.

Moshe chose to leave me the farm and Oded didn't resent it. He preferred the truck to cows, and went on taking me to Naomi's every now and then.

No longer did I fall asleep on the long nocturnal trips. I was an attentive ear for the memories and hopes and dreams he told in loud shouts, with surprising candour, and always with the demand: 'You'll write this, Zayde, right?' I loved to ride with him and listen to him, and that's why I didn't tell him I didn't intend to do what he asked.

Moshe decided to limit the scope of his work. He leased the field to the village cooperative growers and left himself only the milk cows and a pen of calves for meat. I put on my mother's old apron, tied the blue kerchief around my head, and like her, I worked in the cowshed and the kitchen and the house and the yard.

I didn't desert the crows. One of my teachers in Jerusalem, the red-haired professor, the one Naomi called the 'head rook', sensed my disgust with the laboratory and my penchant for watching and appreciated my ability to climb, endanger myself, and observe. One day, a few months after I dropped out of school and went back to the village, he showed up at our house and gave me some follow-up work to do for him in the Valley, mainly in the subject of the crows' processes of settlement among human beings and the damage they did to the local population of small songbirds.

In those years, the villagers had already despaired of me. They watched me while I watched the crows, added my name and my seclusion to that, seasoned it with memories about my mother, stirred it and tasted it, and determined my character. In that community, whose most important doctrines were fertility and furrows, I, too, was considered a rather strange bird.

One way or another, in 1963, I was still studying zoology in Jerusalem. I state that simply as a chronological fact, because my studies neither add to nor detract from the story I want to tell. The laboratories of Terra Sancta and the Russian Compound bored me. Out the window I saw the crows gathering and hatching eggs in the thick pine trees, and my soul yearned to climb up and peep into their nests instead of into the preparations placed under my microscope.

'I hate their microscopes,' I told Naomi. 'Everything I need to know can be seen with the eye.'

'And what do you love?' asked Naomi.

'You I love, Naomi,' I said. 'You I've loved from the day I was born. I remember the first time we met. I was zero years old and you were sixteen. I opened my eyes and saw you. I looked at you and I told you.'

'And what are you waiting for now, Zayde?' she asked.

'I'm waiting for you to get to my age,' I said.

Naomi laughed. 'I know what you're waiting for,' she said. 'For me to be old so that I can't get pregnant, that's what's scared you all the time, that you'll have a son, then a grandson, and then the Angel of Death, you're such an idiot, Zayde.'

She and Meir have one child. He was born when I was ten, and I've already said that I don't want to tell about him. Especially since he was born very close to my mother's death and he doesn't have anything to do with the history of her life.

After staying in Jerusalem a few months, I already knew most of the groups of crows there. I regularly visited the flock at the Moon Grove and the Leprosarium, and the big group of the cemetery in the German Colony and the small group of the Beit-Israel neighbourhood. From Yemin Moshe, I peeped at the assembly tree in the Armenian Quarter, over the border.

And at the end of the second year, I left them and my boring studies and the cold city, and returned to the village.

2

At our first meal, Jacob was about fifty-five years old, I was twelve, and the two of us were very embarrassed.

At the second one, after I got out of the army, I was amused and mocking and Jacob was older than his years.

This time, I'm over thirty and he's over seventy. I held the invitation to the third meal in my hand, and my heart clenched. It was a printed invitation, rather florid. I knew he had gone to the printer to print this solitary invitation, and I was filled with affection, compassion, and excitement.

'I'm waiting for you outside in the cab,' said the driver who came to get me, the same driver who had brought me the invitation to the second meal, and who still drove Jacob to sit at the bus stop.

'Come in and have a drink while I get ready,' I suggested to him.

'No need. I'm used to waiting for him.'

I told Moshe I wouldn't be with him at the milking that night; I polished my shoes, took a shower, shaved, put on a white shirt, and went.

This time, Jacob greeted me in a suit he had inherited from Rebecca's second husband. Splendid and expensive it was, but on him it looked like a rag. As he walked around his big, state-of-the-art kitchen, he looked like a beggar who had chanced on a house of philanthropists. But his trembling hands and his shaking head that threatened to slip out of joint hid the adroit movements of a virtuoso. He knew how to turn over a steak with an imperceptible flick of the wrist and skillet, could estimate the internal redness of a roast with his eyes closed, and when he kneaded the dough for the *kreplach*, he rolled up his sleeves and worked with all ten fingers, the cushions of his palms, his middle fingers, even his elbows.

'It's important to do many things together. To work with two pots and a skillet together on the stove,' he said. ''Cause that way you use the time good.'

'Not just in the kitchen,' he added later. 'People think time goes just with them and just for them. But at the same time that you're milking the cows in the village, in the meantime the grapefruits on the tree are turning ripe, and the laundry on the clothesline is drying, and somebody's soul is leaving him very slow. And while you're sleeping, the earthworms are working in the ground, and clouds are slowly sailing in the sky, and a child is growing in his mother's belly, and somebody in America is riding on a train to another woman. And in the summer, very slow, the fruit on the roof dries. So know, Zayde, at the same time that one apricot is drying itself out, a bird has time to lay eggs, to grow chicks, and to look for a new bridegroom. Once, in the war, I read in the paper: the Allies are attacking on all fronts. I liked that a lot. At the same time and on all kinds of fronts, all the Allies are attacking all together. Just imagine if every one of them would start only after the other one got through – till today, the war would still be going on. And if that's how you see the world, all of a sudden you can get a lot more time inside that little box. Did you ever think about that, Zayde?'

The pots boiled, aromas of evaporation and seasoning, delicate and slow, rose from Jacob's hands to the skin of my face. He preferred to acquire flavour by touching and curiosity, not through conquest and assimilation. Experience and dexterity didn't fill him with pride, but with respect – for the green cucumber, the fresh egg, meat, and fruit.

'I already told you who taught me to cook? It was my fat worker, who used to dance and do voices of people and animals, and was a very great chef. You knew that? He told me that feelings in the heart should be mixed together one into the other, but seasonings in food should be one next to the other. And that's why, Zayde, cooking salt is better than table salt that dissolves altogether. But in the soul, love with worry and with hate should be mixed together, and anger with longing with fear with a little joy should be mixed together. Otherwise, it cuts you up in pieces.'

'And you should never forget, Zayde,' he added, 'cooking and a meal and food isn't your goal. They're only the way to the goal. 'Cause it's so boring to cook, maybe only working the land is more boring than that.'

And suddenly he dipped his finger into the boiling pot and I almost leaped up.

'That doesn't hurt? To dip your finger in the pot like that?'

'Hurt?' he put his finger in his mouth to taste if it was good. 'What more can hurt this body? I don't hear good anymore, I don't see good, pains I almost don't feel, and I don't remember so good, either. It looks like pains and memory are a sense like hearing and seeing, eh? This morning I thought that somebody who doesn't remember so good, simply forgets to die, too. And so we trudge on and on, and finally nobody knows what our name is and what we did in our life. 'Cause what's an old man got outside of old age? Strength he doesn't have and sense he doesn't have and a woman he doesn't have. Just a little memory he's got, that breaks his whole body.'

And a few seconds later, he added: 'And if God gives you more years, what He gives you after all is a chance to do more foolishness.'

'There in the village near the river was a very old *goy*. At the age of a hundred, all of a sudden he got scared that they wouldn't take him in the next world, 'cause even in the next world they like young men more. Maybe that's why the Angel of Death was so mad at your mother for giving you that name. He thought he had a nice young *yingele* by the hand and all of a sudden, such a Zayde, what a *brokh*. So every Sunday that old man starts going to church and yelling at their god he should take him already, he was fed up, he was waiting so long and all the time people was cutting in line ahead of him. You know, to be old you don't have to study and you don't have to work and you don't need sense for that and there's no success in it. All you got to do is wait and it'll come. I, for instance, stopped shaving with a mirror a few years ago. Ask me why, Zayde, come on, ask . . .'

'Why?' I asked.

'So I'll tell you why. 'Cause first of all after so much time the hand knows the face good enough and doesn't need a mirror. And second of all, at my age, one way or another, you see another human being in the mirror. So let him shave inside the mirror and I'll shave outside the mirror. And one more thing that's good about old age, all kinds of people around you all of a sudden aren't there. Some disappeared 'cause I just got fed up with them, and some disappeared 'cause I forgot them, and that's the best way to get rid of people, and another part disappear 'cause you just don't see them no more, and all the other ones disappear 'cause they just die. And then you know it's the Angel of Death who's trying to hit you. Like artillery officers shooting cannons from far away – the first times they hit near the target, and then slowly, they get closer and closer until they hit it. And meantime, like Robinson Crusoe alone on the island, that's how I live. That's what old age is like. An island. And every place I go, my island comes with me. That's why nobody talks to an old person in the street, he walks like a solitary island with all that water around. Sometimes you see a ship far away. You make bonfires and you jump and you yell: Here I am! I'm alive! But only the errand boy from the store comes, and the cleaning woman, and once in ten years Zayde comes. It's lucky the Village Papish comes here sometimes, from his island he swims to my island. To talk he comes and even more to look at the picture of Rebecca and to yell at me. Once he used to come to me on the bus, and now he calls on the phone and I send my cab driver to him to bring him like a lord. Just recently I told him that in me the brain is already like a rag, and you know what he says? He says: "You shouldn't be scared of that, Sheinfeld, 'cause you were already an idiot by the age of thirty." And he still laughs at how I talk. Is it any wonder I talk like this? While he was studying in *Heder* and the *Yeshiva*, I was a slave in my evil uncle's shop. But it's mainly because of Rebecca that he's mad at me. To this day he's mad at me because of her. He comes, sits here and looks at her picture, and sighs. Once he said: "Do me a favour, Sheinfeld, maybe you'll describe to me that beauty how she looked with no clothes on." Believe you me, that's what he wanted. Everything I should describe to him, every point, every line. Shameless he asked.'

I felt a slight, strange tension pulling at the corners of my mouth, as if a baby's fingers were touching me there, and even though no baby ever touched my lips, I knew I was smiling.

'Well, Zayde, if you're lucky, this is gonna be our last meal and no more father of yours will pester you no more, eh?'

He stood up with a great effort and walked to the big black oven which had been slowly rustling all the time, and when he opened the heavy door, the warm swallows of rosemary and wine, olive and garlic soared out of there, and their wings fluttered over my nose until I grew dizzy with pleasure.

'What did you make there, Jacob?' I asked.

'A poor lamb. There's an old blind man in the village of Illut who I once knew, and he sent me the lamb with his grandson. You wouldn't believe. All of a sudden some Arab boy is knocking on my door, and says, "This is for you," and he goes away. And I see a lamb standing there. All by myself I slaughtered him behind the house and all by myself I hung him up on the tree and skinned him. Would you believe it? Slaughtering and skinning a lamb here on Oak Street in Tivon? Here, if you throw a sweet wrapper in the street they look at you, but nobody noticed it. Not even the lamb. That's an interesting thing. Sheep and goats don't notice it when they go to slaughter, but cows do notice it and become sad and weak. Someday I'll teach you how you skin a lamb. It's like a lot of other things a child needs a father to teach him, 'cause if you know how to do them it's very easy and if you don't it's very hard. A pure lamb. You never tasted such a thing. So soft you can eat it with a spoon.'

He smiled to himself and set the table. He served me the lamb and the seasoned rice and himself his omelette and his salad with olives and cottage cheese.

'Ess, meyn kind.'

The meat really was very tender and good. A gamut of colours and tastes, an embroidery of field and springtime.

'If you want, Zayde, I'll feed it to you from my fingers, like you were a baby or a woman.'

'No need, Jacob.'

'Feeding a person from your fingers is like seeing him without no clothes on. Someday watch a person when they give him food like that. The eyes look, the nose opens. Saliva comes in his mouth. His lips separate, his chin drops down a little bit, his tongue comes out a little bit to get the food, and if you ever feed a woman like that, remember to pull your fingers back fast because after all that the bite comes all by itself. Take, Zayde, take.' And a small, fragrant, bewildered piece of meat was brought to my lips.

I flinched and Jacob sighed and put the meat back on the plate.

'You like it?' he asked.

'A lot,' I said. 'Like a peacock's tail spreading out in your mouth.'

'That's a very beautiful thing, what you just said. It's like the beautiful words the Village Papish says about the beauty of the woman. May you be healthy and enjoy . . .'

And those pleading words – my son – that also wanted to be said, remained unuttered, fluttering in the air of his lungs, stifled in his throat.

3

Once, the old people say, a paper boat disappeared on the slope of the river.

'That's the worst thing. A fellow whose boat sails off far and disappears will never have peace again. Even if he gets married to somebody, he'll never have peace. That boat will go on sailing in his head all his life and every night it'll come to another woman.'

Sixty years later, a young woman nobody knew came to the village and went straight to the house of a farmer named Nozdryov, who was about eighty years old and no woman wanted him anymore.

'Ever since his paper boat disappeared, four times he got married and four times his wife died right after the wedding. If a thing like that happens it's a sign that God is trying to tell you something.'

The woman pulled the bell cord a few times, but old age had dimmed Nozdryov's hearing. She knocked and yelled and finally she opened the door and went inside. When she touched the old man's shoulder, he turned to her with a smile that spread over his face even before he understood why, and only then did he recognize the handsome young woman who had been residing in his dreams for so many years and so many times now he had seen her expelling strange women from them.

Tears rose in his eyes. He knew he would wake up right away and the woman, as usual, would melt away and vanish. But the guest wrapped two very fragrant and real arms around his wrinkled neck and pressed his meagre body to the warm lust of her breast that made him weep.

Her tongue didn't find a single tooth to strum in his mouth, but that very day, the two of them appeared in church and the woman showed the flabbergasted priest the paper boat that had been thrown into the river many years before she was born, and had come to her, with sharp folds and clear letters, a journey of sixty years and two hundred miles east of where it was put in the water.

'And ever since then, I've been walking here, to him,' she said, pointing to the old man. 'Walking and searching along the river.'

'And she had a little branch in her hand,' said Jacob. 'People who search walk with a little branch like that. There are people who know how to find water in the ground like that, you know that, Zayde? They walk along like everybody else walks and they search. They wait for the branch to bend, for a little boat to come, wait for our heart to yell at last, for our *shvantz* to point, for our eyes to see deep in the ground. Your mother used to walk like that in the field. She'd put on a beautiful dress and walk from the path in the field to the road and disappear in the hills for half a day. She didn't take food along or a stick. And she didn't take Naomi, either. Only her calf Rachel she took. The little girl used to run after them until Judith used to tell her to go back home and Rachel used to push her with her head, go home, Nomele, go on, go. That cow, she was like a male calf, by the time you knew her she was already old, but back in those days, all the time she used to jump and play and bleat like a *tsigele*, and if you just tried to put a hand on her teat, she could kill you. She had the body of a bull and the sense of a calf, but with your mother, she was soft like butter. Once Judith even hitched her up to a cart. Believe you me, Zayde. Hitched her up to a cart and went down to the field with her to bring clover. And at sundown, they'd come back, with a bottle or two she bought. See, you know she loved to drink a little bit sometimes, see, that's no secret. There were some people that didn't look kindly on that, but she knew her limit and she never got drunk. For our wedding, when I prepared everything, I even searched and found where she got her grappa, it was from a monastery in Nazareth, where an Italian man used to make the drink, and only the devil knows how she found him. She used to go with the cow on foot from here to Nazareth, through all the mountains and the villages, without no fear, and all anybody had to do was get close to her. To make a long story short, the dealer, the minute he found out she loved to drink a little, he right away started bringing her some drink now and then. Like a mole who sees some crack and attacks it to make it wider. They used to sit and drink in the cowshed, but she left the doors wide open so people wouldn't talk and mainly so the guest wouldn't get ideas, you understand? She really hated him with a mortal hatred, Globerman, and he, behind all his evil instincts and coarseness and greed, he was in mortal terror of her, but they did drink together. Really slow, not much, but it was a little bit like a contest. Not a contest of who would get drunk first and fall down like the *goyim* do, that they didn't do. That was a contest of who would look first at the other one and smile. It's only now I understand that he was the smartest one of us all, the dealer, that he was the only one who knew that love isn't just giving but is also a lot of taking, and he was the only one who knew that you daren't show how much you love, 'cause for one moment of weakness in love a person will pay afterwards all his life. On the table between them there was always a little something to eat that he used to bring with the drink. 'Cause somebody who drinks – you need to know that, Zayde – knows how to give every drink its own food, the companion that goes hand in hand with it. The companion of cognac is something sweet, the companion of schnapps is something salty, and vodka is everybody's companion. To make a long story short, it's good to have something next to the drink, 'cause then you drink slow, take more time, you don't spill every glass into your mouth like that. You understand that, Zayde? You drink slow, you smell, you breathe, you taste a little something, you talk, you chew, you think what to say next. Sense he never lacked, the dealer, and of course he knew all those little shtiks that if you eat a little and drink a little, really slow, then you stay more time together. And then the words start coming out, and you can talk, think, and once I even saw them making "le-khaim" – to life – to each other, glass against glass, and the dealer said: "May the ears of Lady Judith also enjoy," and the glasses rang with a sound the village wouldn't hear at all 'cause, here in the village, the most delicate ring is a cow's horns on the iron yoke. And she smiled at him all of a sudden like I never saw her smile. I would have fallen down and cried from such a smile, but the dealer, that bastard, just looked at her and didn't budge. If he fell down from that smile, it was only inside his body he fell down, and if he cried, it was only inside his soul that he cried. Meat dealers – you need to know this, Zayde – they've got a special way to act with women. Back home, they used to say: a *fleysh handler* knows when to cry with the widow and when to dance with her. Not like us, that if, let's say, the sun was in another hour, and if I wasn't in the citrus grove when she came, and I saw her, let's say, only a week later in the street, or in the morning at the supply warehouse – everything would have been different. But I did see her there sailing in the field on the wagon, in the yellow-green sea of flowers, and right away I knew: here's what God sent me, here comes my boat, my bird, here's the woman who will give me wings. Just stretch out your hand and take, Jacob, that's what I said to myself, stretch out your hand and take, so you won't punish yourself afterwards all your life, 'cause a woman you loved and you let her go, that's the most awful thing that can happen.'

He stood up and walked around the room and I felt his pain in my throat, but I went on eating, chewing, swallowing.

'All your life you'll punish yourself for it afterwards. A thing like that is even worse than a boat that disappears. That's even more loneliness than Robinson Crusoe's. You understand what I'm saying? Zayde, these words about loneliness? Alone I was on the River Kodyma, alone in my uncle's shop, alone I immigrated to Eretz Israel, and even with Rebecca I was alone. Who can be together with beauty like that? So beautiful she was that even I already forgot how she looked. For Judith I just have to close my eyes and I'm with her, but with Rebecca I was, like they wrote in the Bible, like a sparrow alone on the top of the house. And I wasn't a child no more, Zayde, every time I used to say the "*she'ma*", to pray, I used to think that only the God of the Jews is more alone than I am, and that's why they call Him the one God. Hear O Israel, the Lord our God the Lord is alone. Poor soul. How much one God and how much He's alone. And once I said that "Hear O Israel" of mine and my uncle raised his hand to me. But by then I wasn't a child no more. Then I was already a man and right away I gave as good as I got, one and another one and another one. For all the times he hit me. That was the first time I hit a man and the last time, too. He fell on the ground, and I got up and went, and before I immigrated to Eretz Israel, I never went back to him. But one Purim back home a drunk clown climbed onto the stage and said that Moses made up the one God so it would be easier for the Jews in the desert. Just imagine trudging in the desert like the Philistines and the Greeks and all the other *goyim*, with forty stone idols on your back, *shlepping* like that with all the statues in a *Hamsin*. Like this, you got one Ark of one God, a little Ark with handles, and two Levite guys dragging it and angels' wings shading them from the sun on their heads, and also you don't need to remember all the names of all the gods and what each one hates and what each one loves.

'The God of the Jews,' Jacob summed up, 'loves lambs, sometimes a dove or fine flour maybe, and something sweet for dessert He don't eat at all, 'cause the God of the Jews loves everything salty.'

And suddenly Jacob burst into loud singing:

And on the da-ay, and on the da-ay, and on the da-ay, and
    on the day
And on the da-ay of Shabbath
And on the da-ay, and on the da-ay, and on the da-ay, and
    on the day
And on the da-ay of Shabbath
And on the da-ay of Shabbath
Two lambs without blemish
And on the da-ay of Shabbath
Two lambs without blemish
Ay ay yeh yeh Adonai
Ay yeh yeh yeh yeh yeh
Yeh yeh ay yeh yeh yeh Adonai.
And two-tenths of fine flour
Mingled with oil
Mingled with oil
He-he-he sa-aved for hi-im
And two-tenths of fine flour
He-he-he sa-aved for him.

4

For a time, the dealer left the truck in Yakobi and Yakoba's
yard, and whenever he came to the village, he would visit it.

'It needs to get used to me,' he explained, because he didn't
want to admit that he couldn't drive.

When everybody started making fun of him, the dealer steeled
himself and started teaching himself to drive on the dirt roads,
and water jets soon began appearing in the fields, marking the
pipes he fractured. After he killed a donkey, annihilated a field of
watermelons, and broke three apple trees – he was warned that
the village council would outlaw him if he didn't get a driving
instructor.

Several candidates hastened to offer their services, but Globerman didn't hesitate a moment and chose Oded Rabinovitch, who

was then only eleven years old, but was already known far and wide for his driving.

Naomi told me that her brother agreed to go to first grade only so he could read *Motor, Car, and Tractor* and write letters to the importers of Reo and International. And so, Oded read about cars and thought about motors and dreamed about transfers and compression ratios and transmissions with such concentrated yearning that he learned to drive all by himself, and without ever sitting in a car, because in his imagination he had already executed and practised every operation thousands of times: he engaged gears and released clutches and accelerated and decelerated and braked and turned, and all of it with the devotion of lovers who savour their longings and prepare to realize them.

'If you go on making car noises all the time, you'll wind up with lips like a Negro,' Uncle Menahem warned him.

But Oded didn't heed his warning and by the time he was eight years old, he was arguing with surprised grown-ups about air cooling as opposed to water cooling and about 'V' engines as opposed to linear engines. In those days Arthur Ruppin came to visit the village and Oded took advantage of the turmoil and excitement, and while the leader was kissing the children in their crowns of wreaths and his driver was trying to make out with Rebecca Sheinfeld, he sneaked up to his long Ford, started it, and fled into the fields.

He drove it like a seasoned pro, and even circled on its axis, raised waves of dirt, did some juggling, and brought up pillars of dust. Finally he abandoned it in one of the orchards and ran away to the eucalyptus forest, returning on foot only the next morning, because he didn't know what admiration and pride he stirred in the hearts of everyone who saw him and he was afraid they would punish him severely.

Now he tried to convey the lore of driving to Globerman, and the livestock dealer obeyed all his instructions.

'An auto isn't a cow, Globerman!' The thin shouting voice rose from the truck when the dealer veered from the road into the fields. 'You don't spin it around by the tail, it's got a steering wheel!'

Fortunately for the dealer, the green truck, with its six gigantic, slow pistons, and its three long gears, was very tolerant. The motor never choked and the thick sheet metal was strong enough to endure the many trials and collisions its new owner subjected it to.

And to his credit, we must add that after all was said and done, the dealer was a law-abiding man. He also took himself down to the Mandatory court in Haifa. There he went to an official who was an expert in such matters and exchanged fifty pounds of fine shoulder roast for two driving licences, one for him and one for his little teacher, which included all possible vehicles: motorcycle, bus, private car, and trucks of every size and kind.

'A licence for a train and for an aeroplane they didn't have,' he bleated with a laugh.

And even though he already had a driving licence, he went on studying with Oded, until the boy told him it was time to stop.

'Now I know how to drive?' asked the dealer.

'No,' said the boy. 'But better than this you'll never know.'

But Globerman persisted, and one day Oded returned home carrying a big bouquet of multicoloured roses in his hand.

'That's for you,' he said to Judith. 'It's not from me. It's from the dealer.'

Judith took the bouquet and saw at once that it wasn't a bouquet of flowers, but a flowered dress. She spread it out between her hands and despite her anger, she had to admit that the dealer had good taste and wasn't tight-fisted with his money.

At dusk, Globerman came into Rabinovitch's yard and managed to open the door and enter the cowshed right at the very moment when Judith was standing in front of the mirror, trying on his gift.

'I ask you, Lady Judith,' he exclaimed triumphantly, 'a person who can tell the weight of a cow with one look of one eye, he can't fit a dress to a woman without measuring it on her?'

It wasn't the coarse comparison that offended her, but the fact that the dealer was right. The dress was very becoming.

'You didn't knock!' she sputtered.

'Here is a cowshed, Lady Judith.' Globerman pulled himself erect. 'Here is my work. At the village grocery store, do you knock on the door before you go in to buy?'

'Here is not only a cowshed. Here is also my home!' said Judith.

'Rabinovitch knocks on the door of your house when he comes to milk?'

'That's none of your business, filth.'

With a marvellous weasel step, Globerman wound around and approached her, even though his feet didn't seem to move at all.

'All I ask of Lady Judith, who is wearing the new dress and looking so beautiful, and feeling how the fine cloth touches her whole body, that she'll think at the same time about the one who bought it for her,' he said.

'Get out of here!' she said to him. 'Nobody asked you for gifts. I'll give it to Oded tomorrow to give back to you.'

'Not tomorrow! Now!' shouted the dealer. 'Now, take it off and give it back to me.' And he leaned impudently on the wall of the cowshed.

'I'll wash it first,' said Judith. 'So you can give it to some other woman. After all, you've got a cow in heat in every village.'

'Don't wash it, Lady Judith.' Globerman knelt in front of her. 'Give it back to me as it is, with your smell folded in the cloth.'

Off to the side, Rachel lowered her head and a deep gurgle of rage rose from the depths of her chest. Globerman smiled. He stood up, went to the cow, and ran his hand over her neck, and from there his knowing fingers hovered, hypnotized, over her spine until he tapped the end of her tailbone.

His tongue clicked with pleasure. 'He's growing nicely. A butcher who understands will pay me a lot of money for him,' he said.

'That heifer you'll never get, bastard,' said Judith.

'He's registered with me,' said the dealer, taking out his notebook and going through it. 'Rachel, right? A funny name for a male calf. Here he is. All taken care of. No mistake. I should have gotten him when he was half a year old, but Rabinovitch keeps postponing it.'

A sharp and wise man he was, and he sensed that he had exposed a crack between Judith and Moshe.

'A good *fleysh handler* has to be well organized,' he said to Rabinovitch a few days later. 'Here she is. Registered and waiting in my notebook. When will you sell her to me, Rabinovitch?'

'I'm still thinking about it,' said Moshe. 'It's not so simple.'

'What's not so simple here?' mocked Globerman. 'There's a dairy farmer, there's a cow, and there's a dealer, right? The dairy farmer and the cow think about the Angel of Death, but the dealer thinks about money, period. And that's why the dealer always wins, Rabinovitch, because to lose life is easy, it's only once and you don't suffer anymore, but to lose money is very hard. 'Cause that can happen a lot of times and every time you suffer again.'

He looked at Moshe, and as he expected, he saw rage darken his eyes.

'A calf!' He grinned at him. He knew that people built like Moshe aren't quick to anger, but when they are inflamed, they are harmful. Now he tapped and pinched the flesh of Rachel's shoulder, estimated the thickness of the layer of fat and the strength of the muscle hidden underneath it. 'What a beautiful shoulder you've got here, Rabinovitch, so when will you sell me Rachel?'

'I can't do that to her,' said Moshe.

'To who? The cow? What are you, the Humane Society?'

'To Judith,' said Moshe.

'To Lady Judith?' the dealer wondered in a loud voice. 'Who's the boss here? You or your worker?'

And Moshe's eyes became dark with anger again.

5

Oded didn't like my mother while she was alive; he teased her and pestered her, and saw no reason to regard her death as a sufficient cause to change his attitude. Nevertheless, I'm fond of him and I feel good with him. He drives me to Naomi and takes me back from there, brings her the packages and the letters and the observations reports for the 'head rook', and keeps on telling me about his father and my mother and his sister, and sometimes also about Dinah, the woman who was his wife.

'I got married to Dinah at the age of thirty-seven and a half, and I got divorced at the age of thirty-eight. How's that, Zayde?'

Dinah's husband was killed in the Sinai Campaign of 1956, and Oded met her through some friends.

'Everybody's got friends like that. They got their own crappy marriages, so they've got to get everybody else paired up, too.'

I remember Dinah. She was eight years younger than Oded and about an inch and a half taller, and even though she wasn't pretty at all, the blue sparks of her hair and the copper of her skin cast melancholy and restlessness into the men who had eyes to see them.

One night, a few months after their wedding, Oded went out on his run and was suddenly filled with such a strange and painful uneasiness that he was afraid to go on driving. He braked the tanker on the side of the highway, sat and thought for a few minutes, then continued on his way, stopped again, and finally turned around and went back to the village.

At the village hall, he killed the motor and silently, like a gigantic metal marten, he slid down the slope until he stopped at his house. A strange, dusty Matchless motorcycle, its motor warm and still smelling, was parked under the tree. Oded got out of the truck, peeped in the window, and saw Dinah riding on somebody, her thin, muscular body gleaming with her special dark gleam.

A soft sponginess pervaded his joints and muscles. He stumbled back to the tanker, started it, and drove it up to the centre of the village. There he got out, opened the big valve under the tank, locked himself in the driver's cab, and hung his hand on the horn cable.

A jet of milk, terrifying and white, flooded the street. The mighty horn of the tanker and the bleating of the young calves who were jolted awake by the smell of milk telling them their dreams had come true, woke the whole village.

'That was the best moment of my life,' he told me. 'That was a whole lot better than going into the room and killing the two of them. It cost me a lot of money, the milk and the divorce, and the trials and everything, but what can I tell you, Zayde, it was a real pleasure.'

'You want to honk the horn?' he asks again, as he always asks me.

Of course I want to honk. I stretch out my hand and pull, from the lap of the dewy grass the toads answer, and a waning moon accompanies us, pushes off the downy embraces of the clouds, and filters between their soft openings.

At that hour, Oded's radio returns from its shrieking journeys in distant Yugoslavian and Greek stations, and once again speaks Hebrew. But I don't need it. Clocks signal to me from every corner. Once again I seek and find the small hand of big time, the hand of the years and their seasons, and the big hand of small time, the hand of the hour of the day. The hues of the leaves tell me late autumn. In low places the chill of dawn is poured into invisible puddles. The lacework of the east turns pale and tells me ten to five.

'You don't need a watch, Zayde, look how many watches there are in the world,' Mother told me.

Every farmer in the village can tell what month it is from the mute lightnings of autumn and the blooming of spring in the field, but I could tell time by the shade of the darkening old crows' nests and by the moulting feathers of their maturing fledglings.

'The village is a room full of clocks,' I wrote to Naomi in Jerusalem to remind her, so she wouldn't forget.

And she wrote to me that she had only one clock: the religious milkman of the neighbourhood, who appeared every morning at six-fifteen on the dot, pushing his cart of milk cans, groaning and proclaiming his merchandise with two drawled-out, weary vowels, 'Mi-ilk,' that echoed in the narrow staircase.

And just a few weeks ago, I wrote to her about our ruined village hall – a mighty index of the passage of time, with the dry ivy clinging to its walls, the seven-branched lamp embellishing the roof with its destruction, the pigeons nesting in the corners of its auditorium.

Swallows fly in through the ventilator holes to feed their fledglings, and in the old projection booth owl droppings reek. That's not a clock with hands, nor is it an hourglass. It's a clock of strata, and it measures time by the thickness of the dried secretions, the scabs of rust on the balcony banister, and the cushions of dust on the floor, where the maggots of ant lions dig their slippery funnels of death.

Wooden boards are nailed over the openings, but here and there they've been broken into, and when I go inside and wait for my eyes to grow accustomed to the gloom, a thin and loathsome smell of human faeces and its disgrace rises to my nose. Weariness assails me and I sit down on one of the filthy chairs and the shrill squeak of the wood rouses a great flapping of wings in the dark space.

Once I surprised the Village Papish here. He also visits the village hall sometimes, enters and tramps around in the pigeon droppings and mutters mutterings and groans old heart-breaking and body-aching groans. Only a few years ago, the final show was put on here, and Papish, as I wrote to Naomi, 'gave one of his greatest performances there'. A theatre troupe came from the city, and a young actress, whose well-known beauty summoned young men from the entire valley to the village – the melting beauty that doesn't stir lust or love, but only the desire to be fruitful and die – appeared on stage and treated us like some goddess, who has an hour of goodwill and is decent enough to be revealed to those who worship her.

And suddenly the Village Papish stood up – and he is very old and heavy – and yelled furiously in a loud voice: 'And we had Rebecca Sheinfeld many years ago, and she, young lady from the television, was much more beautiful than you!' And he exited.

He was angry at the village for the ruin of the village hall and he was angry at Jacob 'because his love for Rabinovitch's Judith made his Rebecca abandon the village and took all her beauty with her and left us with nothing, wallowing in our ugly mud.'

The hut that was once the house of Yakobi and Yakoba and afterwards the house of the albino is also a ruin now. The winds and the rains have eaten its roof, worms and dews have melted its boards, and what the sun didn't evaporate the earth absorbed. Everyone saw the hut shrinking, and after it disappeared only the anemones growing there indicated that it had once been.

But the house the albino built for his canaries and left to Jacob is still standing. No one fills the feeding troughs and basins, the cages and the door are always open, the canaries come and go as they please, and Jacob doesn't return there to visit his past, either.

'In the morning and in the evening,' I said, 'time goes most slowly.'

'It slows down at the turns,' laughed Oded, 'so the world won't turn over.'

We were approaching the turn to the village. Oded shifted down, one gear after another. His feet danced on the big pedals and the truck moaned and shook.

'There. We're back home.' He turned in a big circle and started driving on the narrow entrance road.

Once the road had been a dirt path. In summer wheels and hooves ground it to dust, and in winter it became thick, dark mud. Then it was covered with crushed basalt stones brought from the mountain, and when it was widened, it was paved and became a thin, straight asphalt road, about a mile long, and casuarinas amassed dust at its edges.

On the side of the crossroads is a bus stop, simply a small tin awning and an iron pole with a sign on top. On the cement bench sat Jacob Sheinfeld, a small wrinkled mummy of love, wearing blue pants and a white cotton shirt. In the shade of the trees, his regular taxi was parked, its driver asleep in the back seat.

Oded braked the truck, turned off the motor, and the silence poured into our ears. He stuck his head out the window and yelled: 'What's up, Sheinfeld?'

'Come in, come in, how nice of you to come, friends. Come in,' said Jacob with the warm expression of a bridegroom at his wedding.

'And where's the bride, Sheinfeld?' yelled Oded.

But Jacob's look passed us by and wandered off.

'Look at him,' Oded repeated his diagnosis. 'If he was a horse, they'd have had to shoot him a long time ago.'

A green car passed by on the road.

'Come in, come in . . .' Jacob said to it. 'Come in, we've got a wedding here today.'

And he smiled, and nodded in greeting, ran his eyes over the road, and didn't pay any more attention to us.

6

Even liars know well that truth and fiction are not at odds with each other. They're good neighbours, and each is interested in the well-being of the other, and they lend one another whatever they need.

I heard that once from Meir – apropos of what, I don't remember – and then he smiled and added that the lie and the truth are not north and south, but rather the magnetic pole and the North Pole.

I say that to explain that I don't want to make up or erase parts of my life. Nor do I want to explain them, to camouflage them, or to re-create them. The whole purpose of this story is to put them in order: a furrow directed for an ox's hooves, channels for water to creep in, cement walks for footsteps.

And whenever I get disgusted with the chaos I'm doomed to hover over, and fed up with the abyss of assumptions and the wind of conjecture, I console myself with the wonderful course of small events. So, that funny character who bought the dead albino's five black suits reappeared in the village a few months later. Without a word, he went into the secretary's office and put on the table five notes he had found in the five inside pockets of the suits. On every one of them were the words: 'The birds go to Jacob.'

Sheinfeld was called to the secretary's office. Even though he had taken care of the canaries since the day the albino died, his heart was pounding now like a sledge-hammer, hard, with fear and joy. Without a word, he went to the canary house and from there to his own house, got into bed fully dressed, and didn't wake up until the next afternoon, when Rebecca woke him with the first shouts that had come out of her mouth since their wedding day, and demanded to know what was happening.

Jacob looked into her eyes, whose transparent colour became rough and opaque as plaster, and with complete calm, he announced that the albino had bequeathed him the poor canaries and from now on they were his.

For one moment, the most beautiful woman in the village wanted to fall down on the floor and scream, but she immediately felt an invisible arm supporting her back and strengthening her knees. All at once, all the mysteries she had solved long ago were clear to her: her husband's insomnia, his sighs, his devotion to those silly canaries whose song, let's admit it, is not so pleasing to the ear.

And Judith's journey in the green and yellow springtime field, and Jacob's trembling, and his talk in the rare, brief slumbers he managed to get, and the days when the colours changed in the irises of his eyes – riddle after riddle, they were all deciphered for her, and a third eye seemed to be opened in her forehead; she walked straight out behind the hut, stretched a precise hand, and pulled out of the space between the floor and the ground the yellow wooden canary hidden there, and threw it away.

From there she carried the picking ladder to the canary house, propped it up and climbed it, once again stretched her hand, and from the space between the ceiling and the roof, she heaved up the small notebook where Jacob had written with the ox's back-and-forth movement: Judith Judith Judith Judith Judith Judith Judith Htiduj Htiduj Htiduj Htiduj Htiduj Htiduj Htiduj Judith Judith Judith Judith Judith . . .

And from there, she walked with complete confidence to the citrus grove, where the rustle of the leaves was associated with such clear sighs, Judith Judith Judith Judith, and she went past the rows of trees one after another, back and forth, Judith Judith Judith . . . Htiduj Htiduj Htiduj Judith Judith Judith . . .

And there, at the third tree in the third row, she dug and found the blue kerchief of Rabinovitch's worker, stolen on a dark night and with a pounding heart off the clothesline in the yard.

A smile spread over Rebecca's lips, cleared her brain, and stretched the lines of the solution between all the dots that had punctured it.

'And beautiful as she was, she was seventy times more beautiful then. All of us were dazzled,' said the Village Papish.

That very same day, Rebecca left the house and the village, with her dress and her hatred and her beauty and her wisdom on her back, and returned to the home of her mother, Mrs Schwartz of Zikhron Ya'akov. The Village Papish followed her out of the village, coaxing her in vain to stay and let him remove all obstacles, no matter what they were.

'One fine day she went off and disappeared,' he said. 'Nobody knew where, nobody understood why.'

> She flew off as the nightingale
> soars from her nest,
> before anyone suspected,
> before anyone guessed.
>
> A cold rainy day will come,
> a second and a third,
> and every eye will weep,
> mute sadness can't be heard.

The Village Papish recited the poem sadly and solemnly, his thin lips took on the precise shape of the words, and his eyelids marked the yearning of the rhyme at the end of the lines.

Mrs Schwartz – practical, wrinkled, and active – didn't rest for a single moment. Letters came and went, messengers and carrier pigeons appeared and disappeared, and then a chauffeur-driven car climbed up to Zikhron Ya'akov and took Rebecca and her mother to the ancient port of Tantura.

A small ship, well-shaped and white, with the name *Rebecca* golden on its rib, emerged clearly from the warm mist rising from the sea. A boat was put down and approached. Two sailors took Rebecca from the shore.

Haim Green, a wealthy English merchant, who had once been a young English lieutenant and had waited whole nights at her house in Zikhron Ya'akov, was waiting for her on deck.

Rebecca spun around, spewed two clouds out of her two chimneys, and slowly went off. Mrs Schwartz waited until it vanished, and then she got in the car and returned to her village.

For twenty-five years neither *Rebecca* the ship nor Rebecca the woman returned to the Land of Israel, until one day a picture of 'Sir Haim and Lady Green', who were 'immigrating to our Land to build and be built in it', appeared in the newspapers. The two of them were photographed on the dock of the port in Haifa, both with striped collars, gleaming smiles, and captain's hats, and the Village Papish, who had never forgotten those features, went shouting into the surprised street of the village: 'She came back, she came back, she came back!'

And Lady Green was indeed Rebecca, and Sir Haim was her husband, whom the years had changed from a young and wealthy English merchant into an old and rich English banker.

'He was an important man and a courteous man,' said the Village Papish. And indeed, Sir Haim contributed money to schools, established laboratories in universities, supported poor students, and bought the beautiful house on Oak Street in Tivon. And by virtue of the polite generosity that characterized all his ways, he also hurried up and died so his widow could bring back her first husband and live with him, an old winner, indulgent and tearful as she was, in the last year of her life.

But on the day Rebecca abandoned the village, 'and we all looked like a face with a gouged-out eye', Jacob was the only one who didn't pay any attention to her departure. He closed himself in the storeroom, busy building a gorgeous wooden cage, painted sky blue and gold, with an enamel trough and basin and two seesaws.

In the evening, when he came out of the storeroom and went into the house, he called out, 'Rebecca . . . Rebecca . . .' a few times, and when there was no answer, he made himself a cup of tea and went to sleep, and before dawn, he got up and went out without noticing the emptiness and the chill that had lain next to him all night long.

He hastened to his urgent romantic affairs, and that evening, when Judith returned from watering the calves, she found a wooden birdcage hanging on the central beam of the cowshed. A big friendly roller, who could sing short fragments of operetta and was the most beautiful of all the male canaries the albino had left behind, hopped and sang, and on the wall gleamed a note that said, or maybe quoted, a hackneyed saying of lovers: 'The birds sing what a human can't say in words.'

7

I said before that Bathsheba called her husband Menahem a 'decent bird'. Moshe, on the other hand, called his brother a 'crazy fowl', but he loved him, appreciated his good mind, and even revealed to Menahem that at night he searched for his braid – which Menahem remembered just as well as Moshe – that and nothing else.

The two brothers were very different from one another, but that difference brought them close together and didn't drive them apart. Menahem, his wife, and his sons often came from the neighbouring village to visit his brother, and Judith, Moshe, and Moshe's children frequently went to visit him and Aunt Bathsheba in their village.

Oded hitched the wagon and put sacks of straw on it to cushion the jolting on the wooden boards. A sturdy and responsible boy he was, and demanded to hold the reins.

Everybody sat down in the wagon and Naomi laughed at Rachel's worried face looking at them from the cow yard.

'C'mon-c'mon-c'mon-c'mon,' called Judith, and Rachel jumped lightly over the fence and accompanied them, striding on her long legs, lingering now and then to pick herself a bunch of clover and flax blossoms.

Lines of rage crept onto Moshe's forehead: 'Why does she follow us everywhere like a dog?'

'What do you care, Father? Nobody will talk about you. She's following Judith and she doesn't bark,' said Naomi.

And Judith said: 'Meantime, she'll eat a little grass on the way and that saves you money, Rabinovitch.'

'It's undignified,' grumbled Moshe.

The dirt road meandered along the old pipe that had once brought water from the spring to the village. A lot of castor oil bushes grew there in those days, and at the edge of the field was a big, chirping colony of field mice. At night, the jackals would hunt them and then come and wail in high voices, dripping blood, right under the windows of the houses. Your heart would fill with dread and cold and the village dogs, even though they were bigger and stronger than the jackals, were also terrified by the savagery of the truth evident in their wailing, and they knocked on the doors of the houses, pleading to be let in lest they be bitten or tempted.

Years later, when I dropped out of school and returned to the village, I worked here ploughing the common field. Four days I sat on the old D-6 and ploughed the way I like to write: back and forth and back and forth and back and forth. Falcons hovered over me, cowbirds and crows, who knew the ploughing seasons by now, flocked together, and hopped behind me, gleaning worms and insects the plough turned up onto the soil. And when I came here, I allowed myself to veer from the furrow to the edges of the field. The blades of the plough burst into the burrows of the field mice and the birds made an awful slaughter of them.

At the end of the field bunches of nests marked the curve of the channel of the wadi. The water deposited an abundance of silt here and a lush growth flourished in it.

From the time of my childhood to this day, I have come down here. On Saturdays in autumn to gather blackberries, and in the spring to pick anemones and narcissus.

In winter Moshe didn't let me go there. The water turned grey then and rose, the mud became deep, and the riverbanks became slippery and treacherous.

'Why do you send him there alone?' he yelled at Mother.

'Nothing will happen to him,' she answered. And to me, she said: 'Go, Zayde, and don't come back late.'

I went, and sometimes I'd see them, my three fathers, peeping at me from a distance and scared about my safety.

By now, Moshe let Oded hold the reins even across the wadi. Silence prevailed. Moshe didn't talk to anyone about his Tonychka, but this was the wadi, that was the water, and here was the place.

Even the horse, the horse Rabinovitch bought to replace the mule that replaced that she-ass, hesitated a bit before he crossed the channel. He went down with recoiling hooves, his nostrils expanding and his neck bristling as if he knew, too. But when he came to the water line and wanted to retreat, the slope of the bank and the weight of the wagon and Oded's scolding would push him from behind and force him across.

The hooves sank in the shallow water and generated precise mud roses. Their reflections shuddered, riding on drops of spreading nacre, and the wheels immediately rumbled and churned up the river. The dragon-flies took off and the muscles of the horse's big fragrant thighs were outlined under his skin as he strove to climb the opposite slope.

The back wheels came out of the water, the thin waves were absorbed in the banks, the silt slowly sank. Like the flesh of a woman, the channel returned to its previous state, and not a single trace remained in it.

For a few more minutes, thick brown drops streamed from the wheels to the dust and left clods and tears of mud in it, and Oded now shouted, 'Whoa', and stopped the horse at the railway station, where they had once picked up Mother.

'Let's stop here and have something to eat,' said Moshe. 'It's not nice to come hungry to people.'

Everyone got out of the wagon and stretched their legs. Naomi spread an old sheet on the grass. Rachel grazed on the side, tried to butt butterflies, ate flowers, and breathed sighs of satisfaction. Judith opened the basket and took out the egg sandwiches with green onion that smelled like a travelling family, and she was still turning out their exact copies years later, when everyone was older, and I had come into the world and would ride with them.

We sat in the shade of the mighty eucalyptus trees of the station and ate.

Rotten wooden sockets were piled up on the side. The railway tracks had been pulled up and removed by then, became rails for cattle pens and beams for building haystacks.

The train that had brought Mother no longer travels here, and the nearby camp, where Italian prisoners-of-war had once been interned, has now become a gigantic melon field and remnants from a stone chimney of an old army kitchen are all that can still be seen there.

I climbed the water tower of the station. In its days of glory it had launched steam locomotives, and now its walls were split and it had become a kingdom of lizards and owls. They looked at me with their round eyes, bowed and gurgled in a ridiculous ceremony of intimidation whose rules I didn't understand. I used to crumble their dry vomit and the findings are still recorded in my old childhood notebook: 'Field mouse skulls, lizard vertebrae, feathers of miserable sparrows.'

From the treetops, crows watched us curiously, waiting for us to go and leave scraps. The bolder ones had already hopped onto the ground not far from us with their erect necks and their black eyes. I knew some of them, because they were among those who gathered in afternoon confabs on our eucalyptus tree, which, in those days, was still standing in the yard in its full power and height.

In Uncle Menahem's carob orchard, the fruit was already swollen and their green was pierced with brown, and in Uncle Menahem's throat the vocal cords were already muted.

'Hello, Zayde, how are you?' he wrote on a sheet of his notebook, pulled it out and handed it to me.

'Fine, Uncle Menahem,' I took out the note I had written beforehand, as if I were also mute. I don't know why, but I always called him 'uncle', even though I never called his brother 'father'.

Uncle Menahem's whole body shook with inaudible laughter, and his hands stroked my head. I knew what he would do now. He took a big handkerchief out of his pocket, folded it sideways into a triangle, folded it again, point on point, turned it over and rolled it, and his fingers were already poking the tail of the handkerchief into its folds until a kind of cloth sausage remained in his hand. Then he released the ends and tied an imaginary knot of two ears on one side.

'A mouse!' I exclaimed excitedly, and Uncle Menahem put the cloth mouse on his left wrist and with the quick fingers of his right hand, he made it jump into my face so suddenly it scared and delighted me every time as it had the first time.

His springtime muteness was so complete that not even a shout, a laugh, a sigh, or a groan managed to escape from his throat. By now he knew how to prepare himself for the weeks of silence that were in store for him. As far as the farm was concerned, he gave his sons orders beforehand, like someone ruling his household, and ahead of time, he prepared the notebook he would use to communicate with anyone he needed. At the top of every page, in red ink, was the sentence, 'I have lost my voice,' so that he wouldn't have to apologize and explain.

Time had made him so accustomed to his allergy that he started enjoying it and even looking forward to it. It was clear to him that during the spring silence, he worked better, had time to read, listen to music, immerse himself in smells and sights. A pleasant smile often illuminated his face, a sign of wonderful thoughts, the kind that relinquish the need to ride on words.

A few weeks after Passover, Uncle Menahem's voice returned to his throat. It was preceded by a sense of ripe fruit forming around his heart, but the return of speech itself was usually revealed to him in the middle of the day, when a thought he thought suddenly surprised him by being heard outside his skull, as if someone else had said it in a voice like his. Or in the morning, when the mirror said something to him in the middle of shaving. Or in the middle of the night, when he would turn over and wake up because he dreamed he heard himself talking in his sleep, and only when the words bounced back from Bathsheba's back did he understand that he had really said them.

He jumped up immediately and got dressed and ran to us through the fields, hoping that one of the hoors would come out of his wife's jealous vision, put on skin and flesh, and he'd get lucky and could talk to her and melt her flesh with words.

'Moshe! Judith! Children!' he shouted as he came into our yard, and the words, which had been waiting for him all spring, flew out of his mouth in excited orbits, just like those swallows that fly and shriek at the height of their power and who never land.

8

Rachel grew up and became a cow whose masculinity was unmistakable. Her muscular shoulders were unusually high and much broader than her rump, her udders were tiny, and the rose of hair on her forehead was lower than a calf's and made her look like a hooligan. Her ways were the arrogant ways of a young, playful bull and embarrassed Moshe to the point of open disgust.

'That's not how a cow behaves,' he kept repeating.

He kept talking about his intention to sell her to Globerman and whenever he said that, Judith would pretend he was talking on her deaf side, but a revealing cloud of anger darkened her forehead and her eyes.

Uncle Menahem, who knew how much Judith's soul was tied to the soul of her cow, and who, unlike his brother, recognized a person's right to behave even in strange and amazing ways, suggested she consult his neighbour, Samson Bloch, the livestock expert I mentioned before.

'Just don't let him ask you his nonsense,' he said.

The people of the Valley loved and appreciated Samson Bloch, but he infuriated them with his popular research on rutting seasons in cattle, which he accomplished by pestering the women of the Valley with intimate questions.

'The professor at the university operates on a mouse to know what happens in a human being, and I ask the woman a few questions to know what the cow feels,' he explained.

'A woman in love is not a cow in heat,' Bathsheba yelled at him one day.

'A female is a female and a male is a male,' said Bloch. 'Balls and ovaries, noise and turmoil. What difference does it make if they walk on four legs or on two? If they chew the cud in their belly or they chew the cud in their mind?'

He took one look at Rachel and shook his head: 'A waste of time.'

He brought out a measuring tape and measured her height and the length of her body, from the shoulder to the end of the tailbone and the hoof of her front leg.

'Exactly the same,' he said. 'Look for yourself, Judith, the height is exactly the same as the length. This is a *tumtum*. Not a bull and not a cow.'

'I want that cow,' she said. 'And if she doesn't give milk, Rabinovitch will sell her to Globerman.'

'That's the fate of cows,' said Bloch. 'How much milk can come out of this udder?'

'Even a little bit, that'll help.'

'There's only one way,' said Bloch. 'To milk her and milk her and milk her until one day maybe something will come out of there. Sometimes it works and sometimes it doesn't.'

Judith went back home and started milking Rachel.

At first the cow complained, shook, and kicked. But Judith coaxed her with words and caresses until she gave in.

Rabinovitch, who saw her doing that and knew what was said, told her she was wasting her time and energy.

Globerman couldn't help saying: 'Maybe you'll also milk the other calves, Lady Judith, they'll love you for it a lot.'

'This cow I'll milk until milk comes out of her udder and blood comes out of my fingers,' answered Judith. 'And you won't get her ever.'

9

On the window, on the window,
a pretty bird has come to stay.
A boy runs to the window—
the pretty bird, she flew away.
Cry, boy, cry,
a pretty bird did fly,
a boy runs to the window—
a pretty bird did fly.

In the big wooden cage hanging on the beam of the cowshed, Jacob's beautiful canary struggled.

At first he sang faithfully and strong, but like hired wooers, he was ashamed and fell silent when he noticed that no one admired his singing. A few weeks later, his feathers started moulting at an embarrassing rate. Judith opened the door of the cage for him and he flew off – annoyed, ashamed, and happy, as far as mixed feelings can nest in the heart of a bird – and returned to his master.

When Jacob saw the canary, he understood that love isn't a matter for proxies, but for the person himself, and since he didn't find in himself the boldness to appeal to Judith with words, he performed a deed. He went to the city, bought himself some yellow sheets of paper – 'yellow is the colour of love', he replied to my question, amazed at my ignorance of such basic things – and cut them into squares of various sizes, which were quickly filled with words, turned into love notes, and piled up and buried in a locked drawer.

Every afternoon, Mother indulged in a little nip, and immediately put her bottle of grappa back in its hiding place and went out to work.

Once she forgot, and Globerman, who always managed to come at the wrong time, peeped into the cowshed and saw the bottle on the table. He didn't say anything, but on his next visit, he asked: 'Maybe you'll raise a glass with me sometime, Lady Judith?'

'Maybe,' she answered. 'If you know when to come and how to behave.'

'Tomorrow at four in the afternoon,' said the dealer. 'I'll bring a bottle of liquor and I'll know how to behave.'

At four, the familiar pounding was heard, and the green truck was braked by the trunk of the eucalyptus.

Globerman, shaved and polished, without the rope and without the *baston*, in clothes and a hat that were surprisingly clean and made it hard to recognize him '*oysgeputzt*', was Jacob's adjective, knocked at the door of the cowshed with a thin shiny stick and waited patiently and politely for it to be opened.

Judith, in that flowered dress, opened the door and the dealer wished her good day. His eyes and his shoes sparkled with excitement. The skin of his face and hands smelled of a delicate eau de cologne, roasted coffee, and chocolate. When he turned from the doorway, he entered and presented a green bottle on the table; next to it he put two thin balloon glasses and announced: 'French cognac. And *pettitt furs* I brought you, Lady Judith, they go good with the liquor.'

They sat and drank the cognac, and for the first time, Judith was grateful to the cattle dealer, who changed from head to toe, drank moderately and in silence, and was wise enough not to

make brutal and coarse statements and not to mention his desire
for Rachel.

When he took his leave of her, he asked if he could come again
the following week, and from then on, he would come every
Tuesday with his liquor and his *'pettitt furs'*, would knock on
the door of the cowshed, and wait until she invited him in.

'Maybe you'd like me to tell you stories?' he asked, certain
she would agree.

'In every person, there's something left from the time when
he was a child,' he explained to me many years later. 'And with
that something, you can win him over. With men, it's usually
some toy, with women it's a story, and with children themselves,
you'll be amazed, Zayde, it's learning something, period.'

He told Judith about the women in his family, who 'throughout all the generations', the colour of their eyes changes when
they make love. 'And that's how the father knew when they had
plucked his daughter's flower and the husband knew when his
wife had cheated on him.'

He told her about his youngest brother, who was fastidious
and sensitive and so disgusted with dealing in meat that he
threw up in their father's butcher shop and in the end became
a vegetarian.

'The intellectual of our family, shy and delicate like a flower,
a chick, a poet!'

Ultimately, the young intellectual of the Globerman family
went to study art in Paris, and once his friends got him drunk
and put a girl in his bed to deliver him from his virginity and
his melancholy. In the morning, when he felt the warmth of her
skin and the soft pricking of her nipples and the ring of flesh
tightening over his flesh, he fell in love with her even before he
opened his eyes.

That day, the two of them got married in the city hall, and
it wasn't until after the wedding that he discovered she was the
youngest daughter of a butcher.

Globerman burst into a roar of laughter. 'And today he's not
a vegetarian or an artist anymore. His love and her father made
him into a pig butcher and a great expert in horsemeat sausages,
because from fate and from blood and from inheritance, Lady

Judith, nobody has yet managed to escape. And everybody who does escape, the Lord sends His big fish after him to catch him.'

'You tell me some story,' he asked after Mother didn't say anything.

'I don't have anything to tell you about, Globerman.'

'Everybody has a little *peckele*, a pack, on his shoulders,' said Globerman. 'Just tell me something small. Tell me about the fish that swallows you every night, Lady Judith – where does it take you? About your hands, tell me, Lady Judith, about your memory, about the beautiful line between your eyes, about something you left behind.'

'Here are my hands, Globerman,' said Mother, and suddenly stretched out her hands to him. 'Let them tell you by themselves.'

Globerman held her hands. His heart fluttered. For the first time in many years, he felt fear flooding his heart.

'Where did you come from, Lady Judith?' he whispered.

'*A nafka mina*, Globerman,' Mother pulled her hands back. 'Who cares.'

'And why here?'

'Because here the big fish vomited me out,' laughed Lady Judith.

Rabinovitch just stared at the wall of the cowshed and didn't say a word. But Jacob, who didn't hear these words but only the laughter rising from the window, was filled with a growing despair. One day, he lay in wait for Globerman in the field, and when the truck appeared, he jumped in front of it and shouted loudly and bitterly: 'Why do you take her away from me? You've got money and you've got meat and you've got women everyplace. Why?'

But the shout didn't come out of him, it just echoed in the chambers of his heart and strove upward, and Globerman, who miraculously succeeded in stopping the truck about a foot away from the canary breeder who stood trembling in front of him, got out of the driver's cabin and asked: 'Have you gone nuts, Sheinfeld? Find better drivers to jump at like that.'

'Everything's fine,' said Jacob, and ran away.

In the days that followed, his yellow notes started creeping out of their locked drawer. At first they dropped onto the floor, then they were stuck to the walls of his house, and then to the fence of his yard, and from there they spread over the whole village: tacked to the administration bulletin board, nailed to the wall of the dairy, tied to the electric pole with grafting straw, and impaled on tree trunks.

'Where I got courage for that, I don't know,' he said.

He decided to turn his love into a matter for the whole village and he had no shame. His notes were seen everywhere, gleaming in their bold colour and their shining words. The expression 'on my bed at night' was said there, 'deep as the sea' was whispered, 'will my torments end' was shouted.

'Where did that ignoramus find such beautiful words?' sneered the Village Papish.

But Jacob wasn't offended and one day he even came to the general assembly, and in the middle of a discussion about paving the access road to the village – in those days only the basalt path was there and the winter rains turned it into quicksand every year – he got up and started talking eagerly about the winding paths of his love, and amazingly he wasn't called to order or expelled from the assembly.

In general, the village doesn't need weighty reasons or professional opinions to decide that some member or other is an idiot or a lunatic. But for some reason, that wasn't the case with Jacob. A gauze of a dream was woven in the scorched eyes of the farmers as he was talking, it rose and overflowed onto the rind of their cheeks. Their coarse fingers, whose skin was hardened by scythe handles and scarred by leaf blades of maize, drummed with sudden softness on the tables. Everyone wanted to imagine the victory of his love.

'Love, what?' the Village Papish shouted. 'All of a sudden you've got something to wait for besides the rain, eh? First let him bring Rebecca back here!'

But Jacob drew valour and encouragement from the smiles and nods that started lighting up in the audience like small candles of pleasure, and in the following days he dared address the village bulletin, and started sailing over its pages a series of letters and articles whose titles were 'To Judith' and whose lines were pleas and love.

He got up, rummaged in the drawer, and took out a note.

'And one day I burned all the notes,' he said. 'Just this little one happened to be left. Look, Zayde, what beautiful words.'

A big X was hoisted over the note, and underneath, it said: 'At sunset I shall wait for you at the field of anemones. Please don't disappoint me this time.'

'Why the X?' I asked.

'In Russian that's the letter for "ch",' said Jacob. 'Every time she didn't come to a meeting, I put a "ch" on top. Ch and another ch and another ch and another ch. In Russian, that's the laughter of fate.'

Judith didn't come, and one day, at five o'clock in the afternoon, Jacob came to her.

Judith was milking Rachel, and Jacob wanted to smile and tell her he had patience, and that he could wait, that the two of them could calm down and even enjoy the expectation. But as soon as Judith asked him what he wanted, his knees buckled like the knees of a condemned man, and he stumbled – 'like an idiot', he said – on the calves' watering bucket, fell down, and hit his forehead on the corner of the trough.

The blow made a deep wound in his forehead, he blacked out for a minute, and his face was flooded with blood. Judith rushed to him, cleaned his forehead with her kerchief, and sprinkled cow sulpha on him, and before he knew if he had come to, his mouth was already wide open and frightening and painful words were rolling out of it.

'All of a sudden I told her all the dumbest things, that if I was a woman, I would be her. Like a stupid bastard I laid on the floor in all that blood, I am you, Judith, I am you.'

10

At that time, Naomi was about eleven years old, and understood what was going on. She asked Judith what she thought of Jacob and Judith said: 'Nomele, Sheinfeld is a *nudnik*. Take a good look and don't forget, because every woman needs to know what a *nudnik* looks like.'

'And who do you love best?' asked Naomi.

'You.' Judith smiled.

'No, Judith, which one of the three do you love the best? Father or Sheinfeld or Globerman?'

'Of the three of them, I love you and Rachel the best,' said Judith. 'And now, Nomele, let me rest a little by myself.'

'I miss that "Nomele" of hers,' Naomi told me. 'I miss the smell of lemons from her hands, I miss a lot of other things of hers.'

I told Naomi what Jacob told me, and she said he was right, men don't seek in their wives the mother or the daughter or the virgin or the whore 'and not all the other nonsense written in books'.

'It's their sister they seek,' she said. Their twin buried inside them, so close, so touching, so naked – and unattainable. 'And you're all so stupid.' She hugged me. 'We're the only ones dumber than you. That's your good luck.'

'How will we end up, Naomi?' I asked.

'You men?'

'Us, me and you.'

She laughed. 'The same thing: I'll ask you what your name is, you'll say "Zayde", I'll understand that there's a mistake here and I'll go sleep with somebody else. That's what's happening to us now and that's what will happen to us later on, too.'

Years before that, when I was seven or eight years old and Naomi and Meir were still living in their small first apartment, I woke up in the middle of the night at the sound of their talking.

After a few minutes, there was silence, the door of their room opened, the wall of the corridor lit up, and Naomi came out of the room naked.

I saw her. She crossed the corridor, closed herself in the shower, and turned on the faucet, but her weeping was clear and lived above and below and within the sound of the flowing water.

Then she came back. The light from the bedroom shone obliquely on her naked body, from the hollow of her neck to the golden dune of her hip, it sliced and served me a gleaming triangle of her flesh.

I didn't tell anyone about the eternal picture of mine, but a few years ago, when I asked Uncle Menahem what he thought about the search for the twin sister, he said there was some truth in that but there was nothing new in it, and the ancients had already said that. But things are much more complicated and become clear to us only when they're no use anymore.

And the Village Papish snorted contemptuously and said that men are so ugly, that not one of them, at any rate he hopes, has a twin sister. And then he added that it's only a lack of choice that makes those monkeys lovable to their mates.

And Globerman burst out laughing and said: 'Well, Zayde, congratulations, that's how it starts. First tales about a twin sister, then a hand job in front of the mirror, and finally maybe you'll want to sit down on your own *shmuck*.'

And Jacob, lying wounded and stunned on the filthy floor of the cowshed, looked at his love. In his excitement, he had forgotten that she was hard of hearing in her left ear and he interpreted the expression of amazement and concentration on her face as disgust with the blood pouring from his wound. He got up and fled to his house and there he burst through the door and shouted, 'Rebecca, Rebecca, help me,' and only an echo replied from the empty hut and from the cold half of the bed and from the incubator, whose cases were filled with tiny dry chick carcasses.

Only then did he realize that it had been several days since he had seen his wife and he understood what the whole village already knew: that she had left him and he wouldn't see her again.

He groped his way to the trough, washed the sulpha and the coagulated blood from his eyebrows and his forehead and his eyes. Then he sat in front of his small shaving mirror, dipped a needle and thread in alcohol, clamped his jaw, and stitched together the torn lips of his wound.

The thread seared its way in the flesh, the edges of the wound shook until they were fastened to one another and tightened. The awful pain pierced Jacob's brain, made his bones shudder, and poured a stream of tears from his eyes.

From now on, he decided, lying and shaking in his empty bed in his empty house, he would give up the exhausting stages of conversation, bouquets of flowers, embellishments, remonstrances, jests, and beautiful words, because he didn't have any special talent for them anyway. From now on he would challenge Fate. He would grasp it by the horns, bend it to his will, or be gored to death.

'Now I'm gonna tell you something about Fate, Zayde. I'm gonna tell you something about Fate and you're gonna eat and you'll listen. Back home, there was a rich Jew who played with fate. His name was Haim, but everybody called him "L'Haim", because he liked to make toasts banging glass against glass. Globerman used to raise a glass with your mother in a refined way, they'd clink the crystal and he'd say: "May Lady Judith's ears also enjoy." But this Jew would bang it real hard, and then he'd lick the blood and wine off his own fingers and off the woman's fingers until both of them together would melt with pleasure. A person like L'Haim I never saw in my life. One day he came to us in town, a Jew sixty years old, without a wife, with two carts and two children, and nobody knew who it was or what it was, where he came from or where he was going. Money he had like water and all his cases was full of silk and furs, and in a loud voice he announced so everybody should hear: "When I die, these children won't be left to ask for charity. Each one of them will have something to start life with." And so it

happened what always happens, that family and money get
mixed up – the children grew up and started waiting for L'Haim
to die already and L'Haim started hating the children, and so
much he hated them that he finally decided to stop working
and to use up all his money to the very end of his life, so there
wouldn't be one red cent left for the children. That's how it is,
when somebody's crazy, he can't stop. All he can do is move his
craziness in another direction, but crazy he'll stay. He sold his
big house and his most beautiful furniture, and for himself he
left only one little house and two horses to go from place to
place and one maid, and he figured he had another seventeen
years left to live, and he figured out how much he'd need for
clothes to wear and food to eat: so many pounds of meat, so
many pounds of flour and salt and sugar, and so many quarts
of liquor and so much wood for heating, and so many crystal
glasses to drink a toast with more women and to cut more
fingers. And he was so precise he even figured the secret charity
a Jew should give, and the tithe for the rabbi, and Sabbath and
holiday feasts, and from the seventeen years he had left, he
remembered to subtract the food for the Fast of Gedalia and
Yom Kippur, and Ten Teveth and Ta'anit Esther, and Seventeen
Tamuz and Tesha B'Av, and since he was a firstborn son, he also
had to fast on the eve of Passover. You never even heard of all
those little fasts, Zayde? All that together was seven fasts times
seventeen years, altogether take away a hundred and nineteen
days of eating, and that's also quite a bit of money and a little
more life. And how many bars of soap he'll need and all kinds
of other little things, 'cause here and there sometimes a button
falls off a garment and rolls God knows where and you've got
to buy a new one 'cause no matter how hard you look for it, it
don't help. And he also figured out how much it would cost him
to feed the horses, and he left enough money to buy new horses
after he'd send the old ones to be skinned, and even snuff and
milk for the cat and seeds for the bird L'Haim took into account.
And then, when the children understood he was serious, they
started hollering: Father is stealing our inheritance! And they
went to the rabbi, but the rabbi said: There's nothing to do. A
man's money is his own and his will is to be respected. The sons

said: And what if Father lives longer than the money and will be old and won't have anything and will fall on our shoulders? And L'Haim said: I won't live long. With me, everything is numbered and measured, when the money runs out, I'm going to die, and when I die, the money's going to run out. And to make doubly sure, he went and ordered himself a big hourglass in the city of Makarov, with the amount of sand and the width of the hole for seventeen years on the dot. I remember how they brought that hourglass on a wagon, upside down and tied to boards and wrapped in cotton. They put it in the yard and L'Haim saw that everybody already came to see, and then he lifted up his hand and he brought it down and he shouted, "*Itzt*, now!" and two special men turned the hourglass over so everybody would see how the time started running to the end of L'Haim. 'Cause that's what's beautiful about an hourglass, that it don't measure the time of the world. It measures its own time and isn't interested in what happened before and what'll happen after. And so many people came to look and he talked so much and was so proud of the accounts of his life and of his hourglass and of all the money he left for himself, and he told how before the end he's going to sit next to the hourglass and watch the last grains of his soul leaving his body, until all around that's the only thing people were talking about. And one evening, nine months and one week after L'Haim stopped working, he was sitting on his money box and eating his herring and smiling at his sand, and all of a sudden, two robbers came into his house and broke his head in one blow with an iron pole, and they broke the hourglass with one blow, too, and all the money they took with one blow, too. And so everybody saw that L'Haim was right. His time and his money and his life all ran out in the same moment, and as L'Haim himself said, nothing was left for his sons after him. 'Cause when Fate decides to take a hand in some game, Zayde, even if you made up that game, then he sets all the laws and all the rules. And Fate and Luck and Chance, you should know, Zayde, they're not where people look for them, in cards and dice, not at all! I'm telling you, Zayde, they're in life itself. And that's why I'm also telling you: never ever play cards or dice! Only chess you play, 'cause we've got enough dice in life when somebody else is throwing and we've got to make a move. And enough in life there's somebody else shuffling the cards for us. So you don't need that in games, too.'

11

All that time Judith kept on milking Rachel's empty udders, and one day Bloch's miracle happened and milk appeared. At first in a thin dripping and then in jets that grew stronger from day to day.

'Like a real milk cow she'll never give,' said Moshe.

'The main thing is she'll pay for the food you give her,' said Judith. 'That's what's so important to you, isn't it?'

'Calves she won't ever give, either,' Moshe persisted.

When the rumour of Rachel's milk reached Globerman's ears, he wrote it down in his notebook, but he didn't give up hope. He knew that Moshe couldn't bear the weird cow, and he guessed correctly that he was a bit afraid of it, and he never passed up an opportunity to mention to him his wish to buy her.

He was a wise man, and years of trading had endowed him with a subtle understanding of the human soul. He deciphered the minuscule signs of distress in a person's neck, discerned the hidden spasms of the diaphragm, and read the cloud maps of the forehead.

Those were hard times, and whenever he came to buy a cow, the livestock dealer also looked at the owner's children. He saw the patches in their clothes and noticed the toes of their worn-out shoes cut out with a knife so that the growing child could wear them another season. He pulled a cookie out of his pocket and assessed the eagerness in their held-out hand.

'Look,' he'd say, 'all kinds of things they say about Globerman in the village, but what after all does Globerman do? Hocus-pocus I do. You look and see, here's a cow, hocus-pocus, what comes from the cow? Three ten-pound notes.'

Now, as winter approached, Globerman started commenting

about the weather and about the heavy mud of the Valley and oy-oy-oy what rain and cold are in store for us this year, Rabinovitch, oy-oy-oy how much coats and boots for the kids cost.

He talked about his own children, children no one had ever seen and no one knew if they really did exist, but all he had to say was the phrase 'coats for the kids' and worry appeared on the farmer's brow. Globerman saw it before the farmer felt it, and knew this was the time to pull out the *knippl*, hold it out, and riffle the bills.

But Moshe feared Judith's anger and she kept on milking Rachel's parched udders and trying to get her in heat. On Uncle Menahem's advice she brought her carobs to sweeten her food, and on Samson Bloch's advice she even caressed her immodestly with a warm damp rag, on her rump and under her tail – in vain.

'Bring her to Gordon for a few days,' Bloch finally suggested. 'Let her look a little bit at my *Krasovitch* and maybe she'll feel like it.'

When the two of them arrived in his yard, Bloch came out of the shed in his rubber boots, smiling happily.

'To me or to the bull?' he asked ingenuously.

Mother couldn't help smiling. 'Is Shoshana at home?' she asked.

'She's in the hatchery.'

'I'll go to the kitchen and put on the kettle.'

By the time Shoshana returned from the hatchery, Judith had already poured two cups of tea.

'Did you ever see such beautiful chicks?' asked Shoshana. 'We bought Sheinfeld's incubators. All of a sudden he up and sold them.'

Judith didn't answer.

'It's very hard for him now, ever since his wife left.'

Judith stirred the tea. Her eye was caught by the black leaves spinning in the cup.

'And what's with you, Judith?' asked Shoshana Bloch.

'Everything's fine,' said Judith.

'Still in the cowshed?'

'I feel good there.'

'It's not good for you,' said Shoshana. 'And it's not good for Rabinovitch, and it's not good for the whole village.' She put her hand on my mother's. 'It's not good, Judith. You're not a young girl anymore. How much longer will you live alone in the cowshed?'

'I feel good there,' repeated Judith.

'Now you're still strong and healthy. But what about in ten or twenty years from now? And the heart, Judith? And the womb? What about them?'

'A *nafka mina*,' said Judith. 'The heart is empty now, and the womb is used to it.'

She drank another cup of tea, hugged Rachel's neck in parting, told her she'd come back to get her in a week, and went to pay a brief courtesy call at Uncle Menahem's.

From there she returned home, her feet treading fast, to keep her from thinking.

12

For a week Rachel stayed with Gordon, and didn't get in heat. Once she wanted to break through to his fence, and Bloch, who was sure his plot had worked, quickly let her in there. But Rachel's heart wasn't set on love. She just wanted to spar with Gordon and almost brought him down. Only with jets of cold water did Bloch manage to get her out of there.

'A waste of work and money,' he told Judith. 'Boys don't interest that girl. Take her back home and try milking a little more.'

It was a winter day. There was no rain, but a flat grey rind covered the sky. Strong smells of crushed grass rose from the treading of the boots and the trampling of the hooves. Angry pairs of lapwings flew above them, rising and falling, splendid and violent at the sight of their black-and-white passing, with their hidden stilettos and their horrible, shrill shrieks.

They crossed the wadi. The cow gulped the water, gasped with all her big, male body, and her nostrils exhaled steam into the cold air. Now and then she gently butted Judith's thighs and back, as if prodding her to play, and Judith responded to her, tapped her on the neck, laughed, and ran beside her, but a stone lay in her chest and tears of cold and worry gathered in the corners of her eyes.

Panting, they came to Sheinfeld's row of walnut trees. The naked branches painted a delicate picture on the sheet of the sky, and the dark blocks of the crows' nests were visible in them like brush drippings on the canvas. Beyond them appeared the tall figure of Globerman, striding along and singing in a loud, confident voice.

The dealer noticed them, stopped singing, waved his *baston*, lopping off the purple head of a brier. He smiled because he knew that nothing would prevent the encounter.

Judith, who was furious for the very same reason, stood still. All her old loathing stirred in her. Outside the framework of the weekly drinking in the cowshed, Globerman was still as dangerous and as filthy to her as always.

The dealer approached until a dozen steps separated them, and then he stopped, peeled the filthy beret off his head, pasted it onto his chest, and bowed.

'Lady Judith . . . the calf Rachel . . . what a surprise . . . what an honour for a poor dealer.'

'Were you following me, Globerman? Who told you I was here?'

'A little bird told me.' Globerman smiled. 'When Lady Judith leaves the village, the wind stops blowing, the birds stop singing, men stop breathing . . .'

He pulled a little package out of his pocket and held it out to her: 'A little something for you. For two lovely ears. *Oyringlakh*, earrings, of pure gold.'

'I never asked you for anything and I don't like your gifts,' said Judith. 'I'm willing only to drink with you, Globerman, once a week, and that's all.'

Rachel swayed her thick neck, snorted, and dug her hoof in.

'Never does any lady have to ask Globerman for anything.

Globerman always knows himself, all by himself, and from the start, what suits every lady, period.'

He bent over, and with his outstretched hand, held the earrings to her, but Judith didn't stretch out her hand to take them and Globerman smiled to himself. 'Where is Lady Judith going? Did you take the calf for a walk?'

'She's in heat.'

'She's in heat?' sneered the dealer. 'She's in heat? That cow isn't in heat and won't be in heat. Just look at her, Lady Judith. She's got the body of a male calf and the face of a male calf and the little feet of a male calf. In the end, they'll still have to call Globerman, God forbid, eh? And then you'll see, after we slaughter her and take her apart, that inside her she's also got two balls of a male calf.'

He approached Rachel, who bent her thick neck menacingly, but retreated.

'She smells Globerman like an old man smells the Angel of Death,' said the dealer. 'Did you ever see an old man a few days before he dies, Lady Judith? How restless he gets, walking around the house like a mouse, sniffing in corners, doesn't sleep? Look at her. She's now smelling something we can't feel. Signs we can't understand. That's how an old man is before death, when he's like an animal that wants to be alone, and that's also how a woman is two or three days before giving birth, when she suddenly starts cleaning up the whole house, and that's also how it is when they smell the Angel of Death.'

And suddenly the dealer took a step forward, flung out his hand, and ran it over Rachel's back, with his hypnotic 'tappen' movement, examining how thick the flesh was between the vertebrae and the skin.

The touch of his hand set off a cold chill in the backs of both of them.

'Oy-oy-oy, that's the best meat in the world,' the dealer chanted a chant of longing. 'There's no better meat in the world than the meat of a barren cow. Even the best chefs in Paris don't know that. Only we, who were born on the butcher block, know that. But they don't, all those dummies in restaurants with their white hats. They season, straighten, soften, feed the cow with all kinds of spices, I heard that in Japan they even give the *kelbelakh*, the calf, beer to drink, and in France they give them a bath with cognac. And there's only one thing they don't know. That that's the meat fit for a king, period. A barren heifer, a *tsvilling* of a calf, with the body of a male and the smell of a baby that will never be in heat, and they'll never jump on her, and she'll never give birth.'

From the east, the big flock of starlings appeared, returning from the fields to their night's lodging in the big trees next to the water tower.

'Here they are,' said Judith. 'It's quarter to five now. I've got to go.'

Like a mighty disc that measured a quarter of the sky, the flock flew and whirled, became a gigantic cloth, and turned over. A string branched out of it and pulled it into a broad ribbon that wrapped around itself and became a gigantic sail. Myriads of wings and beaks set up a wave of noise. The air shook and turned dark.

'That cow you'll never get, Globerman,' said Judith.

'All cows come to the dealer in the end,' said Globerman.

'Not this cow,' said Judith. 'This cow is mine.'

'We're all yours, Lady Judith.' Globerman put on his hat and started bowing and stepping backward. 'We're all yours and we'll all come in the end. Everyone to his dealer and everyone to his slaughterer.'

13

'So how come I fell in love with her, you ask? Come on, ask, Zayde, and I'll answer you. 'Cause in a village like this, where the work is always the same work, and the mud is the same mud and the same sweat and the same milk and rain, where everything is always the same thing, so not to fall in love with her? Every year the same thing. Again the sprout sprouts and the flower flowers, and again crops and slops, and lopping and chopping, and summer and winter, and to a place like this a woman comes all of a sudden, so if you ask me how come I fell in love with her, I'll ask you a question back: is this a life for a Jew? They took us out of the synagogue where the prayers and commandments are all the time the same thing, and they took us to the Land of Israel and to this Kfar-David and here, too, it's all the same thing, and very fast I understood the principle here, that today and yesterday and tomorrow are as alike as brothers, and like a bird I fell into the trap. Eat, Zayde, eat, you don't have to stop eating to listen, that's what's good about a meal, that you can eat and also listen. It's not the hard work that bothered me, and waiting didn't bother me, either. I, bless God, from a very young age have been working, and patience I've got enough for ten men, to work for love all Jacobs know. Years are like a few days in our eyes. And somebody who waited for love like I did, he's also got enough patience for horses and geese and trees and rain and mainly for time. 'Cause patience for time, that's what's important, not patience for each other and not for love and not for work and not for nothing else, just patience for time. Both for time that goes in a circle, like the seasons of the year, and for time that goes in a straight line, like a person's age. But there will never be oranges in summer here and no rooster will ever lay eggs and no hen will ever give pears. At most, sometimes it will be a little hotter, or sometimes there'll be a little more rain. And the Village Papish, who I never agreed with about anything, and he thinks I'm an idiot and I think he's a sage and both of us are quite wrong, so the Village Papish, two years after we came here, he said: What's going on here, comrades? What kind of life is this? How long can you see every year at the same season on the same tree the same yellow lemons? Like a joke he said that, but in fact it's a very sad thing. Once Globerman told me how he saw in Nahalal two women guests from the city standing at a pen of big calves. Standing and looking, excuse me, where in a grown calf there's something to see. They stood there and looked and finally one of them opens her mouth and asks: And what do they do with the milk from the calves? What do you say about such a thing, Zayde? Well, after all the villagers finished laughing, the second city woman wanted to show how much she did understand, so she says to her: What a dummy you are, they don't have milk yet because they're still small. Funny, eh? I see you're laughing, so I'll tell you something, Zayde – you laugh, but that story is really sad and not so funny. 'Cause you can stand on your head all day long, the calf won't ever give milk. And sometimes some calf is born with two heads or a chicken with four legs, and right away there's a fuss, people come, take pictures, ask who-what-why, and the four eyes are already closed, and the two heads have already fallen, and the poor little *kelbel* is already dead, and his two little souls, poof, gone, each one from its little head, and all the visitors, too, poof, gone, and everything in its place, poof, came back safe, and what was under the sun, like what I told you, poof, it is also what it's going to be. So you ask me how come I fell in love with her?'

Now the other door of the oven was opened and this time a smell of baked strudel rose from it. For half an hour it had been tormenting my ability to pay attention, and now it burst out to the tunnels of my nose and entangled my senses.

Jacob stuck a toothpick in the crisp crust, took it out, licked it, and chuckled with satisfaction. Then he pulled the pan and with unexpected expertise separated the cake from it with a thin strong wire, and slid it onto a metal rack.

A wonderful smell of flaming rum and burnt sugar and lemon rind and apples and raisins rose from it.

'You see,' said Jacob, 'cake you cool on a rack and not in a pan, and then it don't stay wet underneath like a rag.'

'How do you know those things?' I asked.

'There was my worker here and he taught me all I need.'

A new tone, of false teeth, rose from his jaw. He poured the two of us a strong and very clear drink that tasted of pears. And then he said he was tired, that I shouldn't touch the dishes. 'Tomorrow, the cleaning woman will come, Zayde, and she'll do everything.'

He lay down, almost dropped onto the bed.

'What are you thinking about, Jacob?' I asked.

'About a wedding.' His voice shook. 'About making matches. Of food and digestion, and of flesh and soul. It's harder to make a match between the body and the soul than between a man and a woman. From a match like that, even to get excited is impossible. Only to commit suicide it's possible, but what good is that then? Body and soul have to know how to grow together, to get old together, and then they're like two poor old birds in the same cage, and neither one of them's got any strength in his wings. The body is already weak and falls. The soul already forgets and regrets, and to run away from each other is also impossible. Well, the only thing left then is knowing how to forgive. That's the wisdom that's left after all the rest of the wise things are finished: knowing how to forgive each other. If not to forgive another person, at least to forgive yourself.'

He groaned and fell silent. I sat on the chair next to him and didn't know whether to go on talking or not.

Jacob lay on his back with one hand crooked behind his neck. To my amazement, the other hand suddenly crept into his pants, at a depth that couldn't be mistaken. When he noticed my embarrassed look, he pulled it out, but a few minutes later, the hand sneaked back into its nest as though it were placed there on its own.

The two of us felt uneasy and finally Jacob said: 'Look here, Zayde, this is how it's comfortable for me to lay, and please don't be offended, that's how we hold and comfort each other. Both of us are soft and old now and enjoy memories. How many friends does a man still have left at this age?'

And the two of us laughed.

'Look at her,' he said after he had fallen asleep for a few minutes and had awoken when I stood up. 'Sometimes I look at that beautiful picture and I don't remember who it is. Her smell isn't on the sheets anymore and the touch of her skin isn't on my skin anymore, and her memory isn't in the heart or the head. If I say to myself Rebecca Schwartz or Rebecca Sheinfeld, I immediately correct myself – Rebecca Green. Everything she wanted he did for her, that Englishman Green. He took her away, he brought her back, he bought her this house, and right away he died, 'cause she wanted to stay alone. In England, he was a great figure, really half a lord, but in this story, he was like a small extra from the theatre. His part ends and he goes off without complaints. In a play, you've got one part. A little one or a big one. But in life you get to be in a lot of plays and you've got a lot of parts. If somebody did a play about the life of the Village Papish or about Rabinovitch, I'd have a very small part in it, but if somebody made a play about the life of your mother, there I'd have a bigger part, eh? And you can have one starring part, the big part in the play about your own life. Never, Zayde, don't let nobody ever take the main part in the play of your life, like I did.'

'How did he live with her? After he gave her up back then?' I wondered. 'I don't understand that.'

'I can't hear,' yelled Oded into the roar of the motor. 'What did you say, Zayde?'

And after I shouted, too, he laughed. 'Don't be a baby, what's wrong with that? What did he have left after the canaries went and after your mother didn't want him? In a house in Tivon, there was a beautiful room waiting for him, and good food, and the clothes of her English husband that fit him to a T, and a cleaning woman cleans his room, and a nursemaid wipes his ass, and a taxi takes him whenever he wants to sit at our bus stop, and the driver waits for him until he finishes sitting there and saying come in come in, and in the kitchen he's got a beautiful picture of his wife, and next to his bed he's got a beautiful picture of your mother. So what doesn't he have?'

'And Rebecca agreed to all that?' I said. 'That he loves another woman?'

'Loves another woman, so what?' shouted Oded. 'Let him love whoever he wants to. That one's dead and this one's alive. It doesn't matter who he loves, the main thing is who he's with.'

He killed the motor. A big, tormented gasp blurted out, and a big lizard of silence crept in its wake.

'When you see the end coming close you start thinking different,' Oded bisected that silence with his shout.

But Jacob didn't see the end coming close and didn't start thinking different, and the love didn't fade from his body or from his soul.

'Now, at long last, they feel good together,' he told me, his hand moving slowly in his pants, doing good and forgiving, examining and consoling. 'Now the soul and the body know each other real good. I know where it hurts and it knows where I hurt.'

14

Every day he got up early for his birds, changed the water and the bottom of the cages, prepared the mixtures of greens and fruits, the sesame seeds and the beets, the egg yolks and shells, gave poppies to the nervous ones, hashish to the gloomy ones, and honey to the hoarse ones.

'Should I tell you something?' he said to me. 'I didn't like their singing very much. Outside there are birds that sing much much better than them.'

It was the routine of the work that he liked, and the loneliness and the serenity, and every day he went out to his wooing and his yellow notes, which he continued to hang on every corner of the village.

And since the notes were visible and their colour stood out and attracted, and their words were clear and open, the villagers would study them and express their opinion, and they soon started hanging their own notes on the village bulletin board: anonymous sheets torn out of notebooks, fragrant wrapping paper for oranges, thick strips ripped from powdered milk sacks by hands that wanted to write and speak. First about Jacob's love for Judith, and then about love in general.

Ultimately, the committee put up another board next to the old one because that one was loaded with so much nonsense and clichés that the various announcements of the secretary, the film projectionist, the sower, and the education committee disappeared among them.

The new board was devoted solely to the issue of Jacob and Judith, and you could always see people near it, arguing, laughing, exchanging opinions and truths about love, and sighing.

And one evening the Village Papish went into Rabinovitch's cowshed and said to Judith: 'You don't have to give in to him, all you have to do is show up for one date, you'll chat a little bit, explain to him whatever you have to, like a decent woman should do in such cases.'

Judith was quick to turn her deaf ear to him, but the words 'decent woman' got around her, surrounded her head, and burst into her consciousness from the good ear.

The blood rushed from her face. 'I am a decent woman,' she said furiously. 'It's not my fault that that man is crazy. I am a decent woman. Did I ask for that love of his? Did I separate him from his wife?'

'About such things, Judith, you don't talk logically,' the Village Papish answered her. 'Because now it's only a matter of good manners, but in another two weeks, God forbid, it will be a matter of saving a life.'

'Stop pestering Judith, Sheinfeld,' Moshe Rabinovitch warned Jacob. 'She came to work here and not for your craziness.'

The articles in the leaflet and the announcements on the board didn't bother him. But the yellow notes swooped down on him from every corner and pierced his eyes. His heavy fists clenched and his forehead shook and wrinkled.

One day such a note appeared nailed to the big eucalyptus tree in the yard, and Moshe didn't even bother to read it. Its place and its colour were enough for him. He tore it down and ran to Jacob's canary house, pounded the door with his short, thick hands, and it was torn off its hinges and knocked down.

The canaries were startled. They started fluttering and struggling in the cages. Feathers and shrieks flew and Jacob looked back at Moshe with pure and innocent eyes and said to him: 'Stand quietly, Rabinovitch. You're scaring the poor birds.'

Moshe was amazed and stood still and didn't say a word. Jacob calmed the canaries, and since he knew that the shouts would make them hoarse, he started preparing the appeasing mixture of lemon juice and honey for them. Moshe was embarrassed and hurried to repair the hinges of the door, and after he left, Jacob bathed and shaved, changed his clothes, and went out for another one of those meetings in the field that Judith didn't come to and they all ended with 'ch'.

15

That whole time, despite Rachel, and in spite of the harsh words exchanged in the field, Judith and the livestock dealer went on meeting once a week for an hour or two of sitting and drinking together.

The bottle of liquor and the glasses Globerman left in the cowshed, and once, when Judith told him that she didn't drink from that bottle except when he was there, his heart was filled with unexpected delight.

'That's our bottle,' he said in a soft voice. 'Just for the two of us. Here's to us, Lady Judith.'

'To us, Globerman,' she said.

'You want me to tell you some tale about my father?'

'Tell me about whoever you want to.'

'Everything I know I learned from my father,' declared the dealer. 'And mainly the most important rule for a *fleysh handler* is that principles and livelihood you mustn't put in the same drawer.'

'I already noticed that, Globerman,' said Judith.

'To buy a cow I learned from him, to check, to haggle, to cheat, and to win. When I was ten years old, he used to send me to sleep in the owner's cowshed, to see that he didn't give the cow salt so she'd drink a lot before the weighing, and to watch that he didn't make money from her shit. You know how they make money from shit, Lady Judith? The night before the weighing, they give the cow something for constipation and so all the shit stays in her belly and is weighed like meat.'

Globerman senior would buy cattle from the Arabs of Kastina and Gaza.

'He was a great dealer. He sold to the Turkish army and then to the English, too. Every time he would buy twenty, thirty head from the sheikh from Gaza, pay him a few pennies in advance, and the rest, he would tell the sheikh, he would give him when every cow arrived safely. That sheikh had a stupid herder, and he would bring the cows from Gaza to Jaffa, walking with them along the shore. Every time with five cows in case, God forbid, robbers or wild animals or a flood would come, the whole herd wouldn't be lost.'

When the first group of cows came, Globerman senior received the herder with great honour, served him food and drink, and took care to put a small chilled bottle of Lebanese arak aside.

'What's that? The herder wondered, running a knowing and delighted finger over the tiny dew drops thickening on the side of the bottle.

'Cold water,' said Globerman senior, who was familiar with the prohibitions of his guest's religion and the weakness of his faith.

He poured him a generous drink, and the herder swallowed it and almost choked on the flame and the sharpness.

'Good water,' he groaned with pleasure.

'From our well,' said Globerman senior.

'A good well,' said the herder.

'May you be healthy.' Globerman senior touched his forehead. 'Ashrab, drink some more, my friend, you're thirsty from the road.'

He tossed slivers of ice into the liquor glasses, he served olives, peeled cucumbers, and fresh bunches of parsley stems, he speared and roasted pieces of meat on a tray of hot coals made of sour orange wood, and when the two of them finished eating and drinking and groaning from the good taste of the water, Globerman senior took a sooty firebrand and scratched five vertical lines on the wall of the butcher shop and a horizontal line going through them all.

'Those are the five cows you brought today,' he said to the herder. 'Now go and come back with five more, and we'll eat some more meat together and we'll drink some more good water from the well together, and we'll write another five lines here on the wall. And so you'll bring all the cows here and on the last round, the lord sheikh will also come, and see with his own eyes and make the account himself.'

They dipped their hands in ashes and stamped their signs on the wall to confirm the group of cows, and the herder parted from his host with words of gratitude and peace, treated himself to one last sip of water before he set out, and returned to his city.

A week later, he came with the second group. Once again he ate and drank his fill, and once again Globerman senior made five charcoal lines on the wall of the butcher shop and the two of them confirmed the group by stamping their handprints.

With the last five cows, the sheikh who owned the herd also came to get his money and discovered – here the dealer thumped his boot with his stick and cackled a choking laugh – 'and discovered something awful'.

'Well, you tell me, Lady Judith.' He winked. 'What did he discover?'

'What?'

'He discovered that that week, Father plastered the butcher shop ... Three layers of whitewash over the signs and over the stamps and over everything, and now go and argue with somebody who was born on the butcher block about how many cows he got.' Globerman roared with laughter.

Judith sipped from her glass and smiled. She untied the blue kerchief and her hair dropped onto her shoulders.

Outside, the afternoon wind began blowing. The rustle of the eucalyptus grew stronger and the dealer knew that in a little while, Lady Judith would get up and say: 'Well, Globerman, it's now half an hour to five and I've got to go to work.' He stood up, put on his hat, and touched the fingers of his right hand to its brim in farewell.

'I better go now, and that way you won't have to throw me out afterwards,' he said. 'And another story I'll tell you next time.'

He went out into the yard, glad that he had succeeded in having a conversation without saying 'period' even once, and he shouted, 'Oded, Oded!' so the boy would come and manoeuvre his truck out of the yard for him.

'If it wasn't for our eucalyptus tree, he would have gone

straight into Papish's geese,' said Naomi. 'Look how many marks he left on it.'

When I look at the scarred stump that was once a tree, where crows nested in its crest and Oded built himself a house and Jacob stuck love notes on it and the dealer's truck braked at its flesh and Moshe sits on it today and straightens nails – my imagination makes its lopped-off past flourish. The branches bloom again, thicken and split, the foliage rustles again, the branches grow long, and I already hear the premonition of that cracking, and bend my neck and wait for the smash of the break, the roar of the fall, the dread of the blow, and nothing shakes me out of my dream and wakes me from her death.

It would have been good if he had uprooted that stump from its place and burned it, so it wouldn't stand here like a tombstone. But Moshe loves the lopped-off trunk, a memorial to his vengeance, as he loves his rock, the testimony to his strength. Sometimes he goes to the rock and taps it with the affection of old-time foes, and on autumn days and in late summer, when a cool afternoon wind comes down from Mount Carmel and blows in the open haystack, he comes to the eucalyptus stump, with a strong hand he rips off every new branch and growth from the edges of the cut, and once again he tells the eucalyptus that this is its punishment: 'To die you won't die, and to bloom you won't bloom.'

Then he sits down on the trunk and starts working. His wooden board is on his lap and on it is a pile of crooked nails. A pile of straightened nails quickly rises next to it, and as the one declines, the other grows.

He is an old man. He's short of breath and his face is always red, as with an invisible effort. Senescence distorts his lips and makes him look like a child who can't understand the world. But yearning for his braid still fills his heart and his awful strength still bubbles in the muscles of his arms, and even though I have known him for many years now, I still find it hard to believe my eyes when I see him straightening nails between his thick fingers as if they were metal wires.

'It calms him,' says Oded.

After Rabinovitch finishes the job of straightening, he polishes the nails with sea sand and used motor oil. When they shine new and gleaming, a smile of pleasure rises to his face.

He was always fond of sparkling things, that's what Uncle Menahem told me, and when he was a little girl, he would modestly raise the hem of the frock his mother dressed him in, kneel down, and insert nails in the wooden floor of the house with precise hammer blows.

The mother, who feared for the floor, but knew that little girls have longings that mustn't be dammed, scratched a square on the floor of the kitchen, a yard square, and allowed Moshe to pound his nails only there. Within a few weeks, the whole area was filled with dense nail heads that were polished until they gleamed and were smooth as glass.

'Moshe was a very nice little girl,' Uncle Menahem concluded that story about his brother. 'And a boy who was a girl and wore a dress and had a braid, will beat every other boy in every contest of love.'

16

One day, Aunt Bathsheba came striding up vigorously from the fields, her face white from rage and her body black from her dress. The sight was so bold and bizarre that no sooner had people peeped out of the windows than they came out of the houses and followed her.

'What happened?' Moshe rushed to his sister-in-law. 'What's that dress?'

'That's a widow's dress,' Aunt Bathsheba announced. 'You don't see? Menahem died and I'm a widow.'

'What do you mean, died?' yelled Moshe. 'What are you prattling about? Lunatic!'

With a fearful heart, he climbed up onto the horse's back and galloped to the next village. His brother, safe and sound, came out to meet him, wiped the horse, made sure he didn't drink too much, and poured some water for Moshe, too. Then he told him that he did indeed sometimes cheat on his wife, but despite her jealousy, suspiciousness, and sleuthing, Bathsheba never managed to catch him in the act.

'That was a mistake on my part,' said Menahem. 'I should have given her a chance to catch me once with a "hoor" or two and she would have calmed down. If a woman has only suspicions and no proof, she just goes crazy.'

One day Bathsheba questioned him until he broke down and admitted that he had a 'hoor' from time to time.

'Where?' asked Bathsheba.

'In my dreams,' said Menahem, and burst out laughing.

He thought that she'd laugh, too, because dreams are a legitimate and acceptable haven and even tyrants don't impose their rule over them, but Bathsheba set up such a ruckus that Menahem's soul revolted against her and her jealousy. This time he took an unexpected act of revenge against the force of her gall: he started meeting with his 'hoors' in the most annoying place – in her own dreams.

'You didn't leave me any choice.' He smiled when she accused him of that. 'If you'd let me meet them in my own dreams, we'd get out of yours.'

'Absolutely not,' said Bathsheba, and in the following days she discovered that her dreams were starting to invent for her husband not only places to meet, but also new 'hoors' to satisfy his passions.

She tried to stay awake, but then her defiant husband expanded the scope of his activity and also started cheating on her in daydreams, too. And this time – she saw it clearly, for daydreams are illuminated by daylight – Menahem was also making love with Shoshana Bloch, one of the only women she had never suspected.

'I saw you with Bloch's "hoor"!' she yelled.

'Maybe you'll describe to me what we were doing.' Menahem was astounded, and when Bathsheba took a deep breath and opened her mouth wide, Menahem put a gentle hand on it and blocked it and requested: 'But very slow, so I'll enjoy it, too.'

Bathsheba went outside, looked directly at the sun, and blinked a few times, and since she couldn't get the adulterous couple out of her eyes even like that, she rode on the bus with them to Haifa, went into Kupershtok's clothing shop, and asked for a black dress.

'When did your husband pass away?' asked the salesman, sympathizing with her grief.

'He didn't pass away, I'm passing away from him,' said Bathsheba.

'I don't understand,' said the salesman.

'For me he's dead and I want a widow's dress!' declared Bathsheba. 'What don't you understand?'

The dress fitted her very well and gave her great pleasure. She returned on the three o'clock bus, got off in the centre of the village, made sure to show off her black to everyone, and after a long walk and a stop at every one of the neighbours' houses, she reached her husband's carob orchard.

Menahem, still emanating the revealing smells of the semen of his trees, was pruning dry branches on one of the treetops, and suddenly noticed his widow standing under the tree.

She raised her eyes to him, twirled around, and asked venomously: 'It suits me?'

'Very well,' smiled Menahem.

Suddenly he was filled with lust for that handsome widow, who was wrapped in black and rage. He came down from the tree, yearning to bend over, roll up her skirt, and spread and kiss the white thighs on her dark dress.

But Bathsheba retreated and started shouting.

'For me you're dead,' she shrieked. 'You and all your "hoors". And now everybody will see me with this dress and know that that's it, that there is no more Menahem. Menahem died and his wife is a widow!'

That's what she shouted and she kept it up all day long, and continued following him around and shouting in the house, too, and Jacob, who was enclosed in his own affairs of the heart and didn't know any of that, came to Menahem that week of all times, because he wanted to consult with him about Judith, and he also saw her storming around in her yard.

'What happened?' He was frightened.

'He died!' shouted Bathsheba. 'You don't understand what it
is when somebody dies? You don't know when a woman wears
black?'

But the late lamented peeped out the window and beckoned
to Jacob to meet him in the haystack.

'What do you think about her?' he asked.

'Maybe I'll come another time?' Jacob apologized.

'No, no,' said Menahem. 'Now is a good time for problems
of love.'

Jacob described all his efforts and struggles, showed him some
of his notes, and complained about Judith meeting Globerman,
listening to his stories, and drinking cognac with him.

Menahem laughed, then he became glum, and finally grew
impatient.

'You're concerned with trivialities, Sheinfeld,' he told his
guest. 'That's love? A few little notes and a few birds? Listen
carefully to what I'm telling you, listen and remember because
I won't talk anymore: for a great love, only great plans help, a
great love is influenced only by great things. And now, excuse
me, Sheinfeld, my wife is mourning for me and I have to go and
console her.'

17

A long time has passed since those days. Many of the deeds
that were done and the feelings that were felt back then in the
streets of the village have been forgotten by now. Jacob's scar,
burning in his forehead like a scarlet thread, turned pale with
the years. Apparently the stitches worked well and the scar is
visible only when memories flush Jacob's face and it stands out
with its pallor.

One way or another, Jacob decided to do something great.
One blazing hot day in late summer 1937, at twilight, the
canaries were heard singing excitedly and very loud, and by
the time the people caught on that it wasn't coming from inside

the breeding house but outside it, the singing had already moved across the village.

Everyone hurried out of the houses and saw that Jacob Sheinfeld had hitched the wagon, loaded four big cages full of canaries on it, and was heading for Rabinovitch's yard.

One by one, the people moved out and accompanied him with a silent procession that grew as it went along the street.

Jacob drove the horse to the cowshed and called out: 'Judith!'

A late summer twilight, hot and dusty, stood in the air. This was the season when the first pomegranates swell up and burst with longing. This is the time when the turtledove drips the beads of his voice from the gloom of the cypress. In the top of the eucalyptus, the crows gathered for their daily meeting. In the cowshed, Judith was washing the jugs and Moshe Rabinovitch was stacking fodder in the troughs for the evening milking.

'He's coming to you,' he said to her.

Judith didn't answer.

'Go out to him. I don't want that leech here!'

Naomi says he was jealous of my mother, but I think Rabinovitch loathed Jacob's wooing and couldn't stand that persistent cloying sweetness anymore.

He felt anger and weariness and knew that if he went out to Jacob or if Jacob came into the cowshed, the whole thing would end badly.

Judith straightened up over the bucket of disinfectant, took the blue kerchief off her head, wiped her forehead and her hands with it, and went out of the cowshed.

'What do you want?' she shouted. 'What do you want from me and what do you want from your poor birds?'

And then the deed was done that will never be forgotten, and the best proof of it is that even people who didn't witness it remember it well.

Jacob took hold of the rope that was cleverly tied to the locks of all four cages, and raised his hand.

'This is for you, Judith!' he shouted.

He pulled the rope and the four doors gaped open all at once.

Judith was amazed.

Moshe, on the other side of the cowshed wall, was also amazed.

Jacob, who hadn't believed he would do it until that very minute, was amazed, too.

Silence reigned. The people fell mute as they always do in the presence of a great deed of renunciation and sacrifice. House pets and wild animals fell mute because the border between freedom and captivity was violated. And the wind fell silent all at once, as if to clear the way for the yellow wings that would soon fly off.

The canaries, who had indeed imagined that something great was going to happen from the moment their cages were loaded onto the wagon, were also stunned and stopped singing. But they immediately recovered, and when Jacob repeated his shout, 'That's for you, Judith!' the silence that closed over his words was broken by the exultant yellow flapping of a thousand wings soaring to freedom.

The escorts all groaned in unison, and Judith, deceived and angry, felt as if a strange and bold fist were shrivelling her heart.

'Now you won't have any more canaries, Jacob,' she said. 'Too bad.'

Jacob got out of the wagon and went to her.

'I'll have you,' he said.

'No you won't,' she took a step back.

'Yes I will,' said Jacob. 'You just now called me Jacob, for the first time.'

'You're wrong, Sheinfeld,' said Judith emphatically.

But Jacob was right. That was the first time she had called him 'Jacob' and not 'Sheinfeld', and the taste of his name in her mouth was like the taste of the bitter almond – sudden and annoying.

'It's you who are making a mistake,' said Jacob, shaking and knowing that the whole village was looking and listening. 'After the poor birds, I don't have anything greater to give you, all I've got left is my soul.'

'Your soul I don't want, either.'

And she turned and went back to the cowshed, and Jacob,

who knew her ways and knew she wouldn't come out again, held the horse by his bridle, turned the empty wagon around, and went back home.

Inside the cowshed, Moshe Rabinovitch stopped milking, straightened up, and leaned against the wall.

'Well, Judith,' he said at last. 'So now maybe you'll agree to meet with him once.'

'Why?' she asked, surprised.

'Because after that, all he can do now is commit suicide. What's left of a person who gave honour and work and property and everything for love? He didn't keep anything on the side for himself.'

Even though he didn't know that, he spoke from the sympathy that only two men competing for the heart of one woman can have for one another, and a slight nausea climbed into Judith's throat.

'Don't worry,' she said. 'Someone who really loves a woman doesn't commit suicide for her. Suicides love only themselves.'

'How many men do you know who would do what he did for a woman?' asked Moshe.

'And how many women do you know who want such martyrs?' asked Judith. 'And how many women do you know at all, Rabinovitch? And since when did you become such a *maven*? And why do you poke your nose in it? I'm only your worker. What you've got to say, you say only about the milk I milk and the food I cook. That's all.'

Outside, the people were still standing around crowded together, and it took a while until they started scattering in a funereal silence. The murmuring died down. The dust settled. A feeling of impending disaster stood in the air.

18

'When I was a boy,' Oded told me, 'Father used to sit at night and polish brown pennies until they gleamed like gold coins, and I was scared the crows would go crazy and break the windows to steal them. I'm amazed you didn't find a coin like that in their nests to this day.'

'They don't hide sparkly things in nests,' I said. 'They bury them in the ground.'

Oded's left arm, the more sun-tanned arm, is lying on the rim of the steering wheel. His right hand dances between the gearstick and all sorts of buttons and handles, and now and then it rises in the air to explain or to emphasize something.

His face is flushed, the grey undershirt is stuck to the potbelly that settles in folds as he sits. His sandalled hairless feet are on the wooden pedals.

'For the wheel of the old Mack, you had to have arms of steel. Now, with power steering and the hydraulic seat and the retarder and the half automatic and all those luxuries, the only exercise I get is smacking the alarm clock every night,' he told me, and burst out laughing.

'I told Dinah once, "Come on, let's go to America and we'll take a horse of a semitrailer, without the wagon, the biggest Peterbilt horse, with a cabin that sleeps two and a refrigerator and a fan and a radio and a shower and whatever gimmicks they've got." That horse, when you release it from the trailer, it just sings aloud, it's the best, most comfortable, strongest car in the world. And to tour America with it, Zayde, to look at the scenery from on high – what could be better? Mile after mile passes by, forests and deserts and fields and mountains, and when you measure in miles instead of kilometres, the whole thing looks altogether different. A mile is a mile and a kilometre is a kilometre. All you've got to do is hear those words, "mile" and "kilometre", to understand the difference between them. 'Cause what can a driver do here? Transport a little milk and a few eggplants and eggs and peppers, maximum from the Jezreel Valley to Jerusalem, like a grocery store errand boy with a bike and a carton. It's lucky they still call me from the army sometimes to tow a few tanks in the reserves, from Sinai to the Golan and from the Golan to Sinai, that's maybe getting close to something. Not that I look down on it, God forbid, but in this country, a semitrailer can't make a U-turn, you've got to do a little in reverse not to cross the border. And over there, an endless country, big, wide, not stingy with anything. Over there when they say "the Grand Canyon", it is a canyon and it is grand, and not like where they took us once, an outing of village kids to the end of the Negev near Eilat, and a whole day we walked in the sun to see a canyon, and in the end that whole canyon was just like the crack of an ass – small and red. Over there a canyon is a canyon and a mountain is a mountain and a river is a river. Like the Mississippi, for instance, is really a sea. You know how to spell Mississippi, well, just look at you, Zayde, a brain from the university, getting along with all the p's and s's ... So, listen, Zayde, there's a little song – m-i-s, s-i-s, s-i-p-p-i – somebody taught it to me, some girl, a hitchhiker I once picked up, a tourist from America. And over there when you go with a truck into a gas station, you've got good food and clean bathrooms, and music, and they fill up your coffee cup when you finish it, a refill they call it. I saw that once in some movie – a driver is sitting at the counter in a gas station, stretching his legs in his boots, drinking his coffee, the waitress comes, a real woman, not some dumb kid, a woman who has learned something from her life, with white shoes like a nurse and a little apron, and when he's at about a fourth of the cup, she asks, listen, Zayde, what she says: "Would you like a refill, sir?" Not like here, where they're so stingy about everything and give you a cup of mud coffee, and a wet sandwich with a carcass of a tomato inside and the bathroom is full of *drek* and the paper you've got to bring yourself. Because who needs a bathroom in a gas station here? Wherever you go, wherever you are – you're always a pee away from home.'

A white vapour and a good smell of warmed resin rose from

the pine grove on the flanks of the mountain. The sun climbed up. The big truck slid down the slope of the road, turned left at the top, and after a short climb it turned and all at once the Valley seemed to be spread out under its wheels.

Oded filled his chest with air, turned his face to me, and smiled. 'Every time I visit her in Jerusalem, Naomi asks me about this moment, when you come out of Wadi Milek. You go up to the left and turn right and suddenly the valley opens up. Here's Givot Zayid, here's Kfar Joshua, Beit Sha'arim, and there's Nahalal, in the distance Givat Moreh. The Valley. Then she asks me and I say to her, "Do you miss it, sister? Just tell me and I'll come take you back home." And you should see Meir's face when I tell her that.'

From the heights of the cabin lies the land of Naomi's regrets stretched out as far as the eye can see, to the blue walls of the distant mountains. In the checkered fields a big oak tree stands out here and there, souvenirs of the glorious forest that used to be here.

'You know very well that I and your mother weren't friends. But about Meir we were in full agreement,' he said.

We crossed the indolent channel of the Kishon, went through Sadeh Ya'akov, turned right, and climbed with a loud groan to Ramat-Ishai, which Oded still called Jeida. We went down and we went up and near the old British police station, Oded told me for the eightieth time about the exploits of Sergeant Shvili, who used to wander around among the Arab villages with the Kurbatch and make order.

'You'll write about all those things, Zayde,' he shouted. 'Otherwise, why am I telling you all that? You'll remember and you'll write.'

19

'They'll all die in the end,' said the Village Papish. 'Those spoiled housebirds don't know what weather is.'

But Jacob Sheinfeld's released canaries endured sun and wind, rain and hail with surprising valour.

They dined on thistle seeds and on the offal in the troughs, nested on every tree, and didn't recoil from owls, cats, or hawks. And those creatures did bring down starlings and tit-mice, but Jacob's canaries they didn't attack. Now the canaries were seen on every pole and every roof in the village, and at the end of winter, they started mating with the gold finches and the green finches, and the *bandooks* they gave birth to also caught the mission of wooing and the ungrateful fate of hired serenaders.

Like a thousand yellow postmen of love the males flew around singing, like yellow notes stuck to the branches of the trees, like a host of yellow cantors bearing an ancient supplication with no end and no beginning.

Nevertheless, Judith didn't grant his plea, and a whole year after their release, when the desperate birds returned to Jacob, admitted their failure, and asked for their old cages, the village's wrath was kindled. Rabinovitch's Judith, everyone said, had gone too far this time.

But despite the villagers' prophecy, Jacob didn't take his life. In the year that began with his release of the canaries and ended with their return, he had already stopped his public wooing. His notes no longer turned the village yellow and his figure crossing the street became a rare sight. Everyone was dazed and amazed and Jacob was calmer than ever. He let the canaries back into their old cages, but he didn't lock the doors anymore and the birds started coming and going to their hearts' content. They sang less now and Jacob heard only a flapping of many wings, like the rustle of blood a person sometimes hears when sleep won't come and he lies in the dark, counting memories and listening to the veins in his temples.

Sometimes Jacob climbed the hill near the village, stood there under the big doum-palm, and looked into the distance, as if wishing for someone to come. If the wind blew in the right direction you could hear the shouts and songs and melodies of the Italian prisoners-of-war in the camp, and Jacob listened and smiled knowingly to himself.

But usually he would go to the edge of the road, sit there on a stone, and wait. In great expectation, his skin quivered like a horse's hide, his eyes filled with tears from the dust, and his fingers were clasped. In those days, there was no bus stop there yet, and when they built it, it was decided to erect it where Jacob Sheinfeld sat, because drivers and passersby were already used to stopping there and exchanging a word or two with him, and an atmosphere of waiting, befitting a bus stop, already prevailed there.

When he returned home, he went into the canary house, cleaned the troughs of seeds that had sprouted and died, and washed the abandoned basins of the salt sediments that amassed on their sides.

'Only great plans and only great things,' he repeated to himself. 'Only great things influence great love.'

The empty cages with their open doors and the dry putrefaction in them told him that things yearned for really do wait until the world and the time are right. That knowledge was frightening, like the thoughts about the size of the universe and about the passage of time and about the invisible ropes of gravity, and all other thoughts where abysses are gaping at their feet and black lanes of fog trail behind them.

'Like the bud that waits and opens only on the exact day it has to,' he explained to me, pacing in the kitchen. He was impatient, like a poet seeking consolation in metaphors. 'Like on one day in winter, all the snails come out of the ground. Everybody in his own place. How does that happen, Zayde? How do they know? All kinds of people will tell you it's God. So I ask you, Zayde, doesn't the God of the Jews have anything more urgent to do than take care of them? But the light together

with the heat together with the time and together with the water
in the ground, and everything is right and everything is ready
and waiting, so the snail don't have no choice and he comes out.
And back then I said to myself, You, Jacob, you will prepare
everything just so, and she'll have to come.'

He took me out to the porch of his house. It was dark, but
Jacob pointed to the edge of the west, beyond the invisible ridge
of Mount Carmel, and declared: 'The Prophet Elijah knew all
those secrets a long time ago.'

If you put the wood right, he said, fire will come out of it by
itself. And if you hold all the ceremonies for the rain, the little
cloud will come and the drops will fall.

Now he got excited and sad at the same time, stood up and
sat down, wrung his old fingers, talked about the 'natural order',
and about the sublime expressions of that order: the force of
gravity of the earth, great, clutching, annihilating, embracing,
and making sure everything is in its place.

Things pull and push each other, he said. Trees don't walk.
Cows don't fly in the air. The water of the sea doesn't overflow
its basin. The stars, unlike humans, don't smash each other.

And because of those laws, he claimed, if you put all the pieces
of the mosaic together, the last, lost, longed-for piece would go
on and be set in its place.

'And that's how I understood what Menahem Rabinovitch
told me, the issue of the great love and great things. That if
the whole world is ready – the tables and the benches and the
wedding canopy and the dress and the food and the rabbi – then
the bride has to come, too. And then I knew that everything I
did before, with the canaries and the gifts and the notes and
the pleas, all of it was wrong. It wasn't her love I should have
chased, not her heart, not her body. I should just have prepared
the wedding. Prepared so good that she would have had to come.
At first I understood those things like in a dream, but then my fat
worker came to me, Joshua. And when he came, I knew: that's
it, Jacob, now you'll learn how to do everything that has to be
done for the wedding. Now you'll prepare everything that has
to be prepared for the wedding. And then everything will come
in its place, like it should.'

20

Rachel was sold to Globerman in the winter of 1940, in that week of the east wind that sometimes comes in early March and sometimes in mid-February, and always amazes the Valley with five turgid, rainy nights and six days of deep blue skies and fresh gleaming sun.

Judith took advantage of the third clear day and went to Haifa with Naomi to buy a few things for the house, and Moshe took advantage of their absence and sold the cow.

The heart and the mind, each in its own way, want to know why. But that question isn't important, and if it does have an answer, it doesn't teach us anything. For even if many of us won't achieve our heart's desire, only a few will release a thousand canaries for it, and a few sold a barren cow that was loved by the woman who worked on their farm.

Perhaps Moshe gave in, and maybe he rebelled, and possibly he wanted to show that he was boss? Or maybe he just needed money? As for me, I have no explanation for it, just as I have no explanation for many other human acts, except for what Globerman himself often repeated to me: 'A mensh trakht un Gott lakht – man makes plans and God laughs.'

And yet, even if the reasons are trivial, the results are important. Rachel was sold for slaughter, Mother rescued her and brought her back home, and nine months later, I, Zayde Rabinovitch, came into the world.

Naturally, the sale of Rachel was secret and hasty.

Rabinovitch, who was filled with a sudden boldness, and the dealer, whose lust for lucre overcame any other feeling that lodged in him, didn't shirk. This time, Globerman, who was always strict about counting money in front of the owner, stuck a messy and uncounted fistful of bills into Moshe's hand and wanted to get away fast with his plunder. He tied his rope to

Rachel's horns and waved his *baston* close to her nose because he feared that the barren cow – manly and unexpectedly strong – would attack him when he pulled the rope.

'On the face of a bull you can see what he's going to do, but with a *tumtum* like that you don't know anything,' he said to Moshe.

But without Judith, all of Rachel's strength left her. She followed the dealer at three paces of capitulation, and suddenly she bleated in a weepy voice and sat down on her behind in a human, spread-out position, as if all at once she had turned from a sturdy lad into a dead-tired old woman.

Rabinovitch and Globerman had enough experience to know that in such a case the cow was liable to hold them up for hours, and the two of them feared Judith's return and her rage.

'You've got to help me now, Rabinovitch!' said Globerman.

Usually the farmers only helped the dealer to lead the calves they sold him. When a milk cow was sold, her owner went home so as not to witness her being taken away, and if the cow was especially beloved, he would go far away into one of the fields, where he would talk to himself and the trees and the stones, or he would go to the middle of the village and bother people there until the dealer and his victim had gone and the bleatings had died out in the distance.

That was obvious and accepted, and the dealer never asked the dairyman's help. But this time Moshe jumped behind Rachel, wrapped her tail around his fist, and twisted it hard. The surprise and the pain made her jump and she got up and followed her purchaser.

At dusk, Naomi and Judith returned from Haifa. When they saw Rachel's empty place, Naomi started shouting and crying, but Judith told her, 'Go into the house now, Nomele,' and not another word did she say.

She milked with Moshe in a silence that dried his tongue and turned the joints of his fingers to stone so that he hurt the cows. Then she went into her corner and pulled the curtain over it.

Moshe, who had prepared himself for a fight and a quarrel and had filled his quiver with arguments and justifications, retreated to the house, to eat dinner with the children. Oded sat at the table with him, but Naomi lay in her bed with her eyes shut and was silent.

Oded said: 'Very good that you sold her, Father. She wasn't worth anything anyway.'

'Go to bed, Oded,' said Moshe.

He himself walked around the house for a while, then he went out and tramped back and forth in the mud next to the northern wall of the cowshed, and when he finally went in, he saw that Judith wasn't there. Worry and relief filled him, but didn't blend with one another, and so they oppressed him many times over. He returned to the house, lay down in his bed, and waited.

A gusty wind blew outside. The pungent smell of wet cypresses stood in the air. The eucalyptus swayed mighty arms.

Rain began to fall, drumming on the roof, humming grief in the gutters, silencing and swallowing other noises.

Moshe pricked up his ears and shut his eyes until he heard distant breathing, carried on the storm, and a banging that sounded like heavy hooves in the mud, approaching and not arriving. A few times he jumped up from his bed and went outside and finally he put on his boots and, clad only in his nightshirt, he ran into the rain through the fields to the eucalyptus forest.

The mud held his feet, the cold air singed his lungs, and when he got there, panting and tired, he didn't dare cross the forest. With heavy steps, he returned to his house, undressed, and lay down in his bed and clamped his eyelids shut.

'C'mon-c'mon-c'mon,' he heard, and also his own name – '*Maydele*' in his mother's mouth and 'Rabinovitch' in Judith's mouth and 'my Moshe' in his Tonya's mouth filled with water. But he didn't know if he really heard or maybe it was only the rain and the wind, maybe the leaves of the groaning eucalyptus, maybe the surging of pain in his own skull.

And when he went back out into the yard, naked and shivering with cold under the blanket he wrapped around himself, he didn't see anything there. And it was only about an hour later, when he had fallen asleep, that the bolt of the cowshed rang in its socket with the clear ring of unmistakable dreams, and Moshe understood that at long last he was sleeping, and two minutes later, when he wrapped himself in the blanket again and strode with a slow flight and eyes closed to the cowshed, he saw the two of them there, drenched and cold as ice.

Rachel, her nose steaming in the cold, stood in her usual place, her head leaning over to Judith, lying at her feet on the filthy cement floor, either sleeping or swooning.

'What is the cow doing here?' shouted Rabinovitch.

Judith didn't answer.

She was frozen, her skin bristling and her eyes cold and hateful as the eyes of a dead fish.

Moshe woke up. He ran home and found that the bundle of money the dealer had given him for Rachel was in its place.

His heart turned to stone. When he returned to the cowshed, Judith had already gotten up off the floor, lit the wood in the half-barrel, and was wiping Rachel with dry sacks.

The two of them were groaning with fatigue and cold.

'Where did you bring the cow from?' shouted Moshe.

Judith sniffled and her whole body shivered.

'That's none of your business, Rabinovitch, and don't raise your voice to me,' she murmured.

'What money did you pay him?'

'It didn't cost you a penny.' She wrung water out of her hair. 'I bought Rachel back, and now she's mine.'

'The dealer returned a cow?' exclaimed Moshe. 'The dealer has never returned a cow before. Who ever heard of such a thing?'

Judith didn't answer.

'You stole her!'

Judith laughed, and so much scorn and malice creaked in her laughter that Moshe was terrified of the truth that was closing in on him.

'If you didn't pay him with money, what did you pay him with?' His voice shook as if the answer was choking him even before he heard it.

'Now Rachel is mine,' answered Judith. 'Her milk you can take for the food she eats and for the place she takes, but this cow is mine now.'

'*Kurve*, whore, how did you pay for it? With your *pirde*?'
Moshe suddenly shouted, unexpectedly coarse and with a feeling
he didn't know was in him, and he didn't believe his lips and
tongue knew such vulgar words.

The words nailed Judith to the spot. Only her head moved as
if it were on a hinge, revolved slowly, and turned to him.

'I heard words like that once,' she said with complete calm,
picked up the pitchfork leaning against the wall and walked
toward him.

She didn't slow down and she didn't assault and she didn't
feint and she didn't threaten. She struck a blow with the pitchfork without any hatred, but only skill, and Moshe, who immediately understood that she didn't intend empty intimidation,
retreated, stumbled, and when he wanted to hold onto something
his foot slipped on the shovel of the dung runnel.

The blanket slid off his body and he fell on his back into the
frozen dung heap. Once again the pitchfork was aimed at him
in that efficient and practical way of thrusting into a pile of hay,
and this time he didn't manage to get out of the way and one of
the tines pierced his arm.

The wound was deep and surprising and Moshe yelled in
pain, but Judith's face remained calm and chill. She extracted
the pitchfork from the flesh of his arm and when she brandished
it a third time, Moshe rolled aside, stood up naked, and fled the
cowshed.

In the house, he locked the door, collapsed onto the floor, and
then crept and washed the blood and mud and dung off his body,
and poured alcohol on his wound. It wasn't weakness that shook
his body, but the novelty of it. He bandaged his arm, lay down
in his bed, and slowly understood that the fingers choking his
throat when he wanted to swallow or sleep were not anger or
fear, but the simple stroking of jealousy. An alien and strange
feeling was this envy, which he had never felt in his life, either.

Once again he fell asleep, and once again he woke up, because
he didn't hear Judith's wailing and wondered why, and wanted
to get up and go back to the cowshed, but the pain in his arm
and the pounding swelling under it reminded him of what had
happened and told him that he better stay in his bed. He closed

his eyes and started dreaming that he was choked by something pressing on his chest, but there wasn't anything there, only the hands of the angel and the dream of his strong thighs clasping his body, and his nipples searing his chest with a double brand of possession, and his finger that was laid on his face and said to him, 'Shaa . . . shaa . . . sleep now, shaa . . .'

Lips whispered in his neck, 'Sorry,' and a warm wet silk grazed and beat and stroked his flesh pleasantly, and the delight was so great that the dream went on even after he opened his eyes, and now the pain in his wounded arm became unbearable and his fever rose high.

A good, heavy smell, forgotten and remembered at the same time, covered his face like a spread-out dress.

'Who are you?' he asked, and no woman answered.

Outside, the storm had stopped now and robins began the chirping of night's end. One from Tonya's pomegranate tree and his foe from Papish's yard. Rabinovitch knew he was left alone and could sleep another hour. But when he woke up the second time, the sun had already crossed the windowsill and the sparrows and crows had already stopped singing the dawn song and the doves had already returned from the mash warehouse of the village and were now humming the hum of the full gullet, and the air was already clear and warm and dry and only the wet smell of the earth wafting from his body and from the open window testified to him.

Judith served him a big cup of tea with lemon in bed, examined his wound, and said: 'Don't get out of bed today, Moshe, I've already milked for you.'

'All by yourself?' asked Moshe.

'I went at dawn to Sheinfeld and he came and helped me,' she said.

From that night on, Judith's wailing was no longer heard.

'There are women who feel it the minute they get pregnant,' Naomi told me. 'And I'm sure that's how it was with her. Like an animal she was in those kinds of things. Even the time of ovulation she knew exactly to the second. She told me that herself, when I got my first period and she gave me a woman's talk. So, if she slept with the three of them that night, or if she got pregnant without sleeping with anyone, only she knew exactly how that happened. But now, Zayde, it really doesn't matter anymore. That secret of hers she also took with her to the grave. It's very crowded, Zayde, in your mother's grave, with so many secrets.'

One way or another, the wailing wasn't heard anymore. There were those who heard laughter rising from the cowshed and there were those who didn't hear anything, but everyone understood that something had happened, and in the village they started talking.

As usual with us, you don't know if reality nourished rumours or vice versa, but the proof increased and became clear: the whites of Judith's eyes grew turgid, her breasts rose, her waist hadn't yet swelled, but several women saw her gathering and eating wood sorrel.

And one morning, about two and a half months after that night, when Moshe entered the cowshed and saw her leaning over Rachel's neck and throwing up in the runnel, he knew that all the gossips were right.

A few weeks later, Globerman and Sheinfeld came to him, as if they had agreed on something, and said: 'It can't be, Rabinovitch, that Judith will bring up a baby among the cows.'

The three of them went to the cowshed to talk with her, but Judith said she felt good and comfortable in her corner there, close to her beloved Rachel. So the three men looked into one another's eyes, went into the house, and started arguing and measuring and drafting plans. And the next day, Globerman and Sheinfeld went to the city in the truck and Moshe Rabinovitch went out and started digging ditches for foundations.

In the afternoon, the truck returned, bowed down under a burden of sacks of cement and sand and gravel and loaded with rubber bags and tools and boards for casting, and Globerman went into the cowshed, took out his and Judith's bottles of grappa and cognac – 'It's not good for our child in the belly' – and filled the closet with flowered maternity dresses, dried fruit, his *pettitt furs* and sausages.

Construction of the new cowshed went on for about two

months, and after the cows were transferred there, Rabinovitch took the twenty-pound hammer and destroyed all the concrete stalls and troughs in the old cowshed, Sheinfeld and Globerman cleared out the shards, and in the next weeks, they built new internal walls that created two rooms and a kitchen and shower, broke out some more windows, and stretched a net for a new ceiling.

Finally, the owner of the store who had sold them all the building material appeared, and thus the City Papish, the alleged brother of the Village Papish, was revealed and confirmed and went from a joke to reality right before the eyes of the whole village. The City Papish had shouted arguments with his brother about every subject in the world and meanwhile he floored and whitewashed and plastered the walls and stretched electrical cables and water pipes, which breathed life into the structure and made it a house, the house I was born in, and in it my mother brought me up, this is the house that was once a cowshed, whose bricks subdue its memories, and a soft smell of milk rises from its walls.

That whole time, the men didn't talk much, but in the shrunken space of the cowshed, the three of them were very close to one another. Sometimes their shoulders touched, sometimes their hands, and when the dealer brought a cast-iron stove from the Druze village on the mountain, he called Moshe, who carried it in his arms from the truck to the cowshed, and Jacob went and cut down two trees in his abandoned citrus grove and brought a full load of heating logs.

'That's for you, Judith,' he said. 'Oranges burn strong and give a good smell.'

21

'Who got her pregnant?' Naomi asked Oded.

'Her? All of them!' answered Oded.

'Who got her pregnant?' Naomi asked her father.

'Nobody,' said Moshe.

'Who got you pregnant?' Naomi asked Judith.

'A *nafka mina*,' said Judith, and when Naomi persisted and kept investigating and wept, she finally said to her: 'I got pregnant by myself, Nomele, by myself.'

'You remember the day you were born here? You remember, Zayde?'

'Nobody remembers the day he was born.'

'I remember. I was here.'

'I know.'

'Maybe I'll stay with you here and not go back to Jerusalem?'

'You've got a child, Naomi, and you've got a husband in Jerusalem.'

Warm smells of a village night rose in my window. My heart soared from my rib cage and a rustle of clothes taken off was heard in the dark.

'Don't turn on the light,' she said, because she didn't know that my eyes were closed.

She got into my bed and asked: 'What's your name?'

'Zayde,' I said.

Outside, the blackbirds started chanting, their voices melting the chill of dawn and painting the east with the orange of their beaks.

'Your eyes have become blue, Zayde,' said Naomi. 'Open them and you'll see yourself.'

An old grief looked out of her eyes. Her tears gleamed. She got out of bed, gleaming in the dark of the room.

'In the middle of class, I got up and ran here. She was already on the floor and that smell was in the air, like the smell of Uncle Menahem in the fall, but it was from Judith's water, which had already broke. The smell of that water only women and doctors know.'

'Don't be scared, Nomele,' said Judith. 'Don't call anybody, go to the house and bring clean sheets and towels.'

Her face was contorted with pain.

'Don't die,' shouted Naomi. 'Don't die!'

And the smile turned Judith's lips pale.

'You don't die from this,' she said. 'You just live more.'

And she started laughing and groaning: 'Oy, how much I'll live now, Nomele, oy, how much I'll live now.'

In their mud dwellings in the corner of the roof, the swallow fledglings shrieked and gaped the red of their jaws. Rachel, in the cow yard, bleated and butted the iron door.

'And now,' said Judith, 'the *kurve* will give birth to a new little girl.'

Lying on her back, she rolled her dress over her belly, dug her heels into the floor, spread her thighs, and raised her behind in the air.

'Fast!' she ordered. 'Put the sheet under me.'

Naomi looked terrified into her gaping groin, which seemed to be shouting.

'What do you see there, Naomi?' asked Judith.

'Like a wall inside,' said Naomi.

'That's her head, right away she'll start coming out and you'll help her very very slow. Just don't worry, Nomele, in just one more little minute she'll come out. It'll be an easy birth. Just wait for her with your hands and you'll catch her.'

'It's boy,' said Naomi.

'And then she simply tore her dress,' she told me, her words and her lips in my neck and the warmth of her thigh on my belly, 'and the buttons flew into the air, and she said: "Fast, Nomele, fast, I can't anymore, put him on my chest." And I put you on her chest, the white chest of a dove she had, and then she wailed.'

Naomi wanted to flee from the cowshed, for until that moment, Judith was cool and very decisive, while now, the final night wailings were extracted from the depths of her belly and came out of her mouth.

She stepped back, wiping her sticky hands on one another until the wall supported her back, looking at the woman twisting in the swamp of straw and blood, her scream running out of her throat and her son clasped in her arms.

Sheinfeld, Rabinovitch, and Globerman came to the circumcision in their best clothes and didn't leave me for a minute.

Jacob, who didn't know how to sew then, bought me some baby layettes.

Moshe Rabinovitch built me a cradle that could be stood on legs and also hung from the rafter.

And Globerman, true to his way and his values, brought a big bundle of bills, wet his finger with saliva and started dividing them into five small piles, and called out to the guests: 'One for the child, one for the mother, one for the father, one for the father, one for the father . . .' Until the Village Papish and the City Papish stood up and shouted at him: 'Give the present already and shut up!'

22

Shlaf meyn Zaydele, meyn kleyne,
shlaf meyn kind un her tsikh tsu,
ot dos feygele dos kleyne,
iz keyn andere vie du.

Sleep, my Zayde, sleep, my little one,
listen to your mama, little one, do,
for that bird, that little bird,
it is you, my child, O, it is you.

'If the Angel of Death comes and sees a little boy named Zayde, he understands at once that there's a mistake here and goes to somebody else.'

And I, with complete faith in the name she gave me, grew up and became a man, convinced that on the day I became a grandfather and justified my name, the Angel of Death would come to me, his patience run out, his face flushed with the wrath of the deceived, would call me by my right name and pour out my life on the ground.

*   *   *

I remember small, very clear pictures, pictures of infancy.

Once I woke up at night and saw her lying on her back. It was a hot summer night, the sheet had slipped off her, her arms were spread out, her chest was bared. The severity of her face had departed. Even the line on the bridge of her nose was softened.

I got up to cover her, and when the sheet hovered over her body, she stretched and relaxed and smiled in her sleep and waves seemed to pass over her naked flesh. I fluttered the sheet again and let it drop onto her until a soft sigh escaped from her throat and when I raised the sheet a third time, her eyes suddenly opened. They were hard and clear, just like her voice, which said: 'Enough, Zayde, go to sleep.'

I said: 'But I want it nice for you.'

I remember how Mother got up and took my arm and led me firmly to my bed and went back and lay down in her bed and both of us knew that we were both awake.

And I remember that Jacob taught me to read and write when I was three and a half years old, after I complained that I was the only one who couldn't read Uncle Menahem's springtime notes.

And I remember that Globerman gave me thin, salted, very tasty slices of raw meat to suck.

And I also remember the game of the 'awful bear' with Moshe and the first time I fell out of the eucalyptus tree. Everybody, including me, was sure I was dead, and when I opened my eyes and sought God and the angels, Mother said to me: 'Get up, Zayde, nothing happened.'

Her stories penetrated my memories and were decanted into them. The she-ass, for instance, died of old age even before I was born, but I clearly remember how she was clever enough to steal barley from the horse: when the horse gathered a mouthful of barley, she bit his neck. He tried to bite her back and the seeds fell out of his mouth and the she-ass gathered them up from the floor.

'And I remember that, too,' said Naomi. 'And I also remember how we used to eat pomegranates together – first we sat down on the rock and then on the walk Father paved for her. And I remember how she used to send me to catch doves and how she used to kill them. She pulled their necks with two fingers until there was a kind of little click, and then she'd bite her lower lip between her teeth.'

We were standing next to the crows' meeting tree in the cemetery of the German Colony in Jerusalem, and Naomi laughed
and challenged me to a tree-climbing contest. 'At falling you're
better, but at climbing I'll beat you.'

And then she said: 'I have to visit Meir's mother. Will you come
with me, Zayde? She lives nearby.'

Naomi called her mother-in-law 'Meir's mother' or 'Mrs
Klebanov', so I don't know her first name. Maybe I did know
it when I was five and Naomi and Meir got married, and
since then I've managed to forget it. In her garden, she had
a fabulous rosebush, a thin old almond tree, and a creeping
honeysuckle.

The rosebush was unique. It was tall as a tree and had thorns
like a cat's claws. So big and sturdy it was that it didn't need to be
tended or watered, and it smelled so strong that people stopped
by it, thunder-struck, and gnats swooned in the deep tangles of
its flowers.

Even during the days of war and siege, when all the flower
gardens died of thirst, as Mrs Klebanov related proudly, its leaves
turned green and didn't wither.

Mrs Klebanov was a widow, and even though she was determined to age fast, her features preserved the lines of an old
beauty, the kind that waits for deliverance.

'I remember you,' she said. 'You're the worker's son. You were
a little boy at Meir's wedding, weren't you?'

'I was also at that wedding,' said Naomi. 'Me you don't
remember?'

'You've got a funny name, don't you?' Mrs Klebanov questioned me.

'My name is Zayde,' I said.

'And how old are you?'

At that time, I was twenty-three.

'A person your age whose name is Zayde, he can only be a
liar,' Mrs Klebanov decreed. 'Tell me, please, you lived there
in the cowshed with the cows, you and your mother, didn't
you?'

'Something like that,' I said. 'I didn't really live with the cows,
but in a house that used to be a cowshed.'

'That sounds very interesting,' concluded Mrs Klebanov. 'I remember talking about that afterwards with my husband's relatives. A woman with a child and she lived with the cows.'

From the porch came a strange metallic banging, and the echo that answered it was even louder than the banging itself.

'That's the birds pecking the water tank. They're the only ones who come visit me,' grumbled Meir's mother.

I glanced out the window. On the porch a big tank stood on four blocks. A Jerusalem water storage in case of emergency. Mrs Klebanov would scatter breadcrumbs on it and the sparrows would gather and peck them off the tin cover. They were grateful, as befits small hungry birds who live in a cold, hard-hearted, close-fisted city, and Mrs Klebanov was pleased to see the gratitude beaming from their round eyes. The echo that answered the banging of their beaks, she said, told her how much water was left in the tank.

Sometimes a heavier and stronger beak was heard, and she knew that the crow from the big cypress had come and chased the sparrows away and was pecking at their bread.

Mrs Klebanov didn't like black animals bigger than her hand. She immediately burst onto the porch, justice trampling at her side and a bristling broom in her right hand. With a shout of 'Get out of here! *Kishta!* Get lost!' she got rid of the thief.

Her face flushed, she returned to the room and went to the kitchen to calm down and make us some tea. Naomi whispered to me that her mother-in-law usually shooed dogs away in Hebrew, goats in Arabic, and cats in Yiddish, but with crows, she didn't know what nation they belonged to or what language they spoke. So she used them all.

We drank the tea, which was sweet and tasty and very hot, and we left.

'To take her to Jerusalem is like plucking a flower from the earth and throwing it onto the road to get run over,' Oded told me.

The time that had passed since his sister married Meir hadn't blunted his anger. Often, ever since I was a little boy, he drove me in the village truck to visit them in Jerusalem. Sleepy and excited, I would run in the dark to the dairy. Oded allowed me to climb up onto the tank and check the lids and, as we were leaving the village, to pull the cable of the horn over his left shoulder.

Then I would fall asleep and not wake up until dawn, when Oded would manoeuvre the gearstick at the entrance to the yard of Tnuva, the marketing cooperative, in Jerusalem. Naomi was already standing there waving, Oded replied with a loud honk of greeting, and the supervisor rushed out of his office and shouted: 'Shut up, pleesh! Don't hong the horn! At five in the morning, people are shtill shleeping in Jerushalem!' And Ezriel, the driver of Kfar Vitkin, shouted: 'Shamshon, Shamshon, you sut up yourshelf!'

Oded stopped with a mighty gasp, jumped out of the horse cabin and hugged his sister, and immediately went back to the cabin and took out the package that Judith had sent her from the village, which was always wrapped in brown packing paper cut from a powdered milk sack and tied with a rope, and in it were fruits and vegetables, pomegranates in season, sour cream and cheese and eggs and a letter.

'That's from home, Naomi. Here, this is just for you, you hear? Eat it all up yourself and don't give him anything. I'm serious, why are you laughing?'

'If I had been there when he came, it wouldn't have wound up like this,' he declared. 'He wouldn't have taken her, she wouldn't have gone with him, he wouldn't have even gotten into the yard. Came from the fields, that lowlife, like a jackal who comes to steal from the chicken coop. I don't understand how your heroine of a mother didn't catch on and throw him out of there.'

And two or three days later, on my way back to the village, I would always wake up there, when the big truck came out of Wadi Milek, and the Valley, warm and beloved and spacious, was spread out before me again. Oded told me again about the train that used to run there and about the ravenous herds the Arabs used to set loose on the village fields, 'and we'd go out to them and drive them away with whips', and about the old anti-aircraft posts of the English and the adventures of Police Sergeant Shvili, and the legend about the destroyed stone chimney in the field, remnant of the Italian POW camp, whose guards didn't do any work and smells of cooking, and how songs were always rising from there.

'You'll write about all those things, Zayde, right?' he yelled.

23

Jacob boiled a pot of water on the fire, cracked an egg into the palm of his hand, slipped the white between his spread fingers, and put the yolk into the bowl. A little wine, a little sugar, and the whisk was gleaming in his hand, steam rose, and the warmth emitted the smell of wine in the air.

'The yolk of the egg,' he said, 'that's strength and that's mother and that's life.'

His hand, so quick and steady over the bowl, started shaking as his finger began moving in it and bringing tastes up from it.

'Don't ever forget me,' he said suddenly.

'Of course not,' I said.

'And Globerman, too, don't forget him, and Rabinovitch, too, don't forget.'

'You tired, Jacob? You want me to go now?'

'Open, if you please, the door of the closet.'

I opened it.

'Take out, if you please, the box,' he said.

A white cardboard box, flat and long, was there, standing like a ghost behind the clothes hanging up. I remembered it and I knew what was inside it.

'Open it,' said Jacob.

A fog of an old white cloth filled the box.

'That's your mother's wedding gown.' His voice shook. 'You remember it? With my own hands, I sewed it.'

My body recoiled and my eyes became moist. Even though Mother wore it for only a few minutes, the empty dress seemed like an empty skin she sloughed off in the field, waiting for the flesh of its mistress, just like me and like Jacob.

'On the way to me she was, with that dress on her, and her

inside it, and something all of a sudden happened. Everybody was sitting at the tables and waiting for her, and you, Zayde, came instead of her. A little boy of ten with that box in your hand with that dress inside, you don't remember? You came and you gave it to me in front of the whole village and you ran away without looking in my eyes. And afterwards, all the guests left and I went into the house and I closed the door and I fell down on the bed with that bridal gown, and all the dishes, all the nice German china, still stayed outside on the tables for the sun and the flies. A whole week I lay like that. Not sleeping, not dreaming, and my heart was as cold as ice, and when they came back they came back right before the big snow, of February nineteen hundred and fifty. You was a little boy then, Zayde, but you must remember that snow. Who doesn't remember the big snow of nineteen hundred and fifty? All over the country it was. Even in the Jordan Valley a few inches fell. What can I tell you, that was really some big surprise. Here in the village trees broke, chickens died, two calves froze, in the transit camp not far from here, a few new immigrants were killed because the whole roof of the kitchen fell on their head. But for us, who came from snows fifteen feet deep and sleds with three horses and wolves as big as calves, and we'd stick our tongue on the iron handle of the well that was so cold – for us that snow was child's play. Here there's snow? Here there's sleds? Here there's wolves? Here we built sleds for mud to take the milk to the dairy, and once the Village Papish shot a wolf who came into the yard with the geese. What can I tell you, Zayde, Papish called it a wolf, but it was as big as a cat. If he hadn't said wolf, I would have said it was a jackal, maximum. Never mind a little bit of snow in Jerusalem or in Safed, but here? In this little village? In this hot valley? Who would even dream of such a thing? Who was ready? Especially the trees weren't ready, and especially that eucalyptus. That's a tree for snow? I ask you, Zayde, a eucalyptus like that from Australia, is that a tree for snow? The apple tree and the cherry tree and the *beryozka*, the birch tree, them I saw standing in the snow, but a eucalyptus like that, with its wet and soft flesh, and its leaves stay in the wintertime, and it holds a lot more snow than what it can take on, it just broke. One flake and another flake and another flake and another flake, until the last flake that said: *Itzt!* Now! And the whole big branch at the top broke and fell down, and the creak they heard all over the village, and the wind whistling in the leaves when it fell down, they heard that, too, and then the blow they heard. And everybody got up and ran there. 'Cause who didn't know Rabinovitch's eucalyptus, with the crows' nest in the top, you used to climb up to them when you were a little boy, and Globerman and Rabinovitch and I used to walk around like lunatics below worrying that God forbid, you'll fall, and Judith used to laugh because a child named Zayde, nothing will happen to him. Only now you should watch out with your name, 'cause you're not a little boy anymore, and the Angel of Death won't forgive you for cheating him. He's waiting and waiting and waiting until the moment comes. Everybody, I sometimes think, has his own Angel of Death. He's born with you and he lives next to you and he waits for you all your life, and because of that, if somebody really is old, he'll get a lot more years 'cause his Angel of Death isn't so young anymore, either, and he doesn't see so good, either, and his own hands shake, too, and in the morning he also gets up with aches all over his body, and finally, when he succeeds at last, he dies himself one minute after he kills you, like a bee that stings and also drops dead. And here's a woman alone, your mother, not a great beauty, but with an open, clear face, like a window looking on the garden. And the line of pain she had between her eyebrows, that's the line of a woman whose love cut her flesh, too, and not only her skin, and if you see her milking a cow or cutting vegetables for a salad or washing a child, you right away understand how good those hands can be. And how come I fell in love with her, you ask again? What did I want from her, you want to know? And anyway what does a person like me want from a woman? So excuse me, Zayde, it's not the *tukhis* he wants and it's not the *tsitskes* he wants, and beauty is already starting not to be so interesting, and the electricity is already starting to run out, and not only the mind, the whole body is starting to be bored and like Globerman used to say: from most girls the *shvantz* already yawns aloud. So good hands, that's what he wants. Good hands of a woman to caress him, to stir the scum of the basin of his soul, hands like water passing, speaking, I'm here, Jacob, I'm here, shaa . . . sleep now, Jacob, you're not alone, shaa . . . Jacob . . . shaa. Sleep.'

Fourth Meal

1

The fourth meal Jacob made for me in 1981, a few weeks after his death.

A quiet and simple death it was. The death of someone whose soul was slowly removed, didn't flee from his rib cage, didn't flare up and flicker out like hemp, and wasn't ripped out of his flesh. His regular taxicab driver found him fully clothed, lying on the sofa in the living room. He said that Jacob's face was calm and his body was already cold but still soft, and neither struggle nor pain was obvious either in his expression or in his position.

'I'm not a young man, either,' the driver told me, 'and that's the kind of death I'd wish for myself.'

I was in Jerusalem when Jacob died. I lay awake in the guest room of Naomi and Meir's house, and all of a sudden the phone rang and lopped off their nighttime conversation. They always conversed at night, I always listened to their conversation, and I never managed to fish up words from the stream of quiet, bitter murmuring.

That was no longer the small apartment in the housing project where I had visited them in my childhood, but the handsome, spacious stone house where they live now. Once Naomi and Meir used to sleep in one twin bed in one room, then in one double bed in one room, then in two twin beds in one room, and now they sleep in two double beds in two separate rooms. That's also a way to measure the passage of time.

As is always my habit, I lay and watched the door that won't open anymore and a triangular blade of light that won't come from it, won't slice and won't serve up to my eyes the golden slice of a body and a corridor.

Whenever Jacob would describe the young girls doing laundry

in the river and would declare proudly that that was 'the eternal picture of love', I thought of that eternal picture of mine, of the woman at night, her cheek moist, her waist cut out and her skin glowing. I wanted to return to that room and whistle to that time to come back, and to see again that naked body glowing in the dark that will never return.

But innocence has already left my flesh, youth has forsaken her flesh, and anyway – there's nothing more miserable in the world than restoring. Better than that is imagination, and better than imagination is fiction, and better than all three of them is memory.

Meir picked up the phone. 'Yes,' I heard him say, 'he's here.' And he immediately called out: 'It's for you, Zayde. And please tell whoever it is that it's four in the morning.'

'I'm here at Tnuva Jerusalem,' said Oded on the other end of the line. 'I thought you might want to know. Sheinfeld died.'

'When?' I asked, surprised by the sharp pain that stabbed me in the stomach.

'Yesterday morning.'

'Why didn't they tell me? Why didn't they call before?'

'Who is this "they"? Who exactly should they have called?' asked Oded sharply. And then he said: 'They already buried him. Yesterday afternoon.'

'When are you going back to the village?'

'Wait for me at the exit from the city. I'll be done here in half an hour.'

All the way I thought about that one thing. About the secret only we knew, only she and I, the secret of her final refusal of his love. Ever since the day she died, I had been trying to work up enough strength to reveal it to Jacob. I told him as I walked in the street, my lips moving and my voice inaudible, I whispered it into the old observation-box I had already outgrown, I shouted it into the distant forest, my mouth wide open and my voice horrible, but the deed itself I couldn't perform.

Oded, who sensed how repentant and agitated I was, didn't talk to me all the way back.

Even when I suddenly said aloud, 'It's better this way. If I had told him, he would have died a long time ago,' he pretended that the roar of the motor swallowed up my confession, and didn't respond.

A few days later, I was summoned to a lawyer's office in Haifa and informed that the beautiful house on Oak Street in Tivon, its garden, its kitchen, and everything in it belonged to me.

'What will you do with the house?' the lawyer asked me.

'I'll rent it out,' I said.

'I'd be glad to rent it from you.'

'In ten days you can move in.'

The lawyer lowered his eyes and cleared his throat. 'In the kitchen, there's a picture of a woman on the wall,' he said in embarrassment. 'I'd be grateful to you if you could leave it hanging there.'

'Did you know her?' I asked.

'Mrs Green? Not in her youth, unfortunately, but in her old age,' he said. 'I was their lawyer, hers and Mr Green's. Years ago, when she passed away and I summoned Mr Sheinfeld here and gave him the keys to the house she had bequeathed him, he told me that he was her first husband. I must admit I was surprised. And now you're inheriting that house, Mr Rabinovitch. Excuse me, please, if I ask you a personal question: how are you related to that family?'

That night, Mr Rabinovitch slept in his new house.

As usual, he fell asleep only at dawn and didn't have any dreams.

The next day, there was a loud knock on the door.

'Who's there?' asked Mr Rabinovitch.

'From the store.'

A young man who smelled of bay leaves and sausage came in. He seemed to know the place well. He headed straight for the kitchen, put a few wrapped packages in the refrigerator, vegetables and fruits in their bins, the bottles rang in their places.

'No charge for this,' he announced, and on the table he left the store's business card and a sealed white envelope with my name on it.

At the door, he turned to me, took a deep breath, and said:

'We're very sorry, Mr Rabinovitch Zayde. Mr Sheinfeld Jacob was a good man and he really knew a lot about food. He couldn't say the names of wine, but his frying pan laughed and his knife danced in his hand. My boss used to go just to smell the air near this house whenever he would cook, and then he would come back to the store and say: It's an honour for us to sell groceries to Mr Sheinfeld Jacob, because he's a person who can cook even with three copper pots at the same time. My boss also asked me to tell you that if you, Mr Rabinovitch Zayde, stay to live here, we'll be glad to serve you, too.'

The fellow concluded his speech, which was delivered in one breath, and left.

Mr Rabinovitch Zayde started searching and rummaging around.

In the envelope was a recipe for preparing the fourth meal.

In the drawer of the nightstand next to the bed waited Mother's blue kerchief.

Her splendid wedding gown hung in the closet, outside the shell of its box. White, smooth, and odourless.

Mr Rabinovitch Zayde took it out of there, spread it on the bed, sat down in the big easy chair, and fell asleep.

2

How clear the memories are: the maple leaves turned yellow and dropped, and like amputated hands were swept up in the water. Farmers dismantled the net trap for geese and collected from the roofs the fruit they had placed there to dry.

How regular things are: a wind came from the north, thin sheets of clouds, a first snow fell, and in the morning wolf tracks came very close to the village houses.

The earth revolved. The winter ended. How obedient are the spring birds: the nightingales of the reeds sang, the apple blossom wafted its train and bridesmaid bees caught it, right in front of

Jacob's eyes white butterflies moved to and fro, drunk, caught
in the webs of his memory.

Gold and green prevailed. The sun ascended, and already –
how familiar, how handsome are the pictures – a tiny kingfisher
hovered over its reflection, a wind capered in the leaves of the
birches, the girls came out to launder clothes and bedsheets on
the rock at the bend of the channel.

Then, Jacob told me, the basic colours of love were painted
in his heart, for in the love of a little boy, he stated, wonder
is greater than lust, amazement is greater than jealousy, and
greater than all the loves that will come, for it is as strong as
the whole body and as heavy.

In those childhood days, he added, he loved not only one
woman, but all women, and he loved the earth that bears the
yearning of their weight, and the sky that forms a canopy over
the splendour of their heads, and the One God of the Jews, who
put them on his doorstep.

He lusted for their knees bent on the black slate. Their breasts
sang to him from the cages of their blouses. The shining eddies
of water kept on getting entangled in his heart. The place and the
angle made it look like the girls were floating on great expanses
of water gilded by the sun. The wind played with the dresses,
tightened, softened, outlined.

'The eternal picture of love,' Jacob repeated to me, enjoying
not only the memory but also the expression his clumsy tongue
had managed to shape.

3

I have no penchant for cooking and no special interest in food.
Like everybody else, I, too, enjoy a good meal, but I don't
delve into the mysteries of how it's made, I don't wonder
about its ingredients, I won't travel especially for it. I believe
in Globerman's decree: 'Good food is food you clean your plate
afterwards with a piece of bread, period.'

The table awaited me, flat and patient. The big white plates that were now mine were gleaming on it. The copper pots reddened like suns setting on the wall. In the cabinet the knives held their breath. Which of them will be chosen by the new hand that will open the drawer?

I hung Jacob's recipe in front of me, and I tied his apron around my waist.

At first I was afraid because all I knew about cooking, as I said, was summed up in Moshe's and my simple meal: scrambled eggs, salad, mashed potatoes, and boiled chicken. But Jacob's instructions were simple, the meat was obedient, the seasonings and vegetables were arranged and ready. The ladles moved in my hands by themselves, the skillet and the pot responded to me, and I quickly felt confident enough to control more than one burner at the same time.

Joy and mourning were not blended in my heart. The steam and the drops of oil didn't touch one another. One next to another, things happened, neighbours in the same box of time. I cut while I fried, I stirred while I squeezed, I smiled in time of grief, I steamed, I mixed, I sprinkled, I boiled, I remembered, I cried, I seasoned.

And when I finished, I finished with a measure of ceremony, which people allow themselves when they're all alone. With a spin on my heels, I untied the apron, bowed, and turned off the burners.

From the wall, Rebecca looked at me with a curiosity whose meaning I didn't understand until I recalled that I was now much older than she.

'*Ess, meyn kind*,' I said to her, mocking, and served myself the last meal.

4

'What did she have inside her, what was under the skin, what are the secrets a woman remembers not in her head but in her flesh – that nobody knows? Even you, Zayde, don't know nothing about your mother. What do you know? That she came on a train and raised Rabinovitch's kids, and cooked and laundered and washed and rinsed and milked and did everything a woman does in the village, but she lived by herself in the cowshed and at night she wailed. That's all you know. Sometimes I thought she came here to atone for something. And her calf she also raised, how come a person raises an animal like that and calls her Rachel, if not for forgiveness? But never did you hear a word from her and nothing did you see on her face. Her face was open like a window looking on the garden, but on the other hand it didn't reveal nothing to you. That was her way of hiding. She was hiding a lot back then, and I'm still hiding a lot for her today. What did you think, that I told everything? Rabinovitch maybe knew something, but he'd never rummage around in such things, and he also lived for so many years inside his own disaster that other people's disasters didn't interest him no more. Only once, when somebody came to the committee complaining about her wailing in the night, Rabinovitch came to the secretary's office and this is what he said: "Do those screams dry up your cows? No? So what do you care and what business is it of yours? Everybody screams, Reuben screams loud and Simon screams quiet." That's what he said and then he turned around and left. At first I didn't understand who was that Reuben and that Simon, until the Village Papish explained to me that those are names you give for example. And then I thought to myself that a name like Jacob is never going to be an example for nothing. And every night she'd cry like that until your heart would break. And sounds at night, those are things you can't hide. It's not like some Zayde that you can't tell who his father

is. It's not like a woman's secrets – where did you come from?
Who do you love? All those secrets that if they don't leave signs
on the flesh, so where do they leave them? On the soul? What
sign can you leave on the soul? Sounds like that wait all day to
be heard at night. She used to lie in the cowshed, next to her
cow, one chews the cud of clover and the other chews the cud of
memories, and that wailing . . . every night . . . like the soul of a
wolf it flew over the village, rising, and falling, and seeking . . .
and seeking . . . what can I tell you, Zayde – there were people
here, no need to mention names, who said: if Rabinovitch's
Judith goes on wailing like that, the jackals will come to the
village to look for their relatives. And stories were going around,
one nicer than the next. One said it was some woman's thing,
pains men can't possibly understand in places they don't have.
One said it was matters of love, one said it was just regrets in
sleep, see, everybody regrets all kinds of things, big things or
little things, and there are people who regret quietly and there
are people who regret with screams and there are people that
all they do in life is just regret. I once knew a *goyish* carpenter
who sometimes regretted something he ate and sometimes he
regretted somebody he loved, and sometimes what he said, and
sometimes what he did. Is there any lack of reasons for people
to regret? Sometimes he would come to people's houses to redo
some commode he made them a week before, and twice they
caught him in the cemetery digging 'cause he regretted the wood
he made the coffin out of, and two or three times a year he would
change his name, and leave the old name to deal with all the old
problems, like a snake sheds its old skin in the field. See, Zayde,
you always used to complain about your name when you were
a child, so how come you didn't change it? See, you could have
gone to the government, too, and said: Don't want to be Zayde
no more. Want to be Gershon, want to be Solomon. Want to
be Jacob. It would be great if you were Jacob. But that's very
dangerous, 'cause names like mine and yours are Fate. With
names like ours you don't fool around.'

5

It was the end of the world war, and one night a strange and bizarre man appeared at Jacob Sheinfeld's house.

'That was a very weird guest, but a guest who couldn't come by chance. Right away I understood that he was sent. Like her and like the viper and like the albino accountant. And just like them, he came from the fields and not from the highway.'

One way or another, a hasty and pleading finger knocked on the door of his house, and when he opened it, a fat and ugly giant stood there in the dark, his sparse hair pulled back and his eyes small and scared like the eyes of a mouse.

The man wore blue overalls which Jacob recognized immediately as the clothes of the Italian prisoners-of-war, from the camp the English had set up not far from the village. The POWs in their blue garments were often seen strolling in the fields. They had a breach in the fence that everybody knew about, and through it they went out, picked some herbs for seasoning, and romped like children.

But the eyes of that POW scurried about in their sockets and his skin was flooded with sweat. He knelt down and, puffing and scared, said in Hebrew: 'They're after me. Hide me here, please.'

'Who's after you?' asked Jacob.

'Hide me, sir,' the POW repeated. 'Just one night, please.'

'Who are you? Are you a Jew? How do you know our language?' asked Jacob suspiciously.

'I can speak any language I hear,' said the man, and Jacob was amazed because now the POW was speaking to him in his own voice. 'If you like, I'll teach you, too. Just let me come in and close the door and I'll tell you everything inside.'

'Can't just let a person in like that,' Jacob persisted. 'I've got to inform somebody.'

The man straightened up to his full height, pushed Jacob inside gently but firmly, followed him in, and closed the door.

'Don't inform, don't tell,' he pleaded.

'And you know, Zayde, how come I felt sorry for him? Not because he escaped from the POW camp and not because he suddenly spoke in my voice. But because he sat down at the table and three fingers he put into the bowl of salt and put some for himself on the palm of his other hand and from there he licked the salt with his tongue just like a cow from her stone in the trough. I knew that very well. A person who does that is really weak and in despair. My mother used to do that in her last year before she died. She always had a small stone of salt on the table and another smaller one in her pocket. People like that, when they feel weak, like other people need sugar, they take a little salt in their mouth, otherwise their knees buckle. I always dreamed how one day I'd make so much money I'd buy my mother some thin, white salt like the rich people have, and not a grey stone to lick like a cow. And when I saw the poor Italian doing that, I understood that he really needed help.'

Jacob sliced some bread and cheese for the escaped prisoner, fried him an egg, watched him as he ate, and then took him to the old canary hut.

He brought him two old bags of sawdust from the hatchery and said: 'Lie down here. Tomorrow morning we'll talk.'

The next day, Jacob woke up earlier than usual because the canaries were singing at the top of their lungs. For a few minutes he lay awake and at last he got out of bed. A thought that was half decision and half desire had taken shape in his heart and didn't let him fall back to sleep.

He went to the canary house and saw that the Italian POW was already awake and lying with his eyes wide open on the sacks of sawdust, conducting the birds with two fingers as big as rolls.

'What's your name?' he asked.

'Salvatore.' The POW stood up and bowed.

'Salvatore what?' asked Jacob.

'Just Salvatore. Someone whose mother and father are dead, who has no wife, and who will never have children, doesn't need a last name.'

'Salvatore,' said Jacob, 'sit down, please. It's not nice that you're standing.'

The POW sat, but even so, he filled the room.

'Where do you live in Italy?'

'In a little village, in the south, in Calabria.'

'So you know, Salvatore, how it is in a little village, that it's impossible to hide anything from anybody and everybody knows what's cooking in everybody else's pot? To hide you here even in the ground I can't. But you speak our language, you look like everybody else here, we'll give you one of our names, we'll dress you in local clothes, and we'll say that you're my worker.'

So, from an Italian POW with no last name, Salvatore became a Jewish worker named Joshua Ber.

No one knew who he was because Salvatore was a marvellous imitator, and aside from his mother tongue, he spoke fluent Hebrew, German, English, Russian, Yiddish, and Arabic. With Jacob he spoke only Hebrew and addressed him only as 'Sheinfeld', and when Jacob mentioned that to him, he answered that he didn't dare call him by his first name, 'because, after all, I'm your worker, and also because of the name itself'.

Jacob bought Joshua work clothes so he wouldn't go out in the blue POW overalls. He knew how to milk, prune vines, pour cement, mow with a scythe, exterminate tree parasites, and fix the plumbing, and within a few weeks, everybody in the village knew that Sheinfeld's new worker had golden hands. Now and then they would call him to work at one of the farms for a few pennies.

He was grateful and wanted to serve Jacob and help him any way he could. He cooked, washed the dishes, cleaned the house, and tended the garden. He found the remnants of the roses the albino had put up near Yakobi and Yakoba's hut, rescued them from the deadly embrace of the ivy, and grafted new strains on them.

Everybody was amazed when he demonstrated his ability to kill mole rats, which he could slay in their burrows with a blind thrust of a pitchfork. They thought he had a rich agricultural and technical experience, and they didn't understand that it was his talent for imitation, the talent that helped him learn languages, that provided him with those skills, too. All Salvatore-Joshua had to do was spend one minute watching a person milk, trim, build, or mow, and he could carry out the same activities and movements with surprising skill. Even difficult and professional work, like levelling tiles on a new floor or hoofing cows, he learned with a look and carried out like an old hand.

Only Naomi Rabinovitch suspected something. One day she said Sheinfeld's worker was 'funny', and when they asked her what she meant, she said: 'He doesn't look like a Joshua, he's looks like a Noshua.'

Ever since then, that nickname stuck, 'Noshua', and that's what everybody called him.

Once Noshua managed to anticipate Globerman and say in Yiddish and in the dealer's voice the exact weight of a cow for sale.

'How did you do that?' Jacob asked him afterward when they were home alone.

'I imitated his face when he looks at the cow, and then it came out, period,' said Noshua.

'Don't do things like that no more,' Jacob told him. 'Globerman is a dangerous person. He's not a little boy. He's got a lot of sense and hasn't got no compassion at all. If he suspects you of something, it'll end up very bad.'

But he himself kept questioning Noshua over and over about his talent for imitation. Finally the worker laughed and answered that he himself didn't have any real talent for imitation, and in fact, he imitated the talent for imitation from his father, who was a 'great artist' and had a travelling puppet theatre.

The POW was a sensitive man, and the tears that flowed from his eyes when he mentioned his dead father were so big they overflowed onto his cheeks and dripped onto his thighs.

'My height I also inherited from him, but he was thin and I'm so fat.'

Jacob asked him how he got so fat, and Noshua told him that once, when he was young, he had a lover.

'Every night I would make him and me zabaglione, for strength

and for love. Later we broke up, but I went on making zabaglione
every night for the memory and to eat it for the regrets. And
that's how I got fat.'

Jacob was embarrassed. Never had he heard a man talk about
loving other men and he didn't know what the word 'zabaglione'
meant, it sounded ridiculous to him, both rude and strange. And
then Noshua brought two eggs, found a little bit of sweet wine,
separated the yolk in the palm of his hand, added sugar, boiled
water, stirred it up, and gave it to Jacob to taste.

'That's good,' said Jacob, excited and amazed. 'How is it that
such simple food and so little work ends up in such a splendid
result?'

'If you had good wine here, Sheinfeld, it would taste even
better,' said Noshua.

'Tell me some more about your father,' Jacob asked.

And Noshua told him that his father was so inundated with
imitations that he had forgotten his own voice and would always
speak in the voice of the last man he had talked to. And that was
how his wife found out about all his carousings and love affairs,
for he would come home late at night and talk in his sleep in the
voices of his best girlfriends.

'He wasn't like me,' he said. 'He loved women and women
loved him, because he could imitate any man they wanted.'

'Who did he imitate for them?' asked Jacob eagerly, expecting
an answer that would shine and dissipate the fog over his
own love.

'You surely think, Sheinfeld, that he imitated Casanova for
them. No, they all wanted him to imitate their own husbands.'

Jacob didn't understand why.

'They hoped he wouldn't succeed so well, that he would be
only a little like him and not really the same thing,' laughed
Noshua. 'Every woman loves her husband, she just wants a few
small improvements.'

'And what did he die of?' asked Jacob.

'A *nafka mina*,' answered Noshua and his voice was the voice
of Jacob. 'One day he came back from a friend's funeral, didn't
talk to anybody, got into bed, and died himself. At first nobody
believed it, they thought he was imitating the friend and didn't

disturb him, and it was only when he started to stink that we knew that this time it was for real.'

About three or four years old I was in those days and I remember him vaguely. Sometimes Sheinfeld's worker would come to the kindergarten, cut out little figures and paper dolls for us, imitate the silly chorus of turkeys, the instructions of the kindergarten teacher, and the war honks of the geese in the Village Papish's yard.

By then everybody knew about his talent for imitation. Some were happy about him and others asked him to demonstrate his ability, and for some his imitations broke out of the fences of their world and they were enraged.

The imitations were so authentic they even surprised the livestock and the poultry. Noshua scared the chickens with the hungry meowing of cats and put them to sleep with the long *Hamsin* lament of swooning brood hens. He dried up the milk cows with perfect quotations from Globerman. He excited heifers in heat with an imitation of the rutting of both Gordon and Bloch. And he reached the pinnacle when he started calling like the jays, the noisiest and nerviest of all winged creatures.

It had been ten years since the jays had come from the forest to the village in their blue and shrieking flight of gypsies. They easily adapted to the new place, stole food, watched and learned, and quickly assumed a monopoly of all pranks and imitation and deception: they uttered terrified cries of mothers; they whistled whistles agreed upon by lovers, and shouted 'giddyap' and 'whoa' at the horses at the wrong times.

Now came the Italian POW and repaid them in kind: he mixed up their ways of life with calls of wooing and seduction, which he uttered right in the middle of the laying season, in the afternoon he pestered them with the dull hollow death rattle of the owl, and at the height of coupling he frightened them with screams of distress from the nestlings.

6

Oded still keeps his driving licence from the time of the British Mandate, and when he showed it to me in the middle of the trip and told me again how he had got it from Globerman when he was still a child, joy stirred in me along with a strange regret for the cattle dealer, whom I, like Mother, loathed and liked at one and the same time.

'He was a big bastard, that *drek*. Too bad you got only his feet and not his head,' shouted Oded.

At one-thirty in the morning, when I get to the dairy, Oded is there already, detaching hoses, closing valves, leaping onto the roof of the tank and tightening the covers.

Then we set out. The pungent smell of toothpaste and shaving cream fills the cab. Oded's cheek is flushed from his midnight shave and I wonder to myself if his left cheek is also like that. For so many years I have been riding on his right that his other profile is as much a mystery to me as the other side of the moon.

He isn't as strong as his father – few men are as strong as Moshe Rabinovitch – but he did inherit a few hints of his structure, and as often happens in a father and son, the observer can't know if the son is an improvement and refinement of his father or if he hasn't come up to his level. Oded excelled in Indian wrestling contests in the village, but he never succeeded in picking up Moshe's rock. He kept trying, and after people began making remarks, he shifted his attempts to the night hours, before he set out on his run.

And once Sheinfeld's worker saw him and asked what he was trying to do.

'To pick up this rock,' said Oded.

'A person can't pick up a rock like this,' said Noshua.

Oded showed Noshua his mother's faded sign, which was still stuck to the rock, but since the talent for imitation doesn't extend to the science of reading, and the Italian POW was afraid to give away his secret, he ran home and asked Jacob what was written there.

Jacob recited the sentence that every person in the village knew by heart – 'Here lives Moshe Rabinovitch who picked me up off the ground' – and Noshua got excited and said that if that was so, he would also pick that rock up off the ground.

'You haven't got a chance,' Jacob told him. 'Many have tried and all have failed.'

Noshua returned to the rock, tried a few times, and he failed, too, but that didn't affect his good mood. His new life was already blessed with the daily routine of a villager, and now he added to it the daily attempt to pick up Rabinovitch's rock. In the morning he got up, drank a raw egg and a cup of chicory, put on his work clothes, and went out to the field and the yard, and at noon he put on a dress he had sewn himself from Rebecca's old clothes, tied an apron around his waist, and cooked lunch. In the afternoon, he put his work clothes on again, went out to work in the yard again, and at dusk he drank another egg, went to the rock, and didn't succeed in picking it up.

7

Noshua slowly sneaked into Jacob's life.

'You don't really like the food I make you,' he complained one day when Jacob left his plate almost full.

'It's very good food,' said Jacob, 'but it's food for Italians. People are used to eating what they used to eat at home.'

Noshua went to Aliza Papish and asked her permission to watch her while she was cooking, and the very next day he slaughtered a chicken and made Jacob soup with fragrant drop-lets of gold floating in it, mashed potatoes with fried onion, sour cream, and dill, and sprinkled coarse salt on the plate.

Jacob ate and enjoyed, and after the meal Noshua dropped a few drops of green oil on his big hands, told his boss to take off his shirt, and kneaded his shoulders and his neck.

'The flesh between your shoulders is very hard, Sheinfeld,' he noted. 'Maybe there's some woman who doesn't return your love?'

Jacob, with the special pride of disappointed men, didn't want to admit, and Noshua didn't ask any more questions. But a few weeks later, as the POW was cutting dough for the *kreplach*, he suddenly asked, seemingly in all innocence: 'How did you say the man who picked up the stone is called?'

'I already told you, he's called Moshe Rabinovitch,' said Jacob. 'And that's also written on the stone.'

He was angry because he felt the Italian's looks piercing and examining him.

'In his cowshed I saw a woman sitting and drinking grappa.'

Jacob didn't respond.

'Who is that woman?'

'That's Rabinovitch's Judith,' said Jacob, and even though he was tense and ready, he couldn't hide the tremor that the question and the answer poured into his voice.

'Never did I see anyone in this country drinking grappa,' said Noshua. 'Where does she get it?'

'Globerman brings it to her.'

'Why does the dealer bring it to her, Sheinfeld? Why don't you bring it to her?'

Jacob was silent.

'And she's also got a little boy,' Noshua went on. 'Every day he comes to see me how I don't succeed in picking up his father's rock.'

'It's not his father!' shouted Jacob, and understood immediately that he had made a mistake.

'So who is his father?'

'None of your business,' said Jacob.

'It's a child who looks like he himself hasn't decided yet who he looks like.'

Jacob was silent.

'I feel a wound here,' said Noshua. 'I can help you.'

'I don't need your help,' said Jacob, and suddenly, without believing his own ears, he heard himself saying: 'No matter what, she won't be mine in the end.'

For a moment he hoped it wasn't he who had said those words, but Noshua who had said them in his voice. But the POW looked at him and said: 'Sheinfeld, you know by now that I don't love women, but precisely because of that there are things I understand better than ordinary men.'

'I know,' said Jacob.

'And mainly I know the most important thing, the secret you don't know.'

'What's that?' asked Jacob.

'That there are rules for love. That love is not a free-for-all. There are rules, otherwise love would kill you like a horse that feels there are no reins on him. It's very simple. The first rule is: a man who really wants a woman has to marry her. And the second rule: a man who wants to get married can't sit at home and wait for God to help him.'

'Where did you hear free-for-all?' Jacob smiled.

'Don't change the subject, Sheinfeld,' Noshua's face became serious. 'I'm talking to you now about your life, so don't ask me about my words. In love there are rules, and where there are rules, the world is simpler. A man who wants to marry a woman has to know how to dance the wedding dance, to know how to cook the wedding food, to know how to sew the wedding gown. Not to sit at home, waiting and saying: No matter what, in the end she will be mine.'

Jacob trembled. The POW had formulated so clearly and simply all the foggy ideas about harnessing and driving fate that had lodged in his brain for years, but had been scared to strip off the clothes of metaphors and fly into the air.

'Look, please, at the crows in the sky, everywhere they act the same way. Here and in Italy. The crows are the wisest birds. Look and learn how they woo.'

'I know how they woo.' Jacob got angry. 'I know birds a little better than you do.'

'Now he has a good wind to put on an act.' Noshua peeped out the window. 'Go outside with me, Sheinfeld, and let's see what you know about crows.'

They went out. The male crow took off high into the air; for a moment he tottered on the warm air and immediately pulled in his limbs and sank like a stone. Right in front of his beloved, dark and excited on one of the branches, all at once he spread his tail and his wings. A small bang was heard, the grey-black body braked in the air, turned over, and soared.

So fast and skilled he was that he didn't seem to lose any speed as he turned over. Now he fell again, spinning around and struggling as if he were wounded and dropping to his death, and just before he hit the ground, he took off again.

'That's what they do in all places and all times,' said Noshua. 'And even if he and she live their whole life together, every year he will woo her anew. Those are the rules. And if some other crow sings her a serenade or brings her grappa, she won't look at him.'

'On the ground he's so ugly,' said Jacob.

'That, Sheinfeld, is why he woos her in the air and not on the ground. First rule of wooing: wooing you do where you're beautiful and not where you're ugly.'

Jacob argued that he was ugly both in the air and on the ground, but Noshua said: 'Everybody has one or two places where he's beautiful.'

And then he added: 'Love is something neat and wise. It's a matter of brains. Like you build a house and like you drive a car and like you cook food and like you write a book – that's how you love.'

'Heart or mind,' said Jacob wearily. '*A nafka mina.*'

'It's very *nafka mina*,' the worker persisted. 'But here I see that you're laughing, Sheinfeld. So you still have hope.'

And Jacob, who had been moved and swept up into unexpected and unformulated waves of his love for so long, at long last felt good and nice, in the deliberate and assuring arms of rules, and with that big strange man, who knew them so well and knew the way to the solid dry land beyond them.

'You helped me when I needed help, Sheinfeld, and for that I shall return the favour. I'll get you the woman from Rabinovitch's cowshed. You'll just have to dance, cook, and sew. Those are the rules.'

'I don't know how to dance and I don't know how to cook and I don't know how to sew,' said Jacob.

'Dancing and cooking also have rules,' said Noshua. 'And everything that has rules can be learned.'

He finished washing the dishes, shook his hands over the sink, and wiped them on the apron he wore over his dress, and suddenly he came to Jacob, stood him up, and said: 'Forgive me one moment, please.'

He put one hand on Jacob's scalp and with the other hand, he held his shoulder.

'Please don't fall,' he ordered, and with a slight and confident push he spun him around like a top.

Jacob closed his eyes because of the pleasant whirlpool and the frightening orange stripes that were drawn in its darkness, and even though he didn't say a word, he heard his own voice saying: 'You'll know how to dance.'

At dawn, Jacob entered the old canary house, grabbed a few fine *bandooks* which slept there, and asked Globerman to take him and his loot to Haifa in the truck.

'You started again with your birds?' asked the dealer.

'I'm selling them,' said Jacob. 'I need money.'

All the way he thought of how he would manage to find that English officer, although he didn't even know his name, but when they got to the navy base, he saw the officer standing at the gate as if he were waiting there for him all those years. He looked just the same as in the days when he came to the albino, but gold stripes were added on his sleeve and a silver stripe in his hair. Jacob gave him the *bandooks* and the officer paid generously for them.

From there they went to the Arabic fabric store across from the railway station and Jacob bought the big, colourful sheets Noshua had instructed him to buy. And from there, they went up to the music store on Shapiro Street, and Jacob bought a big gramophone with a bronze handle and a giant earphone on instalments, along with the four records Noshua had told him to bring.

'There are rules for love,' Jacob informed the amused Globerman when the dealer asked him the meaning of his purchases. 'You thought only you and Rabinovitch know that? Now the two of you will see that I know it, too. Love is something neat and Judith will be mine in the end. She and the child, too.'

When they returned to the village, Jacob saw people gathered at the fence of his house. The trunk of a young eucalyptus tree, thin and tall as a mast, which Noshua had cut down in the forest and dragged to the yard, was standing there, stuck in a pit and held by taut cables. The worker quickly unrolled the cloth sheets Jacob brought, and with skilled and strong movements, he spread and stretched them, tied and built around the mast a big, colourful tent that looked like a giant flower and that smelled good and fresh.

Like a big cat, the POW climbed the electric pole on the roof of the cowshed, a screwdriver in his pocket and a pair of pliers between his teeth.

'Watch out for the electricity,' said Jacob.

'Don't worry.' Noshua laughed. 'Once I saw how an electrician works.'

He cut, screwed, wrapped, and pulled a wire from there to the tent. The gramophone he put on a wooden box and the four records he put next to it. He lit the bulb, closed the sheet of the tent, stood across from Jacob formally, and said: 'Now we shall begin.'

All over the world, stated Noshua, there are no more than four dances, and in them there are no more than four basic movements.

'The turn, the jump, the back, and the forth,' he enumerated.

'And the right and the left?' asked Jacob.

'The right is the back of the left, and the front is the left of the right,' said Noshua very compassionately, and went on to explain that all other dances are merely versions, imitations, and hypotheses of the four basic dances: the waltz, the dance of memory, the dance of war, and the dance of touch, the tango, the most sublime and exalted of all dances. 'And all the rest,' he said contemptuously, 'all those dances of shepherds and harvesters and hunters and the rain and wine dances, and all the dances where people hold hands and form a circle, those aren't dances.'

Jacob laughed and as he laughed, he realized that that was the first time he had laughed aloud in many years, ever since Judith had come to the village. And Noshua joined him with a laugh so much like his own that it seemed like its frightening echo, coming back to him from the crest of the big body.

'And precisely because of that, Sheinfeld, you will learn the tango,' said Noshua. 'Not to please her and not to touch her. You will learn the tango because that's the rule: the bridegroom has to dance a tango with the bride.'

He wound up the gramophone, put on a record, and Jacob scurried to his feet, for he thought that now he would be ordered to dance, and his body was embarrassed. But Noshua put a heavy hand on his shoulder and sat him down again, and instructed him to listen to the notes of the tango without moving and without getting up.

'Just sit and listen, Sheinfeld, sit and don't move at all, so I won't have to tie you up!' he warned him. 'You just listen and listen and listen, and don't you move. That's what we will do every day until your body is full.'

At first Jacob listened to the tango with his ears, then with his diaphragm and his stomach, and a few hours later, when he wanted to rebel and stand up, it was already too late. His body was soft and slack and his muscles couldn't move his new heaviness.

He stretched out on the floor of the tent like a person lying in a warm rain, and in the evening, when Noshua suddenly stopped the gramophone and helped his student out to the yard, Jacob discovered that his flesh had overflowed its banks and his feet strode with steps so new to his body that he laughed in surprise and bliss and all the muscles of his body laughed with him.

8

Now Noshua called the shots in Sheinfeld's house.

He set the agenda, cooked the meals, prepared Jacob's studies, and followed his training. He ordered when to go and when to come, when to get up and when to lie down.

'This agenda is very important,' he kept repeating.

Sometimes Jacob felt him staring at him with discerning eyes and even sniffing him with an expression he probably copied from the faces of the orange growers before picking, as if he wanted to determine how ripe he was.

'There are rules for love, Sheinfeld,' he kept issuing his decree. 'A very important rule I already told you, which is that love is a matter of the mind and not of the heart. And another important rule I will tell you now: in love you have to give a lot, but you never peel off all the skin and you don't reveal everything to the end. And what I already told you – that for love, as for all work and exercise and art, you need an orderly life with hours of rest and proper food.

'Now you won't go out into the street anymore,' he said. 'You won't see people anymore, and you especially won't see her. You will walk only in your house and in your yard and in your field. Just like this. One two three four, one two three four. No, Sheinfeld! You won't count, I'll walk with you and I'll count, one two three four. Numbers come from the brain, and the brain, don't forget, isn't good for the tango. A waltz is a dance for the brain, a one-step is for the brain, a Charleston is also a dance for the brain, for the stupid brain, but still for the brain. Even our tarantella is for the brain. But a tango that says touch, a tango is a dance for here, here . . .'

And all of a sudden the POW's body moved like a broad, quiet flash, and he was standing behind his student, his blacksmith's chest clinging to the back of Jacob's neck, the strong belly to his back, the big hands to his ribs, and from there he slipped down hard to Jacob's waist and to the bulging bones of the loins, and above them he slipped to the sensitive, scared inside of his thighs.

'Here,' he said. 'That's the tango. To touch.'

He tightened his hold. 'From here it comes and for here it goes.'

Jacob felt his behind scared and shrivelling and his breath fleeing from his rib cage.

'Not with the brain,' said Noshua at the back of his neck. 'If you had a brain, you wouldn't have called me, Sheinfeld, and I wouldn't have come.'

Jacob wanted to say that he hadn't called him at all, but as if from his belly came the knowledge that that was pointless. The POW's hands held him, his legs led him. A lot of water, yellow-green springtime water, flowed around him and didn't cover him.

9

Time passed. The world war came to an end. Jacob pondered the possibility of keeping that from Salvatore. But ultimately, he took pity and told him.

The POW took a deep breath and said, 'I'm going for a little walk,' and an hour later he came back and said he wanted to stay.

'I thought you would want to go back home, to your little village in Italy,' said Jacob.

'Someone whose father and mother are dead, and no wife is waiting for him and children he will never have, doesn't have to go back to any home,' said the POW. 'They call me Joshua. I make repairs and I heal wounds and I cook and sew and clean and dance. Now, Sheinfeld, we've got work to do.'

The end of the war returned home the sons who had been mobilized into the British army. They brought new ways to the village: they drank beer, they sang songs in English, and told stories of regrets and alienation. Now and then guests appeared in the village, army buddies, and so one day a fellow from Jerusalem showed up, one Meir Klebanov.

That day, Oded was on the road, Judith was cooking in the house, Moshe was in the mash storehouse, and Naomi was sitting on the roof of the cowshed replacing broken tiles. When she straightened up and wiped her forehead, the sun gleamed on the body of a distant car, glanced off it, and made it shine like an eye, opening and shutting as it moved.

A car wasn't a common sight in the Valley in those days and Naomi looked at it and saw it stop next to the old police station on the highway.

A tiny dot got out of the car and moved in a straight line in the lot, and Naomi looked at it and didn't know that within fifteen minutes the dot would arrive from the fields to the yard, and that a few months later that dot would marry her and take her to Jerusalem. From the distance she couldn't even know if it was a man-dot or a woman-dot.

The little figure made its way along the edges of the sorghum field, advanced and grew bigger along the row of old pomelos in the citrus grove beyond the wadi, crossed the channel, and slowly became a young man whose name was not yet known, but whose features became clear and whose walk became light and carefree.

Even though Naomi couldn't hear, there was in his stride a hint that he was whistling, and now she already figured out that the route of his walk would bring him to the yard. And indeed, the soft whistling was soon heard and even grew louder, and Naomi recognized one of the soldier's songs brought back by those who came home from the war.

Now the walker was close enough for Naomi to see a fellow of about twenty-seven; his hair was thick and smooth and combed like city boys did with a parting in the middle, his skin was thin and fair, his features were neither handsome nor ugly, and the crease in his khaki trousers was sharp and precise.

'Are you looking for somebody here?' she asked when he passed the cowshed.

The whistling stopped. The fellow's eyes searched all around. His crepe-soled shoes were polished so hard they shone even though he had been walking in the dust of the fields.

'This is a private yard,' said Naomi.

Now the stranger understood that his interlocutor was standing on the roof and he raised his eyes.

'Excuse me,' he said, 'I'm looking for the Liberman family.'

He had a pleasant baritone and he articulated clearly. A wind suddenly blew and Naomi's hands clasped her skirt to her thighs.

'Go out of the yard to the street, turn left, and it's the sixth yard from here.'

'Thanks,' said the fellow, and after a few steps he stopped, turned back, and asked: 'When will you come down from there?'

'Later.'

'I'd come up to you, but I'm scared of heights.'

'So you'd really better stay below.'

'What's your name?'

'Esther Greenfeld,' answered Naomi.

The fellow took a notebook and fountain pen out of his pocket, wrote down something, tore off the page, and laid it on the ground. He put a small stone on it so it wouldn't fly off in the wind, and he straightened up: 'Left and the sixth yard from here, Liberman,' he said and left.

Both of them knew she couldn't help coming down from the roof to see what he wrote for her, and both of them knew she would wait until he left the yard and disappeared, and wouldn't see how she jumped from the roof to the bales of straw and leaped down from them and rushed to the note.

'Too bad Esther Greenfeld will get all the letters I'll send you,' was written there.

Two hours later, when the fellow came back to the yard, he searched and looked in all directions and walked around the cowshed with his face turned up, Naomi said: 'Now I'm here.'

She had already finished repairing the roof tiles and now was sitting and eating pomegranates in Oded's old 'Tarzan hut'. The branches of the eucalyptus hid her from the guest. Between the leaves she saw him approach the mighty trunk, walk around it, and look up.

'Do you have any hours when you come down to earth?'

And then Judith came out to him and asked angrily who he was looking for.

'Esther Greenfeld.'

'There's no Esther Greenfeld here,' said Judith. 'There's no Esther Greenfeld in this village. Go look for your Esther Greenfeld someplace else.'

Naomi was surprised at her flinty voice, for Judith was usually generous to passersby and always offered them a glass of cold water.

'Did you hear? There is no Esther Greenfeld here!' the fellow shouted up, and his voice was high and jolly. 'You're Naomi Rabinovitch. I asked at Liberman's who was the girl on the sixth yard to the right of there, and they told me. You're Naomi Rabinovitch and I'll send you letters.'

And as he talked he walked backward, and Judith walked up to him as if she were pushing him with her eyes, her hands moving back and forth over her apron, with firm wiping movements hinting that she was ready for war.

'I'll come back,' cried the fellow. 'My name is Meir Klebanov, and I'll come back.'

And that's how he made the whole long way to the road, a backward walk that pulled behind it an invisible and unbreakable web, waving his hand and stumbling a bit and throwing kisses that got farther away and smaller, until they gathered together again in that dot, which crossed the wadi and retreated along the line of old pomelos in the citrus grove and on the edges of the sorghum field behind it, reached the road, and was swallowed up in the three o'clock bus.

Two days later came the first letter from Jerusalem, a pioneer at the head of a long blue non-stop caravan of envelopes. In the village they started saying that Naomi Rabinovitch had a 'fellow in Jerusalem', and a few weeks later Meir returned for a visit.

Once again Oded was on a trip and Judith, clearly angry and hostile, said, 'That fellow, he's not for you, Nomele,' and she didn't allow her to let him into the house.

Naomi brought food for her and Meir out to the yard and the two of them ate in the shade of the eucalyptus.

'She's a character, your mother,' said Meir.

'She really is a character,' said Naomi, 'but she's not my mother.'

Meir enjoyed the food and didn't ask or demand anything. Afterwards, Naomi accompanied him to the highway and kissed him under the dusty casuarinas.

'And one minute after that, I came from Tel Aviv with the Mack,' laments Oded. 'And on the other side of the road stood some fellow hitchhiking. But Naomi wasn't there anymore and I didn't understand what or who it was. Here's what one minute can do.'

10

'There's something not good here in the house,' Noshua grumbled again.

He sniffed and searched and found the collection of yellow notes that had once been addressed to Judith. His face contorted and he demanded that Jacob burn them.

'You see, Sheinfeld?' He warmed his hands over the small bonfire. 'Look and you'll see by yourself. Love letters burn like any other paper.'

Before noon, Noshua worked in the yard a little, and sometimes he hired himself out to other farmers. But most of the hours of the day, the two of them spent together. And at twilight, Noshua went to Rabinovitch's house to try to pick up Moshe's rock.

Back then I was about five or six and I remember the picture very well: the worker would emerge from Sheinfeld's house, rub his big hands together, and give himself roars of encouragement. He walked very quickly until he started running toward Rabinovitch's house, and all the village children hurried at his heels. He had broad, springy steps, which no one would have expected in his lumbering body, and as he ran he bowed amusingly and clenched his fist in the air at imaginary rivals.

'Max Schmeling,' said the Village Papish. 'The spittin' image.'

When he reached the rock, Noshua didn't delay even one second. He bent over, he grabbed, he groaned. He flushed and panted and clasped and moaned, but Rabinovitch's rock, which had already defeated Jewish butchers and Circassian blacksmiths, loggers from Mount Carmel and Salonikans from the port of Haifa, knew how to distinguish between genuine effort and imitation effort, and didn't move one single tenth of an inch.

The villagers expected that Noshua would also kick the rock and break his big toe, but Noshua didn't get angry, didn't kick, didn't break, and didn't limp.

'You mustn't get mad at a stone,' he said. 'The stone doesn't understand and isn't to blame. That's the whole issue of intelligence. In the end, I'll pick it up just like Rabinovitch.'

And he went back to his tent, to his student, to his records, and to his dances.

'All day long all I do is dance,' Jacob complained. 'We also talked about cooking and sewing.'

'Soon, soon,' said Noshua.

They were walking in the field and Noshua said: 'This little citrus grove, you don't need it anymore, Sheinfeld.'

And indeed, grapefruits and oranges were already dropping from their branches, fruit flies buzzed on the trees, and weeds were growing up between them.

'Orange trees make good wood for cooking,' Noshua went on. 'They've got hot coals and a good smell. The time has come for us to chop down these trees and after they dry, we'll learn how to cook the wedding food on them.'

In the warehouse, Jacob bought two axes and a big saw, the kind that's made for two people, and he and Noshua chopped down the citrus grove, the same citrus grove that years before he and his wife had planted, where he had stood the day Judith arrived in the village, and underneath the third tree in the third row Rebecca had discovered the blue kerchief of her rival.

All his muscles ached. Blisters rose on the palms of his hands. His eyes were scorched by the pungent oils from the stumps of the citrus trees. Noshua looked at him and laughed. 'Do what I do,' he said. 'Imitate a person who doesn't get tired.'

He lopped off the branches and arranged them in tight piles. 'Here, Sheinfeld,' he said, 'now you don't have a citrus grove to go back to anymore.'

I stood up, boiled a little water in a pot, and cracked two eggs into the palm of my hand. I spread my fingers and let the whites slip between them into the sink. I mixed and beat the yolks with sugar and wine and the sweet reflections that awaited them in my memory.

Without stopping even for a minute, I placed the bowl on the pot of boiling water and went on like that for another two minutes. The yolks warmed up, absorbed the wine and their own liquid, turned into a smooth froth, and all at once the rich fragrance of zabaglione rose in the air. When I finished sucking my finger, I stood up and slid my tongue over my top teeth, from right to left and from left to right sweet sweet sweet sweet sweet sweet sweet sweet sweet sweet sweet sweet sweet sweet sweet sweet teews teews teews teews teews teews teews teews teews teews teews teews teews

And then I stuck my tongue to my palate and drank the saliva that filled my mouth.

I sat down at the table again, my belly full and my head light. Then I put the dishes in the sink and washed them.

The window-panes above the sink were very clean and a soft sun of already-seven-in-the-evening-soon-I-will-set healed the garden. Bubbles of memory burst one by one, exposing and caressing, and Jacob's face beyond the transparent light in the glass was softer than regrets.

'How come I fell in love with her, Zayde?' He smiled as if to himself, because I hadn't asked the question, or at least, I hadn't asked it aloud.

'Not only me,' he went on. 'Globerman loved her, too, and Rabinovitch loved her and Naomi also loved her. All of us together, every one of us in his own way, we loved her, and

that's how she raised you with three fathers but without one
father, and from the day you was born three men think you're
their son and they watch over you, and so each one watches
over the others. When Globerman died, I went to his funeral
not only because of custom and grief, but also to see that this
time he really was dead and not trying to lower the price of a
cow. And you think Rabinovitch wasn't there for exactly the
same reason? We watched each other and the whole village
watched us. Everybody talked and asked whose child it was,
and I was the only one who didn't understand what all the fuss
was about. See, when there's love, even in a dream you can get
pregnant. But just to make sure, one day I waited for her in the
street and I grabbed her by the hand, and these are the words I
said to her: "Judith, maybe you came to me in the night? And I
didn't notice it? Back then, the night Rabinovitch sold the cow?"
You know that sometimes a woman, when she wants a child a
whole lot, can do things like that. At night she comes, and the
man doesn't even feel and doesn't know, or he thinks he's having
a dream and he's scared to wake up, like what happened to me
a lot of times, I'm lying with my eyes open and dreaming she
comes, and she's with me, and her hands I feel, here, and here,
and her lips on mine, and, excuse me, Zayde, her nipples right
on mine. See, they always ask why men have nipples on their
chest, and there's all kinds of answers to that. First of all, they
say it's to remind us of where we come from, and B, they say it's
to remind us of what we could have been, and C, they say it's
so we can make a miracle and give milk. See, sometimes, Zayde,
you want to make a miracle, but you've got nothing to make it
with, so the God of the Jews already thought of that and that's
why He gave you nipples. If He brings water out of the rock, so
He won't bring milk out of a man? And I'm telling you, Zayde,
all of them are just stories. Nipples on a man, it's only to line
himself up right, across from the woman. If his mouth is on her
mouth and the nipples are touching one across from the other,
then the eyes are also going to open one into the other and all
the rest of the body fits to a T. So maybe in a dream like that
you really came to me? See, with my eyes open I was dreaming
that you were with me, and also around the neck, Judith, around

the waist you hugged me, with all the arms and legs, all of you, Judith, you were with me. A lot of times I dreamed like that, but that night I shut my eyes and I saw it was real and everything was facing everything: chest facing chest, and mouth facing mouth and eyes facing eyes and her hands caressing my whole body, like in water, passing and saying: "I'm here, shaaa . . . Jacob . . . shaaa . . . shaaa . . . I'm here . . . you're not alone, sleep now, Jacob, sleep." And from all that shaa and that Jacob and that sleep, I finally got up and went with her to the cowshed, and half awake and half asleep I helped her milk there. Then, afterwards, facing that whole belly of hers that grew, I thought maybe it was true, maybe it really was with me, 'cause you know that: in the end you wake up, and then on the one hand she wasn't there no more, but on the other hand you feel, excuse me, that you were wet with a layer of semen and the smell of autumn you feel filling all the air. And that, for somebody who understands, is a sign that the time of love has come. That's what Menahem Rabinovitch told me. The autumn, when the animals search for food to get fat for the winter, that's the time for human beings to search for somebody to sleep together with them in the cold, and in the spring it's only to jump and be happy and make children. That's why, in the spring, people take their own lives, 'cause they don't all want to take part in all that joy. It's like how they used to sing here at Purim, "you've got to be happy", until once Rabinovitch, dressed in his Tonychka's clothes, the one who died and he looked just like her, got up on the stage and showed everybody what it means to have to be happy. So why were we talking about autumn, Zayde? Because of that smell of carobs? Well, so is there better proof that you were with me? Does a layer of semen come out of a person all by itself? All that I told her there in the street, and she pulled her hand out of my hand really hard and said to me: "Sheinfeld, don't make yourself a laughing-stock. I didn't come to you, not at night and not by day, and in this belly you don't have any part or parcel and don't even think about such a thing." "So who does have a part and parcel? Come on, you tell me, Judith, who does?" And my whole body was shaking. "Nobody you know and nobody you think," she told me. "And don't think that if at night I came

to you and in the morning you helped me milk, that you've got
any rights." But I didn't let her alone, 'cause the belly and the
anger they were hers, but the dream and the semen they were
mine. So I used to come see her and she used to throw me out.
Once she said: "You see this pitchfork, Sheinfeld? If you don't
stop talking about my belly, in one more minute, you'll get it
in your belly." I couldn't bear it that she called me Sheinfeld.
Only three times she called me Jacob and not Sheinfeld: once
when I let all the birds fly off for her, and once when she was
with me then at night, and the third time I'll tell you about in
a little while. You think I was scared? Right away I opened
my shirt and I said: "Come on, stick in the pitchfork, Judith!"
Because a pregnant woman's got crazinesses and you got to take
them into account. She wants to eat something, let her eat it,
she wants to fight, let her fight, she wants to stab you with
a pitchfork, let her stab you with a pitchfork. And then she
laughed. Like a lunatic she laughed. "What will be the end
of you, Jacob?" And like that, with the pitchfork in her hand,
that was the third time. And a few days before the birth, I
went and bought things you need, and a wooden yellow bird
I also made, so you'd have something to play with, and after
you were born again and again I came and again and again I
told her: "I'm going to forgive you, Judith, just tell me, whose
baby is it?" Until one day she raised her hand and smacked
me: "You *nudnik*! I don't need your forgiveness, not yours and
not nobody's." *Nudnik* is a very offensive word in a situation
of love, and my question she didn't answer. Until the end she
didn't say. We came there and saw half the eucalyptus already
on the ground, and the poor crows' eggs broken in the snow all
around, and the black feathers and the blue kerchief, it was all
there, but there was no answer. And Rabinovitch stood there
already sharpening the axe, like that would help, like the tree
did it on purpose. And then I thought, Zayde, maybe it wasn't
Fate, maybe it was his bad brother Chance. I already told you
that once? Two brothers Fate has. The good brother is Luck
and the bad brother is Chance. And when those three brothers
laugh, the whole earth quakes. So it was Luck that she came,
and it was Chance that she died, and it was Fate that she was

on her way to the wedding I made for her, wearing the bridal gown I sewed for her, and on the way something happened. So a eucalyptus like that in the Land of Israel, that's not Chance? Snow like that in the Land of Israel, that's not Chance? And that you, Judith, came to me at night, that's by Fate or by Luck? And a paper boat like that which reaches this girl, is that on purpose or by Chance? Well, what can I tell you, Zayde, all that doesn't matter now, *a nafka mina*, like she always used to say. The whole village came to her funeral, and I was the only one who didn't go. Come on, ask me why I didn't go. Let's put it like this: 'cause I felt that if that funeral was a wedding, me they wouldn't invite. You understand? So I didn't go. And the heart of this old man, who all his life was alone, will be alone a little while more. It's already used to being alone, so let it be alone a little while more.'

11

'And when are we going to sew the bridal gown?' Jacob worried, when they finished chopping and arranging the lopped-off branches of the citrus grove.

'Everything in its time, Sheinfeld,' said Noshua.

'And when will I finally dance with a woman?'

'When the day comes, Sheinfeld,' said Noshua.

'And why do you call me Sheinfeld all the time? Why not Jacob?'

'Everything will be in its order,' said the POW. 'The dress and the woman and the name.'

'You're having fun with all your games, but I'm never going to learn.'

'First of all, having fun is no disgrace, and second of all, you will learn and you will know,' said Noshua. 'And meanwhile, you don't need to dance with a woman. With the tango, it doesn't matter whether there's a woman or not . . .'

'You said that the tango is touching,' said Jacob.

Noshua smiled. 'Women, Sheinfeld, are so much like one another that it really doesn't matter, and the tango really does say touch, but it's not like other dances. You can touch together and also alone, with a man and also with a woman.'

Another few weeks went by. Jacob's movements kept on improving. Noshua observed him with satisfaction and smiles that kept on getting broader, he praised him and uttered meaningless rules and strange slogans, like, 'In the tango, when you're together, you're really apart,' and 'You don't lead her, you lead yourself with her,' which mixed up Jacob's feet and agitated his heart.

But the Italian knew what he was doing, and one morning he got up and declared: 'The day has come!' And Jacob understood that the day before his teacher had visited the Village Papish because Papish spoke those very same words and in that very same solemn voice the day he first went into the pen for young geese with the fattening tube in his hand.

Jacob was sure that now he could at long last dance with his mate, but Noshua bowed to him, held out his big arms to him, fluttered his eyelashes, and said, 'May I have this dance?' so graciously that Jacob burst out laughing despite the fear that suddenly filled his body.

He took heart, approached his teacher, and in a wink found himself trapped in the Italian's confident and pleasant embrace.

His heart pounded, but his feet and his hips were already accustomed, and his body, suddenly its own master, was clasped to Noshua's solid belly, and they were dancing.

'That's how it is in the tango. Sometimes you're the man and I'm the woman, and sometimes you're the woman and I'm the man, and sometimes both of us are women, and sometimes both of us are men,' laughed the POW.

A good smell rose from his mouth, and Jacob was embarrassed by the touch of that big, skilled body and by the broad, guiding hand on his back, and by the strong, demanding belly that pushed him and played with him, and he was even more embarrassed by the instructions pouring down at an increased pace:

'A woman isn't a piano that has to be shoved!'

'A woman isn't a blind man who has to be shown the way!'

'A woman isn't a stone that has to be picked up!'

'A woman isn't a balloon that has to be held so it doesn't fly away!'

'So what is a woman?' Jacob suddenly shouted.

And Noshua smiled into his ear, and while spinning, dipping, pulling, and stepping, he whispered to him: 'One two three four. A woman is you, is you, is you.'

A glass of cognac slipped through my fingers. A small smash was heard, a thin strip of blood poured, soap bubbles turned pink.

Outside the owl hissed. A short flutter of death was heard among the branches. A wind of already-four-in-the-morning-soon-I'll-calm-down rustled in the leaves.

I returned to Jacob's bed, sucked my cut finger, and couldn't fall asleep. I got up, stopped the old gramophone's spinning, and wandered around the rooms of my new house.

The chill air told me that in twenty minutes the birds would start singing the songs of dawn, and I, as I said, all I had to do was hear the voice of the first early-rising bird to know the season and the hour and how much time I had left to live in the world. In winter, it's the robin who starts in the five a.m. dark and wakes up the swallow and the warbler, who join him, and by six the voices of the blackbirds and the jays are heard. At the end of spring, the larks and the falcons are the first ones up, and in midsummer only the warbler is up before them. The crow, like man, has no fixed time, but as soon as one crow wakes up, all his friends follow suit.

'At night the world is covered up and sleeping,' Mother told me one morning, when she got up to distribute the mash in the troughs and saw that the child Zayde, the immortal bastard, was already awake and listening, 'and in the morning the birds peck at its blanket and poke holes in it.'

12

Sometimes Jacob felt that Noshua knew the house and yard even better than he did.

'Maybe you were here before?' he kept asking, and pretended to be joking to hide his fear.

'Maybe,' Noshua would keep answering, and one day, after he returned from Rabinovitch's rock, he headed straight for the storehouse in the yard, and with the confidence of a prophet he rummaged around and burrowed and dug and tossed out, until he found what he was looking for – the albino accountant's heavy old pots and pans.

He assessed their weight in relation to their thickness and smiled happily.

'These pots and pans are yours?'

'They belonged to somebody who once lived in the house next door,' said Jacob. 'Now they're mine.'

The pots and pans were filthy dirty. Noshua scratched them with his thumbnail a few times and his eyes lit up.

'A good chef would sell his son for pots like these,' he said.

He sent Jacob to bring some steel wool while he made mixtures of ashes and oil, lemon and sand, all kinds of pastes for scraping and scouring. And when he rubbed the pots and pans their gleam began to emerge through the black and the dirt, until dull beams of red copper – the most exciting, warm, and human of all metals – burst out.

Noshua explained to Jacob that copper pots and pans are intended for master chefs, who are cold-blooded and hot-tempered, and for women who eat with patience and strength. He hammered nails in the kitchen wall and the skillets hanging there looked like three suns setting.

'Now I'll cook you a special meal,' he said. 'Go outside, Sheinfeld. I'll call you when everything's ready.'

Jacob went out, but he walked around the house and peeped

through the window and saw the POW tie Rebecca's old apron around his waist and his big nimble hands cutting and mixing, stirring and pouring, and all of it with a confidence that brought a smile to Jacob's face, for he understood that Noshua had once seen a master chef at work, and now he was amusing himself with his imitations.

And suddenly, right in front of his amazed eyes, the POW dipped his finger – with no hesitation or grimace of pain – into the boiling sauce bubbling in the pot. He left it there a few seconds and then put it in his mouth. His face, the mask of a curious child, became thoughtful. He seasoned and stirred and dipped his finger again, licked it, and nodded and called Jacob to the table.

The food was fragrant and tasty and unlike anything Jacob had ever eaten.

'Chew a lot and eat a little, Sheinfeld,' said Noshua. 'And you may leave a lot on your plate. That's a good custom.'

And when he saw Jacob's questioning eyes, he added: 'A really loving couple never eat too much. If you see a couple in a restuarant eating too much, know that they hate each other, that they want to kill each other by eating, and mainly that they fill their belly so they'll have an excuse not to go to bed together afterward.'

And after a brief silence, he said: 'And the most important thing, Sheinfeld, both in food as in love, are the rules. In a house where there are no rules, Fate goes wild, Luck tarries, and Chance visits. But in a house where there are rules, Fate does what it's told, Luck you don't need, and Chance stays outside, knocking and yelling and can't come in.'

A few big yellow sheets of paper that hadn't been cut into notes remained in the house. Noshua found them and instructed Jacob to write on them the do's and don'ts of cooking – some of them were very strange – and to hang them on the kitchen wall:

'Don't keep flour together with seasonings.'

'A knife should be longer than the diameter of the cake.'

'Cilantro is parsley's crazy sister.'

'The light for eating should be as bright as the light for reading.'

'Pears should be kept so they can't touch one another.'

'The front part of the cow is eaten in winter and the back part in summer.'

'Every beverage for drinking has a companion for eating.'

And one summer morning, out of the blue, as the two of them were sitting in their underwear in the tent and reciting the rule 'Eggs are first poured into a small bowl and only afterward into the big bowl,' the Italian suddenly smacked his forehead and shouted: '*Cretino! Cretino! Cretino!* How didn't I think of that before? I know how to pick up Rabinovitch's rock.'

And from that day on, he forbade himself any imitation of man or beast or bird, and for a few days he even spoke in a new voice, which was so strange that Jacob imagined it was his real voice.

A new stage began. He no longer played with the village children and no longer pestered cows and jays. From now on, the Italian POW devoted all his free time to studying Moshe Rabinovitch's movements and memorizing how he did and what he did.

13

One day a letter came from one of Naomi's friends, a girl from Nahalal who was studying at the Moshav Movement Teachers' College in Jerusalem. She invited her to come visit for 'a few days'.

'You're going to him?' asked Judith.

'I'm not going "to him".' Naomi got angry. 'And who is this "him" anyway? I'm going to my girlfriend, and maybe I'll visit "him", too.'

Oded took her to Jerusalem in the milk tanker.

'Where are the two of you sleeping?' he asked in a restrained tone.

'In the street.'

'I'm asking you where you're sleeping, Naomi, so answer and don't get fresh.'

'I'll go up to strange men with a gold tooth in their mouth and nicotine stains on their moustache, and I'll ask them if I can sleep at their place, and if they say they don't have any room for me, then I'll say: "That's just fine, sir, the two of us can crowd together in the same bed."'

'If you go on like that, I'll turn the truck around right now and take you back to the village.'

'You won't turn any truck around and you won't take anybody back. The milk will get sour in the tank.'

'And where is your girlfriend?' asked Oded after three hours of silence, when dawn bloomed on Jerusalem.

'She'll be here right away,' she said.

And indeed, the girlfriend from Nahalal did come and take Naomi to her room in the nearby Bukharan neighbourhood, where Meir was waiting for her and took her for a cup of strong, sweet tea in a restaurant for night workers in Beit Israel.

The dawn cold stood in the air. Noami clasped her hands around the thick, small cup, so different from the thin Russian tea glasses in her father's house.

The sun began to rise. Bells pealed. She and Meir bought some fresh bagels and Naomi couldn't help eating two of them on the way to his room. Going down Princess Mary Street, Meir removed the three sesame seeds that had stuck to her lips – one with a cautious finger, the second with a light puff, and the third with a delicate lick.

He lived fairly close to Ludwig Meyer's bookstore, in a rented room with thick walls that delighted her immediately with its red carpet, its deep window ledges, and its low bed. A smell so similar to the smell of Meir's body came from the pillows on the bed that you couldn't tell who took the smell from whom.

'You're a fool, Nomele,' said Mother.

'You're the last one who can give me advice,' said Naomi.

I heard them weeping in close but different voices that didn't blend into one another, and a few months later, in the spring of 1946, the wedding was held under the big eucalyptus in Rabinovitch's yard.

I remember the funny clothes of the strange guests from Jerusalem and Tel Aviv, and the chorus of wild canaries that suddenly descended on us along with the exulting riffraff of gold finches and green finches that joined in. And I remember the big gramophone – Sheinfeld's worker brought it on his shoulder from the colourful tent, set it up near the wall of the cowshed, and kept on turning its handle and playing tunes on it.

Jacob didn't dance. He sat off to the side and suddenly called me to come to him.

Six years old I was at the wedding of Meir and Naomi, and it seems to me that the first speech I heard from Jacob I heard then, when he sat me on his lap and made a remark that didn't suit my age: 'Every human being, Zaydele, feels death when his child is born and when his child marries and when his parents die. Did you know that?'

'No,' I said.

'Well, now you do.'

I wanted to get off his lap and go on walking around among the tables, attracting looks, candy, and amazement, but Jacob tightened his hold on me and went on with his strange speech: 'Three fathers to die before you, you got, Zaydele, and a special name against death you got, and children, I'm afraid, it looks like you won't get. That you inherited from me. I don't have no children, either. I just have a part of a child. I just have thirty-three and a third percent of you, but when you was born, I cried like a father cries for a whole child. People say we cry from joy, but it's not from joy, Zaydele, it's from sadness we cry, 'cause a lot of signs of the Angel of Death we can't understand, but that sign we do know. That's his sign to announce that your turn is coming. Well, Zaydele, I feel that you want to go now, so run off, play, be happy. We got a wedding today, we got to be happy.'

Meir's relatives looked at me with ironic, questioning eyes, conferred in whispers at the sight of Aunt Bathsheba's black widow's weeds, and were scared of Rachel, who suddenly burst out of the cowshed and strode into the divided sea of terrified guests and tottering tables to where Mother was sitting.

Embarrassed giggles were heard when Uncle Menahem, whose spring muteness had struck three days before the wedding, began distributing to all the strangers his notes saying: 'I have lost my voice. I am the uncle of the bride and the husband of the widow. Congratulations!'

Then he beckoned me to him. His pleasant hand tapped encouragement on my shoulder and another note of his was placed before my eyes, saying: 'What do you care, Zayde, let them look at us.'

Meir's mother, puffed up like a brood hen, kept grumbling about the smells rising from the Village Papish's goose yard and about the mire that stuck to her shoes. At last, Globerman grabbed her arm and took her off for a dance that made her face flush with the effort and the closeness, and because of the sudden affront to her body. His gigantic feet moved like wild animals around and between her feet, his hand investigated the stunned slope of her spine, his fingers estimated the submissive layer of fat at the bottom of her back.

'You shouldn't believe in age, Mrs Klebanov,' whispered the dealer. 'You're a beautiful, soft, and tasty woman, and a woman who's got such a fine hill at the bottom of her back shouldn't have to do such things to herself.'

Mrs Klebanov couldn't imagine that the strange and attractive smell emanating from his neck was the smell of blood. His hand rose up again, examined the thorns of her vertebrae through the fabric of her dress. Suddenly she sighed softly. Drops of warm and forgotten gold, annoying and shameless, rose in the most treacherous tissues of her flesh.

'Which side are you from?' She blushed.

'Rabinovitch's,' said Globerman.

'You're Rabinovitch's brother?'

'No,' said the cattle dealer politely, 'I'm the father of Rabinovitch's son.' And he pointed at me. 'Say hello to Meir's mother, Zayde.'

Two children guests, or 'petits bourgeois', as Uncle Menahem called them in a mocking note, wearing dark blue berets and low shoes, pulled out a pocketknife and wanted to carve their names in the soft flesh of the eucalyptus. But Mother went to them and hissed in a voice only I heard: 'Leave that tree alone, little carcasses, or I'll take your knife and I'll cut off your ears.'

Rachel lowed, the children fled, the crows, nervy and fearless, dived and pecked at what fell from the tables.

Two days after the wedding, the sky turned gloomy with spring clouds, a heavy late April rain fell, and the first big quarrel between Meir and Mother erupted.

I don't remember what the quarrel was about, but at dawn, Naomi packed clothes in a suitcase and books in a fruit carton, and Oded, frozen and pale with rage, drove his sister and his new brother-in-law to Jerusalem.

Even at the wedding, Noshua watched Moshe Rabinovitch, observed, and learned. By now he had stopped his attempts to pick up the rock and concentrated solely on Moshe. That year he had already acquired most of the Rabinovitch ways, both the big ones and the small ones, but he hadn't showed them to anyone, not even to Jacob.

And one day, after Sukkoth, when the days had grown short and the air was already laden with a smell of water and the first touches of cold, Noshua walked behind Moshe in the dark as he was returning from the dairy.

Moshe sensed something but didn't know what. Once, twice, he turned his head around, striving to see and understand, and then he felt her all over his skin and all over his flesh, his Tonychka, his twin reflection, who had risen from the dead and was walking in his wake, and his flesh shuddered.

Noshua, who didn't know all those ancient, concealed things and didn't imagine that in his attempts to imitate Moshe he would also become like his dead wife, walked in his wake again the next night, too.

And then, when that feeling struck him again, Rabinovitch didn't delay and didn't hesitate, but turned around and ran into the gloom behind him, grabbed the stunned worker by the neck, and shouted at him: 'Where's the braid? Now you'll tell me where's the braid!'

Noshua almost collapsed. Moshe was a head and a half shorter than him, but his grip was like the grip of an iron vice.

'If you had told me, you'd still be alive today,' shouted Moshe.

And his hands, suddenly despairing and weak, slackened and dropped. Noshua fled, choked and triumphant, laughing and coughing, to the house of his student.

Meanwhile, Jacob started learning the next stage, the very difficult one, of the tango: while dancing, Noshua posed riddles to him, told him stories, asked him questions, and argued with him, so his brain would be busy and leave his body to itself.

At first it was very complicated. If, for instance, the POW asked him what was two hundred thirty-five less one hundred seventeen, Jacob's body grew stiff and his knees were startled and got tangled up in each other. And things had come to such a pass that, one day, when he asked him, while dancing, the well-known logical conundrum about the man who meets at a crossroads the man who always lies and the man who always tells the truth – Jacob's legs gave out and he fell face-down.

But his legs quickly acquired experience and were now confident enough to give up the contact with his brain and his thoughts. Within a few months, he had succeeded in reciting the six laws of overlapping triangles while doing the 'Paso Doble' of Buenos Aires, and in carrying on a heated argument, even with some mockery, about the unity of the body and soul while doing the most vigorous turns of 'Jealousy'.

14

By that time, I was in school, and all the children there, both big and small, used to make fun of me, my name, my three fathers, and my mother. Because of their pestering and their cruelty, I sought shelter in the crests of the village cypresses and eucalyptuses, in heights that people with regular names didn't dare scale. That's how I discovered the crows, their nests, and their children.

'Well, Zayde' – Jacob Sheinfeld grabbed me in the street – 'maybe you'll find with the crows some gold jewellery and bring it to your mother as a gift.'

I told him, with the seriousness of children, that there was no scientific proof that crows steal jewellery. And he burst out laughing and declared: 'The crow isn't a scientific bird.'

'You want to come in?' he asked when we reached the gate of his yard.

His worker was cooking in the kitchen, and when I entered he bowed to me comically and barked like a dog. Jacob poured tea and told me that in his village, the village on the banks of the Kodyma, there was one *shaygets*, one gentile, who rode the train to the city every year, 'for there were very, very rich people there'. In the city, the *shaygets* searched and found abandoned crows' nests and took jewels and precious stones from them which the crows had stolen from rich women who left their windows open.

'Thieving from a thief is not a theft,' declared Noshua from the stove.

'Only male crows steal jewellery,' explained Jacob. 'And they don't hide it in the family nest. Only in an old nest or even in the ground, 'cause they don't trust nobody, not even Mrs Crow and certainly not baby crows. And when nobody sees, they come all by themselves to look at their treasure, to play and enjoy. And that *shaygets*, you should know, Zayde, he used to ride to the city without a ticket on the roof of the train, but coming back to the village, he rode first class, with a case full of gold and two gypsy women on his lap.'

In the middle of winter, when the rain was still falling, but the days were already starting to get longer, the crows started breaking dry branches off the trees and building their nests with them. On the rough skeleton, they placed thinner twigs and the concave surface they padded with straw and strings, ropes and feathers. They were so firm and bold that I frequently saw them swooping down and plucking off strands of hair from an angry cow. They didn't use their old nests anymore and those remained strong and stable and falcons and owls often took possession of them.

Then the female crow started hatching the eggs, and the male crow guarded her from his lookout point on one of the nearby trees.

By now I could distinguish the revealing direction of his look as well as the tail of the mother, sticking out like an oblique black stick over the rim of the nest. When I climbed up to the nests to look, the male crows would surround me furiously and would take off to a nearby tree and make do with loud protests. Once I discovered two fledglings thrown into the tree trunk, two victims of a cuckoo. They were small and ugly, their eyes were blue, and their pinion feathers were only just beginning to sprout on their wings.

Two grades ahead of me was a child who pestered and abused me a lot and called me names. I told him it was possible to take a fledgling like that home, raise it, and make it into a tame crow. The minute he picked up the fledgling, the crows swooped down on him in flaming fury, beat him with their wings, and pecked his head until he fled home crying and yelling. That whole year, they lay in wait for him in the schoolyard and in his parents' yard, and tried to wound him every chance they got.

That has nothing to do with the story of my mother's life, and so I shall make do with a brief and parenthetical statement, that that was the first and the last time I took revenge on anybody, and I discovered that even though I value and respect the instinct of revenge, satisfying it doesn't give me any pleasure.

Sometimes we'd stand around Jacob's yard and hope the worker would come outside, put on a little show for us, or resume his war with Rabinovitch's rock. Our eyes tried to penetrate the sheets of the colourful tent and our nostrils tried to pick up the lids of the pots. The smells of the dishes Noshua cooked were different and better than everything that was cooked in our own houses, and his ways were distinct and attractive. We knew he was a foreigner, but none of us suspected that Sheinfeld's worker had been an escaped Italian prisoner-of-war. The war was over by now, the camp was dismantled and ploughed up, the worker spoke our language, dressed like all of us, and only later did we find out that Globerman had arranged all his necessary documents and papers, at Jacob's request.

Suddenly Sheinfeld came out to the yard, spun around, and walked with strange steps, and the children stared at me, as if they were trying to see what I thought about my mother's obstinate suitor. Their parents also looked at me like that, for they, too, wanted to know what I thought about my mother. But I had no opinion, and Mother didn't tell me anything about that, and I didn't ask her.

'So maybe you, Zayde, maybe you know whose you are? Maybe now, so many years after she's gone, somebody will say at long last? Maybe you'll make a test in a hospital to know? I heard they got a special microscope for that. But in you, they see everything even without a microscope. Here, look at yourself and you'll see what inheritance means. You got big feet like Globerman, blue eyes you got like Rabinovitch, drooping shoulders you got like me. Too bad, if it were the other way around, it would be much better. Even in a normal family a child doesn't always look like father or mother, sometimes he looks like an uncle and sometimes like a brother of the father of the grandfather. Back home, one woman once gave birth to a daughter who looked just like her husband's first wife. What do you say about something like that, Zayde? If she would have given birth to a daughter who looked like her first husband, that's not so nice, but it's not so hard to explain, either. But such a thing? Where does it come from? Interesting, Zayde, the whole business of looking alike. See, they say that it's not only children and parents, husbands and wives also come to look like each other over the years. Maybe it's their blood that gets mixed? Maybe it's his semen she gets and is absorbed in her inside there? Maybe it's from her liquid that he absorbs? See with both of them that's very delicate skin there, and with some women it's just like a sweet river there, believe you me, and you even have to hang the sheets outside to dry afterwards. There was a *goya* back home like that, and the whole village

used to count how many times a week they'd hang up the wet
sheets, and the clowns in the synagogue used to say about her
and her husband "the horse and his rider hath he thrown into
the sea". Moths used to come and die on those sheets in the dark,
and dogs, even from villages very far away, used to always come
there to wail and go nuts. So, Zayde, what if I had stayed with
Rebecca all the years, maybe today I would look like her and
be a handsome man, eh? Moshe and his Tonychka really did
look like each other, but that it seems was even before they met.
From birth they looked alike and that it seems is why they fell in
love, 'cause with a man there's nothing that attracts him more
than a woman who looks like him. Right away he wants to get
into that body without knocking on the door. Right away he
feels like he's got permission from God to do everything. I wish
I also had such a simple and good answer to my love. What can
I tell you, Zayde, those matters of looking alike, they're very
complicated. And here, with Rabinovitch, something even more
interesting happened. Judith and Tonya's little girl came to look
alike. The little girl got Judith's walk, and her face, don't tell me
you didn't see how much they looked alike. Real slow it came,
that looking alike, until in the end, you'd look and swear Judith
and Naomi are really mother and daughter.'

The sun broke forth. I opened the closet. The big mirror looked
at my yellow hair, my drooping shoulders, my big feet.

In fact, I said aloud to myself, there really aren't any answers
in me. Just more questions.

The sand pouring out of her eye sockets, the cypress shadows
creeping over her grave, the white of her bared bones.

'May I have this dance?'

His old, dead, shrivelled arms reach out to me.

His feet stumbled. His cold hand sought support on my back.
A trace of his brittle chin was laid on my shoulder. The sun rose,
and I shook him off me, went back to bed and closed my eyes,
ripe and ready for my brief sleep.

'And to the wedding, see, you know, Zayde, she didn't come.
Everybody came to the wedding I made, everybody ate the food
I cooked, she put on the bridal gown I sewed, and all alone I

danced the dance I learned. How did that happen, Zayde? See, she was on her way to me, so what happened?'

15

Noshua went on searching and found the albino's old scythe. He honed the curved blade, mowed the grass of the yard, and raked it into a pile along with the straw and the old briers that time had amassed there. Then he took a crushed cigarette out of his shirt pocket, and even though nobody had ever seen him smoke before, he lit it. He inhaled the smoke with great pleasure; and he didn't blow out the match, but tossed it onto the pile. The fire caught with a roar and with flames, and turned a new generation of curious faces red.

'And now, food for the wedding,' he declared.

He turned up the ground with the pitchfork, inserted posts, stretched wires, dug beds, and sowed vegetables. Behind the canary house, onions and eggplant, peppers and squash quickly sprouted. In the front of the lot grew the garlic and the parsley and various kinds of leaves and grasses whose good smell was twined with the notes of the tango and the chirps of the canaries, and a few ancient poppies, which had been waiting in the ground in violation of every law, also decided to show up among them.

Noshua instructed Jacob to fertilize the vegetables with blood, but Jacob was scared of the idea. 'Why blood? Are we lacking manure here? With all the cows and chickens?'

'And why dung?' Noshua marvelled. 'If you were a tomato, which would you choose?'

The slaughterhouse, the small active kingdom of the butchers, and the cattle dealers, was beyond the eucalyptus forest, and the figure of Jacob, with two small jars hanging from a pole on his shoulders, was seen there three times a week.

Flies of cadavers, lusty and ravenous, flew behind him like a greenish bridal veil of death. Martens and jackals, their eyes shut, rubbed against his legs, mad with the smell of blood rising from the jars.

At that time, Jacob gave me the observation-box, and I often hid there, watching the birds who came to eat their fill of the offal from the knives of the ritual slaughterers and the porgers.

And humans I saw, too. I saw, I heard, and I remembered.

'If Lady Judith knows that you are watering your garden with cows' blood, you won't ever see her again,' Globerman said to Jacob, when the two of them met on the path leading through the forest. 'Please remember, sir, what Globerman says.'

Jacob didn't answer.

'So what, Sheinfeld?' the dealer changed the subject. 'You are still dancing?'

'Yes,' answered Jacob with the seriousness of lovers, that naive seriousness that wards off all mockery.

'You're a fool, Sheinfeld,' said Globerman. 'But that's nothing, there are a lot of other fools besides you. He who is a fool is never alone, he's in a very big company.'

'With Judith, we're all fools,' said Jacob, and with a sudden daring, he added: 'With Judith, even you are a fool, Globerman.'

My heart pounded, shook my ribs and the sides of the box. The steel tip of the *baston* gently tapped the toes of Jacob's boots.

'Yes, Sheinfeld,' murmured the cattle dealer. 'With Judith we're all fools, but only you are also an idiot. You act like an idiot and you love like an idiot and you'll also end up like an idiot.'

'And how does an idiot end up?' asked Jacob.

'An idiot ends up exactly like a fool, but it's an end everybody sees, period,' said the cattle dealer, and after a brief, cold pause that fell on the two of them, he added: 'And because you are an idiot, I'll give you an example that will help you, Sheinfeld, that even an idiot like you can understand. Your love is like walking around with a hundred-pound note in your pocket. That's a lot of money, right? You think you can make a life with it, right? But you can't make anything with it. With a hundred pounds you can't drink a glass of beer, you can't eat a sausage, you can't get into the movies, you can't even go to a whore. Nobody's going to give you change for a hundred-pound note, and nobody's going to sell you nothing, period. That's exactly like your love.'

'With great love only great things work,' declared Jacob proudly. 'Not small change.'

Pity and scorn were all mixed up in the cattle dealer's voice: 'I don't know what your dancing-clowning worker is teaching you or what Menahem Rabinovitch tells you when you run to cry to him,' he said. 'But love, you should know, Sheinfeld, you have to change it to pennies, not to think so big, not to talk too high, not to sacrifice your whole life all at once. All your canaries you released for her and you didn't get nothing in return. Not her did you get and not the change from the birds did you get.'

'Shut your mouth,' said Jacob.

The cattle dealer waved his hand in well-acted despair. 'Why I give you advice I don't know. After all, I love that woman, too, and her son I want, too. But I feel sorry for you, Sheinfeld, 'cause you're an idiot and you're confused. My father used to say about somebody like you that God had mercy on you when He put your balls in a bag, or else you'd lose them, too. So at least know how to use the advice I'm giving you now. You've got to know how to bring something small here, tell a little story there, that's what works, Sheinfeld, something small, and many times.'

16

The Israeli War of Independence broke out. Men disappeared from the village. Shots were heard from the road and distant smoke rose beyond the hills. New graves were also dug in the village cemetery. But Noshua, with a perfect Galilean accent and with bare feet that left traces, went to the nearby Arab village and came back, bleating in the voices of ewes, and a trusting little lamb trotted behind him.

After two weeks of fattening, leaping in the field, and games of hide-and-seek, Noshua led the lamb to the walnut tree, tied its hind legs with a rope, hung it head-down on one of the branches, and before the lamb understood that this wasn't a new game, he picked up an old sickle that had lost all its teeth, stretched his victim's neck, and cut off his head in one smooth movement.

Even before the decapitated lamb's spasms stopped, the worker had already cut the joints of his limbs, right above the hooves, placed his lips to the pieces, and blown hard.

'Pay attention, Sheinfeld,' he said to Jacob, tapping the entire small body with both hands.

Blowing air separated the skin from the flesh, and when Noshua cut along the lamb's belly, he stripped off the skin like a coat.

'If you know how to do this, it's very easy, and if you don't know, it's very hard,' he said.

Excited by the fragrant proximity of death, the crows hovered and hopped around. Lust and impatience made them so bold they came close and pecked Noshua's blood-soaked shoes. He tossed them the intestines and he baked the lamb in the aromatic ashes of what once were the branches of the orange trees in Rebecca and Jacob's citrus grove.

'Sit here, Sheinfeld,' said Noshua. He picked up a small, fragrant piece of meat with his fingers, blew on it to cool it, and put it to his student's lips. 'And remember that there are rules,' he went on. 'You will look into her eyes and her eyes will look at you, and then very slow they will close. That's the sign that she trusts you, and then, very slow, the lips will open, and very careful you'll offer it, but you won't yet really put the meat inside. You'll wait a minute and then there'll be a sign: her tongue will peep out a bit, like a little hand, to accept the gift. Then you'll touch it with the meat and she'll open her mouth and take it. That's great trust and that's great love, you should know. To open your mouth like that and to eat with your eyes closed, that's more trust than to lie together with your eyes closed.'

Jacob's eyes closed, his jaws spread apart, his tongue peeped out. Trusting and groping and smelling the fragrance and the warmth, it took and gathered its booty into his mouth.

'Eat now, Sheinfeld, eat,' and another small piece was put in his mouth.

'After the wedding, you'll sit together at the table, the whole village will watch and you will feed her just like this. Not a lot, not with a fork, just a bit and only with the fingers. You'll look at her as she chews, and she'll look at you.'

And Jacob opened his eyes wide, looked and chewed and swallowed. The scar blazed on his forehead. Saliva and tears, milder than all the other liquids of the body, made what he swallowed slide to his jaw, his thighs trembled, and his heart melted.

Noshua noted the expression of pleasure and love on his student's lips and hurried to extract his fingers before he was bitten. He stood up and put a record on the gramophone and Jacob couldn't decide whether the tune fitted itself to the POW's movements or whether the Italian placed his feet on the notes as schoolgirls can get into a skipping rope.

And then Noshua turned his head to Jacob and asked: 'Finished with the mouth?'

Jacob nodded.

'Now the two of you will dance.'

And he gathered him up in his arms, pressed him to his body, and together they danced the tango, the dance of restrained lust, dried saliva, and the pain of regrets of the flesh.

The endless notes of the dance and the scents of the vapour and the seasoning and the mixing and the thickening rose from Sheinfeld's yard and hovered over the earth. Everybody understood what they meant and knew what their purpose was, and yet mystery surrounded the house and the tent and the two men who lived, studied, trained, and prepared there.

A thin covering, like a fabric that envelops hired killers, alchemists, and very young widows, veiled all their ways.

Many people stopped at the house and tried to crumble its walls with their looks. Others only slowed their pace and gulped the air.

'In the Land of Israel young men are killed, and those two are playing over her,' said Oded, who came on leave for a few hours.

He was serving in the Harel Brigade as a convoy truck driver, and brought letters to Naomi and from Naomi into besieged Jerusalem.

Jacob announced that he intended to enlist in the war, but they told him officially that he was too old and they told him less officially that he was crazy. Relieved, he went back to his tent, his dancing, and his cooking.

The cooking smells didn't take any account of the direction of the wind, and always came from Jacob's house to our window. But Mother wasn't impressed by them, never lingered to look at the tent, and didn't lend an ear to the music. Even worse, she didn't even change her normal route to avoid passing by there. She walked by them with her erect stride, her passing profile, and her flapping dress, turned to them the armour of her back and the chill of her deaf ear.

Rabinovitch's Judith milked Rabinovitch's cows, laundered Rabinovitch's clothes, cooked Rabinovitch's meals, and received her salary from Rabinovitch. Once a week she met with Globerman and drank with him from the common bottle, and twice a week I went with her on her walks with her cow Rachel, who was a very old calf by then, and had to be shown the way home, because sometimes she forgot.

The old cowshed was now a handsome little house, with bougainvillea twined around its cheeks like colourful side curls, swallows fluttering yearnings at its windows, and a soft smell of milk rising from the cracks in its walls. Rabinovitch's Judith raised her son there and paid no heed to anybody.

In Jacob, this behaviour stirred an understandable fear, but Noshua wasn't at all interested either in Judith or in her behaviour. He acted according to rules no woman could ignore, and according to slow and calculated schedules that Chance can't influence and Time can't deviate from.

At the first cease-fire, the two of them went to Haifa to buy cloth for the bride's gown, and while Jacob was feeling fabrics, Noshua was attentively observing the cutters and seamstresses who were working there.

'He's sewing the dress for me,' he told the women, propping his elbow on Jacob, who was thoroughly embarrassed.

The seamstresses laughed and, in the high voice of the village nursery school teacher, Noshua sang:

> Who knows who knows
> How the tailor works
> Threads a needle so it goes
> The machine it sews and sews
> That is how he works.

The seamstresses applauded him, sang along with him, and enjoyed themselves so much they didn't suspect anything and allowed him to stay with them and watch their work as much as he wanted. And at night, the POW returned to the village an expert at measuring, cutting, and sewing.

'Now we'll start sewing the gown for the wedding, and next year everything will be ready,' he said.

'You don't have to measure it on the bride herself?' asked Jacob.

'Enough with the bride already!' said Noshua, unexpectedly sharp. 'What does the bride have to do with it? You don't have to see the bride and you don't have to dance with the bride and you don't have to measure the bride!'

He spread big, rustling sheets of paper over the floor of the room.

'Now just describe her body to me in words,' he instructed.

Jacob described and the POW crawled and drew the parts of the dress with a pencil, cut out the paper with scissors, and then spread the cloth on the floor.

That whole stage, which only takes a few lines and seconds in the story, lasted many months. It started with buying the cloth and continued with preparing and calculating, and drawing and cutting, and as it went, showers fell, fruits ripened, the moon filled and waned, and birds migrated, and at the end, Jacob washed his feet and dried them with a rag and after he trod on white paper, to show Noshua there was no dirt on them, he walked on the plot of the fabric.

His heels and big toes burned, but we can't say if that was from heat or cold. He put the papers on the fabric and cut the parts of the dress according to them, his tongue poking out, the air held in the cage of his lungs, and only his fingers moving.

Afterwards he felt a great weariness and lay down to sleep. And a few days later, Noshua went to Aliza Papish and asked to borrow her Singer sewing machine.

'Give it to him, give it to him,' the Village Papish said to his wife. 'It's prevention of cruelty to animals.'

Noshua returned, carrying the heavy sewing machine on his shoulders, and in the days that followed, he stitched together the parts of the dress and Jacob didn't stop talking with him about Judith.

Very slowly, the dress took shape, and was white and pure and empty.

'You feel it already? You feel?' asked Noshua, and Jacob felt with his whole heart and his whole body the longing of the cloth for the skin and the fabric of the gown for the flesh, and those yearnings, which he thought only he had, to be filled and to hold.

And when the POW finished basting the dress and laughed and let Jacob measure the gown, Jacob felt his skin burning despite the coolness of the cloth, and the cry of surprise and pain that blurted out of his mouth was unintentional. Noshua didn't let him wear the bridal gown for more than two minutes, and then he sat him down at the sewing machine and together they began the task of the final sewing.

Globerman, the only one who understood where all these things were leading and was very amused and curious, supplied Jacob with 'important addresses' of food profiteers. The dealer, who had lent his truck, his cunning, and his connections to the War of Independence, 'for any national need that comes up', resumed his normal procedures during the period of shortages. He made a fortune smuggling meat on the black market and selling it to restaurants, where government officials ate in the back rooms, and so he knew where you could buy groceries for a wedding.

He also promised Jacob to get him a discount, and even to lend him all the serving pieces needed for a wedding, the gorgeous Dresden and Prague dishes of the German Templars, and so he

confirmed the suspicions about the legendary plunder he had
made in their houses after the expulsion.

'To help you is against my own interest,' he said. 'But at my
age, sometimes curiosity gets the better of love.'

Meanwhile, all the villagers commented that they hadn't seen
Jacob in a long time, that he had stopped pestering Judith, and
no longer waited across from Rabinovitch's yard, and didn't
hang yellow notes on trees and walls, and didn't lie in wait on
the paths where she walked, and in fact wasn't seen anywhere,
because he was closed in his house and his yard and was busy
with his preparations and his studies and his examinations:

All day he cooked and sewed and danced, fertilized and sowed
and watered and planted, and at midnight he went to bed and
lay there awake and asleep, reciting and dreaming, opening and
shutting his eyes, ploughing and returning back and forth, like
the whisper of an ox: Judith Judith Judith Judith Judith Judith
Judith Judith Judith Judith Judith Judith htiduj htiduj htiduj
htiduj htiduj htiduj htiduj htiduj htiduj htiduj htiduj htiduj
htiduj Judith Judith Judith Judith Judith Judith Judith Judith
Judith Judith Judith Judith.

Evening smells emanated from the kitchen cabinets, delicate
goblets rang on their shelves, red skillets shone on the wall in
endless sunsets.

And myriads of dense tiny stitches were sewn, until the gown
was completed and waited for the longed-for body to come, to
accept it, to don it, and to fill it.

Noshua stroked the gown and folded it and put it in a long
white cardboard box.

'Now everything is ready for the wedding.' He put the box
in the closet. 'All we have to do is wait for the sign.'

17

Like all those who wait, Jacob asked Noshua and himself what the sign would be.

The shriek of a swallow when swallows don't tend to shriek? Or maybe the shriek of a swallow when swallows do tend to shriek? Or maybe a crow will be the herald? Or a peach will ripen in winter? Or maybe the sun won't set in the evening? Or maybe it will shine as usual in the morning? Or maybe a leaf of an apple tree will be the sign? A yellow leaf, that will fall in the autumn from one of the trees in the orchard, like its thousand brothers?

And how to prepare for it? To sit at home and wait? Or to come and go, to work and live?

Noshua and Jacob, like all those who wait, watched for a sign, and the sign, like all signs, tarried and didn't come.

'Once, just because of that there used to be angels. But these days angels don't do those things no more and you got to guess the sign all by yourself. So two people I told about my whole plan so they'd help me. Globerman I told and Menahem Rabinovitch I told. Menahem told me it was a very beautiful plan, and when I asked what was so beautiful, he said: "Every plan to win a woman is a very beautiful plan, and I hope for your sake that you succeed." He wasn't the same Menahem anymore. After his younger son was killed in the War of Independence, he was a broken man, and soon after that he also stopped being mute in the spring and that broke him even more. "Here," he told me, "now I'm talking in the spring, but not a single hoor comes to hear." But the dealer just started laughing. I told him: "See, you and I want the same woman, so maybe once and for all you'll listen and not laugh and just tell me what you think?" And from beginning to end, I told him the whole idea, that if I prepare everything, the wedding and the food and the dancing and the bridal gown and the rabbi and the bridal canopy and the guests,

then she'll come, too. There's a rule like that in nature, that if
everything is ready and only one piece is missing, then that one
last piece has got to come, too. Oh, how he laughed, Globerman,
when I told him about that plan of mine. "All your money you're
going to use up on that woman, Sheinfeld," he told me. "Your
money and your life and your strength and everything." And in
that he really was right, that's what happened and I really did use
up everything. I was like that man I told you about, who figured
out the money down to the end of his life. I was like the ship in
the French book, I forget its name, that used up all the coal in
the middle of the sea and then started burning the wood of its
body and finally, when it arrived, there was nothing left of it,
just iron beams like a skeleton of a carcass in the field. But in my
dreams about Judith, I saw what Globerman didn't understand
– that she had no choice, that Fate had already tied the rope on
her. Otherwise why, all of a sudden at night, did a person who
came all the way from Italy and fought in the desert and fell
prisoner and escaped and came to me – how come he shows
up at my house? He came to teach me to cook for the wedding
and to dance a tango for the wedding and to sew the gown
for the wedding. And when I told that to Globerman, suddenly
he turned white as a sheet and his lips became thin with rage,
and he started hollering at me: "Right away you're going to tell
me, Sheinfeld, that Hitler may-his-name-be-wiped-out started
that whole war just so that parrot Italian of yours would fall
prisoner and come here and make you a wedding?" He really
was furious. Maybe because in Latvia so many of his family
were killed by the Germans. Like a sheet he turned white
when he hollered. "Children weren't burned in the ovens in
that war and soldiers weren't killed and there weren't orphans
and widows and camps? There's only some *farkakte* Italian who
came to make a wedding for Jacob Sheinfeld and Lady Judith,
eh?" But then I wasn't paying attention no more to such words,
because not everybody who knows about livestock also knows
about human beings, and besides that, what is the dealer talking
about war and about life and about death? See, he himself is the
Hitler of cows.'

*   *   *

And then, one day, as if some bubble burst inside him, during one completely normal afternoon nap, Noshua suddenly turned over and got out of bed. No angel appeared, but Noshua got dressed, left the house, and started walking on the road he hadn't walked on for some time, to Moshe Rabinovitch's rock, which he hadn't visited for some time.

Slowly and quietly he walked, he didn't leap and he didn't clench his fist. His chest rose and fell with deep breaths and his small eyes were almost shut.

A few children who saw him started tramping to the village and shouting: 'Noshua's going to the stone, Noshua's going to the stone!' And by the time the POW reached Rabinovitch's yard, onlookers had already gathered.

Noshua didn't wait a single minute. He went to the rock and said to it: 'Please wait just a minute, right away I'll call my Moshe and he'll pick you up from the ground.'

Everyone was scared. Even the rock, half buried in the ground, seemed to shudder. Even Noshua was surprised because he didn't know where the words came from or whose voice he said them in.

He wiped his hands on his pants with the dead woman's unforgettable gesture, then knelt down and embraced the rock, and with an amazing Rabinovitchy groan, he uprooted it from its place, picked it up, and carried it like a baby, close to his chest.

Thus he walked with it in the village street, and everyone walked behind him in a procession of triumph and smiles.

'Don't follow them. Come in the house at once, Zayde,' shouted Mother from the window of the cowshed.

I didn't follow them and I didn't come in the house, either, because the male and female crow dived from the crest of the eucalyptus to the rim of the deep crater left behind by the uprooted rock. I went there, too. Startled earthworms were burrowing into the wet earth, globules and moss rolled around. Pot-bellied ants, transparent yellow ones, were crawling. The crows started pecking and swallowing, and suddenly one of the black beaks uttered a thud, and I bent down and put out my hand to find out what it had struck.

My mind didn't understand and didn't imagine, but my heart was pounding even before my fingers told me what they were touching. I scraped off the damp earth and I felt the square corner of a box. I removed a few clods and I saw mother-of-pearl and wood.

Noshua carried the rock to the middle of the village, walked around the big ficus trees near the community centre, and started retracing his steps. With a shout he dropped the rock into its crater and returned to Sheinfeld's house. Without a word to any of his stunned escorts he went in and said: 'That was the sign, Jacob. The day has come.'

He kindled the wood in the oven, warmed water for washing, showered, ate, and fell asleep.

In the evening he got up, put on the old POW's overalls, took down the tent, and picked up the white box with the bridal gown lying in it.

'Good-bye, Jacob,' he said.

'Good-bye, Salvatore,' said Jacob.

The Italian went to Rabinovitch's house, knocked on the door of the cowshed, and handed Judith the white box and the gown inside it.

'*Questo per te*,' he said. 'That's for you, Judith.'

He didn't wait for her answer, but for her arms. And when those, against her will, rose and reached out to him, he laid the box on them, turned around, and walked to the centre of the village, and there he hung a big yellow announcement on the board, saying: 'Rabinovitch's Judith and her heart's desire Jacob will enter into the covenant of marriage on the 14th of Shevat this year, Wednesday, February 1, 1950, at 4 p.m. Friends are invited.'

From there, Salvatore went to the highway, left the village, and was never seen again.

18

'So by then I knew how to dance and how to cook and the dishes were ready and the gown was ready and the Italian picked up the rock and called me Jacob for the first time, like he was promoting me, from Sheinfeld to Jacob, from just a poor simple soldier to a great general of love. And the whole village came to read the announcement he put up for the wedding. The words were so beautiful and so simple. Covenant of marriage . . . her heart's desire . . . and the date, both the Hebrew date and the regular date, and the hour, and the day, and the month, and the year, so everything would be clear and Luck and Fate and Chance couldn't mix in. And a few days later I took the bus to Haifa with a fine chicken to give the rabbi, to tell him also about the date and to make sure he wouldn't forget to come, 'cause you know how it is with those pious jerks, money for a *mitzvah*, a commandment he's forbidden to take, but a fat chicken just to remind him he's got to do the *mitzvah* – that's all right. Then what, Zayde, all the time you kept asking me how I learned to cook and sew and dance? Now you know. And never mind what Globerman said – the world war was for that. So the English would capture Salvatore in the desert and bring him here to the prisoner-of-war camp so he'd escape and come to me and teach me all the things and all the rules. 'Cause if the war wasn't for that, what was it for? I ask you, what for? Doesn't my love deserve a big war? At first I thought he would teach me to cook Italian food, with all their noodles and tomatoes and cheese, but no. He himself told me that for a Jewish wedding you also got to cook Jewish food, and he went and watched Aliza Papish to see how she cooks, and right away he cooked like he himself was born in the Ukraine, he cooked and he also taught me. And that's how I made three kinds of herring, one with sour cream and green apples for the appetite, one with onion and oil and lemon for the soul, and one with vinegar and oil and pepper and bay leaves for regrets, with bread and butter and schnapps. And chicken soup I made with *kreplach* with little droplets of fat smiling at you like gold coins and with the dill cut up so thin you all of a sudden heard all the people sighing over their bowl because everybody saw his mother like a picture shaking in those little droplets in the soup. And the dough for the *kreplach* I also made all by myself. Because with *kreplach*, what's outside is more important than what's inside. And that chicken, the one that in Russia only the rich *goyim* in Kiev ate, the *Taganka*, that, too, I made, and the borscht of the Ukraine, with potatoes and cabbage and beets and beef. That Italian knew the rules so good he even wrote down for me not to forget to put for everybody half a clove of garlic next to the bowl of borscht to rub on the bread crust. And a salted radish salad I made, rubbed in a grater with big holes and with fried onion burned a little along with its oil. And next to everybody, a little bit of horseradish – not red, white – so strong its tears ran from your nose and not your eyes, and it goes down to your stomach not through the throat but from wherever it felt like. And to drink I put cold beet borscht with a mound of sour cream in every cup, beautiful like a mountain of snow in blood. And pomegranate juice he made before the winter, 'cause I told him how much you like pomegranates, Judith. And three kinds of preserves I made from strawberries and raspberries and black plums from that tree that grows wild on the way to the wadi. And everything was in the beautiful bowls of the Germans, may-their-name-be-wiped-out, which the dealer gave me. What can I tell you, Zayde, a fortune all those things cost me. And I sold a lot of poor birds for that, and a lot of things the dealer gave me, 'cause under all his money and blood and scorn, Globerman is a good man, better than all of us was that evil murderer, and a lot of foodstuffs he gave me really as a gift. See, he made a fortune during the time of shortages. He had all kinds of *shtiks* to cheat in documents of the slaughter of cows, and the government supervisors knew it, but they never could catch him. Food I made for about a hundred people, but from all over the Valley they heard about it and came. A hundred people sat down to eat and the rest stood to watch and smell. And nobody complained, 'cause they didn't come so much for the food, but for curiosity and love, and because of my seriousness about this, 'cause, when love and seriousness go together, Zayde, nothing can stand in their way. And a gorgeous winter sun shone, and for me that wasn't a surprise, 'cause a wedding you prepare down to the very last detail, it will also have good weather. And I went to the village carpenter shop and took boards and put them on trestles, and white cloths I put on them and chairs for the guests, everything all by myself. And then I washed and I dressed and at four o'clock in the afternoon, with blue pants and a white shirt, I stood, in the lovely clothes of her heart's desire, and to everybody I said: "Come in, come in, friends, we've got a wedding here today, nice of you to come, friends, come in." And everybody came in, very serious, and the smell of the food overhead like regrets, for what is food-for-the-soul like it says in the Bible, if not regrets? There is food-for-the-body like meat and potatoes, and there is food-for-the-soul, like a glass of vodka and a piece of herring. And then the rabbi also came from Haifa with the sticks and the canopy and approached the table, and the Village Papish who, I don't need to tell you how much he likes the pious jerks, says to him, "Rabbenu, here everything's not altogether kosher, here there's heathen cooking," and at me he winked with both eyes. See, he couldn't wink with one eye, two eyes used to close when he winked. I was scared if he said heathen cooking, maybe he knew it was a *goyish* Italian and not really a worker named Joshua. But that rabbi was a clever Jew, and right away he looks at the Village Papish and says to him: "Reb Yid, I asked you if it's kosher?" So the Village Papish says to him: "No you didn't ask." So the Rabbi says to him: "If I didn't ask, so why do you answer?" And he ate like tomorrow Yom Kippur and Tesha b'Av together were in store for him, he stuck his hands in and smacked his lips and cleaned his plate with a piece of bread, because say what you will about those rabbis, fools they're not. Afterwards he starts pestering, who's the bride and where's the bride and why doesn't the bride come? And I say: "We've already prepared everything for her and now we hope that we are worthy for her to come." Well, then the rabbi looks at me and says: "Reb Yid" – seems he liked to say Reb Yid

– "it's a bride, after all, it's not the King Messiah." And so I say:
"For me, that bride is the Messiah." That he couldn't stand, and
right away he gets up from the table, and says, really mad: "The
Messiah I don't see here yet, but the jackass I already see," which
is a very very old joke, and he wants to leave, but four men get
up and grab him by the arm and sit him back down in the chair,
and along with all the rest of us, he also waits for her to come.
All of us waited and waited, and what happened there I don't
know, but Judith didn't come. Only you came all of a sudden,
Zayde. Half an hour we waited and only you came, a little boy
with the white box of the wedding gown that you held in your
arms like this, and you came into the yard. You remember that,
Zayde? How could you forget such a thing? You came in all
of a sudden, and everybody got quiet and looked at you, and
you walked straight to me, so quiet you could hear both our
hearts beating, and you gave me the box with the gown and
right away you turned around and ran home without looking
back. I yelled, "Zayde, Zayde, what happened, Zayde?" like a
lunatic and without any shame in front of everybody I stood up
and hollered, but you ran and didn't turn around. You didn't
hear me yelling at you? You don't remember? How can you
forget something like that? You took off and I opened the box
and I took out the wedding gown in front of everybody. So white
and so long and so empty it was without Judith inside it, and a
big sigh came from everybody, 'cause from the wedding gown
they sigh, and it don't matter if the bride's in it or not, and then
the four men really dragged the rabbi to me and held the four
poles, and I stood under the canopy with the gown and I said
to him: "Here's the bride, now you can start." And the tears
were already starting to flow from my eyes like they're flowing
now, and you, too, Zayde, they're falling from your eyes even
though I don't understand why you should cry, too. See, nothing
happened to you and for you it was even better like that. And
the rabbi looked at me and said, "Reb Yid, don't make fun of a
rabbi and a Jewish wedding," and again he wanted to take off,
and again the four men surrounded him in a circle and grabbed
him by the arm. Then it seems he understood that the God of
the Jews was for that wedding, 'cause right away he read like

papa all the blessings and whatever he had to, and I put the ring on the air that should have been filled with her finger, right on the air, and without getting confused, I said, "Behold you are consecrated to me this day according to the ritual of Moses and Israel," and even though she wasn't there, everybody knew who I was saying that to, and she, even though she didn't come, see, she is my wife, consecrated to me, and the whole village were witnesses, and they saw that even though she didn't come, she was there, Judith, you are there and with me and mine.'

19

The wedding of Jacob Sheinfeld and Rabinovitch's Judith is still inscribed on the memory of the people of the village and the nearby villages, and also on the memory of the children who were babies then, and it lives in the memory of their grandchildren, who hadn't yet been born then. There are still people who talk about it, and whenever they see me, they stare at me in wonder and curiosity as if I bear the answer in my flesh.

But there is no answer in me, only a memory.

I was about ten years old then, and despite what Jacob accused me of, I remember very well. I remember how Noshua picked up Moshe's rock, I remember that he came to our cowshed and gave Mother the big white box. He told her something in a language I didn't understand and in a voice I didn't recognize, and he left.

I remember the tremor of her hands, guessing and straying over the white box. Her body, weak as a condemned person when she sat down on one of the sacks. The glow that lit up the whole cowshed when the gown was spread out.

And I remember how she got up and stripped and put the gown on her naked flesh. Her eyes shut, her lips trembled, she hovered in the space of the cowshed, but she didn't go outside.

In the following days, she wore it again and again. For a minute, a few minutes, a quarter of an hour, an hour, and more than an hour. And in the middle of the night, she sneaked to the yard in it and I saw her walking around along the trough like a distant nebula of the stars. She was pondering, shrouded in her gown, and she didn't talk with anyone. Not even with me did she exchange a word.

And three days before the date that Sheinfeld's worker wrote as the date of the wedding, when the whole village was preparing and was covered with clamorous smells of laundry basins and cooking pots, Mother went to Moshe and told him that things were ready, that she was about to stop working in his yard and his house, that she had decided to enter into the covenant of marriage with Jacob Sheinfeld, her heart's desire.

That afternoon, Judith kindled wood and corncobs in the stove to heat water.

'I want to wash now, Zayde,' she said. 'You run off and see what's going on in Jacob's yard.'

I ran, I came back, and I told her that Sheinfeld had put up the tables, spread white cloths, and set out dishes. 'It looks like he's making some party,' I added, pretending I didn't understand and didn't know.

Mother sat in the big tub and steam whispered on her skin. She told me to soap her back and pour water on her head. I did everything she asked and then I waited for her with a towel spread out and with my eyes shut and my heart cold and hating and worrying and heavy.

She got up slowly from the bath, wrapped herself in the towel, sat down and combed her hair, and for a long time she examined her face in the mirror.

'Come here, Zayde,' she said.

I went and stood near her.

'I'm going to get married to Jacob today,' she said.

'All right,' I said.

'He'll be your father.' She took hold of my chin. 'Only him.'

'All right,' I said.

'And we'll stay here in the village. You won't have to part from anybody.'

She got up and held my head to the drops of water between

her breasts, and then she turned aside and put on the white bridal gown.

'You wait for me here,' she said.

And when she turned and left the cowshed and started walking away there, the cold hard hand hit my shoulder and I fell down.

'What's your name?' asked the familar, abominable voice.

'Zayde!' I shouted. 'I'm a little boy named Zayde! Go kill somebody else!' And I got up and pushed him off me and assaulted the sacks of mash and pulled out the box I had hidden among them and ran after her.

Silence reigned in the village. No one was seen. Everybody was waiting for her in Sheinfeld's yard. Everybody except me, and I was running in the street, except Moshe Rabinovitch, who stayed home. The few sounds that sawed in the air were very small and clear. Side by side in the transparent air moved: the beating of my heart, the pounding of my steps, the tempest of my breathing, the shriek of a distant crow.

I didn't call to her to stand still because I knew that her deaf ear and her white gown sheltered her now from the whole world, that she wouldn't hear and wouldn't stop and wouldn't turn around. I ran after her, I caught up with her, I ran around her, I stood facing her, and stretching both hands, I held out the small dirty box to her glance.

The mother-of-pearl and wooden cover was locked, but when Mother stuck her hairpin into the keyhole, it came up obediently, and for a moment the box seemed to hold only her expectations and nothing else.

She put her hand inside it and felt something soft and desired. Moshe Rabinovitch's braid, long and thick, was pulled out, and when Mother lifted it up to her eyes, the ancient ribbons came untied and the golden cascade poured between her fingers.

'He sent you?' she asked.

'No.'

She understood immediately, of course, that that was what Moshe had been searching for all the time. But I assume she didn't yet take in the fact that this was his braid, and she assumed it was a woman's braid, Tonya's or some other lover's. And nevertheless, her hands already felt the pleasant deep warmth that hands feel when they touch the truth itself.

'Where did you find this, Zayde?'

'Under Moshe's rock,' I said. 'When Sheinfeld's worker picked it up.'

We stood in the middle of the empty street. Mother put the braid back in the box, took a few steps aside, turned her back to me, buried her face in her arms, and her shoulders shook.

'Under the rock.' She laughed. 'Under the rock . . . A wise woman she was . . . Why did you look there?'

'The crows from the eucalyptus found it.'

She came back to me. Her fingers covered her lips and hid the quivering of her chin. Her eyes roved around, hunting shelter.

And suddenly she leaned her full weight on me. 'Who could have known, who could have thought . . . under the rock . . . And that's what he's been searching for all the time . . .'

I held out my hand to her and supported her with my ten-year-old body along the silent street of the village, until we returned to our cowshed.

Moshe was walking around between the walls there, as pale and hard as they were, and Mother held the box out to him.

'Is this what you're searching for?'

Her voice was low and firm. She opened the box and without taking her eyes off his, she picked the tresses up from it. Her movement was slow, calculated, like the wave of a fabric merchant's arm, presenting the most expensive silk in his shop.

Moshe's right hand first went up to the back of his neck, with a gesture that Judith knew well but only now understood, and from there, it covered his neck, descended, and kneaded the big muscles of the chest, where he should have sprouted breasts if he had fulfilled his mother's wish, and from there it descended and groped his groin, examining and proving and confirming. And all with a gesture that had no trace of coarseness and with a face that took off all its manliness for a moment.

Only then did Judith understand that the braid wasn't the braid of a mother or a sister or a wife, but was the lost braid of men, the braid of Moshe himself.

'It's yours, Moshe . . . ?' she whispered, half asking and half stating. 'It's yours, Moshe?'

'It's mine.'

I stood there, in the corner of the cowshed, but they didn't notice me.

'Make me your wife, Moshe,' said Mother, 'and I'll give you your braid.'

Small and white were the words in the cold air. Warm and sparkling her tear rolled down her cheek.

'And the boy?' asked Moshe, and his mouth was dry. 'Whose boy is he?'

The boy, hidden among the sack of mash in his dark corner, heard and saw and didn't say a word.

'Make me your wife, Moshe, and give the boy your name.'

She gave him his braid and no sooner had he smelled the hair and put it against the skin of his face than Mother had taken the bridal gown off her flesh.

Her body was very white. Only the tanned triangle of the open collar of her work shirt and her arms were brown. She had a body younger than her years, delicate and strong. Her breasts were small and gleaming, two merry, surprising dimples laughed in the small of her back, and her thighs were long and solid.

She put on her work clothes, leaned down to the floor, picked up the white cardboard box, and put the gown in it.

'Take this to Sheinfeld now, Zayde,' she told me. 'Give it to him, don't say a word to anyone there, and come right back home.'

20

All that night footsteps of people returning from Jacob's wedding were heard in the street. They walked back and forth across from Rabinovitch's house in a kind of silent demonstration until at last they went off.

The next day, Oded brought Naomi and her baby from

Jerusalem. She was happy, worried, and surprised. She called Mother 'Mother', and the two of them wept.

And at night Moshe came to sleep in the cowshed, and Naomi took me to sleep with her and her son in the house, and in the morning, she woke me up for the milking.

'They went to be alone a little, Zayde,' said Naomi. 'And we'll spend a few days here and take care of the cows.'

Mother and Moshe went to a small boardinghouse in Zikhron Ya'akov, with stone walls, gravel paths, and an avenue of waving Washington palms leading to its gates. Ten years later, on one of my leaves in the army, I went there, but I didn't go inside.

'Here, Judith,' said Moshe, 'in a place like this we should have lived all those years, you and I, with carriages and servants.' And he held her fingertips and bowed a polished and amusing bow, whose presence in his clumsy body couldn't have been imagined.

Judith stroked the back of his neck with her hovering fingertips. Dim, trembling notes of a cello and a violin hummed in the air. A girl and three boys were playing there in the music room of the boardinghouse.

A mensh trakht un Gott lakht, no one knew and no one deciphered. Not the quick drumming of the woodpecker on the tree trunks, not the soaring of the vulture, which moved over the sky like a tiny glazier's diamond.

They were there four days, in early February 1950, and Naomi and I took care of the yard and the cowshed.

A dry strong cold prevailed then all over the country, and when they returned on the bus, Moshe told Judith it was the kind of cold he remembered from the winters of his childhood in the Ukraine.

And at the feet of Mukhraka Mountain, when the bus turned left and climbed and turned right and the Valley was opened and its fields spread out before their eyes, Judith sighed and clung to him and said: 'Here, we've returned home, Moshe, it's better at home.'

That night, when Oded came to take Naomi and her baby back to Jerusalem and Mother woke me up to tell her good-bye,

Naomi suddenly said: 'Why shouldn't Zayde come with me to Jerusalem for a few days? On the radio they said we might get some snow.'

'He's got to go to school,' said Moshe.

'It's an opportunity,' said Naomi. 'Here in the village snow will never fall. You'll have a little more time alone and Zayde will see some real snow.'

'He'll miss the Arbor Day party,' said Mother.

'There are enough trees here even without him,' said Naomi.

Mother laughed and made a few more egg sandwiches for the road and packed a small bag for me, and Naomi held my hand in one of hers and carried her baby in the other one.

'Oded has to leave, come fast,' and the two of us hurried to the tanker.

'I didn't get a chance to say good-bye to Moshe and to give Mother a kiss,' I blurted out as we ran.

'Tell him when you get back,' she laughed. 'And as for the kiss, give it to me.'

All the way, I slept. When I woke up I discovered that Oded had changed his habit and had gone right into the neighbour-hood with the tanker, disturbing the dawn peace with the roar of his motor.

'Want to honk, Zayde?' he asked, and before Naomi could get a word out, I had already pulled the rope and the great bleating had shaken the air.

'Because of you two, I'll fight with the whole neighbourhood,' she growled.

'Just don't come back to us a city boy, eh, Zayde?' Oded said to me, honked again, and left.

I was about ten years old then and never in my life had I felt such strong cold. The next day it was even colder. Naomi wrapped my neck in a red wool scarf and Meir took me for a glimpse of the Old City over the border.

We rode in a shaky bus that looked like a cow and was called 'Chausson'. Meir asked if I wanted to give the money to the driver, and I got some funny change, a paper penny I had never seen before in my life. From Zion Square, we walked until we came to a big cement wall and we peeped through the holes in it and climbed up to a big house with a statue of a woman on the roof and chilly nuns hastened along its enormous corridors.

A man of about fifty, with red eyes and white bristles, stood next to us, winding *tefillin* on his arm, looking at the city and at us and humming a monotonous tune with a strong smell of licorice emanating from its lines: 'For Abraham and Isaac and Jacob, and for the memory of King David for a blessing, help me Lord, bring salvation from the Heavens, help to us, and remember the righteous ones, Our Teacher Moses and Our Teacher King Solomon and Our Teacher King David, peace upon them, their repose in Paradise.'

'Parasite,' grumbled Meir, but he told me to give the man the paper half-penny.

21

So many things happened to me that week for the first time.

For the first time I drank hot cocoa in a café.

For the first time Naomi kissed me on the neck and the lips and not only on the cheek.

For the first time I was in a bookstore.

For the first time in my life my mother died.

At night Meir and Naomi's baby screamed. I heard her get up to feed him and I heard her shout of surprise and amazement when she glanced out the window.

'Get up, Zayde.' She rushed to me and shook me. 'Get up, here's the snow I promised you.'

I got up, I looked, and for the first time in my life I saw snow. The ground was all covered and in the cone of light of the streetlamp big feathery flakes whirled weightlessly and aimlessly.

In the morning, the neighbourhood children went out to play in the snow and Naomi said: 'Go outside, Zayde, play with them.'

'No,' I said.

'They're nice kids,' she said. 'There are a few your own age.'

'They'll laugh at me,' I said. 'Did you tell them what my name is?'

'What's your name?' She leaned over to me with a frightening expression and laughed thickly. 'What's your name, kid? Tell me fast before I grab you.'

'My name's Zayde,' I said. 'Go kill somebody else.' And Naomi held my hand and the two of us ran outside.

For a long time we played with the children. Naomi's face was flushed with cold and happiness. The snow kept on falling and its flakes crowned her hair. Her eyes sparkled, a warm sweet vapour rose from her cheeks. Then we built a big snowman, and as Naomi was making him a nose, a small black figure appeared in the distance, came towards us, stumbled, got up, and approached.

'It's Meir,' said Naomi, and her face turned pale until it almost disappeared.

And the figure, black and growing and stumbling, walks toward us in the expanse of the white field.

'Something happened,' said Naomi. 'They certainly told him something on the phone in the office.'

And Meir appeared and approached until he came and took Naomi's arm and led her off to the side, to the fence post, to the horror of the news, to the hoarse shout – Judith, Judith, Judith, Judith – flying, spinning, dropping, and turning dark like a crow's wing on the snow, into the slow fall and into the steam, every single 'u' in every one of those Judiths flew out of her mouth, and Meir picked her up and supported her and said to me: 'Later we'll tell you, Zayde, later.'

And at dawn Oded came in the jeep he borrowed from one of the villagers, after he had made his way for sixteen hours on the blocked, white, hidden roads only he could guess beneath the blanket of snow.

He slept an hour, got up and drank four cups of tea one after another, ate two chocolate bars and half a loaf of bread, and took us – among whirling, hovering, hypnotizing flakes, turned by the jeep's headlights into a spinning and deceptive magic – back to the village, to Mother's funeral.

22

On the morning of February 6, 1950, Rabinovitch woke up and Judith opened her eyes, which were always grey, and now they were blue and very new among the lines of their corners.

Moshe went to the stove to make her the coffee she liked, and as he boiled the milk he suddenly understood what had woken him up: the silence, the still blanket that covered the outside and swallowed up all the usual village morning sounds. Not a chick was cheeping, not a calf was bleating, not a pump was beating. And when Moshe opened the shutter he saw that a deep snow was covering the ground, a heavy and surprising and uninvited snow that had lasted all night.

Soft and white the snowflakes fell, light and hovering they amassed and heaped up. Foreign, northern angels of death, handsome emissaries of Fate that had strayed to the wrong place and anticipated the ugly deaths of that land – the snake's venom, the sun's blaze, the madness of the blood, and the blow of the stone.

The Valley was stunned. Mice and snakes froze in their burrows. Stiff warblers, their heads grey with cold, dropped like stones from the branches of the trees. The Arbor Day seedlings the schoolchildren had planted three days before disappeared. Next to the spring the big leaves of the prickly pear bush were broken, in the orchards trees bent, for no one had ever prepared them to bear such a burden, and at the crest of the eucalyptus in Rabinovitch's yard, a mighty branch counted the clock of the dropping flakes.

The story, I think to myself at night, requires a pattern and a channel and a way out.

A tale of pouring rain and a rising wadi and a lying Revisionist and a husband who tarries and a wife who was unfaithful and lost her daughter, and came to live and to work in the cowshed of a widower whose cows she milked and whose children she raised.

The story, I soothe myself, refuses to be fiction.

A tale of a cattle dealer who couldn't drive, and of a child who isn't ruled by death or lust, of fearless crows, and of paper boats, and of a braid cut off, and of an uncle whose skin smelled of semen, and of two pomegranate trees and a pitchfork whose wound is bad.

One two three four. The story assumes lines of causation.

A tale of a woman who is the most beautiful one in the world and of a white boat that bears her name, a tale of an Italian who could imitate every bird and animal, an expert in dance steps and an expert in the rules of love. A tale of a tree that waited and of a lantern that fell and of a barren cow and of a stormy night and of an albino who bequeathed birds to his neighbour and turned his world upside-down.

Listen, these are the three brothers of the Fate family, laughing and making the earth quake: if not for the liar, if not for the wadi rising, if not for the selling of the cow. One two three four. One two three four. One two three four.

But the braid was hidden and the snake stung and the albino came and the liar lied and the husband tarried and the woman got pregnant, and there, in that cowshed, she lived and worked, slept and wept, and in it she gave birth to her son, the son that death does not rule, who grew up and brought her death upon her.

For man makes plans and God laughs and the rock was picked up and the braid was found and the snow fell and the crest of the eucalyptus, whose big and wide branches whose wet flesh wasn't accustomed to the burden, bent and dropped.

Of course that's how it was. If that's not how it was, then how was it?

'Judith!' shouted Moshe from the window of the house.

She didn't raise her eyes, just bent her neck a bit more, and the expectation of the blow trembled down her spine.

'Judith!' and the man's shout passed over the white silence of the snow along with the shriek of the crow and the crack of the tree breaking like three black whiplashes.

The whole village heard him, but Mother, whose bad ear was turned to him and whose good ear was filled with the wind whistling in the leaves of the dropping branch, didn't hear.

Like a mighty stick, the crest of the tree came down on her and struck her to the ground, and silence immediately returned to the world. It was a thin clear silence, and in the eye of the world, a lucid crystal eye, it stands and doesn't melt away.

People rushed from all over, and came running like farmers run, who run much faster than you'd think from their heavy gait, their hearts struck dumb even before they saw the blue kerchief and the smashed crows' eggs and the crushed brood hen and my mother's dress sprouting from under the green-white avalanche.

The Village Papish's gigantic mare was hitched to the broken branch. The pulley was brought from the carpenter's shop and Oded climbed up and tied it to the root of the thick bottom branch of the tree.

The Village Papish shouted to his mare, 'Giddyap, carcass, giddyap!' as if she were the guilty one. The rope stretched, the pulley creaked, and the branch was raised off Judith.

No one hurried forward. Everybody stood around, eyes staring at the thin ivory neck, whose gleam hadn't been dulled by years or regrets or death, and at the stockings that had rolled down a little from the strong, delicate ankles.

It was cold and the dry wind played with the black-grey nape feathers and with the cloth of the dead woman's dress – tightened it and released it against her thighs as if it were trying to bring them back to life.

For long minutes, the branch swayed above her body and no one dared to budge. Even the mare stood still, her firm feet planted in the ground, her muscles trembling with the effort, her fragrant skin steaming, and her nostrils pillars of vapour.

And then Aliza Papish approached, took hold of Judith's elbows, and started pulling her aside, and Moshe went to the toolshed and brought the stone and the file, and as the crows circled and shrieked revenge on his head, he started honing the blade of the big axe with the measured movements of an executioner.

23

About ten years old I was when my mother died, and more than anything else I remember that trip at night, on roads shrouded in white, wrapped in army blankets and big warm chenille robes, and not saying a word.

Naomi's hand held my hand and her complaining baby screamed non-stop in the arms of his father. He was so annoying and noisy that when we came to the village, Jacob Sheinfeld came and told Naomi that he didn't intend to go to the funeral and suggested she leave the child with him.

'And his screaming won't disturb you to be with Judith,' he said.

'I can stay with him, too,' Meir quickly volunteered.

'You'll come with me,' said Naomi. And she gave the baby to Sheinfeld and thanked him.

The baby screamed at the top of his lungs and Jacob tried to soothe him.

First he whistled like a canary to him, then he folded little yellow boats for him from pieces of paper that once again nested in his pockets, and finally he wrapped him in a blanket he had once embroidered for me, and carried him for a walk in the snowy field.

There, near the place where the village bus stop would be built, he walked around with him, rocked him, and gave him biscuits to suck on. And then, when the disgusting baby finally shut up, Jacob raised his head and saw the people returning from the cemetery in small groups of sadness and talk, and the cart came behind them, writing wheel strips in the snow, punctuated by the mare's hooves.

'Come in, friends, come in,' said Jacob.

He spread his coat on the snow and put the baby on it, knelt down, and wept. A sun suddenly turned yellow through a break in the clouds and brightened the eye of the field, and when the empty cart approached, returning from the cemetery, Judith looked to Jacob as if she were slowly floating on a broad river, a gold-green river that has no banks.